Lifeline

JUDY MCDONOUGH

For Mike.

Thanks for being my lifeline.

ACKNOWLEDGEMENTS

My arrrrsome editor, Jennifer Bray-Weber. Thank you for being such a great friend, teacher, and mentor. I've learned the lot of a pirate's booty from you, and look forward to setting sail with you again on Flatline. Love ya, wench.

The Killion group, Inc. I appreciate your mad skills and patience to design my beautiful covers, logo, and formatting. You're fast, incredibly talented, and super easy to work with. You make this fun.

My street team. Thank you for all you do to help me get the word out about my books. Y'all are amazing and I am grateful for your big mouths.

My Beta-Readers. Thank you for nit-picking my manuscript and being honest with me. You are all rock stars.

My Navy SEAL friend, College. Thank you for sharing your experiences with me and allowing me to integrate them into my own story. And thank you for your service to our country.

My family. My husband and boys: Thank you for putting up with my stressed out, high-strung, distracted, crazy self while I was in editing mode. Momma, thank you for reading anything and everything I sent you and for telling me when Caroline was a being brat.

My friends. Thank you for taking my boys this summer to let them play and enjoy being a kid so I could slave away on my computer to get this book completed. I am truly blessed to have you in my lives.

The Romance Writers of America. Thank you for providing an awesome conference with workshops to help new authors succeed.

My readers. You are why I do this. Thank you for believing in me, supporting me, buying my stuff and spreading the word. Thank you for loving me.

ONE

The familiar crunching of the oyster shell gravel beneath her tires authenticated this moment as Caroline pulled into the long driveway of the white plantation house. She smiled. Home. Her welcoming party waited anxiously on the front porch. Of the four bodies watching, only one commanded her immediate attention. She pressed a little harder on the gas pedal.

Cade, all smiles and eager to greet her, bounded down the steps with his arms outstretched like the picture on an anatomical chart. His broad reach filled most of the entrance of the porch, and his fitted dress shirt bunched across his defined chest muscles. Cade's smile lit up his handsome, chiseled face, and the sun glinted off his golden locks. Landscaping outdoors all spring had lightened his caramel brown hair and darkened his naturally tan skin. Caroline's stomach fluttered with anticipation of feeling those strong arms wrapped around her again, of kissing that delectable mouth.

Caroline glanced at her new watch, a gift from Cade last summer just after she moved down here. Plenty of time to catch up before the party tonight. She grinned, remembering his adorable smirk when he gave her the hand-wrapped box. "Trust me. . .you need it," he said. She laughed. He was right.

1

She'd seen Cade only a few times that semester, and of course he and her dad had come to her graduation with some of Cade's alligator hunting buddies. When her name was called, they'd effectively embarrassed her with their cheering, whistling and hollering. Honestly, that wasn't so bad, but as they cheered, they waved their white handkerchiefs like Pittsburgh Steelers fans with their terrible towels.

Cade winked, and an involuntary smile split her face upon his elation to see her. Relieved to finally be finished with school, now she could focus all her time and energy on her family and her favorite Cajun. Her dad rose from the white rocking chair, flanked by Delia and Delphine, when Caroline's Jeep slowed to a stop. Eddie smiled proudly as he walked to the front of the porch beside Cade and leaned his shoulder against a massive white column. Delia held a large tray with glasses of iced tea, and Delphine held a platter of something resembling a mountain of cookies. They were all happy to see her.

Out of habit she glanced up at the third story window, the room from which her G3 grandmother, Rachel Fontenot, had fallen to her death over a century ago. G3, as in great-to-the-third-power. Caroline chuckled. That was Cade's shortcut for genealogy to limit having to repeat all the "greats." Caroline thought it was adorable and quite genius, really. Until she came to the bayou, she had never thought much past her grandparents, much less her great, great, great ones.

Thinking about Rachel's tragic story saddened Caroline, and her smile slowly faded. Rachel Fontenot fought to live, but evil won out. Caroline had been told she was Rachel's doppelgänger, and she'd seen a young girl in her dreams, but until Caroline saw Rachel's picture with her own eyes, she hadn't believed it.

It had been rumored that Rachel jumped from the window to end her life because she suffered from postpartum depression. But that wasn't what happened at all. Through Caroline's recurring—and freakishly accurate—dreams and the discovery of Rachel's journal, she was able to prove Rachel was murdered. Coincidentally, her death came at the hands of George Callahan, the G3 grandfather of Caroline's ex-fiancé, Trevor. George had been desperately in love with Rachel but insanely jealous that she married his business partner. He had raped and killed her as revenge against the Fontenot family.

Was it Caroline's imagination or had someone just passed across Rachel's window?

Cade opened her car door with a huge smile and a helping hand. He yanked her out of the car and wrapped his muscular arms tightly around her in a bear hug. His clean, masculine smell swirled through her senses confirming the undeniable attraction she'd felt the first time she caught a whiff of him in that library. Actually, it was first in his cabin where she'd trespassed on his naked, freshly-showered body. Caroline smirked with the gratifying memory. She should be ecstatic about finally graduating college, being with her man, and having a large family to celebrate with, but she couldn't shake the lingering melancholy.

Cade pulled back to look at her. She lost herself in the golden-green pool of his hazel eyes taking her in before his lips moved to the crook of her neck, then to her lips with a gentle "welcome home" kiss. Her worries and cares were suspended in time while her slumbering libido roared to attention. His soft kiss deepened for a much-too-brief glimpse of how much he'd missed her, and she longed for more.

"Congratulations, graduate. Have I told you how happy I am to finally have you back here with me on a permanent basis?"

She puckered her lips, thoughtfully. "Um, you might have mentioned something like that a few times, yes. I never get tired of hearing it, though."

He flashed his perfect teeth in a breathtaking smile and gave her another hug. She would never get enough of his raw beauty. The subtle laugh lines, the way his bottom lip was slightly fuller than his

3

top lip, and his naturally-long lashes. The slight dimple in his chin framed by his chiseled, square jaw and angular cheek bones. Cade Beauregard was a living sculpture and he was completely devoted to her.

"Oh, sweet Caroline. I've missed you so much." He wrinkled his nose and pursed his lips. "Oh, yeah. Now that you're an LSU graduate living in Tiger country, you can get rid of all those Razorback T-shirts you're so proud of."

She glared, but he distracted her with another sweet kiss. Though she'd attended the University of Chicago, she was raised in Arkansas and never strayed from her Razorbacks. However, she was now an LSU graduate with a new, very good reason to become a Tiger fan, and he never failed to sweep her off her feet. She loved every part of her handsome, playful, protective Cade.

Caroline's fierce desire to touch every facet of his body overwhelmed her. With his arms locked securely around her, she smoothed her palms over his firm chest and placed a gentle kiss in the valley of his defined pectorals before resting her cheek against the steady drumming of his heart. Cade's embrace was the epitome of comfort. She could stay wrapped in him forever. She finally looked up and nearly swooned from the way his hungry eyes devoured her.

"Beau, come on, man. You're hogging her. Let her come up here so the rest of us can congratulate her, too."

"For reals, though. Get a room." Kristy playfully mumbled and winked as she shut her passenger door.

Caroline had almost forgotten her mom and Kristy were in the car as she ignored her snarky friend and peeked around Cade's broad shoulders to the man for whom she had developed a powerful love in such a short time. "Hi, Daddy."

A proud, fatherly expression lit his eyes, crinkling at the corners. He wore the face of a man who counted his blessings. Her own features reflected back at her through their prominent physical similarities and shared personality traits. She was his spitting image.

4

"Hello, sweetheart. Welcome home."

To have just met last summer, she and her dad bonded especially fast. The obvious connection they possessed with one another linked them psychologically as well as genetically. When he'd left her mother all those years ago, Eddie never thought he would see Caroline again. Yet, here she stood in his front yard where he welcomed her home. As joy surged in her heart, a memory flashed through her mind from the first time she approached those steps. The image that followed stung like a thousand hornets. Trevor. She wouldn't be here celebrating with her family if not for him. A knot of guilt ached in her chest for how it ended between them.

While packing her things this afternoon, she'd come across a patched-up teddy bear he'd once given her to apologize for being a jerk. He'd explained that each patch represented a time he had hurt her, and the soft, white fur a portrayal of her purity. A very thoughtful gift. Her remorse didn't sting any less now than it had then. Caroline was beyond grateful to Trevor for insisting she make this journey that she had once dreaded so terribly, and she repaid him by dumping him on their wedding day. Maybe she should call to thank him. . .to see how he's doing.

Kristy gracefully strutted past Cade and Caroline to give Eddie a hug. "Hey, Mr. Fontenot. Thanks for hosting the big celebration tonight. You know me, I always enjoy a good party."

He returned her hug with a kiss on the cheek. Spinning her around for display, his bayou roots surfaced through his accent. "Ooooh weeee, *sha*. You lookin' gorgeous, as always, Miss Kristy. Always a pleasure."

Laughter cut through the thick humid air, abounding from all bodies present except for one. Emily's grim, worried face accentuated the deep crease between her normally vibrant eyes, her arms folded rigidly across her stomach. Her right arm was angled diagonally across her chest, and her hand gently clutched her throat.

On the car ride to the plantation, Emily had grown distant. It baffled Caroline. There was no rhyme or reason for the sudden change in behavior. One moment, she was as chatty as Kristy, the next she'd withdrawn, a spooked look in her eyes. Caroline had asked if Emily was alright, but she simply muttered she was a little car sick and stared out the window.

Eddie's eyes landed on Emily, and Caroline saw compassion flood his green irises as he noticed her mother's distraught expression or lack of interest. If his breathless voice didn't reveal his nerves, his wavering expression did.

"Emily. How are things?"

"I'm fine, thank you." Emily's forced smile faded when she glanced in Caroline's direction making eye contact. She held her gaze for a heartbeat, then blinked and walked toward the front door.

Disappointment drew creases in Eddie's forehead as he stumbled after her. "Wait, let me get your bag and show you to your room."

Emily waved him off, "No, it's fine. I can get it, thanks. Really. You don't need to fuss over me."

Not taking no for an answer, Eddie glanced at Caroline before asking Delia to show Emily upstairs. He cut Emily off at the steps and flashed his killer smile. "It's great to see you, Em."

Emily lingered a moment, studying his face before a slight grin softened her grim features. "Thank you. It's great to see you, too." She dipped her head, "Please excuse me."

Caroline disguised her worry by asking Eddie about his plans for the party. He kissed her cheeks, oblivious to her concern, and placed his arm around her shoulders as he led her to the front door. Caroline sighed. She was a better actress than she thought.

In the large entry of the house, there stood the one person in this town, this state, honestly—this *country*, that Caroline absolutely despised. April's blue eyes pierced through Caroline like a rusty dagger as her voice shattered whatever happiness Caroline had managed to muster outside.

6

"Caroline. How wonderful to see you again!" April sashayed forward with her arms outstretched. Caroline didn't move. April hugged her anyway as everyone watched with surprise and intrigue. "Congratulations on your graduation. I hope you'll forgive me for not attending the ceremony. I was quite busy. I'm *sure* you understand."

Caroline stepped backwards and shrugged away from her cold, bony arms. "Yeah, April. No worries. I'm sure you *were* quite busy. Aren't you always?"

Her steely blue eyes narrowed for only an instant at the implication, then the façade was back. "Some days are busier than others. You look tired, love. Why don't you run upstairs and do something about those bags under your eyes? I also have a flat iron you could borrow if you'd like to attempt to tame that frizz, dear. Though I'm not sure it would do much good."

Caroline opened her mouth to retaliate, but Kristy beat her to it.

"April, right? Um, hi. I'm Kristy, but I'm sure you didn't remember that." Kristy spoke with an exaggerated valley girl accent, using her hands wildly for emphasis. "I know they say the memory is the first thing to fade with aging."

Caroline choked back the exploding laughter that nearly escaped her throat.

April whirled around to face Kristy, guarded but curious. "Kristy. Of course I remember you. How could I forget how you rushed down here to play nursemaid for clumsy Caroline after her unfortunate accident?"

"April, please," Eddie warned.

Kristy discounted her snarky comment and remained in character. "Right. Of course. I'm curious, have you been to California recently?"

April's annoyance with Kristy's obnoxious behavior was accentuated by the deep crease between her perfectly waxed eyebrows. "No, I haven't. Why do you ask?"

Kristy's expression hardened, but she maintained her smile as she took a couple of steps closer, invading April's personal space. A little taller than April, Kristy looked down her nose. "Well, in passing, I saw a crew filming a new reality show the other day. I would swear I saw you there. The woman they were filming certainly made me think of you. Perhaps you've heard of it. I'm sure you have, it's just your style. It's called *The Diary of a Gold Digger*. I heard it was based on a true story."

April's jaw dropped and her eyes flashed with anger. Eddie and Cade suppressed their smirks while everyone else in the room struggled to contain their giggles. Kristy didn't stop there. "You know, the woman in the show did strongly resemble you, what, with the bad highlights and a fake tan and all, but I see now that she dressed much better than you do. My mistake." She mockingly added, "I'm *sure* you understand."

April took a step forward, slightly stretched up on her toes, her back rigid with fury until practically nose to nose with Kristy. She pointed one bony finger in Kristy's face and hissed. "Let me tell you something, you spoiled-rotten brat. One day that smug little grin on your face is going to be scratched off by someone a lot meaner than me. And neither your looks nor your money will get you out of it." She clenched her fist. "For your information, this is not a fake tan. My mother was—"

She stopped suddenly and looked at all the engrossed faces tuned in to this entertaining verbal exchange, all listening intently to see what came next, but April didn't continue. Instead, she cut her eyes to Eddie, lifted her stubborn chin and spoke with the warmth of a cold-blooded snake.

"I've had quite enough fun. You can all take your petty, childish behavior and shove it up your asses. I'll be in my room. Do yourself a favor and don't bother me." She turned on her heel and hurried up the stairs.

You could have heard a pin drop until she was out of sight, then Kristy turned to Eddie. "Seriously, Mr. F., feed that woman some red beans and rice." Her eyes dropped. "I apologize for being rude in your home. That was out of line. But, honestly, in my opinion, you could do *so* much better. She's wretched."

Eddie shook his head and chuckled, though Caroline could see his disappointment. "You know, she only acts like this when y'all are here. She has a quick temper and can be difficult to take sometimes. You're both young and beautiful. Maybe she's a little threatened. It's best to limit your exposure to small doses. She's a. . .a. . .handful."

Caroline mumbled, "I can think of a different word for her."

Kristy started to fill in her blank. "Me, too. What a bi—"

"I think we all know an appropriate word without having to pollute the air with bad vibes," Cade interrupted. "This is a happy day, remember? You ladies both look beautiful, and we have a celebration to attend. Let's forget about unpleasant things and shift into party mode. Shall we?" He hugged Caroline closer to him and kissed her temple.

"Yeah," Eddie said. "I'm gonna go upstairs and check on your mother to make sure she's comfortable in her room. There are plenty to choose from, so it can be a little intimidating. You kids rest up. You don't want us old folks to show you up tonight."

Kristy sighed. "Alright, Caroline. These Cajun cuties are absolutely right. It's party time, and you still need to look through my wardrobe for a dress," Kristy rolled her eyes. "Since you were disturbingly unprepared. Clearly I've taught you nothing," she mumbled. "Anyway, I need to shower and get ready. Perfection takes time." She glanced at her watch and made a face. "Time that we're running out of. You coming up?"

Cade raised his brow. "What's wrong with that one?" He pointed to Kristy's three-quarter length designer black dress that hugged her curves in all the right places. He stammered, "I mean, um, you're not just gonna wear the dress you've already got on?" A burning twinge of jealousy pulsed through Caroline's veins as she clenched her teeth together.

Kristy smiled, amused and, no doubt, flattered. "No, I wasn't planning on it. Why?"

Cade swallowed nervously and glanced at Caroline. He had obviously been checking Kristy out. He may not have a jealous streak, but Caroline sure did. And now she felt guilty for even thinking about Trevor.

Cade stumbled over his words. "Well, I was just asking. I mean, you look fine in that. I don't see anything wrong with just wearing what you have on. Why do you need to change?" He shifted his weight, nervously glanced at Caroline, and quietly added, "Psssh. *Women*. Changing clothes every two hours. . ."

Kristy ignored him and smoothed her hands over the skirt of her outrageously expensive dress, which, in Caroline's opinion, was a bit much just for a graduation ceremony.

"Thank you for the compliment. It *is* a beautiful dress, but I got sticky and sweaty in this soupy humidity today and would love a shower." Kristy elegantly flicked her wrist in the air. "Who knows, my elusive Prince Charming may show up to sweep me off my feet."

She laughed impetuously as she climbed the stairs. Caroline heard her sigh and mutter to herself. "Of course, *my* Prince is probably doing a photo shoot in Milan as we speak, without a clue that I even exist."

Cade turned to Caroline with liquid eyes full of remorse. "Caroline, I-I am so stupid. I didn't mean to—" She held a finger to his lips to make him stop. His shoulders slumped, and she knew he felt terrible about his awkward slip. Caroline didn't care anymore. She had more urgent things on her mind.

"It's no big deal. I need to talk to you about something else." She flippantly waved her hand brushing aside her jealousy and letting him off the hook. She had more important things to worry about. Figuring out how to explain it would be a different story.

His brow furrowed. "What's wrong? Did something happen?"

She wasn't sure exactly how to bring up the nightmare she'd had last night without sounding ridiculous. After all, it *was* just a dream.

Simply because she'd had similar dreams before and ended up being haunted by a ghost didn't mean it was happening again. What are the odds that she'd be haunted twice in one lifetime? She drew in a breath and held it before exhaling slowly through puffed cheeks. Anxiety tightened her features.

He placed his hands on each side of her face and angled it upward. His eyes searched hers for answers. "What is it, sweet girl?"

She stepped away from his penetrating gaze and paced as she thought aloud. "It's probably nothing. I'm sure I'm just overreacting because of everything that has happened in the past, but I can't seem to shake it." He reached for her hand, but she dodged his grasp. For some very strange reason, maybe nerves, she hesitated telling him anything. But it was inconceivably real. She could still smell the burning musk and sandalwood. Also, she had no explanation for her mother's weird and uncharacteristic reaction in the car, nor what induced it, so how was she supposed to explain that to Cade?

"I suppose it could be an exaggeration from my stupid imagination."

He stepped in front of her pacing and blocked her way. His hands braced her shoulders now, and she couldn't avoid facing him any longer. His hot breath landed upon her forehead, and she focused on the buttons of his dress shirt. She finally looked up with clear resolve but couldn't say anything. The right words evaded her. How could she explain something this ludicrous?

He hugged her tightly and let out an exasperated sigh. "Baby, I'm *dying* here. Please tell me what is wrong before I lose my mind."

His secure embrace comforted her. Nothing could harm her as long as she was in the safety of his astonishingly capable arms. He firmly pressed his lips to her head.

"Please, Caroline. You can tell me anything. I love you. I can't help you if you don't let me in. What is it?"

"I had a nightmare last night," she blurted out. "It was freakishly consistent with the dreams I had last summer."

He didn't react the way she'd expected. Honestly, she wasn't sure *how* he would react, but she certainly didn't expect the lack of concern she received. He stood very still for a moment, then he started chuckling.

"Are you *laughing* at me?" Her pulse throbbed in her ears.

"Is that all that's bothering you? A bad dream? Oh, thank goodness," he breathed. "You had me so scared. I had no idea what you were about to tell me, but the horrified look on your face had me preparing for something terrible, something. . .life-altering."

Positively giddy, he laughed like a damned maniac. His relief only fueled her anger. She shoved him as hard as she could, which only made him take a half-step back and caused him to laugh even harder.

"Seriously? Who *are* you? Are you not the same guy who helped me try to contact a freakin' ghost last year? The same guy who convinced me that my dreams were a result of a ghost trying to communicate with me? Didn't you hear what I just said? I had a nightmare that was exactly like the ones Rachel caused."

He stopped laughing and did his best to wipe away the cheesy grin. He cleared his throat and coughed, trying to cover the few rogue laughs that escaped. "I'm sorry, you're right. This dream—"

"Nightmare," she interrupted.

"Of course. Sorry. This nightmare was exactly like the ones Rachel gave you? Could it not be your subconscious remembering the previous dreams because you knew you'd be coming back here today?"

"I considered that possibility. But I don't think so. It wasn't exactly like the others by content, but more by. . .theme."

He looked confused. "I'm not following you. Can you describe what happened?"

She sighed, still frustrated by his reaction. "See, this is why I was hesitant to tell you. I am not exactly sure how to explain it, and you laughing at me didn't help any."

"Caroline, I really am sorry I laughed. I wasn't laughing at you, I laughed because I was relieved it wasn't something much, much worse. You wouldn't believe the kinds of things *my* imagination had dreamed up. Please, try to explain this dre— nightmare for me."

"I was attacked by someone. But I wasn't running from him, he already had me. Also, this time it was *my* body that was attacked, not me in someone else's body. His mask only revealed his eye color, lips and chin."

Cade focused, more serious now. "If you couldn't recognize the attacker, how could you tell that it was you and not someone else?"

"Because he was squeezing the air from my throat."

At full attention, he stiffened, darkness creeping into his expression.

"This man in your nightmare was trying to *kill* you?"

"It would seem that way, yes, and I didn't say I couldn't recognize him. I grappled for his hands choking me but could never grip them. I couldn't stop him. The strangest thing was that I couldn't see the crowd clearly at all."

"Crowd?"

"We were in front of an audience, almost as if we were surrounded by a mob, but I couldn't see any of them clearly. My other senses worked fine, though. Apart from the pain of being strangled, and my burning lungs, I could hear drums which drowned out the voices from the crowd. Oh, and I smelled candles and herbs burning."

"Herbs? Like. . .marijuana? You were being lynched in front of a group of potheads?"

She chuckled. "No, not *herb*. Herbs. Like, rosemary and sage. Sandalwood. You know, incense and stuff."

"Oh. So, was the mob cheering for the attacker or trying to help you? Did they even notice what was happening?"

"I'm not sure. I couldn't see them or hear what they were saying. I saw feet stomping to the beat of the drums, almost as if they were dancing. The crowd itself is kind of foggy in my head now because I was mostly focused on his hands crushing my windpipe. I woke up clutching my throat, chest aching, gasping for breath, and scared out of my mind."

"So, we have a crowd dancing to conga drumming, candles, *herbs*, and a man trying to kill you. Have you been to any parties recently or taken any prescription pain medicine?"

"Are you mocking me? Seriously, I have done nothing to provoke this subconscious torture. If anyone would believe me I would have thought for sure it would be you."

Apparently amused by her reaction, he smiled and shook his head. "I believe you, cher. I'm just trying to better understand by eliminating all other possibilities. Has anything else unusual happened to you or was the nightmare the only thing?"

She shivered from the chill that shot through her body. Taking a deep breath to calm her nerves, she told him about her drive down here. "Yes. My mom. . ."

Cade frowned. "Your mom? What happened? Did you give her a heart attack with your crazy driving?"

Caroline rolled her eyes. "Very funny. I drive just fine. She was white as a sheet, not moving, not blinking, probably not even breathing." She earnestly placed her hand on his cheek to command his attention. "Cade, she looked traumatized, worried." Caroline shuddered. "My mom and I have been close my entire life, and I've never seen her act like this. Never. She genuinely looked frightened. Something is very wrong."

"What do you think could have happened?"

"That's just it. I have no clue. One minute she's fine, talking and laughing with Kristy and me. When I asked her if she was okay, she responded in a dead, monotone voice and told me she was fine, just ready to get out of the car. I asked again because I didn't believe her, and she snapped at me."

Cade pulled her close and hugged her tightly. "If it'll ease your mind, I will help you get to the bottom of this mystery. Everything

14

will be okay. We'll work together, just promise me you'll be honest and not keep things from me, okay?"

"Well then, there's one more thing I should tell you."

Cade pulled her back to look in her eyes, concern deepening the line between his brows. "What is it?"

"I think my attacker was Peter Callahan. George's father. He's ready for his revenge."

TWO

"How do you know it was Peter and not George if you couldn't see his face? George was the one who killed Rachel."

"I heard his voice."

Cade pursed his lips. "It was just a dream. You've never heard Peter Callahan's voice, how could you possibly conclude that it was him, especially if he wore a mask?"

"It was a black Mardi Gras mask that only covered part of his face, and this man did not have the cleft in his chin like George did. But he had the same color eyes and menacing laugh I heard in my dreams last summer." He rocked his head back thoughtfully, but the smirk he unsuccessfully suppressed proved his disbelief.

She huffed and crossed her arms. "All the Callahan's have those striking blue eyes, Cade. They're hard to forget. Even Rachel mentioned George's eyes in her journal. Plus, this guy in my dream said something about the day of reckoning as he choked me. He's the patriarch of the Callahan family. It was him, I tell you."

"Okay, okay, I believe you. Do you think it was his ghost or Rachel trying to warn you again? What can we do about it?"

"I don't know."

Cade tugged on her tightly wound arms and pulled her into his comforting embrace. "Let's not worry about anything until we have something to worry about. Now that you're done with school and I have you all to myself, I will be keeping a close watch on you, cher.

All of you." He waggled his eyebrows. Caroline's cheeks heated and she really hoped she wasn't blushing. That was getting old, but her body responded eagerly to his hungry inspection of her. "Now, can I get that promise that you won't keep things from me?"

"Okay. If you promise not to laugh at me again."

He smiled, dazzling her. "Yes, ma'am. Promise me something else?"

She was hesitant to promise anything else today. She checked her watch. "That depends on what it is. We've already been down here for almost an hour. Kristy's going to kill me if I don't get up there soon."

"Just one more thing." He kissed the center of her forehead just above her brow line. "Promise me you'll relax and enjoy your party this evening? Your father has worked very hard to make everything perfect for you, and I promised him I would see to it that your happiness was a priority. I told him I would take full responsibility in successfully completing this mission."

"You sound like a covert spy." She smiled, "What's next? Will my message self-destruct in ten-seconds? Is your head going to blow up now?"

He chuckled. "It might if you don't agree and kiss me this instant. Promise?"

She pressed her eyes closed, sighing in defeat. "Fine." When she opened her eyes, his lips were on her mouth, which was already partially opened in invitation for his taste. He scooped his hand behind her knees, sweeping her off her feet and she wrapped her arms around his neck to deepen the kiss. He was about to carry her up the stairs to her room when the doorbell rang. He stopped kissing her and smiled as if he knew who would be standing on the other side of the door.

She frowned, puzzled. "Are you expecting someone?"

He gently set her down and gave her a peck on the lips. "I'm expecting a bunch of people tonight."

"Yeah, but it's only four o'clock. The party isn't until six. Right?"

He ignored her and pulled open the door. The unfamiliar face of the man walking inside took her breath away. He was beautiful, mysterious, incredibly sexy, and about the same age as Cade. But she couldn't tear her gaze away from his unusual eyes.

Cade cleared his throat. She heard it, but it didn't register. What color were those eyes? They glowed in contrast to his dark olive skin tone. If she thought Trevor's were memorable. . .

The stranger stepped aside as Cade closed the door and made a cryptic hand signal before embracing Cade in a brotherly hug.

Her curiosity spiraled out of control. She looked at them expectantly and crossed her arms, pathetically attempting to conceal any attraction to the unexpected guest.

"Caroline, I'd like you to meet a friend of mine. This is Runway. He's the closest thing to a brother I've ever had." Cade presented her with a sweep of his arm. "Runway, this is Caroline. My, um, friend."

"Hello, Caroline." His Hollywood smile lit his face. "I've heard so much about you. It's a pleasure to finally meet the beautiful woman Beau can't stop carrying on about. Congratulations on your graduation."

She reached out to shake his proffered hand and stared into his mesmerizing eyes. Long black lashes encased irises the pale mint green of a ripe honeydew melon. Very exotic. She guessed he was of Mediterranean descent.

With his designer clothing perfectly tailored, accentuating his physique, she immediately thought of Kristy. No doubt her best friend would approve. Especially once she heard his smooth, heavily-accented voice.

"Hello. It's nice to meet you, *Runway?*"

"Runway is his nickname." Cade shrugged, "His name is Matteo, but I've called him Runway for so long, it's a habit."

"You can call me Matt if you'd prefer. I'll answer to either," he grinned.

"May I ask how you got that nickname?"

"Isn't it obvious? I mean, *look* at him. It's like he just stepped off of a runway at an Italian fashion show." Cade laughed, but Runway's cheeks flushed and his eyes rolled toward the floor.

She used the invitation to her advantage. He was as tall as Cade, but less muscular. Less bulky, but more defined, and he was thinner. Thick, coffee black hair, trimmed on the sides and back, and longer soft waves on the top. She understood why they called him that.

He definitely succeeded in emitting waves of sensuality to anyone who looked at him for longer than a millisecond. His lips curved up at the corners providing a constant smirk.

He frowned at Cade, clearly annoyed. "You could have explained it a little better than *that*. You make me sound about as deep as a puddle. *Testa di cazzo.*"

The different language caught her attention, and her eyes cut to Cade who smiled relentlessly. He replied, "*Cagna* sexy," and playfully blew Matt a kiss.

"What just happened? What did y'all just say to each other?" She probed Cade for information; he knew she hated not being in on a joke.

"My apologies, Caroline," Runway said. "I meant no disrespect. But it would be rude to repeat those words in the presence of a lady."

He smiled and tossed a glance at Cade before he continued speaking. "My buddies nicknamed me Runway in boot camp because I prefer to dress nicely and do more with my hair than just shave it all off. I enjoy finer things as well. When I was assigned to my team, the nickname surfaced only once, but unfortunately it stuck. I personally think it's a bit of an exaggeration. I'm hardly a runway model. Beau's nickname was much cooler than mine." He grinned big, but it quickly faded when Cade didn't reciprocate.

"What team? Boot camp? You were in the military?" The pieces of the puzzle were slowly coming together. She'd suspected some sort of special training or martial arts, but the military hadn't crossed her mind.

"Beau and I were both in the Navy. He didn't tell you?" He glanced warily at Cade who quietly studied her reaction.

She tilted her chin up and looked at Cade as she spoke to Runway. "No, as a matter of fact, he didn't. Please, enlighten me. I want to hear everything." He made another silent communication to Cade and waited for an answer. Her head shifted back and forth like a tennis match. Very frustrating. Cade stood still, thinking for a few seconds, and finally answered with a nod before his gaze fell back to her. She was intrigued. She couldn't let this golden opportunity slip through her fingers before she learned about Cade's enigmatic past he refused to talk about.

"Please, go on. I'm dying to know all about the ever-mysterious Cade Beauregard's history and service to our country."

"Beau and I were in the same division in boot camp from the very first day. We started out as bunkmates, and, as we learned more about each other's interests, we realized we had a lot more in common that we thought."

She looked at Cade. "You were in the *Navy*? You never said anything about that. Why didn't you tell me you were in the Navy?"

He shrugged. "You never asked."

Her voice came out louder and higher pitched than she intended.

"Didn't I?" She paused as she digested this information. "I never asked if you were married either. You were in the United States Navy?"

"The subject never came up, and I saw no reason to bring up unnecessary topics. I can print you a resumé if you'd like." Caroline didn't appreciate his sarcasm as he and Runway laughed together. Cade noticed and his smile faded. He shifted his weight, clearly uncomfortable. "I don't talk much about my Navy days." His forehead creased with worry. "Does it bother you that I was in the military?"

"Bother me? Why in the world would it bother me? I think it's awesome. And incredibly hot. It explains so much. You're tidy, self-sufficient, physically fit. It all makes sense now. How long were you in? What was your job? Is that where you learned to fight so well? And shoot? If you were in the military, why do you have these little part-time jobs now?"

Cade placed his hands on her shoulders and chuckled. "Slow down, sweet girl. I will answer your questions in due time, just take a deep breath. You're getting all worked up." He nonchalantly waved his hand, but the tension in his shoulders revealed more than his words. "It's really not that big of an issue. A lot of people don't like the sorts of things I had to do, so I don't flaunt the information to just anyone."

"I'm not just anyone."

"I know, love. I wasn't trying to keep it from you, I swear. The perfect opportunity to divulge the information never arrived, so I didn't see any reason to specifically bring it up. That's all. I will tell you anything I can about it."

"Anything you can? Does that mean there are some things you still can't talk about, even though you're out of the military now?"

"Yes. There are things I *can't* talk about and things I *won't*. I promise to be as open with you as I can. Deal?"

"I suppose that's fair. So, what was *your* nickname?"

He dropped his head. "How did I know you were gonna ask that? I hated it, and those who really care about me know that, so they never mention it. The only people who know it are the guys who served with me. I would love to keep it that way." He gave Runway a warning look to which he nodded in acknowledgement.

"Oh, come on! You can't do this to me. I have to know what it is! It's going to drive me crazy. Come on, Runway. Just tell me. I promise I won't tell anyone else."

Just as she thought he was about to cave and tell her, Kristy called from upstairs.

"Caroline, what are you screeching about now?" She rounded the corner of the banister, her attention solely on her phone, and continued talking. "You know, if you don't relax more you're going to get premature wrinkles and frown lines."

Kristy looked incredible as she floated down the stairs. The dress she had chosen for the party was unbelievable. Obviously designer, ruche satin from top to bottom, stopped mid-thigh and contoured her every curve. The champagne color matched her shimmering skin and fit her so perfectly she could have been naked. The pearl and crystal-embellished line of roses scattered throughout the bodice gracefully climbed her curvy body in an elegant wave pattern.

"Why aren't you getting ready ye—" Kristy glanced up mid-sentence to see if Caroline was listening, and her eyes froze upon Runway. She paused briefly, a look of shock flashing across her perfectly made-up face for an instant. Her undecipherable eyes fixed upon Runway as she continued to the next step. Runway had the same awestruck expression as he stared at Kristy. He might have even stopped breathing.

Just as she was about to introduce the two of them, Kristy's strappy, crystal-encrusted heel caught on the carpet runner. She launched forward, falling down the spiral staircase.

THREE

In all her years of gymnastics, cheerleading, and high school track, Caroline had never seen such catlike reflexes. Runway swooped Kristy into his arms before any part of her body touched the floor. It was as if he'd been rehearsing the move and was readily prepared for it. His speed, reaction time, and ability to act quickly was incredible. Cade wasn't the least bit surprised, but Caroline stood dumbfounded.

"Oh my gosh, Kristy!" Caroline's hands flew to her mouth. "Are you okay?"

Kristy didn't respond, not taking her eyes off of Runway.

"How the heck did you just do that?" Caroline asked of Runway. "You were standing at least six feet from the bottom of the stairs! How did you get to her so fa—"

Cade pulled her back to his side and chuckled. Standing back, she realized what exactly he was chuckling about. Runway effortlessly held Kristy close in his arms, and she had a death grip around his neck. Only, that's not what was funny. Their faces inches apart, both were completely lost in each other's eyes. "Hi."

In the same bewildered tone, Runway responded. "Hi." He slowly lowered her to the ground without removing his eyes from hers.

It was crazy. The energy radiating between the two of them was palpable. She nudged Cade with her elbow and quietly muttered. "And you thought *we* had chemistry."

23

"No kidding." He winked and softly replied. "I wonder if we should step out and give them some privacy?"

"Thank you, for, um. . .saving me from the most embarrassing, and possibly the most painful, moment of my life." Kristy stepped back, straightened her dress and smiled before very formally and stiffly sticking her arm out to shake Runway's hand. "Hello, I haven't officially met you yet. I'm Kristy Tanner, Caroline's best friend."

He flashed his irresistible smile and returned her formal greeting as he pressed the back of her hand to his lips.

"*Ciao, bellissima*. I am Matteo DeLuka, Beau's best friend."

Kristy straightened ever so slightly under the full effect of Runway's smile, charm, and smooth accent. But she didn't waiver, maintaining her act. And Caroline knew without a doubt that it was an act, always detached and cool.

"Matteo DeLuka. Hmmm. . .Italian? It's a pleasure to meet you. Are you here for the party?"

He briefly glanced at Cade, and then his eyes were glued on Kristy again. "Yes, I will be attending the party tonight. It's Sicilian, but you were close enough for my satisfaction. May I ask, is that Giovanni Couture you are wearing?"

Her eyes sparkled. "Yes, as a matter of fact it is." Her breathless voice fooled no one. She was a goner. "How did you know that?"

He smiled again, no doubt melting every barrier Kristy had put up. "I know my designers. Especially the Italian ones. That is the new collection, no? Has it even been released to the public yet?"

"No, actually, it hasn't been released yet. I work in the fashion industry, which has it's perks. This is the summer collection that will be debuted next month. *Very* impressive, Mr. DeLuka."

"Please, call me Matt."

"Oh, no, Kris, your shoe," Caroline said.

Realization dawned on Kristy, and she stared, horrified, at her brand new designer heels. "Aw, man! This is the first time I've ever worn these. The entire heel is cracked."

Runway knelt down at her feet and gently slipped the broken shoe from her perfectly pedicured foot while casually caressing her calf in the process. Most people wouldn't have even caught it, but Caroline's eyes were glued to the unmistakable connection these two shared. "I think I can fix this. Do you have another pair of heels to wear tonight?"

Kristy stared at him in astonishment. "Uh. . .I'm sure I have *something* that will do. I'm sorry, how, exactly, are you planning to fix that? No offense, but I could probably send them back to the store and have a professional fix it."

He answered without looking up at her. "It's a clean break. I can fix it so you won't even be able to tell anything ever happened to it. That is. . ." He stood, now incredibly close to her, clearly invading her personal space, not that Kristy seemed to mind. "That is. . .if you can trust me. Can you?"

"Hmm? What?" her voice a faint whisper.

"Can you?"

"Can I what?"

"Trust me?" he paused and flashed his heart-stopping smile. "Don't worry, *bellissima*, I am very good with my hands, especially when I'm working with such delicate treasures."

Kristy took a step back, laughing loudly as if he'd told a joke. "Sure, why not. I don't know anything about you other than the fact that you're Sicilian, gorgeous and excessively *over*confident, but it's just a pair of shoes, right? Why *shouldn't* I trust you? Go ahead. Knock yourself out." She slipped the other shoe off of her foot and slowly backed up the stairs. "Now, if you'll excuse me. I need to go find another pair of shoes." She turned and quickly scurried the rest of the way up the stairs.

Caroline clasped her hands together in finality of the moment. "I think I'd better go see if she needs any help. It's time for me to start getting ready, too. Pleased to meet you, Runway. See you at the party."

"Kris? Are you okay?" Caroline knocked and slowly pushed the door to her room open.

"Yeah, I'm fine," she mumbled. "It's just a pair of shoes. Even though they were incredible and it took me forever to find the perfect ones for this dress. I'll get over it. Eventually. Maybe."

Caroline rolled her eyes. "Right. The shoes. Gimme a break, Kristy. You know I wasn't talking about your stupid shoes."

She turned away and pretended to dig through her suitcase. "Seriously, Caroline. You may not give a crap about fashion, but it's my life."

Caroline snorted. "I'm talking about the Italian Stallion downstairs who saved you from breaking your neck."

"He's Sicilian."

"Ah-ha! I *knew* it!" Caroline smiled triumphantly while propping on her knees on the bed like a teenager.

"Good grief, Caroline. Grow up. I'm not dead." She grew frustrated and began emptying her suitcase onto the bed. "He's gorgeous. Those hypnotic eyes. . ."

Caroline groaned, "Yes, those eyes. What color would you call them?"

Kristy shot her a stern look. "Hey, heifer. You've already got a man."

Caroline had struck a nerve. This was good. "Yes, I have a man, but I'm not dead either. I can still notice when someone is absurdly attractive and *exotic*." There. Caroline threw back the word Kristy had always used to describe her type. Runway was perfect for her, and Caroline would bet money that Kristy was perfect for him. He could obviously handle a diva. He was probably pretty high maintenance, himself.

"Yes, he's definitely exotic." She moved to the closet and pulled a pair of champagne-colored heels from the base of a hanging bag. They were more simple than the others, but still beautiful. "Whatever color they are, I couldn't stop staring at them. I wonder if he wears contacts. I've never seen anyone with eyes like that."

"So, do you think he could be the prince you were talking about?"

"Oh, please," Kristy said as she slipped on the new shoes. "Stop trying to play matchmaker and focus on your own romantic issues. *If* he's even into women, he's Cade's friend. I'm sure he's from Louisiana, and I live in California. It would never work. I'm not into long-distance relationships. They're impractical, and they always fail. He's probably one of Cade's alligator wrestlers, anyway."

"It's alligator *hunting,* not wrestling. Anyway, you think he's gay? I don't think so. I've met most of Cade's friends from here, and he wasn't one of them. Besides, you saw him. I don't think he's into hunting anything, especially alligators. He looks like he stepped right out of a fashion magazine."

"Yes, he certainly has great fashion sense. He smells amazing, too. If you take all the qualities he possesses and compare them to an ordinary man, he has to be gay. He's too perfect."

"So, he's *extra*ordinary. That doesn't mean he's not into women. Trevor looked like a model, too. And he *definitely* wasn't gay. The extreme opposite, in fact." Caroline smacked her hand on the bed, but Kristy ignored her as she continued pilfering through her make-up bag. "C'mon, Kristy, open your eyes. He's perfect for you. He's beautiful, exotic, Sicilian, dresses like a fashion model, knows fashion designers and lingo and all that other mumbo jumbo you work with. Plus, he was in the Navy with Cade."

Kristy's head snapped up in surprise. "What? He was in the Navy?"

"Yep." She grinned, letting the "p" sound pop at the end of the word. She knew that would get her attention.

"Mmmm, now *that's* hot. He's refined and fashion conscious, yet he's also rugged and athletic, and being a sailor in those dress whites is like the whipped cream and cherry on top. What'd he do in the Navy?"

"I don't know, I only got to talk to him briefly before you came launching down the stairs. I didn't even know Cade was in the military until Runway told me they had served together. They were

27

on the same team, whatever that means. I assume it means they had each other's backs in battle, but I thought just being in the U. S. military meant they were all on the same team. Maybe he meant they had the same job. Either way, it's a great conversation starter." Caroline stepped up behind Kristy, catching her attention in the mirror. "C'mon, hot stuff. Work your magic." She winked, and Kristy rolled her eyes as she brushed past Caroline, pulled a hanger from the closet, and shoved a slinky dress at her.

"Here, wear this tonight. It should fit you like a glove."

Caroline inspected the silky fabric with horror. "This is like a second skin. Can I even wear a bra with that? I may as well be naked," she griped.

Kristy snorted and gestured to Caroline's chest. "Yeah right, honey. You unleash those beasts on these poor, unsuspecting southerners and they may have instant heart failure."

Caroline frowned. "Ha. Ha. Ha. You're just jealous because you had to pay for yours. I would have happily traded, and saved you a lot of money."

Kristy admired her perky size C breasts. "Don't be silly. These babies were worth every penny. Besides, at least you have a good man already. Being single sucks. Keeping up with the dreaded social scene, fishing from the dating pond. . . Lately, that grungy little puddle is full of nothing but scum and piranhas."

"Excuse me, princess, but your Sicilian trophy fish is probably downstairs right now waiting impatiently for you to set your hooks in him," Caroline replied smugly.

"Oh, give me a break, Caroline." Kristy smacked her arm. "Just because he's perfect for me does not mean I'm perfect for him. I didn't exactly notice his heart fluttering upon seeing me." She sighed. "With my luck, he's probably more interested in Cade than in me. What a waste." She sighed again and stared out the window at nothing. "Oh, the things I could do to that boy. . ."

"Are you insane? He was entranced. Completely fixated on you. He caught you before anyone else even realized you were falling."

Kristy shook her head. "That doesn't mean anything. Just that he has quick reflexes."

"Whatever. It means he was watching you very closely and anticipating your next move. He offered to fix your shoe, and, oh! What he said about being good with his hands! That was *definitely* a come-on. He's got it bad for you, sweetheart. There's no denying that." Caroline smirked. "Besides, Cade is mine, and he knows it."

She bit back a laugh and brushed off the notion. "You're exaggerating because you want me to hookup with him so badly."

"Yes, I do," Caroline insisted. "Listen, remember what you said about everyone but me being able to see that Cade and I were perfect together? Well, now you're the one who's not seeing it. Don't blow him off because you assume something. Get to know him better tonight at the party. Please?" Kristy sorted her items on the bed to put them away. "He is your Mr. Right, and he's here now at the exact same time you are. Don't you see? It's fate. And you, being the overachiever that you are, jumped right into his arms before you ever spoke to him. Ha ha! You may not get another opportunity like this, so don't screw it up."

Kristy threw a pillow at her. "Oh, go get ready, you little heathen." Caroline stuck her tongue out and went to her room to get ready. Her mind raced as she dressed.

The Navy. That's honorable enough. Why had Cade withheld this information? What else was he hiding?

FOUR

Caroline padded down the hall looking for her mother's room. She turned the corner and saw Eddie standing outside a door. His forehead against the frame, he sighed visably.

"Em?" Eddie said "You okay?"

Caroline ducked around the corner. Like usual, and not always wisely, her curiosity ruled, and she decided to eavesdrop.

He stepped into the room completely, leaving the door cracked. Caroline sneaked closer to better hear them. She should feel ashamed, but she didn't. She desperately wanted to know what was up with her mother and hoped Eddie might drag it out of her.

"I don't believe you. What's wrong?" His voice was thick with concern. Good. Caroline was relieved she hadn't been the only one to notice.

Emily mumbled, "It's nothing, really. I'm fine."

She was lying. Caroline hoped Eddie knew it, too. She peeked through the crack of the door jamb. Her dad stood behind her mom and gently placed his hands on her shoulders as he spoke softly. Caroline strained to hear.

"Emily, I know I'm probably not your favorite person after all that I've put you through, but I want you to know you can talk to me. I don't deserve the gifts I've already been given by having Caroline back in my life, but I do care about you."

Emily wept and Caroline resisted the urge to go inside and comfort her.

Eddie turned Emily around, and she tried to hide her distress behind her hands as she buried her face into his chest. He tenderly pulled on her hands and lifted her chin so he could see her tear-streaked cheeks. He presented a folded handkerchief from his pocket and dabbed Emily's swollen eyes.

"You know," he said. "You're doing a number on my ego. I don't recall seeing tears like this when I left you on your own with nothing but an infant and divorce papers. The mystery of what could possibly have you so sad is killing me." He chuckled at his self-ridicule and the grace with which he delivered it.

Emily studied his face, her eyes glistening with fresh tears. The crease between her brows deepened and she shook her head.

"What is it?"

"Nothing, I just. . . Well, I've spent the past twenty-something years building up my hatred and bitterness for you so I wouldn't wonder what things could've been like if you hadn't left. Then, seeing how great you've been with Caroline. . . And now you're concern for me. . . You're just being so. . .*nice*. You're supposed to be egotistical and selfish so that I'll hate you more and be glad you left when you did so I wouldn't have spent my life in misery with someone like you. You're the complete opposite of everything I had convinced myself you were for the last two decades."

He laughed. "Thank you. I think. I can't be certain, but I believe there was a compliment in there somewhere."

She smiled and bowed her head in embarrassment. "No, I-I'm so sorry. I shouldn't have said those awful things just now. I'm not myself at the moment. You should probably go."

"No, I think I'll stay."

Yes! Good, Eddie. Don't let her push you away.

"I can tell when I'm needed, and right now I think you need someone to talk to. Or at least someone to yell at. Why don't you tell me what's bothering you?"

31

"Eddie, I don't think. . . Well, I can't—" She let out an exasperated sigh, dropping her hands to her thighs as she sat on the edge of the bed. "I can't explain it. I don't know how."

"Will you try? I've heard some pretty crazy stuff involving ghosts and things over the last year, so I think I can handle it." He snickered, no doubt remembering Caroline's attempt to explain the story of the ghost of his G2 grandmother haunting her dreams. It had been a lot for both of them to swallow, but once Caroline presented Rachel's journal and explained how she found it, Eddie finally believed her.

Emily continued. "Well, you see, that's just it. I don't know *how* to throw it at you because I'm not certain what exactly happened. I'm sure I'm overreacting. No need fretting over something that's probably nothing. I'm just emotional. I just got Caroline back after her living in Chicago for four years. Now that she's finished with college, I'm sure she'll be moving back here before the ink on her degree is even dry." Emily wiped her tears before blowing her nose in his handkerchief. "I'll be okay, I promise." She held up the soiled cloth before tucking it in her pocket. "I'll wash this and give it back to you later."

He knelt down in front of her and held both of her hands in his. "Are you sure, Em? You were way too upset for it to have been nothing to worry about. Believe me, I understand about getting spoiled from quality time with Caroline. It nearly killed me when I learned she was going back to Chicago earlier than she'd planned to rush into a wedding with that controlling, abusive. . . Well, you remember. I wasn't ready to let her go. I'm willing to listen if you just want to get whatever is bothering you off your chest. I promise I won't say anything, I'll just listen."

She caressed his cheek and smiled. "You've already helped me more than you realize. Thank you for everything."

She leaned forward and kissed his forehead. He closed his eyes, relishing the moment.

Caroline's heart swelled. Their affection was too natural and too good for them to have been apart for so long.

Approaching footsteps resounded up the stairs. Caroline bolted back around the corner.

"Well, now, isn't this sweet?"

Caroline cringed at April's shrill voice.

"I guess the old saying *is* true. Like mother, like daughter."

Caroline had had enough and was about to intervene, but Eddie's response kept her rooted in place.

"Shut the hell up, April. You don't know what was going on, so don't stand there haughty and pretentious like you have any ground to stand upon. It's still daylight outside, so keep your snide comments and insults to yourself and fly back to your cave."

Obviously stunned and silenced by the truth he so adequately slapped upon her, April stormed out and retreated to the master bedroom.

Eddie and April's marriage was not as peachy as April would like for people to think. Caroline tiptoed back to the door and peeked through the crack.

Eddie intertwined his fingers through Emily's. "I'm so sorry. I've had about all I can stand of her blatant disrespect. She had no right to say those things to you, and I apologize for putting you in such an awkward and vulnerable position. I'll deal with her, but first I need to know that you're alright."

She blinked back her tears and nodded. "I'm fine. I just need to rest before the party tonight. Thank you, Eddie. I appreciate your friendship. Caroline is very lucky to have you in her life. And so am I."

He cradled her face again and bent his head as if contemplating a loss. "Emily, I was wondering—"

"I think you should go now. . .before you do something you'll regret later," Emily said. "Thank you again. For everything."

He sighed in defeat and pursed his lips. "There's the strong girl I remember. Always in control. I guess this was just a rare and brief vulnerable moment that I happened to barge in on. I understand, though. No worries. If someone had treated me as badly as I treated you, I wouldn't want to let her back in either." He leaned in and left a lingering kiss on her cheek. "You've done well, Em. Get some rest, I'm reserving a dance with you tonight." He turned toward the door.

Caroline zipped around the corner. She poked her head around to capture a glimpse of her dad outside the door, listening, waiting, though she wasn't sure exactly what for, but he clearly wasn't ready to walk away. Sobs carried down the hall. Her dad put a hand to the door, a battle warring in his expression.

Caroline, blown away, was thankful for her curiosity and good-fortune of witnessing a special moment between her parents.

Eddie squared his shoulders and took a deep breath as he briskly walked toward his room down the hall. Caroline's position was close enough to catch everything as he stormed into his bedroom. April's gasp was punctuated by the slamming door. Eddie's low, furious voice carried down the hall just enough to be audible.

"It seems I've obviously caught you in the middle of something."

A drawer smashed shut. "Nothing quite as good as what I caught *you* doing."

"That's it. We need to have a little talk," he growled.

Caroline flinched at the clack of the door lock and she bolted down the hall. She did not want to be caught snooping while Eddie was on a rampage.

"Momma, it's time for you to start getting ready if you want to be downstairs by six."

Emily sat up slowly and rubbed her puffy eyes. It killed Caroline that she didn't know why her mom had been crying.

Her mom frowned and looked around for a clock.

"It's five-thirty. I wanted to let you sleep as long as possible."

"Yeah, I feel a little better. Weary, but better."

34

Caroline chortled. "Weary is better than how you were feeling before? Man, that's depressing. What was wrong with you earlier? I know it wasn't my driving, so don't even try to go there."

She immediately went into mom-mode. "Caroline, I'm fine. I just had an emotional moment, that's all. I'm not a fool. I know you will be moving down here as soon as you can, and, honestly, you'd be a fool not to. I understand that, but it's just going to hurt letting you go again. I'll be okay. Don't worry about me."

Caroline wasn't convinced. Something else plagued Emily. "Well, you don't have to *let me go*. You could always move down here with me. There are plenty of rooms in this house, and you wouldn't have to cook or clean anything."

Her mom gave her a precocious look. "Uh-huh, yeah, I don't think that would work out too well. I've already made quite an impression on your wicked stepmother. She likes me about as much as she likes you. There would be too many hens in this hen house if I moved in."

"Oh, forget about April. She's a wanker."

Emily burst out laughing. It was great to see her mom smiling again. She felt better about leaving her to finish dressing.

Fifteen minutes later, Caroline stood before the mirror smoothing out her sleek, teal blue, halter dress, mentally preparing herself for the evening ahead. The tight fit and type of material didn't allow for undergarments, so Caroline felt somewhat exposed. A thought that flitted across her mind caused her instantaneous shame. She swore under her breath and scolded her reflection.

She had a handsome, loyal, extremely talented, former Navy guy of her own, and he would be waiting eagerly for her to join him downstairs at any moment. Why, why, *why* was she thinking about Trevor?

FIVE

"Dude! You've been holding out on me." Runway's voice cracked like a pre-pubescent teenager.

Smirking, Cade decided to mess with him as they walked through the woods toward his cabin. "I have no idea what you're talking about."

"Oh, it's like that, huh? I see. Come on. You're with Caroline, and she's beautiful. My hopes of Caroline having a hot twin sister were pointless. But you didn't tell me about the fashion goddess that is her best friend. Tell me everything you know about Kristy." He cut his eyes to Cade. "*Now.*"

Cade stopped walking and squared his shoulders. "Or what?"

"You seriously have to ask? Dude, I will take you down."

"Psh. With what? Your looks? You got nothin' on me, bro. Save your energy for shopping or something." Cade laughed hysterically as he dodged Runway's lunge just in time. Runway, missing his target by less than a foot, stumbled to his knees. "Damn, boy, when'd you get so slow? Civilian life isn't doing you any favors."

Cade was poking the bull, but it was too much fun to stop.

Runway brushed himself off and stared Cade down for a moment before a knowing grin spread across his face. He cracked his knuckles and walked off at a normal pace again. Cade watched carefully before following him. Once he caught up, he continued in a casual tone. "So what's with the grin?"

"Oh, nothing. I'll get what I want. Though I'd rather hear it from you. It's cool. I'm sure Caroline will spill it after I disclose your oh-so-secret nickname to her. She seems to be the inquisitive type, and I'm sure it's killing her that no one will tell her. Especially you."

Cade's neck tensed. He called Runway's bluff. "Go ahead and tell her. I don't care because she knows how I feel about it."

Runway frowned, so Cade changed the subject. "So you wanna know about Kristy, huh? She *is* pretty hot, isn't she?"

Runway stopped again. "I've seen more sexy women in my twenty-seven years than most men have the opportunity to see in a lifetime, but none of them have caught my attention that strongly. It's rare for anyone to steal my breath the way she did. If you don't stop screwing around and tell me more about her, I might be inclined to corner Caroline and interrogate her like the tangos we grilled overseas."

"DeLuka, if you so much as fart in Caroline's direction or approach her with the intention of forcing her to do *anything*, I'll have you in a position that'll need the jaws of life just so you can breathe. And you'll learn how we do torture down here. We clear?"

Runway laughed and put his hands up in surrender. "Roger that. Loud and clear. Clearly aggression still doesn't intimidate you, so now I'm resorting to begging." He plopped down on his knees in front of Cade and clasped his hands together. "Please, Beau, I'm begging you. Please tell me everything you know about her. Throw me a line, dude. I'm dying here."

Cade shook his head. "Damn, Runway. Get off your knees before someone sees you kneeling in front of me, man. I've got a reputation to keep around here. I've never seen you act like this before. What's the deal with this one? Sure, I mean, she's beautiful, but letting down your man-guard, assuming the position with your face level to my crotch, and begging like a freak?" Cade shook his head. "Ain't like you, man. How do you know she's even worth this ridiculous," Cade gestured to his compromising position, "and *extreme* overreaction?"

Runway stood and swiped the dirt from his knees. "Since when have you become a homophobe? Don't ask, don't tell, right?" Cade glared at him. "I'm kidding. Relax, brother. Okay, it's like this. You remember when you told me how you met Caroline? How you knew within minutes of talking to her that she was the one for you? Even though she was engaged to someone else, you felt the connection and had no doubt that you two were meant to be together?"

Cade smiled. He was lucky enough to be working the day Caroline walked into the library, helplessly looking for newspapers from the 1800s, and he was smitten. He chuckled, remembering the moment they both had realized she was the one who'd barreled into his stark-naked body as he stepped from his bathroom after a shower. He instantly loved everything about her. Her innocence, how easily she blushed about the smallest things, the panic attack when she realized it was his house she'd walked into. After absorbing what Runway implied, he nodded.

"Well, I thought you were nuts when you told me that. I couldn't imagine anyone knowing something of that magnitude so quickly after meeting a chick for the first time. I didn't believe you. Even when I arrived here and saw how you physically and emotionally lit up when you talked about her, I still didn't believe you. After meeting her and seeing for myself how lovely she is and how great you two looked together, I saw how you would be attracted to her. "But, I still couldn't see how you came to such a conclusion so soon after meeting her. Then, when Kristy began walking down the stairs, and I saw her hair, her face, her incredible body, her sultry voice. . .immaculate fashion sense. The stars aligned and I was blown away. What happened next was just. . . I can't explain it."

Runway rested his hands on his hips and kicked a stump. "My experience with beautiful women like her is usually grouped into two dissatisfying categories. One, they get this star-struck look in their eyes and can't make it past my face to enter into an intelligent conversation. When they learn about my military background, I can usually spot that hero-worship gaze before the first word comes out.

A major turnoff. Two, they assume since I am from California and interested in designer clothes that I'm either gay or as shallow as they are."

He adamantly shook his head. "I didn't get that impression from Kristy. If anything, she seemed. . .*un*interested. I mean, I think she was attracted to me, at least I hope so, but she wasn't consumed with it. She doubted my ability to fix her shoe and didn't even react to my touch or anything. It was. . .it was. . ."

"Humbling?" Cade laughed.

A smile erupted, and the carefree man Cade had met that first day of boot camp was back for the first time in years.

"Well, yes. But it was also intriguing. My entire life, I've never wanted to learn everything I could about a specific woman, and she's got me completely captivated. I don't know what else to do. It's like I can't control myself. My desire. This obsession. This has never happened to me. I have to know her. To talk to her. . .touch her."

"Careful about that last bit. She doesn't hold back and you may get more than you bargained for. Like a knee in the balls."

"Come on, Beau. You know I'm serious about this."

"I know."

They walked in silence for several hundreds yards, Runway patiently waiting for the information. Beau's mind was a thousand miles away before Runway froze. Cade stopped, but shamefully avoided looking at him.

He shouldn't let his buried resentment keep Runway from being happy, right? He and Kristy were a match made in Heaven, and Runway *did* save his life. If he hadn't done that, Cade wouldn't be here to hold a grudge about the other stuff.

Resigned, Runway's voice softened. "Look, I realize we haven't seen each other in a long time, and our last memory was unpleasant for you. But you *know* me. I don't hold any bitterness about what happened in Afghanistan, and you know I love you like the brother I never had."

"Dammit, Runway, this has nothing to do with—"

"I pushed you off of that bomb then, and I would do it again in a heartbeat. It's not your fault my shoulder got shredded, it's mine. And I take full responsibility for that."

Cade watched him plead his case and remembered the first time he'd met Matteo DeLuka. Runway's parents had died in a car crash when he was only eighteen. He joined the Navy three months later, and he and Cade had been inseparable. They went through boot camp together, and did extra pushups, pull-ups, and sit-ups while everyone else polished their boots, or took Hollywood showers. They shared the same drive and passion. Cade was Runway's only family.

Remorse filled him as he remembered seeing his best friend, his brother in arms, fly through the air with the blast that would have killed Cade if Runway hadn't pushed him out of the way. Runway had been lucky it only blasted his shoulder. But their issues went deeper. He still felt guilty for the way he'd cut Runway out of his life after everything they'd been through. And the reasoning seemed petty after all this time. Runway had done nothing that Cade wouldn't have done had the situation been reversed. So why hadn't he let it go? He let out a frustrated breath.

"You know me better than anyone else in the world. You *have* to know that this isn't just some childish crush. If anyone could understand why I have to know more, I would think it would be you."

Cade wasn't interested in dragging up old memories of Afghanistan. "Yeah, fine. You don't have to get all mushy on me. It's not like I can give you permission to marry her or anything. Why don't you just talk to her yourself?"

Runway's shoulders sagged.

Cade sighed. "I guess I can see wanting to do your research before blindly approaching her. But I can't help you much because I don't really know that much about her." Cade stopped walking and pointed at him. "What I *do* know is that she's Caroline's best friend, and if you hurt her, I'll have to jack you up a little. A lot."

40

Runway's brow raised. "Deal. I know you observed more than you're letting on. I don't need her life story, just what you have noticed since you've known her."

Cade broke a twig from a tree and peeled the bark off in strips as he searched his memory. They started walking again, kicking rocks as they shuffled through the brush and leaves. "Let's see, she's originally from Tennessee. A fashion designer with a privileged upbringing, and now she lives somewhere in southern California."

Runway's eyes lit up with satisfaction.

"She's very classy but also extremely high maintenance. That much is obvious. She's very protective of the people she loves. I had a difficult time getting her to talk about Caroline behind her back. She's intelligent, witty and very sharp. There's nothing you can sneak past this chick. She's quick. Doesn't miss anything. I guess you could say she's very intuitive or just keenly observant. And persistent." Cade laughed, "Man, she won't let anything go once she's on the trail." He thought for a moment. "She's open, and honest if she trusts you. Oh, and she's blunt." Cade chuckled.

"Honestly, Kristy's exactly the kind of best friend Caroline needs. As far as I know, she's never been married or even had a serious boyfriend, so she could be afraid or unwilling to commit. I'm not sure." He remembered Kristy's comment about not being as innocent as Caroline. "She's a good girl, but I don't think she's without experience."

They approached his cabin and Cade knocked his shoes on the porch slab. Before inserting his key in the lock, he turned to Runway to issue one final warning. "I'll get you two talking at the party later, but, dude, I swear, if you use her or take advantage of her in any way, you will seriously have to answer to me. I have Kristy to thank for helping me stop Caroline from marrying that prick in Chicago. I couldn't have done it without her, so I owe her. *Big time*."

Runway smiled, and, before Cade realized, Runway gave him a huge bear hug. "Thanks, dude. You're the man. I owe you."

41

He shrugged him off. "Yeah, sure. Okay, that's enough, bro. Damn, I forgot how touchy-feely you were. You gotta keep that California hippy crap to a minimum down here or I'll have to defend myself in more ways than one."

Cade grabbed a beer from the fridge, handed one to Runway, and settled in to check the results from the voice-activated recording devices he had carefully positioned and installed in the Fontenot house. After his unfortunate discovery of a Mafia hit man's intentions to take out Eddie and Caroline, Eddie insisted he place them inconspicuously throughout the house where secluded and/or suspicious conversations would most likely take place. Runway had better connections regarding surveillance, so Cade had called him last summer and asked him to send the latest equipment.

For months, Cade hoped to gain information about the enemy Kenneth Callahan had warned them about after his plot to eliminate Caroline's entire family was foiled. Instead, he listened to mostly muffled noises, clandestine phone conversations of a teenage daughter, or Delphine and Delia gossiping. Nothing more.

Not today. What Cade heard sent chills down his spine, and he immediately picked up his phone to call Eddie. Party or no party, Eddie needed to hear this.

He'd answered on the first ring.

"Hey, Mr. Fontenot. It's Beau."

"Hey, Beau. What's up?"

"Sir, I need you to come down to my cabin if you're able to get away for a few minutes."

"People will be showing up for the party in about half an hour."

"Yes, sir. I know. I promise if it wasn't important I wouldn't ask you to come here."

The prolonged silence revealed his hesitation. "I'll be there in a few."

"Sir?"

"Yeah?"

"Can you make sure Caroline doesn't know where you're going? I don't really want her to know anything's going on."

The urgency in his tone intensified. "Done. On my way."

Cade hung up to Runway's eyes boring into him. "What?"

He raised one eyebrow and crossed his arms. "Your girlfriend's father drops everything to come at your request? Nice. You'll have to let me in on your secret. That's awesome."

Though amused by Runway's impression of his relationship with Eddie, Cade couldn't mislead him. "Nah, he trusts me. He knows I love Caroline, and that I'd do anything to protect her. Plus, he knows about my past. And it doesn't hurt that I saved his family from an absolute tragedy last year. Trust me, it's not at all like what you're thinking. We have a mutual respect for each other. Besides, Caroline's not my girlfriend yet."

Ten minutes later, Eddie didn't wait for him to open the door. He knocked a second before he barged in, concern prematurely aging his face. "What's up, Beau? Is Caroline in trouble?"

Cade held one hand up to reassure him. "She's fine, Mr. Fontenot. It's not Caroline I'm concerned about." He motioned across the room. "This is my Navy buddy, Runway." Eddie nodded his greeting.

"I have something you need to hear," Cade continued.

Confusion clouded Eddie's eyes.

"I picked up something on one of the voice-activated tapping devices in your office, and one in your bedroom."

Eddie's lips pursed and his head rocked back in recognition. His less-than-thrilled expression proved he'd clearly forgotten they'd tapped his house.

"I promise I fast forwarded the conversations in which you were involved. Honestly, I mostly monitored the people who work inside your home, on the grounds, and April. . .which brings me to the now."

Eddie crossed his arms and frowned.

"Sir, has April done anything strange or out of character lately?"

43

"Well, yes, actually. Well, our relationship hasn't been. . .we've struggled for the past couple of years. . .intimately." Eddie shifted his weight, shoving one hand in his pocket while the other brusquely rubbed his smoothly shaved chin. Cade didn't envy him. It had to be tough to find an appropriate way to discuss the intimate details of his marriage with two other guys, one of whom he didn't know. "Yeah, earlier today. Before Caroline arrived, she came to my office and seduced me. Suspicious at first, I questioned her motives, but she can, uh, be quite persuasive." He smirked and shrugged. "But yeah, out of character. She snapped back to normal as soon as everyone got here. Why?"

"The tap from your bedroom recorded something this afternoon that I really think you should hear. You may want to sit down and get comfortable." Cade prepared the recording for playback and sat where he could observe Eddie's reaction to each new revelation.

April's voice flooded the small living room of the cabin.

"How dare he speak to me like that. Especially in front of his ex-wife. They'd have been sucking face if I hadn't interrupted them. That whore. No wonder that little slut daughter of hers is the way she is. Eddie's *my* man. After what I did for him this morning, and now he's all over her? This house isn't big enough for those two and me to all be under the same roof."

Eddie pinched the bridge of his nose and shook his head. They heard the sound of a drawer opening and closing.

Cade poured a highball glass of whiskey and handed it to him, which he downed in one large gulp. They heard the muted beeps of buttons from what was probably a cell phone.

"Joey? It's Apr—uh—it's Ana." Panic laced her voice after the awkward silence. "Morales. Ana Morales."

Eddie's posture was now ramrod straight, his jaw dropped. His wife's apparent alias and noticeable difference in her accent surprised them all.

Still, more silence. "Come on, Joey. Whaddya want me to say? Huh? I'm sorry if I hurt your ego, but I'm married."

Eddie's eyebrows raised in surprise. Cade rubbed his face to hide his grin.

"Joe! Come on. Gimme a br—"

A male voice could almost be heard now. April must have moved directly beside the tap Cade had installed.

"Good. I'm glad that's out of the way then. I need a favor. Kind of a big one."

A long pause and a definite sigh, April's tone dropped. "I know. Things didn't go exactly as I had planned, and I'm sorry about all that. I promise, I'll do it right this time. I didn't know that little tramp would move her ass in with us. Then she started sleeping around and ruined the whole wedding, not to mention her little lover-boy stickin' his nose where it don't belong. I'll follow through with it all on my own if I have to. Talk to him for me, Joey? Please? I'll owe ya big."

A moment passed and April growled in frustration. "Yeah, yeah. I know, I already owe you for sending the last guy.

Eddie's head rocked back with amusement. He glanced at Cade, and they made eye contact in silent recollection. Ivan Baronovsky. The hit man sent to end the Fontenots so the Callahan's could have their revenge. Caroline had been right. Apparently April had her hands in that mess after all. And Ivan had turned out to be like a phantom. None of Cade's contacts in law enforcement were able to find Baronovsky anywhere to question him. His last known location was a boarding school in Moscow from which he disappeared at age ten. Otherwise, absolutely no record of him existed.

"I have a few unexpected loose ends I need to clip before I can successfully execute my plan."

There was rustling in the room, like shoes scuffling across the hardwood. Her voice lowered to a near whisper. "Look, I can't say anything about it right now. Just talk to him for me, would ya? I can't do this without help. Tell him he can trust me the same as he trusted my mother and grandmother."

The muted beep of the cell phone disconnecting was followed by the sound of a door opening and the slam of a drawer. Eddie's voice flowed through the speakers.

"It seems I've obviously caught you in the middle of something."

Cade immediately stopped the recording. Eddie pressed his palms against his eyes. Cade gave Eddie a moment to digest what he'd just heard. He stood and walked toward the door. He paused before opening it and turned back.

"I will think about everything I just heard and decide what I should do about it. Thank you, Beau, for bringing this to my attention. Good work. We can deal with this tomorrow. Let's do our best to enjoy the party tonight, shall we?"

Cade nodded. "Yes, sir."

"See y'all in a bit." He walked out and didn't look back.

"Well, he's a cool guy," Runway said. "Good job, man. You've got yourself a good father-in-law."

Cade shrugged. "He's not my father-in-law. . .yet. But I'm about ready to make the first big move in changing that."

Runway smiled big and nodded his head in approval. "Hooyah, brother!"

Dressed to impress, Cade and Runway walked through the woods toward the party carefully avoiding pot holes and muddy spots, cutting up and reminiscing of good times. A gunshot not too far in the distance echoed through the trees. They froze, their jovial expressions immediately dropped into sober ones. Effortlessly, they picked up where they left off years ago in Afghanistan.

They stealthily headed in the direction of the gunshot, picking up the pace when they heard four more quickly follow. Cade pulled his knife from his right back pocket, cursing himself for not being better prepared with a more suitable weapon. Not to mention having to deal with someone potentially dangerous while wearing restrictive clothing. He hated dressing up and rarely had reason to. And the stiff new shoes that went with his tux were hardly broken in with their slippery soles. Damn leprechaun shoes.

He gave a silent signal to Runway to branch around the perimeter from where the sounds came. Their eyes met across the small field on the outskirts of the Fontenot property. Runway withdrew a small revolver from under his jacket, ready to have Cade's back if necessary. Good, Cade thought, at least one of them came somewhat prepared.

Cade moved closer to the clearing of the field, a pungent odor triggering memories of rotting flesh from his hellish experience in Afghanistan. He cautiously slipped behind a small rundown shack he'd planned to renovate as a hunting blind and never got around to it. The smell invaded his senses causing his gag reflex to angrily protest. The lone window facing the back was missing the bottom pane, the wood frame rotted and unsupportive. The top pane was broken in the corner, chillingly reminding him of a guillotine blade. He drew in a sharp breath as he peeked through the broken window above his head and saw the culprit.

He spied the back of April's bleached-blonde head, her arm outstretched pointing a 9mm pistol downward, as if she had just executed the enemy on the battlefield. She released the clip, letting it drop to the ground, and replaced it in one swift motion before loading the chamber again. She handled the weapon with incredible and surprising skill. April wasn't the ditzy airhead he'd originally thought her to be.

His mind sprinted as he digested this new information about her. What in the world, or *who*, could enlist April's interest in target practice these days? She obviously had some anger issues considering the last four rapid-fire shots at a dangerously close range.

Cade hadn't listened to the rest of the conversation after Eddie had confronted her, but apparently Eddie had pissed her off. Was she so angry she needed to shoot out her frustration? Certain he had a big fat target on his own back for crashing the wedding and causing

Caroline to permanently move in, Cade couldn't understand this extremely aggressive reaction from someone like April. He had severely underestimated her. Cade risked another look to see what else she had in her arsenal.

The decaying wood floor was splattered with blood from half-empty jars along a rickety bench, and a smattering of white chicken feathers trailed through the narrow doorway. Dead snakes hung from the rafters by wire hangers, the skin shredded halfway exposing rotten, fly-covered meat. An uneasy dread swept over Cade. What the hell was April's game? He'd been told about voodoo rituals, even saw some himself, but this didn't look like anything he'd ever heard of before. This was morbid.

Caroline swore she was evil, but until today he hadn't believed it. There was simply no hard evidence of a real threat to cause worry. Sure, she's got an acerbic tongue, but violence just didn't seem like her style.

While he contemplated what to do next, April's cell phone rang. He sank lower beneath the broken window, and motioned for Runway to hold steady. He needed to gather as much information as possible before taking any kind of action. One wrong, hasty move could ruin everything.

"Yeah? I thought I told you never to call me at this number? Are you trying to ruin everythi—" she huffed.

"Listen to me you half-brained, redneck, coon-ass. Backing out is not an option. You knew the details when you agreed to do this job. If you screw this up, believe me when I tell you, those alligators you hunt will look like kittens compared to the monsters I'll unleash. I want him gone. Out of the picture. Dead. Clear enough? Good. Now, don't ever call me on this phone again, or I'll kill you myself."

Cade closed his eyes as the realization sank in, and he wanted to puke. Someone he knew, and most likely trusted, was working with April. But who? Who does she want out of the picture? Him? Eddie? Callahan?

He glanced at Runway and motioned for him to head toward the plantation house as he prepared to sneak back into the cover of the trees. Whatever that chick had planned, one thing was clear. It wasn't any good, and she obviously had friends in high places. Higher than he'd ever imagined. And more heinous. This battle was quickly turning into a war.

Just as he started to move, he heard the unmistakable click of a weapon directly behind his head. He spun slowly on his feet still in a squatted position, and stared up into the barrel of April's 9mm weapon, cocked and ready to fire. Focused behind it, ice-cold eyes danced with intensity.

"Why, hello, Beau. Are you lost? Something I can do for you?" she asked in an exaggerated chirpy tone. She stood on something, her arm stretched through the broken glass in the window aimed down at him. He calmly raised his hands.

"Nope, thanks. Just passing through. If you'll excuse me, I have a party to get to." His eyes remained coolly focused on her face, refusing to show fear or give away Runway's position. Assuming he waited around in the perimeter to see this.

April's face was plastered with her signature fake smile. "Oh, dear boy. I'm terribly sorry, but I'm afraid you won't be attending the party tonight. You see, I think you might have seen or heard more than you should have, so unfortunately for you and your little sweet-tart, Caroline, you won't be going anywhere tonight."

He cursed himself again for not being better prepared. While deciding the best way to disarm her, she withdrew slightly, the weapon out of his reach but still aimed at his face.

"Uh-uh-uh," she melodically warned. "Don't be stupid. Your heroics won't get you out of this one."

Cade did not want her smug face to be his last memory. But before he could move, a shot rang out. He jolted and tensed, ducking to cover his head as shards of glass fell around him. Attempting to get to his feet, his ears rang with the pop of more gunfire, so he dropped to the dirt. Something hot pierced his shoulder, pinning him to the ground.

SIX

"Mom," Caroline called from outside the bathroom door. "The party's already started."

A shriek resounded from the other side. Caroline burst through the door. Her mother clutched her chest with one hand, the other had a death grip on the sink. Horrified, Emily looked as if she had just seen a ghost. Caroline scoffed. In this house, that was entirely possible.

"Momma? What happened? Are you okay?" She didn't answer. Instead, she stared blankly into the mirror mumbling something barely audible. "Mother! Talk to me. Don't you dare tell me it was nothing. What is wrong with you?"

She continued mumbling. "Why? Why is this happening to me? What's causing this? What does it mean? It can't be true. This can't be real."

Frustrated, Caroline shook her shoulders hard. "Snap out of it. What's wrong?"

Emily's expression switched from terrified to tragic. "Oh, Caroline! It was awful! Is he here yet? I need to see him."

Beyond confused, she said, "Who? Is who here yet? Eddie? He's downstairs. Please, tell me what is going on."

Emily shook her head and shoved past her out of the bathroom. "No, no, not Eddie. Cade! Is Cade here yet? Is he okay? I need to see him."

"No, he's not here yet. Why do you need to see him? What's up with you?"

Her mother wouldn't stop. "Momma," Caroline shouted. "Why are you acting so crazy? Did something happen?"

She stopped and turned to her daughter, looking into her eyes with sorrow. "Baby, I think Cade's been shot."

The bottom of her stomach dropped. "What? H-how—Why would you think that?"

Emily mumbled, "I-I-I don't know for sure, I just. . . Call it a gut feeling. I just need to see if he's alright."

Caroline drew in a deep calming breath. A gut feeling she could handle. Facts, not so much. She was sure her mother had overreacted. "Okay, calm down." She reassuringly squeezed her mother's arm. "I'm sure Cade is okay. It's been a stressful day. Just relax. Let's go have a drink and chill out." Caroline pulled on her mom, but she didn't budge. "He'll be here," Caroline urged. She didn't understand her mom's extreme behavior about a feeling. "He helped Dad plan this shindig, so I'm sure he won't skip out on it. If he does, I'll kill him myself. Although, he *is* late," Caroline frowned, as she checked her watch, "which is very unlike him. He's usually annoyingly punctual."

Emily took a slow, cleansing breath and squeezed her eyes closed. "Okay, you're probably right. Um, just out of curiosity, how late is he? I mean, how long has the party been going on?" She fumbled with her own watch.

"He's already forty-five minutes late. I'm sure he and his friend are primping in the mirror like a couple of girls."

Emily's eyes jerked up. "Friend? What friend?"

Caroline shrugged, "It's a guy he knew from the military. Did you know he was in the Navy?" She still couldn't wrap her mind around it and the revelation was a nice surprise.

"Does his friend look Italian with dark wavy hair that hangs to about here?" She motioned to her temples.

Caroline's eyes narrowed. "He's Sicilian, actually. Why? How'd you know that?"

Emily's face paled, her hollow eyes saddened. "Have mercy," she whispered. Her mom reached out to grab her arm for support as they both sank down onto the floor. "Oh, Caroline. I think something terrible has happened. I hope I'm wrong, but I don't think Cade will be coming to your party tonight."

Caroline forced herself to focus. "Come again? Wrong about what, exactly? Why *wouldn't* Cade be coming tonight? Momma, what is going on with you?"

Emily's jaw tightened, and she finally gathered her bearings as she stood and straightened her clothes. "Caroline, come with me. I need to tell you something, but I'd rather go somewhere a little more comfortable and private than in the bathroom."

"Is this necessary? Can't you just tell me what you're talking about without all this drama? You've got me worried now, and I really want to go see if Cade's okay."

Emily stopped and looked into her eyes. Without a word, she smoothed Caroline's face as only a mother can, kissed her forehead, and stroked her hair. "You know what, I probably am just overreacting. It was a bad daydream, that's all. Let's go downstairs, get a drink, and see if your father might know where Cade is."

"Wait a minute. No way!" She followed her mom down the hall to the stairs. "You are gonna tell me what has you acting so weird. You've got me freaking out now."

"Why don't you give him a call? Maybe that will ease both of our minds and then we can enjoy the party." She started down the stairs at rocket speed, and Caroline stopped in her room to grab her phone before scurrying down the stairs after her. She dialed Cade's number and listened to the empty ringing before his voicemail picked up. Worry rattled her mind when she saw her mom in the foyer headed for the receiving room. Why was she acting so weird? Panicked and frightful one moment to completely indifferent the next. Something screwy was going on, and Caroline tried not to worry about Cade, but him not answering his phone was unusual.

Caroline pushed the niggling anxiety to the side for the moment and paused to absorb the beautiful decorations. In the short time they had been upstairs getting ready, Delia had lined the foyer with white cloth-covered entry tables. Each table hosted crystal vases filled with bouquets of fresh-cut red roses. The sweet fragrance filled the air. Trying not to panic, Caroline scanned the rom for any sign of the man she loved. Nothing.

Half a dozen round tables had been set up between the receiving room and the parlor. Large water-filled crystal bowls with red rose petals and floating candles centered each formally set table. Crimson votive candles flickered in small crystal goblets scattered throughout the space, adding a splash of color and light among the elegant white decor. Polished silver candelabras with tapered candles added to the ambience as the flames licked the air with the slight draft of each passing guest.

Strings of white lights led a pathway to the ballroom that was swathed with cascading cream chiffon curtains loosely draped in a tent-like fashion from the ceiling with balls of lights filtered amongst them.

Many people had already arrived and, though some danced to the jazz music provided by a hired deejay, most spilled out through the ballroom doors that led to the festively decorated patio. Through the open doors, Caroline spied strands of lights and lanterns hanging from the surrounding trees. Caroline caught up to her mom, and together they entered the crowded receiving room.

Kristy stood with Caroline's father and plucked a crystal champagne flute from Delia's tray as she passed through the crowd. Eddie hadn't noticed them as he chatted with the small group of people, but Kristy smiled and waved them over.

Eddie's face brightened upon their arrival. "Well, hello ladies. Nice of you to join us." He motioned to his guests. "This is my daughter Caroline and my. . . uh, her mother, Emily." Eddie held her mother's gaze for a moment before swallowing hard and clearing his throat. "Caroline, you remember Dr. Breaux. This lovely lady on his arm is his fiancée, Cecily."

Caroline smiled sheepishly. The last time she saw the handsome doctor, she'd cracked her skull and he'd shaved a portion of her head. Not her finest moment.

Eddie pointed to an older bald man. His white eyebrows and broad shoulders reminded Caroline of Mr. Clean, minus the earring.

"This old geezer is my attorney, Simon Guidry." Eddie winked. "He keeps me honest." They shared a laugh. "Would you like something to drink?" Eddie offered.

Caroline spoke before Emily could without taking her eyes off of her mom. "No, not yet. I think we need to mingle and talk a bit first. Don't you, Momma?" Eddie and Emily briefly locked stares, the mutual longing evident.

"Dad, do you happen to know where Cade is?"

"No, cher, I haven't seen him here yet. Why? Something the matter?"

"No, nothing's wrong. Yet. If he doesn't show up tonight, he might end up in the ER, though."

Eddie chuckled. "Come on, love, don't be too hard on him. He wants this moment to be special for you. That's why he worked so hard on this party. I told him I'd help in any way I could."

"Wait, what? This wasn't your idea? This party was Cade's doing?"

Worried he'd let the cat out of the bag, Eddie stammered. "W- well, yes, um, it was initially his idea. He's proud of you, Caroline. He thought you'd enjoy marking the end of your education with a little *fais do do*. A fun celebration with your friends and relatives so you could dance the night away. Very thoughtful of him, I think."

Though amused, Dr. Breaux and his fiancée respectfully excused themselves to mingle, quickly followed by Mr. Guidry. Caroline figured they didn't want to hang around for a family feud. She didn't blame them.

This new information worried her. If the whole party was Cade's idea, where the heck was he? What kept him? Where *was* he? Something wasn't right. Her imagination ran wild. Just as the panic started rising in her chest, glancing at her watch and seeing they were now an hour late, the door opened, and she heard the sweet familiar sound of his sexy voice. She didn't miss the relief that oozed from her mother as he walked through the door, alive and well. In her own panicked relief, she rushed to him and launched herself into his arms. But when she didn't receive a welcoming embrace in return, she nearly choked on her pounding heart.

Her eyes instantly searched his face for answers as she slowly backed up to take a good look at him. He looked fine. Gorgeous, in fact, in a deep blue dress shirt and scarlet tie with black slacks. He looked like Superman. *Her* Superman. But where was his tux?

She frowned. "Cade, what is it? Are you okay?"

"Everything is just fine, love. You look beautiful tonight." With one arm, he brushed an escaped tendril of hair from her face, slipped his hand around to cup the back of her head, pulling her to him for a gentle kiss. Though marginally reassured, she still couldn't shake the looming unease. Something was off. Way off.

She looked to Runway for answers, but he remained stoic and unreadable. She tugged Cade over to the corner for more privacy, but their audience stayed put.

"Where have you been? Do you realize you're an hour late? You had me worried."

Amused, most likely with her typical, overbearing, girlfriend-type outburst, he smirked and answered calmly. "Runway and I ran into some. . .wardrobe malfunctions on our way here. We had to go back and change clothes. I'm sorry I didn't call."

"Wardrobe malfunction? Seriously? You're guys, what could have possibly malfunctioned in your wardrobe?" Angry for scaring her, she was only warming up for her verbal assault.

Runway stepped up to them and spoke in his butter-soft voice. "Please forgive me, Miss Caroline. It was completely my fault. I take full responsibility for Beau's lack of courtesy and sincerely hope we haven't tainted your special evening with our irresponsible tardiness."

Like a goofy, socially-challenged teenager, she stared at his impossible beauty. Whatever argument she had conjured up to use in her attack effectively dissipated in that instant. Her mom stepped closer and nudged her, and she gave her best smile. By this point Kristy and Eddie had also joined them in the more secluded corner.

"Um, sure, Runway. You're completely and absolutely forgiven. No big deal. I just worried something might have happened to y'all." She cut her eyes at Emily. "You're here now, and despite my unwelcoming attitude, I'm glad you two are okay. I really am happy to see you. Both of you. Sorry for my bad manners."

Cade smiled, his tantalizing eyes caused her to flush from her toes to her nose. Hoping to lighten the mood a little, she changed the subject.

"So, now that your wardrobe is fixed, I owe you this for looking so hot, and for your thoughtfulness in planning this party." She aggressively gripped Cade's collar and pulled him closer, giving him a heart-stopping kiss. "And *this* for lying to me and telling me my dad planned it and you just helped." She stepped back and punched his left shoulder. His reaction was nothing like she expected.

He stumbled back and down onto his knees. Tears welled in his eyes. A string of mumbled curses slipped out under his breath followed by a pained, frustrated growl.

Shocked and breathless, she stood frozen, completely confused. He clutched his shoulder. His face turned purple, and the veins protruded from his forehead threatening to explode.

Runway rushed to his side whispering something she couldn't hear.

She wasn't *that* strong. She snapped out of her daze and rushed to his other side.

"Oh my gosh! Are you okay? I didn't think I hit you that hard. I'm so sorry!"

His jaw clenched and he shook his head, unable to speak.

Her terrified confusion quickly turned into anger. He lied. There was no wardrobe malfunction. Whatever kept him, he lied about it. Runway covered for him. And her mom's premonition and her refusal to talk about it was too much.

Caroline stood and stomped her foot. "That's enough! Somebody tell me what the *hell* is going on here!" Several heads of nearby guests turned their way to see what the commotion was, so Eddie waved them off and shushed Caroline. She only minimally lowered her voice. "I'm sick of all the secrets and half-truths. Cade, you can go first. What is wrong with your shoulder?"

Runway opened his mouth about to speak, but she stopped him with a stern look.

"No, Runway. I'm sorry, but Cade can answer for himself."

Cade still gripped his arm and breathed heavily in through his nose and out of his mouth. Obviously avoiding her glare. She cleared her throat to get his attention. He slowly stood, and, with Runway's help, walked over to a chair in the foyer. The uncomfortable minutes rivaled hours of crippling suspense. Cade held up one finger and she bit her tongue to harness her temper.

"Caroline, it's nothing, really." She started to protest, and he held his finger up again and laughed. "Will you just shut it and let me finish, please?"

She gasped, appalled, but he chuckled. Shaking his head, he grinned at her adoringly. "Woman, do you have any clue how much I love you, everything about you, including that red-hot temper of yours?"

Touched, but reminded how Trevor would always distract her with kisses and gifts, Caroline was determined not to let Cade do the same with his compliments. Her stubborn jaw set and she crossed her arms, waiting for him to continue.

He took a deep breath and nodded toward Runway. "If this knucklehead could hit the broad side of a barn with a bazooka, there wouldn't be any issues to discuss, and we would be sipping champagne, locked in each other's arms on the dance floor right now."

She shifted her eyes to Runway who laughed with Cade. Caroline was sufficiently stumped and bewildered now, and still pissed off.

Runway mumbled, "Hey, dude. I'm no sniper. Besides, I was too far away and didn't exactly have much of a weapon to work with."

Her face crumpled with confusion. Her mother had been right? He'd been shot? By Runway? Caroline breathlessly spat the word everyone was thinking. "What?"

They stared, their eyes wide with guilt like boys with their hands caught in a cookie jar.

Already livid and borderline explosive, Caroline pinched the bridge of her nose and drew in a deep breath. Cade immediately stood and wrapped his good arm around her in a comforting gesture. But it only fueled her anger. She stepped away from him, frustrated and severely put out by his cryptic, ambiguous behavior. Men claimed that *women* were impossible to understand.

"Did you get shot?" She pointed her finger at Runway. "How, and *why*, did he shoot you?" She looked back and forth between them waiting for answers. "Cade, what going on?" The walls closed in on her, it was difficult to breathe. Tears threatened to ruin her mascara. Cade laced his fingers through hers and whispered in her ear for them to go somewhere quiet to talk. She nodded, unable to reply.He bowed his head to Emily and Eddie. "Please excuse us for a few moments. I'd like to talk to Caroline in private."

Eddie nodded, but Emily stared unfocused.

"Mrs. Fontenot, are you all right?" Cade said.

She blinked a few times before acknowledging him. "I *saw* you. I saw the gun. I heard the shot. I saw you fall! H-how. . .this isn't possible."

59

Everyone in their small group, as well as a few curious bystanders, stared at Caroline's mother, none knowing exactly how to interpret the crazy things she said. Behind her, Eddie gently rubbed his hands up and down her arms.

"What do you mean, you saw me?" Cade's brow crumpled, emphasizing his confusion. "Did you have a premonition? What exactly did you see and how? Tell me everything, please," he urged.

Caroline couldn't stand by, silent, anymore. "Wait, you're having visions now? When did this start?"

Emily moved as if she was far older than she was and slowly walked to a chair. She sighed and sank into the cushion, releasing the exhale in a gust, as she worked to prepare her thoughts.

"I'll go get her some water," Kristy said.

"I don't know why this is happening to me. It started in the car on the way down here. Believe me, I've racked my brain trying to come up with a sensible explanation. Thought maybe I had a brain tumor or something." She dabbed her eyes with the handkerchief Eddie had given her earlier.

"The first vision was of something that hasn't happened, so I suppose it could've been a premonition. Lord, I certainly hope not. It was awful. Then, while getting ready for tonight, I had another vision in the bathroom. I was wide awake, just like in the car, but it was weird. Very difficult to explain. Almost like a projector in my head playing a movie and my eyes are the screen. I would never believe that you all couldn't see the movie, or vision, the same as me, except that y'all were completely oblivious to it happening."

Eddie hugged her from behind. "Em, why didn't you tell me this earlier? You could have told me, I would've believed you. Did something happen to trigger these visions?"

"I don't know of anything."

"Have you had any accidents or bumped your head recently?" Runway asked. "I dated a med student who did a research paper on the brain. She learned that any kind of head trauma can cause

60

changes in your vision. Perhaps that might explain your projector-like visions?"

Emily huffed in frustration, and waved off the attention. "I don't know, I'm sure it's nothing. Let's forget it and enjoy the party."

Suddenly, Caroline remembered the accident at breakfast. "What about that can of evaporated milk that fell out of the cabinet on your head this morning. That could have triggered your visions."

"It's possible," Cade offered.

"So what did you see, exactly?" Caroline said.

Distant and slow to answer, Emily wasn't eager to describe her visions. "Well, I saw Cade and his friend." She looked up at Runway. "I'm sorry, I don't know your name."

He smiled and held his hand out to formally introduce himself to her. "Matteo DeLuka, madam. Pleasure to meet you."

"Matteo? I heard Caroline call you Jetway or something."

They all snickered at her flub.

Again, he smiled, his green eyes sparkling. "Runway, ma'am. It's just a nickname. You can call me whatever you'd like."

She looked him up and down, smiled back. "Can I call you tonight?"

"Mom," Caroline gasped.

She looked playfully offended. "What? I'm old, but I'm not dead. A woman can dream, can't she?"

The laughter burst from all parties but one. Eddie only smiled, and failed miserably to hide his jealousy.

Her mom's comment lightened the mood, but it didn't take Caroline's focus off of the matter at hand. "Okay, Momma. Go on with your story. You saw Cade and Runway. Then what?"

She focused again, the deep line between her brows resurfacing. "Well, I saw them walking through the woods talking about Kristy." Cade and Runway shared a glance. Caroline guessed her mom was spot-on. "They joked around until they heard a gunshot." She looked at Cade. "Am I right so far?"

61

"Yes, Ms. Fontenot, you're exactly right. That's amazing. Have you had any other visions? Did you see what happened next?"

Caroline cut in. "Wait just a minute. She told me you had been shot. Is that true?"

"No, Caroline. I wasn't shot. I was fired at, but, thankfully, Runway is a lousy shot."

Runway grumbled. "It was a shoddy weapon."

"Back to my original question. Why did Runway shoot at you? If you weren't hit, then why did you nearly throw up when I punched your shoulder?"

"You don't miss anything, do you?"

"It was obvious to everyone, Cade, not just me. And you're stalling. Get to the point. What happened?"

He took a deep breath. "Runway and I were walking through the woods on our way here when we heard a gunshot in the distance. With a party close by with a lot of people gathered, we checked it out. We headed toward the sound of the shots, the opposite direction of the plantation, to an old dilapidated shed in a clearing near the edge of the property. I'd seen it before and planned to spruce it up as a hunting blind, but I never got around to it. I think someone must have once stored plows or lawn equipment in it. It's not big enough for much else." Cade nervously glanced from Runway to Emily. "I crept up to the shack while Runway stayed in the woods to cover me since he had a firearm and I only had a Buck knife."

His eyes burned with intensity, and he stared at her mom as he finished the story. "As I peeked through the broken window, a huge wild hog came snorting its way around the corner and spotted me. It dug its hooves into the dirt about to charge me."

He looked back at Caroline and sarcasm dripped from his words. "That's when the hero over here decided to shoot at it from over a hundred yards away with a little six-shooter. Of course he missed the hog, but at least he scared it away from me. He did, however, manage to shoot the broken glass above my left shoulder causing a large piece to fall, slicing a deep, four-inch laceration into my upper arm. It bled like a stuck hog, no pun intended."

She raised an eyebrow.

"Okay, the pun was intended, but you gotta admit, it's a little funny."

"A wild hog, huh?" She looked at Runway. "Did you take Cade to the hospital? Is that why y'all were late? A four-inch laceration would have surely needed stitches."

Cade answered for him. "No, I don't do hospitals. Too many people don't come back out after they go in."

"Caden Luke! I just got my degree in nursing, and you're dissing on hospitals? Really? If you didn't go to the hospital, how in the world did you stop the bleeding and properly sterilize the wound? Here, let me see it." She started unbuttoning his shirt and he grabbed at her hands.

"Caroline, stop trying to take my clothes off." He smiled and whispered, "Not here anyway. Your parents are watching."

She playfully smacked his chest, and he winced. A little too close to the wound perhaps. "I'm serious. I need to look at it and properly care for it so it doesn't get infected."

He kissed her fingertips. "It's okay, love. Runway took care of it. He cleaned it, sterilized it, stitched it up and bandaged it like a pro. I'm good, I just don't have pain medication to help with beautiful young women abusing me so."

"Ha. Ha. Ha. That's very funny. While I'm happy that you two are close and have a wonderful history together, I would still like to take a look at it to make sure it's done correctly. No offense to Runway, but someone with proper training should have taken care of you. . .the wound."

Cade winked at Runway. "Nah, we've done this a few times before. I've stitched him up, he's stitched me up, and we've administered I.V.'s to each other. We were required to learn more than just basic first aid while we were in the military. We're better trained than some of the incompetent folks who call themselves

63

professionals. No offense to you, of course." He kissed her nose. "I'm okay. Just don't throw any more right hooks at me, okay, Tyson?"

She didn't realize sailors were *required* to learn more than basic first aid, but she opted not to press the issue. However, she knew there was more to Cade and Runway's story than just being in the Navy together. Something didn't add up, but now wasn't the time for an interrogation. Instead, she rolled her eyes.

"Fine. Be a hero and suffer in pain." She said as she turned to the sound of Kristy's melodic voice coming from the parlor. She expertly carried a tray of sparkling champagne glasses.

"Hello, lovelies. Who wants some bubbly?"

Caroline instantly snatched two from her tray and handed one to Cade. "Here, this will help numb the pain."

Kristy questionably studied him for a split second then moved to Caroline's mom and dad. "A drink for the proud parents?"

They thanked her, and each took a glass. Eddie excused himself, asking Emily to join him in the kitchen to test out the appetizers, boasting of blackened alligator. He securely fastened his arm around her shoulders, and hers around his waist, and disappeared behind the kitchen door. The sight of them comfortably embraced made Caroline happy. Too bad April had to ruin it all.

Kristy then turned to Runway. "Would the handsome stranger like one as well?"

"Indeed he would. *Grazie, bella.*"

She sashayed past him and replied in a sexy, raspy voice. "My pleasure, *amante.*" His eyes widened. He hooked his arm through hers, and they disappeared into the formal living room to be alone.

Caroline looked at Cade in bewilderment. "What in the world did she just say to him? He looked like he wanted to ravish her."

Cade's adorable wicked smile slowly stretched across his face. "I don't think we have to worry about hooking those two up. They're doing a great job on their own."

"I can see that. What did they say to each other?"

"Runway told her, 'Thank you, beautiful.' She replied, 'You're welcome, lover.' I think with that one word she cleared up any insecurities he had of her feelings for him."

"Well, I would imagine so. You can't get much more direct than that." They laughed briefly, and his smile faded.

"What is it? Are you hurting?"

His eyes closed, and he rested his forehead on hers. "Caroline, are you okay?"

"Me? You have a huge and excruciating wound that was stitched with no anesthesia, and you're asking me if *I'm* okay?"

He pulled his head back to look at her again. "Yes. I am. Are you?" She searched his eyes for any hidden meaning, a glimpse into his thoughts. She pulled him to one of the expertly decorated tables and prompted him to sit with her.

"I'm okay. I wish you hadn't lied to me about planning this party. I wish you had come to me with your wound and let me take care of you. I wish I knew what was plaguing my mom. I wish for a lot of things, but yes, I'm okay."

Cade rolled the delicate stem of the flute glass between his fingers as he spoke. "I'm sorry I was late. And that I lied to you." He looked up through his thick lashes, his eyes melting her insides. "I was afraid you would ask me to call it off, and you know how hard it is for me to deny you anything."

"Why didn't you just tell me?" Caroline crossed and uncrossed her arms trying not to fidget too much. "I mean, not just about the party, but everything. Your shoulder, the Navy. . .Runway? If he's the brother you never had then why have you never mentioned him?"

He squirmed, uncomfortable with talking about his past. "I joined the military for a few reasons, but mainly because I felt a strong desire to protect my country and those in the world who couldn't protect themselves. There are still things that I can't talk about because they're either classified or just too painful for me to dredge up."

"Oh. That must be awful." Thousands of questions swam in her head, but she didn't push for more.

He nodded and exhaled. He spoke slowly, as if trying to decide how much he wanted to reveal. "Most of the time I bury it in the back of my mind." He picked up the glass and took a sip. "Occasionally, I'm reminded of some of my experiences, or people from my past will show up."

She smiled. "Like Runway?"

"Yes, only I called him to come out here. He didn't just show up."

"You called him?"

"Last summer. After you called off the wedding, and with all the talk that circulated about Mafia hit men. I couldn't stand knowing someone hunted you or your family. You were so vulnerable and unprotected." He took another drink. "Runway sent some extra surveillance equipment and called in a few favors for me. We've been in contact the whole time you've been here, always watching out for you." Cade smirked, "He's kind of my secret weapon."

He slowly leaned forward and tipped her chin up with his finger while his other hand cradled her face, his thumb brushing across her lips. His intensity commanded her attention and she lost herself in his golden irises. His powerful focus permeated her soul, his silky voice caressing her ears.

"Sweet Caroline, I can't let anything happen to you. I don't think I could survive if I lost you. You are everything to me. You are my reason for waking up every morning. I love you." She'd heard him say that many times before, but she would never tire of it. The warmth and flutters in her heart stole her breath every time those words slipped from his tongue.

"I love you, too." She blinked back the tears as he pulled away to take a drink. She sipped from her own flute, letting the bubbles tickle her nose, the chilled tart liquid sliding down her throat.

"Kristy and Runway seem cozy," he said.

She swiveled in her chair and peered into the dimly lit living room. Their silhouettes were close together—almost one.

"Caroline."

She turned back to find Cade on one knee, his hand in his pocket.

Please, God. Not again.

SEVEN

Caroline hovered quietly outside her father's office door. Even through her dazed stupor, she'd heard her name and slinked against the wall like James Bond.

"Claire, you are way too young. I cannot allow this."

"Why do you even care? I'll be out of your way, then you can spend all of your time with Caroline without having to worry about me."

"Is that what you think? That you're in my way?"

"I'm sorry, Dad. If you won't give us your blessing and sign the forms, then I'll just wait until I turn eighteen in four months. Either way, I'm getting married, and there's nothing you can say or do to stop me."

Caroline never knew Claire was jealous or angry with her, but, come to think of it, she did kind of butt in on Claire's life and take over the father-daughter relationship in the family. She'd probably be angry, too, if put in Claire's position. Caroline made a mental note to talk to her sister.

The door beside Caroline creaked open. Curious, she pushed it open and stepped inside. The inky darkness pressed in around her. Something ethereal crawled up her back. Creepy and unnerving, it was as if someone slowly skimmed their fingers up her spine and started around her neck. Spooked, she darted out of the room and headed for the sanctity of her bedroom.

She threw open the door to find Cade sitting on her bed. Sullen and stricken, he glanced up as she entered, and immediately rushed to her, wrapping his steely arms around her. Suddenly her petty sibling issues seemed insignificant.

"Cade, what's wrong?" He buried his face into her hair. "What is it?"

"Are you okay? Are *we* okay? I didn't mean to freak you out earlier. I wasn't—I mean, when you just kissed me and walked off without a word. . ." he straightened and shoved his fingers in his hair, releasing an exasperated sigh. "I need to know if I blew it. Please tell me I didn't just ruin everything."

"What? No. Absolutely not. I just. . .I need to think about some things before I can commit."

He let out a huge sigh. "Oh, thank goodness. You had me so worried. I just knew when you dashed up the stairs and didn't look back, I had blown everything."

She grinned, nodding much too quickly to be convincing. "I panicked, but I'm okay now."

"You thought I was proposing?" She bit her bottom lip and bowed her head, ashamed for overreacting.

He cupped his hands around her face and stared into her eyes. She felt like the most beautiful woman in the world when he looked at her. Her cheeks heated, and, by his crooked smile, she knew she was blushing. He spoke softly without removing his eyes from hers "So, would you like to talk about anything? Do you have any questions for me? I wasn't intending to scare you. Honestly, I was trying very hard *not* to freak you out. That's why I wrote it out on paper, so I wouldn't say the wrong thing."

She smiled and turned her face into the palm of his left hand. "And I didn't give you the chance." Closing her eyes, she breathed in his masculine soapy scent. "You didn't freak me out. I think seeing you down on one knee gave me a start, but when I saw a piece of paper in your hand rather than a ring box, I was speechless."

He smirked, "Wow, that's quite an accomplishment, huh?"

"Oh, stop it." She started to smack his arm, then she remembered his wound. "You really had me scared. Between my mom's visions, your tardiness, the look on your face when I tapped your arm. . ."

His eyebrow raised. "Tapped? I beg to differ, cher. You hauled off and punched me with everything you had. I think I saw stars."

"Okay, maybe I did get a little overzealous with my punishment, but how was I supposed to know you'd just gotten stitches? By the way, you never did show me your wound. How many stitches did it take?"

He shrugged. "Not too many."

"How many?"

"I'm not sure, maybe twenty or thirty?"

"No way. That's it, let me see it. I have to make sure Runway did a good enough job before I can let it go. And for the record, I don't believe your stupid wild hog story for a second. Surely you're more imaginative than that."

He grabbed her fidgeting hands relentlessly trying to unbutton his shirt and pressed them to his chest. "Do you feel that? It's my heartbeat. I'm alive and well. You've got a house full of people downstairs here to celebrate your graduation and your return to Golden Meadow, and they're probably all wondering where you disappeared to. Now, stop trying to get me naked, because, frankly, we just don't have time."

They laughed and she leaned her forehead on his chest between her hands that were still in his grasp. "Cade, I love you. You know this, right?"

He let go of her fingers and rubbed his hands up and down her back. "Yes, sweet girl. I know that. I just need you to know how much *I* love *you*. I haven't felt this way about anyone since. . . Well, since Jenny. I lost her before I could do anything about it."

Ah-hah. Jenny, his high school sweetheart. The young school teacher who had died in the car accident. Her heart broke for him.

"I can't take the chance of losing you, too. I honestly don't think I could handle it. I'm not proposing." She flinched and immediately regretted it. She didn't want him to think she completely rejected marriage, she just wasn't ready yet for a commitment that strong. He pretended not to see it and smoothly continued. "Not yet, anyway. I'm only asking you to be my girlfriend. Exclusively. I'm asking for a promise. If you are ever worried or concerned about something, anything at all, you will talk to me about it before making a decision to leave me. I would have presented you with a promise ring if I hadn't been afraid the whole ring thing would send you over the edge."

She looked into his eyes. "Yeah, the ring would have probably scared me a little. Besides, promise rings are kind of high-schoolish, aren't they?"

"Maybe, but I haven't been serious about anyone since that time in my life. I don't want to lose you. You've been down the proposal and engagement route before and you're not looking to rush into it again, I get that. But I also know how much we love each other. I told you before, you're worth waiting for, and I'm a patient person. I know a good thing when I see it, and we are a good thing. Together. We bring out the best in each other."

He sighed and ran his hands through his thick hair before he faced her again, pulling her close. "In the Navy, we don't call the thick, heavy rope on the ship 'rope,' it's called 'line.' When someone falls overboard, we throw him a life ring attached to the thick line, and it's called a 'lifeline'. Caroline, *you* are my lifeline. You saved me from a dismal time in my life when I was drowning and didn't realize it. I lived in a miserably dark place emotionally. I had shut everyone out, and you managed to pull me from it." His voice softened as he rested his forehead on hers.

"I want to marry you and grow old with you. I want to make love to you. A lot." She smiled and his hand slipped down to her belly. "I want to see your beautiful, pregnant, glowing body someday as you carry our children in your womb and nurture them as infants into

71

adulthood. I want to sit on our front porch with you and watch our four or five kids play soccer or basketball with each other. I want to watch your hair turn from this beautiful reddish brown to a shiny silver, and I want to see the laugh lines deepen in your skin because you've smiled so much in your happy life. Your happy life with me."

He kissed her forehead, then her nose, and his warm, soft lips rested on hers sweeping her from reality. If she hadn't been one hundred percent sure she was in love with him before, she was certain of it now. Moved and touched by his beautiful speech, it took everything she had to keep the tears from falling like rain. Her lips parted, she took in a breath, and locked her arms around his neck. She passionately kissed him while the flaming embers burned holes in the walls surrounding her heart.

She placed her hands on his cheeks and stared deeply into his beautiful hazel eyes. "Caden Luke, I would love to officially become your girlfriend. And you have my word, I promise to talk to you about everything. Especially before making any rash decisions." She gave him a quick peck on the lips. "I would love for us to grow old and gray together. Most importantly, I want to laugh with you every single day of our lives, because a life without laughter is a tragedy."

They kissed again and she felt light as the air. Euphoric. However, she couldn't escape the annoying little voice in her head that kept screaming.

What else has he not told her regarding his past? His painful experience in the military? What exactly happened between him and Jenny that had him so reluctant to talk about it? So much to learn.

This evasion would need to change before they could officially say their vows to each other someday. He had to answer the nagging questions she'd had since they met, starting tonight.

EIGHT

The best part of the jam-packed party was the food, of course. Delphine had created a wonderful array of hors d'oeuvres for everyone to enjoy. Caroline's favorites being the blackened alligator, crab cakes, fried eggplant cubes, and bacon-wrapped scallops. As she indulged in the savory cuisine, she noticed a familiar face, but couldn't quite remember where she'd seen her.

Caroline leaned in close to Cade with the intention of asking him about the mystery girl, but his warm masculine smell overrode her senses causing her to forget her train of thought. He'd instinctively leaned toward her as well, and when she didn't say anything, he looked at her inquisitively. The heat spreading across her skin explained her silence, and of course he noticed. His amusement was unmistakable.

"What is it, cher? Something on your mind?"

She definitely had something on her mind, but she wasn't about to tell him. She willed herself to remember what she wanted to ask, but the thought was gone. As she tried to recall, the same woman she'd planned to ask about now stood in front of them. Substantially taller than Caroline, she had long, silky, chocolate-brown hair.

She smiled, glancing at Caroline, but settled her gaze on Cade. "Hi, do y'all remember me?" She said, 'y'all,' but by the way she devoured Cade with just her eyes, Caroline knew this chick wasn't talking to her. The man-eating look on this girl's face reminded Caroline of where she'd seen her.

"I remember you. You work at the courthouse, right?"

The girl's face lit up. "Yes! You do remember me. I'm Jessica Robicheaux." She gestured toward Caroline. "You came in looking for records for a girl from the 1800s." Her pretty brown eyes drifted back to Cade and she licked her lips. "Did you, um. . .find what you were looking for?"

Jessica's flagrant flirting with Caroline's now-exclusive boyfriend rubbed her raw. She shot a perturbed glance at Cade and ground her teeth. Amused by her reaction, he smirked.

"Yes, Caroline definitely found what she was looking for."

Jessica giggled, causing Caroline to see red. . .or green. "That's great. How about you? Did you find everything you were looking for?" Her eyelids dropped suggestively and she bit her bottom lip. Caroline turned to Cade and waited eagerly for his response to Jessica's bold invitation. Now it was his turn to be uncomfortable. All those times he relished embarrassing her simply to see her blush. Caroline smirked as she watched for him to squirm. Unfortunately, she witnessed zero discomfort.

Without missing a beat, he smoothly slinked his arm around Caroline's waist and said, "Yes, as a matter of fact, I did. And she's better than I ever imagined anyone could be." He kissed Caroline's temple and turned back to Jessica. "Thanks for your help with that."

The obvious disappointment gleamed in her eyes, but flushed cheeks exposed her embarrassment. As the frequent blushing recipient of Cade's charm, Caroline kind of felt bad for her. She admired Jessica's courage because she could never have done that. Caroline stretched her hand out in greeting. "Caroline Fontenot. It's nice to meet you, Jessica. This is my boyfriend, Ca—Beau."

Flustered now, Jessica fell over herself apologizing. "I'm very sorry, I didn't know you two were together. I thought—I mean, with your reaction to the name similarity that day—that you might have been related. Never mind, it was stupid of me to assume. It's really nice to meet you, too." She pressed her fingertips to her forehead and closed her eyes. "I'm so embarrassed."

Cade smiled and reached to shake her hand. "Don't be embarrassed. I'm flattered. Really. If you ladies will excuse me, I see my cousin just arrived." Cade worked his way through the crowd and shook hands with Josh. Caroline looked for Claire and wondered how Eddie would react to his arrival.

Caroline chatted with Jessica for a while and realized they had several things in common. They planned to meet for lunch later in the week. Caroline really liked her, and she needed a friend in Golden Meadow. Perhaps this would help fill the girl-gap Kristy would leave when she returned to California. At least until she could work things out with Claire.

Eddie interrupted the crowd from their conversation and refreshments to make a speech.

"May I have your attention, please? I want to personally thank my good friend, Beau, for thinking to have this party and helping me organize everything. I also want to thank you all for coming tonight to celebrate with us. My daughter, Caroline, has graduated from college. I know she's been waiting for this day for a very long time. I'm sure she's relieved to be back down here in the bayou with everyone who loves her, but not half as relieved as I am to have her in my life forever. Caroline, welcome home, baby." Applause erupted in the large room, and her scarlet face glowed. She scanned the faces until she found Claire who clapped, but didn't smile. Eddie noticed as well. Especially as Josh stepped up behind her and suggestively wrapped his arms around her waist. Eddie eyed them for a moment before he continued.

"This magnificent party is a joint celebration in honor of another very special occasion. My beautiful baby girl, Claire, has graduated from high school." His eyes filled with caring and sincerity. "Claire, sweetheart, this is an important milestone in your life, and I hope you will choose to make smart choices that pave the pathway for your future. When I graduated high school, my father told me one thing

75

and nothing else. He said, 'Son, life gets hard when you turn eighteen. Welcome to the real world.' Boy was he right."

The crowd chuckled. "Anyway, congratulations to you and Caroline." He held up his glass to propose a toast. "To my incredible daughters. I love you *both*, and may you find nothing but good luck and fortune in your bright futures." Clapping, cheering, and hugging surrounded them. Claire's face had reddened, as well, and she genuinely smiled. Caroline hoped she was truly happy.

Kristy and Runway still talked in the living room, engaged in deep conversation, when Caroline interrupted to ask if they'd seen her mom around. They hadn't. That gentle interruption managed to tear Kristy and Runway apart from each other, and they came to stand with Cade and Caroline in the elegant foyer. Hanging around the front doors presented an easy escape for Caroline to get some much-needed fresh air. Once Josh arrived, the tension was palpable between Eddie and Claire. She and Josh disappeared shortly after Eddie's eloquent toast. Kristy excused herself to the bathroom, and minutes later the front door startled Caroline when it opened directly behind her. Walking across the threshold emerged a well-dressed young boy with a fresh haircut. She almost didn't recognize him.

"Remy! Look at you! Wow. I know I haven't been gone *that* long, but you've changed so much. You look so handsome." She leaned in for a hug, and he kissed her cheek.

His face turned red as he shifted his weight from foot to foot. "S'not a big deal, Caroline. I'm just growin' up."

"You cut off your long bangs. And got muscles. Have you been working out?" She cupped his bicep.

He smiled and intermittently flexed his pectoral muscles making them jump beneath his tight, canary yellow, polyester shirt. "Yeah, I've been hitting the gym after school, and the hair made my forehead break out." Though he stood proud, there was a crack in his newfound confidence. He motioned to Cade with a silent, nervous plea. "Beau, can I talk to you for a sec?"

Cade looked to her for answers, but she only shrugged. He'd turned fourteen shortly after she arrived last summer. She couldn't believe he was pushing fifteen-years-old. She hadn't paid much attention to him after she met Cade last summer. Between the ghost of her G3 grandmother, her fixation with Cade, Trevor's drama, and all her freak accidents, she stayed pretty preoccupied. Standing there in deep thought, she realized they both stared at her.

"What? I have to leave?"

Remy shrugged. "It's kind of a guy thing."

Caroline rolled her eyes and motioned to Runway. "I guess he gets to stay then?"

Remy looked at him questionably. "Do I know you?"

"My bad, Remy." Cade motioned to Runway. "This is my best friend, Matt, but we all call him Runway."

Remy smiled. "Runway, huh? Are you a pilot?"

Runway's handsome smile stretched across his chiseled face. "Don't I wish. I'll step over here with Caroline and give you two a minute."

"That'd be boss. Thanks." Remy waited for us to get just out of earshot, then turned back to Cade who looked uncertain.

She stared at Runway and tried to rein in her annoyance. Remy was *her* brother, and if he needed help with something she hoped she could help as much or more than Cade. She did a decent job with Claire last summer. At least she thought she had. Maybe not. Maybe that's why Claire harbored such resentment?

"I wonder what that's all about." Runway shrugged at her query, which fueled her annoyance even more. "You're not the least bit curious what he wants to talk to Cade about?"

"Not really, no. I don't know him, but he's a teenage boy just starting to work out and focus on his appearance. Beau's a pretty fit, handsome guy. I imagine it's something to do with fitness or girls."

She hadn't thought about that. "If it's about girls, don't you think a female would be better to talk to than another guy?"

He winked. "Not if you're a teenage boy."

She nodded. "I guess. I'm dying here." Suddenly, Cade motioned for Runway to come over there. Now she really wanted to know. "Oh, come on! Remy, I can help you with things, too."

Cade smiled. "Easy, tiger. Haven't you ever heard curiosity killed the cat? We're handling this."

"Handling what?" Kristy stepped up next to Caroline with two glasses of champagne. She handed her one and her eyes widened. "Whoa! Is that Remy? Wow, he's grown up. Hot stuff." Caroline gave her a confused frown. Kristy smiled, "Well, hot in a *High School Musical* kind of way."

Caroline snorted and rolled her eyes. "You're gonna be one of those cougars checking out all the hot college boys when you're forty."

She pretended to be offended, then giggled. "Yeah, probably."

"At least you live in California where all the sexy surfer guys are. You'll have the beach as your playground and can inconspicuously look from behind your sunglasses while you're checking them out."

"Speaking of that, I saw Dr. Yummypants in there. You never told me your doc was such a hottie."

"Dr. Breaux?" Caroline laughed. "Yeah, but he's off the market." Caroline eyed Kristy and cast her bait. "I guess you'll have to stick to your beach bums."

"I don't know, I'm having a hard time taking my eyes off of the Italian Romeo over there. He makes me tingle in places that haven't tingled in a long time."

Caroline raised an eyebrow. "Yeah, I noticed your smooth little innuendo. . .*in Italian*. What'd you do, Google it?"

A mischievous smile swept across her face. "You caught that, huh? Yeah, I looked it up on my phone before I came out with the drinks. He seemed to like it. By the way, I took one of your new toothbrushes because I can't find mine. I might need it in a little while." She winked.

She couldn't believe Kris already had plans with him in her naughty mind. Caroline knew from the beginning Kristy wanted him.

"Are you kidding me? He more than liked it. You nearly brought him to his knees with that simple, one-word invitation. I thought you said he was gay?"

She shrugged, "Eh—the jury's still out on that one. I had a great conversation with him earlier, got some good vibes, but all I managed to learn about him is that he's never been married and isn't currently dating anyone. He lives alone, loves surfing and land paddling, and his favorite designer is Armani."

"Land paddling? What is that? I've never heard of it."

"A sort of surf board on wheels, and you use a really big stick to 'paddle' your way along the street. It's big in Cali. He land paddles along the boardwalk for fun. Kind of like a huge skateboard. It must be great exercise because his body is bangin.' I mean, just look at him," she purred. "He is the definition of sexy." She purposefully shivered, letting out a groan. "The things I could do to make that man squirm."

Caroline and Kristy had slowly inched their way closer to the guys watching intently for any sign of what they discussed. When they saw Runway caress Remy's face, then look like he was about to kiss him, she and Kristy glanced at each other.

"Damn," Kristy sighed defeated and mumbled into her flute glass, "Definitely gay."

Caroline elbowed Kristy's ribs and walked over to them while guzzling the rest of her champagne. Kristy must have stayed back a few paces so not to intrude in the moment, unlike Caroline.

"Hi. May I ask what you boys are doing?"

Remy blushed, Cade laughed, and Runway, frustrated, threw his palms up to the ceiling. With Remy's permission, Cade finally explained.

"Remy has a new girlfriend, and he's never kissed a girl. He doesn't want a bad reputation for not having any swag, so he wanted advice and pointers. I told him he'd be better to talk to the *real* ladies man." Cade pointed to a sulking Runway. "Runway attempted to explain the buildup to the kiss and how you need to caress the girl's face. To show how you should set the mood before you just move in and shove your tongue down her throat." Cade coughed out a laugh while Runway continued to seethe.

Remy was now a deep shade of maroon. "Seriously, he was about to kiss me. I swear it!"

"No, I was not! I was explaining foreplay, showing you how to touch her before. . ." The muscles in Runway's jaw rippled with annoyance. His fierce eyes landed on Kristy. Without removing his focus from her, he spoke softly to Remy. "Young man, watch and learn."

He deftly cupped his hand around Kristy's lower back and pulled her hips against him. His determination radiated heat and a small crowd had stopped to witness the passionate exchange. "May I?" he murmured.

She sucked in a breath. "Please," she whispered, absent-mindedly passing her flute glass to Caroline without looking.

Runway brushed the backs of his fingers lightly across her cheekbone before cradling her jaw with both hands and touching his forehead to hers. His eyes closed as he moved to her neck and inhaled her scent. Kristy tilted her head back as Runway placed whisper-soft kisses along the delicate column of her throat. A faint moan escaped her as his nose skimmed over her jaw to her ear. Runway pulled back to look at her, his iridescent eyes fixated on her mouth as his thumb slipped to her pout, stroking her full bottom lip. He pressed his lips to hers with light, teasing kisses, giving her a chance to respond. When she wrapped her slender arms around his neck and buried her fingers into his thick, raven hair, he deepened the kiss, hands roaming over her curves, slightly bending her backward and igniting the entire room.

Bystanders shifted uncomfortably, but did not look away, and Remy was branding the experience to memory.

Heat crept up Caroline's neck and she glanced at Cade who fervently watched her. He paid no attention to Runway and Kristy. His eyes, molten with desire, were only for Caroline.

People slowly filtered away, one or two at a time, snickering and embracing each other tighter. Finally Cade tugged Remy and Caroline away to give Runway and Kristy some privacy.

"Get your answers, kid?" Cade asked, amused.

Remy smiled, pressing his lips together, accentuating his deep dimples, and mumbled, "And then some."

NINE

Caroline mingled with her party guests until Cade asked her to accompany him outside for fresh air. The lanterns were sprinkled throughout the trees around the house, emitting a soft glow in the darkness, and the faint wail of a saxophone drifted through the open doors of the house. Lightning bugs filled the night sky, flashing their signals in rhythm with the smooth jazz, and bull frogs croaked the bass while cicadas and crickets harmonized with their own tune. She couldn't think of anyone she'd rather share this romantic setting with than Cade.

Cade led her down his newly constructed stone pathway to the duck pond where the trickle from a fountain relaxed her almost as much as his hand in hers. The humidity wasn't too bad yet, so the night air was perfect. Peaceful. Especially with the sweet perfume from his strategically placed gardenia and azalea bushes. Caroline admired his colorful, fragrant landscaping design. He really was an artist.

Several other couples mingled around the yard, congregating in small groups or sneaking away for solitude. Moments passed before Cade's smooth voice perforated the silence.

"You look amazing. And your smell, good Lord." He nuzzled her neck as he inhaled." I could live a thousand lives and never tire of it."

82

She pulled back just a little to look at him. "Thank you. You're the only person besides my dad to tell me that tonight."

He looked puzzled. "Does anybody else matter?" he joked. The corner of his mouth turned up. "You know how beautiful you are, right?"

She smiled as she rested her head back on his chest and listened to the steady beat of his heart. "Yeah, but it's still nice to hear. Every woman loves to be reminded on a regular basis." She smiled coyly, "And I'm not wearing perfume. That's sweat you're smelling."

He burst out laughing and tightened his arms around her torso. "I love your sweaty smell then, and I'll make a point to tell you how beautiful you are on a daily basis."

"Please do, Mr. Beauregard. I can't have you getting lazy in the romance department." She reached down and squeezed his firm buttocks.

He released his grip and stood still as a statue until she finally looked up at him again. He had an amused but stern expression she couldn't exactly decipher. "Lazy? Did you really just imply that I could *ever* get lazy in the romance department? Seriously?"

She opened her mouth to reiterate, but he quickly shut her up by aggressively consuming her mouth like a predator with his prey. One of his hands tangled in her hair, pressing her face against his own, while the other roamed the curves of her body, resting on her behind and gently squeezing. He let out a sensual groan as his tongue danced with hers, earnestly proving his level of passion the best he could with a simple kiss. This particular kiss, however, was anything but simple. He finished by gently biting her lower lip and tugging, leaving her breathless.

"Wow. I take that back. You've never kissed me like that before."

He pulled her hips against his and the unmistakable bulge pressing against her belly set her heart aflutter. "Sweet Caroline, you have no idea how much I've been holding back."

She gasped. Her all-too-brief glimpse last summer of his naked body in a relaxed state was impressive. She could only imagine what it looked like now. What it felt like.

A wicked smile lit his face. "Happens every time I'm with you, cher. Every time." He kissed her neck, nipping at her sensitive skin in between words, his tickling breath lighting up her body like a live wire. "I have dreamed. . .of exploring. . .every inch. . .of your incredible body. . .since I first laid eyes on you." He moved to her ear, "But you were unavailable then."

He gazed deeply into her eyes. "After you broke it off with— well, once you were *physically* available, you were emotionally *un*available. Then, once you became emotionally *and* physically available, you lived with your mother. I'm a man, but I'm also a gentleman. It just didn't feel right making out with you with your mom in the next room. Plus, I don't ever want to push you too far."

Unable to ignore the scorching thirst for his touch, she reached for the hand wrapped around her waist. She kissed his fingers before slipping his hand lower, pressing his palm to her breast. It was the first time he'd ever touched her so intimately, and her heart raced. His eyes ignited with desire. The hazel-green eyes she had grown to love were now an amber color, and his pupils dilated.

Her hands glided over his muscular back settling on his tapered waist, eventually sliding to his belt buckle and downward to explore the result of her touch. She swallowed hard and met his watchful gaze. His impassioned eyes permeated her soul. When he inhaled sharply through flared nostrils, closing his eyes and tilting his head back in pleasure, guilt stabbed her for teasing him. Trevor would have taken this small gesture and pushed her three levels farther until she finally had to stop him. Instead, Cade seemed to revel in this small allowance.

His rugged hands were surprisingly tender as he caressed and circled her breast through her satin dress, squeezing gently. Her body responded with an intensity like never before. She ached for more. Caroline shoved both hands into his hair and stretched to kiss him deeper. She wanted him to know how much she craved his touch, but she didn't know how. They weren't exactly alone out here, and she honestly didn't think she'd want to stop once she got started.

She didn't have to worry. Their kiss was broken by Runway's velvety laughter bouncing off the thicket of the nearby woods as he and Kristy emerged by the pond.

"Get a room."

"What are you two doing out here?" There was a tinge of annoyance in Cade's tone.

Kristy had already changed out of her expensive dress and shoes as she beamed. "I kept trying to seduce him, but all he was interested in was finding you. Perhaps Caroline and I should leave you two alone?"

Cade and Runway looked at each other then quickly stared at Kristy in confusion. Caroline couldn't contain her laughter. Cade searched both their faces for answers.

"We've been trying to figure out all night if Runway prefers males to females," Caroline confessed.

Runway's jaw dropped. "Wait, what? You thought I was gay?" Italian expletives flowed in a lovely melody from his beautiful mouth.

Cade bellowed with laughter and playfully punched his buddy. "You should be used to it by now, right?" He shrugged, "I gotta say, bro, you are pretty hot."

Runway ignored Cade and looked at Kristy, his brow raised and bunched. "You thought I was *gay*?"

She sheepishly nodded. "At first, definitely. After talking with you tonight, the doubt was still there, but that kiss. . ."

He breathed heavily, obviously distraught by her confession and pulled her hips closer to his as he had before. "And now?"

She shrugged and raised an eyebrow. "The jury's still out. My evidence was inconclusive." She cringed, "Sorry."

Cade laughed hysterically. Runway looked back at him with flared nostrils and a steely expression. "I can't believe you, man."

His tone shifted from embarrassed to thick with passion and desire. His wounded ego now on a mission to conquer the challenge, he stared at Kristy as he spoke to Cade. "Tell this delicious cupcake the only reason I wanted to find you was to get the keys to your cabin." The intensity with which he looked at her could have set the trees on fire. He pulled her even closer and locked his arms around the small of her back "One chance to lick your frosting, bella, and you'll never doubt my sexuality again. That'll be all the evidence you need."

For the first time in the eleven years Caroline had known her, Kristy stood undeniably speechless. Effectively under his Sicilian spell and dripping with arousal. Kristy forcefully swallowed and spoke smoothly, much smoother than Caroline would have in her position. "I'm sorry, Signor DeLuka. Circumstantial evidence doesn't stand in this court. I'm gonna need some hard proof before I can come up with a verdict," she purred as she seductively licked her lips. Runway flashed a panty-busting smile and confidently replied, "Ah, *signora*. It will be my greatest pleasure."

Cade gracefully tossed him the keys and told him to clean up after himself. Cade grinned. "Y'all really thought he was gay?"

"I never did, but Kristy was convinced from the moment she met him. I think she used it as a defense mechanism to mask the horrible luck she's always had with men. She's convinced there is no such man who can live up to her incredibly high standards. Although, I would bet she's finally met him. Especially after seeing their chemistry."

"Yeah, Runway is a great guy. He'll treat her right. He's never settled down with anyone, though. He doesn't want to take a chance getting serious with someone who will bail on him after she gets what she wants. I've seen him turn down some beautiful women because he could tell right off the bat that they were only interested in his money, or his looks, or bragging rights because of his Navy experience. He's been with plenty of women, but he's got his own supreme specifications when it comes to keeping one of them."

"What do you mean by his *Navy experience*? What exactly did you two do?"

Cade shifted uncomfortably. "It's really not a big deal." She stared him down, silently persisting. He shrugged, blowing it off like nothing. "We weren't just in the Navy. We were Navy SEALs." He studied her face for a reaction. When there was none, he added, "We had special training that normal sailors didn't have to go through. Needless to say, we had some pretty intense deployments." Cade avoided further questions about himself by focusing on Runway and Kristy again. "You know, Runway grilled me for information about Kristy earlier. This may just work out between them."

"I hope so. Kristy needs a good solid man in her life. She's always setting everyone else up and making their lives work out. It's her turn for something good to happen."

Caroline knew nothing about Navy SEALs, only what she'd seen in movies, and was intrigued about why he changed the subject. But she wanted even more to get back to where they were before they were interrupted. "So, if they're going to be in your cabin tonight, where will you sleep?"

He grinned as he pulled her close. "Who said anything about sleeping?" All kidding aside, the unmistakable desire in his eyes stirred her libido. "I officially have a girlfriend now."

Though she liked the sound of that, she took more enjoyment from the implication of the statement and the hungry look on his face. Her heart raced, her breath hitched, and her pulse throbbed in areas she didn't realize she had a pulse. Her mouth was dry, so she waited for an actual answer before assuming anything.

He sighed. "Maybe I could ask your dad for one of the guest rooms again. If the mosquitoes wouldn't use my body as a buffet feast, I'd sleep in the bed of my truck. I think I have some blankets and netting in the cab, maybe I'll spread it over the top."

"Wouldn't that be terribly uncomfortable?"

He shrugged. "I've slept in much worse conditions."

She shook her head unable to hide her ignorance. "As a Navy SEAL?"

Concern darkened his voice. "Does that bother you?"

"That you were a SEAL? No, why would it bother me? I know it's some sort of special forces, but honestly, I have no idea what that entails. Should it bother me?"

"I've done things I'm not proud of. I mean, they were all part of my job, my duty to my country, but for most people they're still hard to swallow sometimes."

She reached for his hand. "Cade, that's part of who you are. I love everything about you. I just wish you would open up to me a little more."

She hugged him, resting her head on his chest. "I am, after all, a very curious person." She looked up and smiled as he kissed her forehead.

"Yes, you most certainly are inquisitive. I only hope that crazy curiosity of yours doesn't get you into trouble. My new mission in life is to see that you are not the cat in that particular proverb."

"Is that your only mission?"

"What do you mean?"

"I kind of like the mission Runway is on tonight. Will that ever be a mission of yours with me?"

The passion blazed with ferocity in his smoldering eyes. "Oh, yes, ma'am. Someday. When you're ready. I promise. My appreciation for every curve, nook and cranny on your delectable body will be shown in ways that'll have you begging for more. And I'll do it again, and again, and again until you won't want to remember what life was like without me."

Heated from her own arousal, she was seriously rethinking her plans to wait until marriage. "I can assure you, Mr. Beauregard, the memories of my life without you are fading fast."

He smiled, pleased with her breathless state. "Good. That's what I like to hear. Shall we go inside and speak to the man of the house about sleeping arrangements?"

She shook her head. "No, I'm thinking about that mosquito net. Will it cover the whole bed of your truck?"

He frowned. "You would make me sleep outside in my truck before letting me sleep in the house with you?"

She winked, grasped his hand, and lead him back to the house. "Who said I would be sleeping in the house? Come on, let's go say our thank-you's and goodbyes. I want to change out of this dress into something a little more comfortable and. . .outdoorsy."

He chuckled. "Ah, cherie, you're gonna be the death of me. If your father knew what was going through my mind right now, he'd put a bullet in my brain."

"Oh yeah? I wonder what he'd do if he could read my mind, then. Bet mine's worse than yours."

He sighed as he mumbled under his breath. "No shot, love. Not a chance."

When they walked through the front door, Caroline stopped cold in her tracks. Walking down the stairs, April was much more than fashionably late in a blood-red, silk gown. The dress, tight around her painfully thin stature, outlined her hip bones jutting against the material. Her bleached hair was twisted in an up-do of cascading curls, and, apart from looking like she needed to eat something, she looked remarkably beautiful. Uncharacteristically, she smiled. The interaction not too bad—until she opened her mouth.

"Hello, daughter. Beau. Always a pleasure to see you." She smiled, but her eyes defied her genuine happiness to see them. Like a growling dog wagging its tail. Which end do you believe?

"You can cut the act," Caroline grumbled. "There's no one in here to see it."

"Oh, really, Caroline. Is it that difficult for you to tolerate me? I am, after all, your stepmother."

"Yes, you are, and so far you've lived up to the fairytale stereotype."

April's eyes narrowed.

"Excuse us, we have a party to attend." Caroline tugged Cade's hand to leave, but he resisted.

April's steely eyes focused on Cade. "Mr. Beauregard, are you going to allow your girlfriend to act so rudely? It isn't very ladylike. One might question her upbringing."

"She's not mine to control, April. Caroline is perfectly capable of speaking for herself. You might remember that someday. It's also not very ladylike to meddle in people's lives trying to control and hurt everyone around you. One might question *your* upbringing." His hard glare and last words were thick with accusation. They held each other's gaze for longer than was socially acceptable. Cade placed his hand on Caroline's lower back and led her into the parlor.

Something was up between those two. Something happened. Something that smelled strangely of wild hog. . .

Caroline scurried up the stairs in a rush to prepare for her evening. After a grueling hour-and-a-half of thanking and hugging people she hardly knew, she was ready to get out of these ridiculous heels and slip into something more comfortable. A wicked grin surfaced when she thought of the graduation gift Kristy gave her. When she'd opened it, she couldn't imagine wearing it. She smiled playfully, remembering Kristy's response.

"Lingerie? You bought me sexy lingerie? When am I supposed to wear this?"

"Sweetheart, that's not just *lingerie. That's from Hollywood. I can assure you, this stuff will make Victoria wish her secret was a little less classy and a lot more sassy."*

Annoyed with Kristy at first for making it even harder for Caroline to keep the restraining order on her hormones, Caroline imagined Cade's face upon seeing her wear it. The excitement had her considering one little slip. After all, she was in love with Cade, and would most likely marry him someday. Of course, she had actually been engaged to Trevor and wouldn't consider sex. Jealousy bit at her. Kristy was getting some action, and she was too busy being a good girl.

Could she really break her promise to God and to herself so easily? She'd stayed strong through Trevor's flaming passion and expertise, so surely she could resist temptation with Cade, right? Deep in thought, Caroline applied some lip gloss and powder to buff the shine from the humidity. Her indecisive brain wouldn't shut up as her nerves bubbled over.

Was she really going to do this? He was incredible, and she. . .well, she. . .wait, what was she? She was in love with him, sure, but was it so different with him than with Trevor?

It's just sex.

After all, it took two, and Cade may not even be interested. Although, he's a red-blooded man. Caroline doubted he would turn her away.

She remembered how he'd done exactly that last summer. The mood had been perfect and when she tried to seduce him in the beautiful hotel room in New Orleans, he stopped her dead in her tracks. Of course, being engaged to another man at the time played a big part. Cade hadn't felt right about any of it. Now it's a different story.

Caroline shook it off, put her mind on mute, and searched her suitcase for her hairbrush. It wasn't there, so she combed her room, looking beneath the bed and behind the antique dressing table but couldn't find it. With her intentions for the evening, her hair didn't really matter. She twisted it up in a messy bun and slipped her shoes off.

She eyeballed the lingerie again as she reached for the zipper on her dress. She hesitated when a chill crept up her spine and the temperature in the room suddenly dropped ten degrees. The whisper of her name danced in the air, a plea, and the hairs on her arms stood

91

straight up. An instant, irrational, and unexplainable feeling washed over her. Goose bumps cloaked her entire body. *What the—*

Then she heard it. A pop, glass shattering, followed by screaming from downstairs.

Her mother's words replayed in her head. *"Baby, I think Cade's been shot."*

Caroline flew down the stairs, her feet barely touching the steps.

Please, if someone got shot, let it be April. Caroline scolded herself for wishing that fate for anyone, but she couldn't bear the idea of losing Cade. Her mother had been wrong earlier, but her vision hadn't specified when Cade would be shot. Caroline burst through the parlor doors and pushed her way through the crowd. When she saw her mom's horrified face, her entire body went cold.

Caroline forced her legs to move in the direction of the people huddled around a body lying on the floor. Dr. Breaux's familiar voice screamed for someone to call an ambulance.

No! It can't be!

Through the mass of panicking bodies she found the top of Cade's head lying on top of someone. Her dad? *Oh God!*

She'd only heard one shot. Just one, right? Could there have been more, and she just missed it? Surely they hadn't both been injured. Caroline refused to think it might be worse than just an injury. No way could she deal with losing the two most important men in her life.

TEN

Caroline pushed and shoved to make her way through the people, frantically trying to get to Cade, but the impenetrable wall of bodies kept her from them.

She turned, looking for her mother, and saw that distant look in her eyes again. Emily was having another vision. She had to be. Normally, in a crisis like this, her mother was calm and collected, always knowing exactly what to do. This strange behavior was unlike her and extremely vexing. Why couldn't she just snap out of it?

Sirens blared in the distance quickly closing in. Caroline scanned the room for any unusual suspects, but everything moved in slow motion. Her gaze stopped on a pair of ice blue eyes frozen onto her own. Time stood still. Panic sometimes provided brief moments of clarity and Caroline knew what she had to do.

She rushed to her mother to help her to a bench before she fell. Then, she stormed across the room to the scrawny bag of bones hell bent on ruining Caroline's life.

"You did this. I know it."

April shook her head, her shoulders sagged, a look of disbelief frozen upon her face. She whispered without moving her lips. "No."

"Oh, please. Cut the crap, April. You are responsible for this. It's got your slimy name all over it."

April shook her head again.

Unsure from where she gathered the courage, Caroline boldly stepped up to her, mere inches from her face, and placed one hand around her throat. "Give me one good reason why I shouldn't kick your scrawny ass right now. Just one."

April swallowed and looked down at her.

"Come on, *stepmother*, give me a reason."

April stared with conflict and annoyance now. She spoke through clenched teeth, still barely above a whisper. "As much as I hate you, Caroline, I did *not* do this."

She didn't want to, but Caroline believed her. A frostiness chilled her to the bone. Flaring temper and all, she shivered. She let go of April's throat, shoving her back a few steps. The paramedics bustled into the house with their equipment. She still didn't know exactly who'd been shot. She frantically looked around, her gaze eventually settling on her mom. Emily sobbed as she watched the medics load a limp body onto the stretcher. Caroline's eyes followed, but she couldn't see past the wall of backs.

Then the medics lifted the gurney, and Caroline recognized the blood-soaked, yellow shirt. *No!*

Remy's lifeless face would haunt her for the rest of her life. She looked back at April in time to witness a single tear slide down her cheek. Frozen and helpless, she stood by as Dr. Breaux helped the paramedics, followed closely by her frantic father, rush her fourteen-year-old brother with a gunshot wound to his chest into the waiting ambulance.

Surreal. Impossible. Terrifying. Caroline juggled her emotions. April seemed convincing enough. How could she just stand there and calmly watch her son, adopted or not, bleeding profusely from the

94

chest as he was rolled out on a stretcher? If that was her child, Caroline would've been a basket case refusing to leave his side.

April had raised Remy from a baby, and he loved her. Caroline couldn't understand how or why, but the boy loved his momma. April was way too calm. There had to be more to this story. Shock?

As much as Caroline wanted to pin all the blame on April, she didn't think April had a hand in the shooting. But she was guilty of something.

"Caroline!"

"Over here." Cade rushed to her and held her in an unyielding hug. She couldn't breathe. "I'm okay. What happened?"

He released his grip, but only slightly. "I don't know. But I'm going to find out." He urgently kissed her again and she sensed his concern. He looked all around, collectively monitoring everything. Missing nothing. "I called Runway. We're going to find out who did this."

"Cade, go," she urged. "I know you want to go meet Runway. I'll be fine."

He shook his head. "No. I'm not leaving you alone."

"I won't be alone. Mom and I will go to the hospital to be with Remy."

"I'll take you." He calmly glanced around the room again, checking every window and every person left in the room. His control and the ability to handle this dangerous situation with logic and patience was amazing. A trait he must have developed as a SEAL. No wonder he had such control over his temper. Caroline was only a thread away from completely unraveling.

"I insist. I can drive. Walk us to my car and meet me at the hospital after you and Runway have done your thing."

Not thrilled with her solution, he reluctantly agreed, but only after he gathered her shoes and purse from upstairs, and walked Caroline and her mother safely to her car before letting them out of his sight.

Caroline whipped her Jeep into a parking spot and shut the engine off. "Mom. Are you okay? What's going on? Did you have another vision or something?"

Emily stopped digging through her purse and looked up. "What?"

Annoyed, Caroline spoke the words again, slowly. "Did. You. Have. Another. Vision?"

Emily rolled her eyes and began digging again. "Really, Caroline, I'm not stupid. I'm looking for my lip balm. You can speak normally to me, I just wasn't paying attention."

"So I noticed. You're very distracted. Answer my question, please." Silence. She put her hand over her mom's to stop the pilfering through her purse, and held it there until Emily finally looked up again. Emily sighed.

"It was no big deal. Yes, I had another vision. This one wasn't as detailed. I don't understand why I'm having these stupid things, but they're really starting to piss me off. If a can of evaporated milk started all this, maybe I need to have you conk me on the head to reverse the curse."

Caroline couldn't stop her smile at her mother's uncharacteristic language. "I'm sure it's not a curse, and hopefully it's only temporary. Please, don't make me ask again."

Emily gently gave her face a maternal caress and smoothed her hair. "Sweetheart, you really shouldn't worry about me. The vision I had this time was very vague and difficult to decipher. All flashy and cloudy, if that makes any sense."

"Not much," she muttered. "I *am* worried about you. We should take you to see Dr. Breaux while we're here to make sure you don't have any major head trauma or something. Whatever these visions are, or why you're having them, it's not normal."

Emily smirked, "Yes, nurse."

Caroline sat alone in the frigid emergency waiting room and

blankly stared at her trembling hands. Her pulse pounded in her head and she desperately tried to curb her downward spiral into a blubbering mess. She squeezed her fingers to hold them still, but it was no use. This wonderful, momentous day had turned into a nightmare, only for real.

Why were no other people in this waiting room? Wasn't this the Emergency Room? Surely more people needed emergency medical attention?

She needed to think about something else to get her mind off of Remy. Cade. Thinking about Cade always made her happy. Her thoughts sped ninety miles-per-hour. So, he served in the Navy. He was a SEAL.

She knew that was special forces, but her knowledge of the military probably wouldn't fill a tiny 3x5 index card. Knowing his job title in the Navy would do no good. Cade was a puzzle. She had all the flat edge pieces to make the frame, but she lacked too many of the middle pieces. There was still so much she didn't know.

Why was he so reserved about his past. Why didn't he tell her about being in the Navy? And why wouldn't he talk about Jenny? Sure, it's painful, but it's been years. Was he not over her yet? Could he move on with Caroline if he still loved a ghost? Caroline shook her head sadly when she realized what she'd just thought. Apparently ghosts are real, and that possibility was endless. She took a slow, deep breath to clear the shivers invading her inner peace, however temporary the solace may be. Searching her memories for any clues Cade might have dropped, or times his guard slipped over the past few months allowed Caroline to relive the most pleasant experiences from her time with him.

The fall semester she had taken off from school, he took her to New Orleans to show her the beauty of moss filled trees lining the entrances to grand plantations. Some had even been sprinkled with gold dust for an extraordinary wedding celebration. Tables laden with gourmet food had run along the path leading to the great house for almost a mile. Cade taught her a little of the local dialect. Words like *fais do do*, *cher* and *envie* were easier to say after he helped her practice the Acadian accent. Her rolling "r's" were now almost as good as his.

Days had melded into weeks as Delia and Delphine taught her how to cook some of their favorite dishes like seafood gumbo and *riz au lait*, a creamy bit of heaven made from rice, milk and sugar. Practically able to smell the savory aromas from her memories, Caroline breathed deeply through her nose and exhaled. The beauty of the locals, their traditions, and their rich history seeped into her soul. She belonged here.

In the spring when Cade visited the house she and her mom shared in uptown New Orleans, he respectfully slept on the couch. Those weekends were her favorite. Caroline stayed in the living room talking to him until they heard the clanging of the 3:38 streetcar on St. Charles at Broadway.

On foggy evenings, they sat on the front porch, skin balmy and tingling with the rich humidity, and listened to the warning blows of boat captains alerting the docks and other ships on the river of their location. It was peaceful and quite romantic, and she'd ramble on about her boring life. Prime opportunity for him to open up and share, but no. Instead, they passionately made out like teenagers while still keeping it simple, never going too far. Not that she was complaining.

Always the gentleman, Cade never pushed her past her comfort zone, but sometimes she'd have to control her own thoughts not to throw him down and jump his bones. Beyond sexy, he made her question her resolve, and her body betrayed her mind. She always stopped, though.

Had it been Trevor staying on their couch, he would have snuck into Caroline's room to pressure her for sex every chance he had, regardless of her mother sleeping in the next room. At least Trevor was forthcoming about his past. Cade, however, was a walking enigma. Playful, charming, and incredibly sexy, but always mysterious. Why?

Caroline paced the vacant hallway, her feet aching with each click of her four-inch heels. She silently cursed Kristy for insisting she wear them, and wished she'd had the chance to change clothes before all hell broke loose. The sound echoed, grating on her already-frayed nerves, so she slipped them off and looped her fingers through the sling back, relishing in the release of her bare feet on the cold tile. She continued pacing and thinking. Analyzing.

Cade's constant reservations about his past annoyed her. Whenever she mentioned anything about it, he immediately shrugged it off and changed the subject. Perhaps he just needed time to sort things through. She couldn't imagine Cade ever doing anything bad enough for him to be too ashamed to admit or disclose. . .especially to her. Why had he not invited her to spend more time with his family? Was he afraid they would tell her things about his past? Maybe that's what she should do. . .ask his sister or his mom. They seemed to like her, maybe they'd give a little insight into Cade's cryptic puzzle?

As she realized all the things she *didn't* know about him, she became upset. His arrogance last summer claiming he would sweep her off her feet and make her fall desperately in love with him, forgetting all about Trevor, her *fiancé*. Yet, when it came down to opening up to her, he was a book of secrets. What was he hiding? The longer she sat brooding over this, the angrier she became.

She decided to go in search of Cade or her dad, but an unmistakable odor burned her nostrils and set off alarms in her head. Something was on fire. She reflexively looked up for smoke, but saw nothing. Caroline scurried from room to room peeking inside while inspecting the hallways for evidence of fire. The scent grew stronger triggering the urge to cough, so Caroline darted to the end of the hallway ready to pull the fire alarm. Before she reached it, Cade rushed into the hall nearly colliding with her. His strong hands gripped her bare arms to steady her as they spun around.

"Hey, I was looking for you. Where's the fire?" He chuckled.

"I don't know, but we need to pull the alarm now before it gets out of hand," she insisted as she frantically squirmed from his hold.

"Wait. . . Baby, I was kidding. What's wrong?" His grip tightened along with his concern. "Caroline, calm down. What happened?"

"You don't smell that? Come on." She pressed, continuing to resist his hold.

"Smell what?" His nose wrinkled as he breathed deeply without letting her go.

"Smoke." She sniffed the air while scanning the ceiling again. "Something's burning, I just don't know where."

"I don't smell anything. Are you sure?" Cade smoothed his hands down the length of her arms. "I'm sure someone would have already pulled the alarm if there was a fire in a hospital," he reassured. "Besides, there are sprinklers everywhere. Don't you think they'd be soaking us right now if anything was burning?"

He licked his lips and a half-smile curved his mouth as he swept an appreciative gaze over the slinky fabric hugging her curves. "Not that I'd object to seeing you all wet," his hands dropped to her lower back and pulled her closer, "Especially after what you told me at the party. But. . .we should probably double check before we summon the fire trucks. You know?" He winked, "I know the guys in the department and I'd have to personally gouge out the eyes of every one of those horny bastards after they caught a glimpse of you." When she didn't respond he frowned and tilted his head, his sharp eyes missing nothing. "You okay, love?"

He didn't believe her. Gritting her teeth, Caroline pressed her eyes closed and concentrated on the scent again. She wasn't crazy. She was certain she'd smelled smoke. When she inhaled again to prove she hadn't imagined it, only the potent aroma of disinfectant filled her nose. She blinked back the infuriating rush of tears and covered her face. Maybe she *was* crazy. The stress of this evening had finally overpowered her. She'd lost her mind. Without a word, Cade pulled her into his arms and kissed her hair. Her tense muscles relaxed when he hugged her, then she remembered he'd caused some of that tension—before her momentary hallucination, that is.

"I believe you," he whispered. "There has to be an explanation. We'll get to the bottom of it. Together. Everything's going to be okay." She was thankful he showed when he did. She shuddered to think of the chaos that false alarm would've caused. But why, or *how* had she smelled smoke with no fire? Unease chilled her bones and she trembled. Cade squeezed her tighter. "I came to tell you Remy is out of surgery, and they've moved him to recovery. Your dad and I have been in the waiting room down the hall."

"Let's go."

He led her by the hand, but her heavy limbs weighed her down like sandbags. Fatigue danced through her body, and her stomach ached. When they stepped into the waiting room on the second floor, it was empty.

"He was here two minutes ago. He must have gone to the cafeteria to get some coffee or something. If you want to wait here, I can go find him."

Caroline searched her foggy mind for the right words. Where were they? She knew she had something she needed to say, but what? She shook the cobwebs from her head. "No, don't go. Please. Stay here with me. We need to talk." Caroline studied the speckled tile floor.

"Okay." He studied her with his sharp eyes. "Anything you want. What's on your mind?"

When she didn't respond, he lifted her chin to look at him. The tears flowed freely now, and she didn't even try to stop them. He pulled out the handkerchief he always kept in his pocket and dabbed her sodden cheeks.

"Baby, you gotta tell me what's wrong. This is killing me." He kissed her tears before smoothing her cheek with the back of his hand. "I can't stand to see you upset. Remy came through the surgery okay. The doctor said he'll be fine."

Her head swiveled from side-to-side, though she couldn't tell if *she* did it or if it was an involuntary motion her body decided upon. Either way, she looked like she was having a seizure, and her jaws ached from clenching. Snotty, weepy, and twitchy, she took his handkerchief and paused before blowing her nose in it. "May I?"

He grinned. "Of course. That's what it's for." After she soiled his hanky, he placed his strong, reassuring hands on her shoulders. "Now, will you *please* tell me what's got you so upset?"

She took a deep, shaky breath, and, before she could think, her mouth responded.

"You."

ELEVEN

"Caroline, what in the world are you talking about? *I've* upset you like this?" Confusion clouded his restraint as a static alarm echoed in Cade's head. He replayed the evening in his mind as he scrutinized every word she said. Every gesture she made in this moment was a crucial form of communication and he didn't want to miss a thing.

Caroline twisted her fingers into knots. "Yes. No. I mean. . . I don't know. Never mind, just forget I said anything."

She turned to walk away from him, but he grabbed her wrist, pulling her into his arms. He couldn't let her off that easily. She needed him now, and he needed to right this wrong. Whatever it was.

"Oh, no you don't. You can't just walk away after dropping a bomb like that. Tell me what I've done. Please, I need to fix it. It hurts me to see you like this."

Her emerald eyes, greener than normal, flashed with doubt causing his heart to flip.

Confused, Cade's instincts told him—no, *screamed* for him, to tread softly through the minefield of her emotions. "It breaks my heart to see you so upset, especially to know I caused it."

She pulled her hand from his and stepped back, crossing her arms over her chest. She trembled slightly, hardly noticeable for her shifting from foot to foot, but Cade noticed everything. Nervous, irritated, or possibly excited. She was difficult to read in this state of mind.

"I could just keep my thoughts and feelings to myself from now on since that seems to be your preference."

His brows pinched together. "I'm not following."

"I've come to the conclusion that I don't know much more about you right now than I did almost a year ago," she seethed.

If growing up with four sisters hadn't taught him anything else, he'd learned sincerity and eye contact held more weight than anything else in situations like this.

"You've been through a lot tonight. We both have. Please, love, you have to tell me what I did to upset you. I honestly don't know."

Her animated arms flailed around, and she paced. "Words, words, words. That's all I ever hear. You say these things, but do you really mean them? The only thing I know about you now that I didn't know last summer after we'd *just met* is that you were a Navy SEAL. And I just learned *that* tonight."

He tried very hard not to laugh. She was in hysterics. Officially flipping out. He'd not seen this side of Caroline yet, and honestly had to say, it was about time. And cute. She was taking her stress from the evening out on him. Normally, an attack like this would get his back up, raise his hackles and defenses. But he could take it. He'd rather this than have her hold it all inside. Besides, angry Caroline was adorable. It was refreshing. She'd begun to seem a little too perfect, rarely getting angry or argumentative. Last summer she challenged him, disagreed with him. . .denied his advances only to switch roles. Always reserved. . .cool and collected. Today, she had shown a hint of jealousy with Jessica, but apart from that, she never argued or confronted him like before. He missed that girl.

"I mean, you're a little *too* perfect, Cade."

His jaw dropped, but he quickly snapped it shut before she saw. "There has to be a flaw somewhere in you. I can't believe I didn't realize this before now. I'm such a fool. How could I have been so naïve?"

"A fool?" He frowned and crossed his arms. He still didn't understand why she was upset with him. "Caroline, what are you talking about? I'm far from perfect." His shoulders slumped in surrender and he reached out for her. "Sweetheart, please, you're not making any sense."

"Look at you!" She stepped out of his reach and gestured to his physique. "You're gorgeous, physically fit, independent, skilled with a weapon." She mumbled, "Now at least I know *why*." Her volume quickly returned to her former level of hysteria. "You never get angry or jealous, and, aside from keeping secrets from your past, you're completely unselfish. You're confident but not arrogant, you come from a great family that you love, you want a big family yourself, you can cook, you've got impeccable manners. Don't you see where I'm going with this? You're too perfect, Cade."

A chuckle slipped, and, unfortunately, it only fueled her anger. Her green irises burned with hostility. He raised his hands in surrender. "Help me out here. I am, after all, just a clueless man. You're upset with me because I'm awesome?"

"No! I'm upset because you haven't revealed anything of depth about your life. I mean, you *are* awesome, but. . ." she inhaled, somewhat calming down. "I love you, and we have lots of fun together, but I don't really *know* you at all. We've stayed up into the wee hours of the morning talking, but we've only ever talked about me. I feel like you're hiding something from me, and I don't like secrets."

She faced the wall and mumbled softly to herself. He strained to hear.

"I was ready to marry you. But how can I marry you when I have no idea who you really are." She huffed and covered her face with both hands. "And I was going to make love to you tonight."

All humor gone, and a little more forcefully, he grasped her arm and spun her around mere inches from his face.

"What did you just say?"

His swift, strong reaction frightened her at first, then she growled. "Ugh!" She looked up to the ceiling. "Oh sure, *that's* the part that you heard." She avoided eye contact and mumbled to the floor. "You're right, you *are* just a man."

Cade had heard enough. Reining in his temper, fully acknowledging this was fear talking, he still didn't appreciate her insinuation. He straightened up and dropped her arm, more offended than angry. He thought she held a much higher regard for him than that. "You're right, Caroline. You don't know me at all." She stared at her hands for several long moments before finally looking up at him with tear-filled eyes. He hoped those were remorseful tears. Shame for thinking so poorly of him. "If you think your last statement is what caught my attention, you have no clue about me."

Being scared was understandable, but it didn't give her the right to cut him so deeply. He couldn't think of anything to say without hurting her back, so he glowered as he stepped away without saying another word. He wanted her to feel the pain of her accusations. He crossed his arms and turned his back to her to speak to the wall.

If Caroline assumed he had no temper, she was wrong. He'd had years of practice and psychological training to control it. "I already knew you were considering our sexual relationship. You mentioned it earlier, to which I said we would go there when you were ready. And *clearly* you are not ready yet." He closed his eyes and breathed deeply to steady his temper before turning around to face her. They locked gazes and shared a noisy silence. Not a word spoken, but much communicated in that brief and intense moment. Finally, he whispered, "You said you were ready to marry me."

Her eyes dropped to her fidgeting hands. "Yes."

Cade stubbornly crossed his arms again. "I haven't asked you yet."

"Oh, well, I assumed. . . Just. . . Never mind. It doesn't matter if you haven't even thought about it."

He shook his head. This woman confused the daylights out of

106

him. "Caroline, are you kidding me? That's *all* I've thought about since I met you. I've taken things slowly—for *you*. You nearly panicked tonight when I simply asked you to be my girlfriend, all because you thought I was on my knee to propose." He ran his hands through his hair, his shoulder throbbing from the sudden motion. Women could be so fickle.

"I was ready to marry you last summer. I would have gladly stepped in Trevor's place if I thought you would be willing." He grinned smugly, trying to hide the sting of her words. "I knew I was meant to marry you the moment I met you in the library."

"Oh, please. That's absurd."

"Maybe, but I don't think so. I only waited this long to officialize our relationship because you needed time to get over Trevor. I'm still not convinced you're over him completely yet, which is why I'm not rushing you into. . .anything." He cringed, not meaning to hesitate before that last word. He'd been very careful with their physical contact so she wouldn't think that's all he wanted. If she knew how often he walked away in physical pain every time he said goodnight, then she'd think he was as bad as that asshole.

Her voice softened. "I'm sorry." She grabbed his hand and laced her fingers through his. "I just want to know all about you. I want to spend time with your family and get to know them better." Her lips curved up at the corner, engulfing Cade with an overwhelming sense of relief. "I *am* your girlfriend now, so you should bring me around them more often."

He exhaled and dropped his forehead to hers as he brought her hands to his lips. He squeezed his eyes closed and whispered, "Sweet Caroline, I've been waiting for a year to hear you say those words."

"What if your family hates me?"

"They won't."

"You don't know that."

"My parents and two of my sisters have already met you. They already love you."

107

"When they met me I was engaged to another man while kissing and making out with their son. I'm sure they don't think very highly of me."

"They didn't know we were kissing."

Caroline looked up with a raised eyebrow.

"I don't kiss and tell, remember?"

"Right. I'm sure they couldn't tell I had it bad for you when I couldn't take my eyes off you the whole time you sang for us last year at the Fourth of July crawfish boil. Then your sister confronted me during the fireworks show. That was humiliating."

"Wait, what?"

"Nothing, she just knew I was looking for you. Where did you go, anyway?"

Cade puffed out his cheeks in thought. "Yeah, fireworks don't go so well with PTSD. I tend to get a little crazy when I'm around explosives."

"You have PTSD?"

"It's controlled now. You don't really ever get rid of it, but I've learned how to cope with it. Sometimes things will drag me back to that hell, but I'm pretty good about snapping out of it. I haven't had a serious episode in years."

"Oh."

"But, that's because I've learned what I can handle and what I can't. That's why I skipped out when I saw them gathering up the loot of rockets and screaming missiles." He laughed, but she didn't. "I'm okay. Promise. See, this is why I don't like to dredge up details of my past. Because it wasn't all good."

"I'd still like to know."

"Why? So you can get upset like you are now?"

"I'm not upset. I'm worried about you."

"Don't. Worry about Remy and your dad. I'm a survivor. I made it out of hell many times and I don't plan to go back. And my family already loves you because I do." Caroline smiled, so he relaxed and kissed her hand, thankful things were okay between them.

"I'm sorry I flipped out on you. I just don't like secrets, and it seems like everyone around here has dozens of them. Even the ghosts."

He chuckled and kissed her forehead. "It's okay, sweet girl. I understand you're scared. I'm sorry I was the cause of your. . .frustration." He smiled, "Now what can I do to keep that enchanting smile on your face?" he said.

"Promise to stop being so cryptic about your past."

That was the one request he did not want from her. He expected a personal question or something, but not a promise to be an open book. He closed his eyes and took a deep breath as he weighed the pros and cons of his answer. "I promise I'll try. Will that work for now?"

"I guess it'll have to."

He gently brushed her hair from her forehead then cradled her face. "So, you were really thinking about making love to me? Tonight? I thought you were just being. . .flirtatious."

She shrugged. "I was at first, but seeing Runway and Kristy so into each other made me jealous. In my search for a change of clothes, I saw the lingerie that Kristy gave me as a graduation present." She blushed and looked up through her lashes. "The thought crossed my mind to give it a test drive." Between her seductive look and the word "lingerie," his body was at full attention. It had been a very long time since he'd seen a beautiful woman wearing lingerie. . .in person, at least.

"Lingerie? Really? What, um, what kind of lingerie?"

She gave a naughty little smile. "Wouldn't you like to know?"

He nodded, eagerly then scolded himself for acting like a slobbering dog.

She leaned in closely, her breath on his face, and he inhaled her sweet feminine scent. Completely still until he knew exactly what she planned to do, Cade suppressed a chuckle thinking about just how badly he wanted to show her his desire to know. She pressed her cheek to his. "Dinner with your family. This weekend. No excuses."

She backed away, leaving him breathless. Of course he didn't let her know that. Then she said something very peculiar.

"I have a puzzle to piece together."

TWELVE

Shrill beeping echoed off the sterile walls of the waiting room, startling both Caroline and Cade. A doctor and two nurses rushed past them, pushing through the recovery room doors.

"Dr. Bailey," Cade said. "That was the surgeon who performed Remy's surgery."

Caroline whirled around to follow them, but Cade pulled her back.

"Wait, you can't go in there. It's the Intensive Care recovery room. They won't let you past the desk."

"I know, but I need to know what's going on. What if Remy flatlined? What could have happened?" She tugged against his hold, but got nowhere. "Let's just go ask the nurse at the desk. Maybe she can tell us something."

He pulled her close and hugged her tightly. "I don't think they'll tell us because of the privacy laws. The only ones with authorization to know anything is your dad or April."

She knew that. But it didn't make it any easier. "You're right. I should call my dad."

She pulled her phone from her purse to dial, but Cade covered her hand to stop her. When she looked up to see why, his tenderness nearly broke her. "Calm down, cher. Do you really want to worry your dad when we don't even know for sure it was Remy's monitors

111

that beeped? There are quite a few rooms back there, and I'm sure he's not the only patient in the ICU.

She shook her head. "The ER was empty."

He smiled. "The ER *waiting room* was empty; that doesn't mean the exam rooms were. Not everyone has a loving family who will wait for hours in a cold uncomfortable room to see if he's going to be okay. Let's just wait to see what the doctor says. They're back there with whoever was beeping, so I'm sure if it was Remy, he'll be okay."

Caroline knew she was overreacting, but the stabbing guilt for not being there when Remy was shot, not being able to help him in this hospital, ate a hole through her heart. She didn't know what else to do. What's the use being a nurse if she can't use her skills? Here she was fresh out of college with medical knowledge seeping from her brain cells, but she couldn't do anything about it. Her hands were tied.

"You're right. We'll just wait. Waiting sucks, but we can just. . .wait." Rambling. Lovely. She was somehow responsible for this, she knew it. But how? Why? She paced back and forth and wrung her hands again, her spastic thoughts interrupted by Cade's smooth calm voice.

"Caroline."

Her mind in a whirlwind, she just wanted to run and scream and try to make everything go away. She wished she could go back to last spring before she ever agreed to marry Trevor. Would she do things differently? If she hadn't agreed to marry Trevor, she never would have come down here to Louisiana, and never would have met Cade, or had such a great relationship with her dad. Things weren't really as bad as she made them seem, right? She gave in and allowed herself the comfort of Cade's sheltering arms and sobbed. Stupid traitor tears. They made her seem so weak and pathetic.

Cade gently rubbed his hand up and down her back and kissed the top of her head. "Shhh, it's okay, baby."

Caroline straightened and wiped her soggy face, but didn't let go of Cade. He was the only reason she had the strength to stand on her own.

A moment later, one of the nurses walked back through the doors. "Are you the relatives of Jeremy Fontenot?"

She nodded. "Yes, ma'am, I'm his sister."

"Do you know where his mother or father are?"

"No, but I can call my dad. What's going on? What happened?"

Her excessively made-up face wrinkled in a sympathetic frown. "I'm sorry, hon, but I can't tell you anything. I can only disclose medical information to his guardians."

Caroline nodded before the nurse finished speaking, trying her best not to scream. "Right. Of course. I'll call my dad."

She dialed the number and stepped away while Cade spoke to the nurse. Caroline didn't take her eyes off of her, but she could hear bits of their conversation while waiting for her dad to pick up. Cade asked if Remy's monitors had been the ones beeping, and she nodded.

"Hello?"

"Hey, Dad. I need you to come back to the ICU recovery waiting room."

"Is everything okay? What happened?"

She tried to stop the tears as she swallowed the unyielding blockage in her throat, but her voice still shook. "I don't know. They can't tell me anything. Are you close?"

"Yeah, I'm walking there now."

"Okay." Annoyance crept into her voice. "Where is April? Doesn't she care that Remy is possibly dying?"

"Of course she cares. Calm down. Dr. Bailey said the bullet had missed any vital organs or arteries, so I'm sure the nurse just wants to give us an update on his status."

"Yes, but Cade and I heard the monitors beeping like crazy, and Dr. Bailey rushed in there only five or ten minutes ago. Something terrible has happened, and now they want to talk to you."

His voice became quiet. "I'm here."

Caroline turned and Eddie stalked past her to the nurse.

"I'm Eddie Fontenot. What happened? Is my son okay?"

The nurse didn't nod or anything. She simply took a deep breath and looked around as if she didn't want to tell him in front of others.

He spoke more loudly. Urgently. "I want to know what's going on with my son. Is he alright?"

Dr. Bailey walked up. Tall and blonde with an athletic build, she couldn't be more than forty years old. "Mr. Fontenot. There's been a serious complication. When the bullet entered his chest, it splintered his scapula. As a result, a fragment of the bone from his scapula lodged into his spinal cord causing temporary paralysis from his waist down. We were able to remove the fragment of bone, and the nerve tissue wasn't badly damaged. We were hoping that after the surgery we would see an improvement once the anesthesia wore off. . .but we haven't."

Caroline let the briefing sink in. "That wasn't what caused the beeping we heard though, right?" she said. "Not seeing improvement in his legs wouldn't have set off the monitors." Something didn't add up.

"Your son's right lung collapsed," Dr. Bailey said.

Caroline gasped. Eddie's face lost all color. He sank into a nearby chair.

"We're on top of things. He's been moved to an operating room where the best pulmonary surgeon we have is working on him now."

"Is he. . .is he going to—" Eddie cleared his throat. "Paralysis? Collapsed lung? He's so young. Will he make it through the surgery since his body's already been through so much?"

Dr. Bailey placed her hand on his shoulder. "He's a strong young man, Mr. Fontenot. I'm optimistic that the paralysis is temporary and he'll be able to walk again. My biggest concern right now is his lung, but Dr. Johnston is the best. He will see to it that Remy is a priority." Dr. Bailey patted Eddie's shoulder again and walked back through the double doors.

Caroline sat beside her dad and rested her head on his shoulder. "It'll be okay. God is watching over him right now. I know it. I believe it. He's not going to let anything else happen to Remy."

"Twenty bucks," Eddie murmured. He shook his head, his hollow gaze blankly staring at the floor. He leaned forward to rest his elbows on his knees as his weary head hung to his clasped hands. "He asked me for some money and I dropped the twenty-dollar bill. When I bent down to get it. . ." Tears welled up, and he pressed his thumbs into his eye sockets to stop the flow.

They sat in silence with only their tears when April walked into the room. She knelt in front of Eddie, not even acknowledging Cade or Caroline, grasped his hands and looked only at him.

"We will get through this. I know it. We have to."

Eddie's eyes spilled over with tears, and the two of them genuinely cried together.

For the first time since she'd met April, Caroline saw a side to her that wasn't evil.

Cade nodded for Caroline to follow him and give Eddie and April a moment of privacy. She followed him into the hall, curious of his take on April's performance. He stared at the walls deep in thought, and Caroline was dying to know what he was thinking about.

"Well, that was interesting," she said.

Cade didn't speak, only nodded.

"I wonder how long it took for her to actually feel something?" Caroline wondered aloud. "As cold as she always seems I would have sworn her heart was made of ice."

Cade stared into her eyes for a moment, thinking, like he was trying to decide what to say. For a moment she worried she had annoyed him with her snide comment about April.

"You know, for a second there I was almost convinced."

Confused, she asked, "Convinced of what?"

"Convinced that she really cares about him."

"Who, my dad or Remy?"

Without a trace of frivolity, he sternly replied. "Either of them."

Caroline was shocked. "You mean you didn't believe any of that? You don't think she was sincerely upset?"

"Sure she's upset, but I don't think so much about Remy or your dad's feelings." He paced like a caged panther. "Think about it. She didn't say *he,* meaning Remy, would get through this. She said *we,* meaning *her.*"

"And my dad, right?" Caroline sniggered, "Trust me, I *want* to believe you, but she could've been grouping the whole family into that statement."

"I don't think so. Something's up with April. I just don't know what yet. I need to do some sniffing around, but I definitely smell a rat somewhere in this kitchen. I was almost convinced, but then. . .," he tilted his head, "She's good, I'll give her that." Cade rubbed the back of his neck before cracking his knuckles. "But I'm better."

"Wait, you're not making any sense. I suspected her involvement with Kenneth Callahan's hit man last year, and you told me she wasn't smart enough to pull off any of this. Don't get me wrong, I'd love to see her go down, and I thought it myself, but to actually say she had her own son shot. . . That's a serious accusation. What if we're wrong? Do you think she could be responsible for this?"

He stopped in front of her. "I didn't say that. I think she's definitely got her hand in this, but I just don't know how." He started pacing again. "It's just something about what she said and how she said it that's rubbing me raw. If she is responsible for the shooting tonight, I don't think she meant for Remy to get shot." He frowned and shook his head. "No, that wasn't part of her plan. Only, now I'm not so certain your dad was the target either."

Caroline's head spun. "What? If he wasn't the target, then who was?"

Cade rubbed the back of his neck in aggravation. "Me."

The amount of air Caroline squeezed from her lungs to form the words was only enough to create a breathless whisper. "What? H-how? How could you possibly know that? My dad said he bent down to grab some money he dropped when Remy was shot. We don't know who the target was."

"Yeah, I bent down to get it, too. Reflex."

She grabbed his arm as he passed, and he stopped to look at her with an unusual expression. "Cade, what are you not telling me."

He didn't plan to let her in on his revelation. That was evident in the hard shift in his eyes and firm set of his jaw. "I don't know for sure. I have to do some more investigating, but I will tell you. Soon."

Beyond frustrated now, she exploded. "Ugh! No. You see, Cade, *this* is what I was talking about earlier. You shut me out when you need to let me in. Tell me what you're thinking so I can help you."

He grasped both of her shoulders and spoke only inches from her face, pleading. "Please don't be upset. I don't like to reveal my hand until I know what I'm up against. Let me do some more digging, and I promise I will tell you everything. Trust me. Please."

Defeated, she sighed. He kissed her gently and whispered, "I need to follow a lead. I'll be back in two hours. Please, Caroline, wait here for me and don't do anything. . .irrational."

She couldn't promise that, but if she didn't at least acknowledge his request, he wouldn't let it go.

"Fine, I'll try to be good. Just hurry before I change my mind."

"I promise."

Like a flash of lightning, he was down the hall and out of her view. Confused and frustrated, Caroline felt the end of her rope slipping through her fingers. She stared at a fluorescent bulb flickering above her. She thought of Rachel and how her light went out much too early. Caroline puffed out a resigned sigh as she mumbled to herself, to Rachel.

"If you're still watching over me, I could use your help right about now. Maybe a little insight or something? A dream? Anything?" How could Rachel have been so present in her life last year when Caroline didn't really want her there, and now be so absent? She realized Rachel did it to show her the truth. To warn her not to marry Trevor. But this wasn't over yet. The Callahan's still posed a threat to her family.

The sound of her name caught her attention. A whisper, the faintest sigh, easily mistaken for equipment fans or the brush of footsteps against the tile, but articulate. And she was the only warm body in the hall. Her clue. A gush of cool air soothed her as a door swung unnaturally on its hinges more times that it should have. Like someone was continually pushing it back and forth for fun. Only. . .she hadn't touched it, and no one else stood nearby.

Chills crept down her spine and bile rose in her throat. Posted in the hallway of the hospital behind the swinging door hung a framed advertisement for KC Real Estate Investors. Rachel still watched out for her, and this message couldn't be good.

THIRTEEN

Eddie held Caroline's hands, and though he was physically sitting beside her, he wasn't there, hardly moving at all. She wished she could soothe him in some way, to tell him everything was going to be okay, but she had no clue how to begin. His drawn, haggard face made him appear twenty years older. The chaos she brought into his family had worn on him.

Caroline abruptly turned toward him, and he flinched in surprise.

"I'm so sorry."

He frowned. "What in the world are you sorry about? You've done nothing wrong."

Caroline considered telling him about Rachel's creepy, subtle message, but decided against it. Now was not the time. "No, this is my fault. None of this happened to your family until I showed up last year and complicated things. I don't know who shot Remy, but whoever it is must have something against me."

He shook his head, and she saw the anger building in his expression. He stood. "This is your family, too, and you have to stop blaming yourself for everything that is happening here. It's not your fault. We don't know who the shooter was targeting, but I don't think it was Remy. I had my back to the window, and Beau stood right next to me. Could have been either one of us, just the same. It all happened so fast." He looked away, wistfully, his face distorting in pain for an instant before he masked it and cleared his throat.

"Remy clutching his chest. . . That sight will haunt me forever." He shook his head and rubbed his eyes to the point that she thought he would dig them out. He spoke with his palms pressed against his sockets. "Either way, none of this is your fault." His jaw twitched as he clenched his teeth together.

No way could Caroline let him shoulder all the blame. "Dad, Remy could die because someone is trying to kill my family, one by one. You. The head of the Fontenot family fortune. I can't handle. . ." She swiped at the flood of tears streaming down her cheeks. "I can't lose you. I just got you in my life."

The stupid lump that had recently taken a permanent residence in her throat threatened to choke her, but she forced out the next three words. "I love you."

He drew in a sharp breath, wiped the tears from her cheeks, and whispered, "I love you, too, baby."

She studied his handsome weathered face. He carried the burdens of the world upon his shoulders. She wrapped her arms around him again. "Oh, Dad. I'm so sorry. I just can't believe this."

Sobs racked his body. There were only a few things Caroline couldn't handle, and a grown man crying was one of them. She broke down right along with him and refused to release her hold from around his waist.

"I'm just so glad you're okay," he whispered between sobs.

She jerked her head back, blinded by the endless supply of tears. "Me? Forget about *me*, I'm glad *you* are okay. I can't believe this is happening. It's all my fault."

He forced her back holding her shoulders tightly in his large hands. "No. Didn't you listen to me? None of this is your fault. Do you hear me? You are in no way responsible for any of this. I am. Whoever shot Remy meant to shoot me. If I hadn't dropped that money and leaned down to pick it up, it would be me in there fighting for my life instead of my child!"

"This isn't your fault either. Do you have any idea who would want to kill you?"

"No, I don't. The only thing I can think of is a possible hit man sent by our friends, the Callahans. I really can't be sure, though. I have no evidence to be throwing around accusations and assumptions."

She hugged him again. "This is terrible. Will we be living in fear for the rest of our lives then?"

Resting his chin on the top of her head, he mumbled, "Not if I can help it."

"Seriously, I don't know what I would do without you in my life now." She wept into his chest, the sound muffled by his shirt.

He kissed the top of her head. "Caroline, I will always be here for you. I promise. Once Remy pulls through this, nothing else is going to happen to him, you, or Claire. I'll make sure of it."

"Where is Claire, anyway?"

"She and Josh went to his parents' house. I told her I would call her with updates as I get them. I know she'd rather be anywhere else but here." The glum, distant look in his eyes, reflected the argument he and Claire had earlier. "Anyway, she's fine. Thank goodness you, Claire and your mother were nowhere near me. I'm going to make sure nothing like this happens to anyone else. I'll have Beau call in more of his guys. The instant we heard the gunshot, he tackled me to the floor. He said he was fairly certain whoever pulled the trigger was aiming for me."

She huffed. "Now he's not so sure. He told me he thinks he might have been the target." Eddie vehemently shook his head. "What exactly did Cade do in the Navy?"

"He hasn't told you?"

"No. I just found out today that he was a Navy SEAL, but he didn't offer many details."

Eddie rubbed the back of his neck when Caroline refused to let it go. "Honestly, does it really matter?"

"If you tell me, I won't have to drag it out of him, and it may explain why he never wants to talk about his past."

Eddie sighed and fidgeted with his wedding ring. "I wonder if it might change how you feel about him."

That got her attention, and she sat up. Why did he think it would change her feelings? What could have possibly been so bad? "He said it was no big deal, that he had special training and pretty intense deployments, but I think he's keeping something else from me. Something that may have happened during his military career."

Eddie quietly studied her, but still didn't answer.

Caroline exhaled and the defiance left her posture. "Yes, it matters to me, and I really want to know. He is so dismissive of his past. He always changes the subject or skips around my questions when I ask, and, frankly, I'm tired of everyone knowing about him but me."

His lips pursed into a grin. "Beau was a highly-trained Navy SEAL. They're supposed to be secretive." Not amused by his candor, Caroline impatiently raised an eyebrow. Finally, he conceded. "They have special teams that conduct dangerous missions. He wasn't the leader of his team, but his job was crucial. He was a sniper." He paused to gauge her reaction and continued when she failed to freak out. "The best. Very important people requested his services for top secret missions all over the world. They wanted the most accurate sniper possible, and he had to be able to drop everything and assemble his team to go on a moment's notice. He's extremely talented, quite lethal, with his hands as well as a weapon, and I'm certain the Navy was sad to see him go."

Her mind raced. *A sniper?* That explained a lot. Like the incident last summer when he shot a rattlesnake from a far-away tree moments before it sank its fangs into her flesh.

Being a SEAL also explained his quick reflexes and how he came away with barely a scratch in a fight with Trevor.

"I don't understand why he didn't just explain that. Why wouldn't he have just mentioned before now that he was a SEAL? Isn't that an honorable thing?"

"Well, yes, but many people are threatened knowing SEALs are highly trained to kill people with their bare hands." Eddie tipped his head, genuinely impressed. "Quite easily and in many different ways." He stared blankly at the wall, deep in thought.

"I don't know much about his past, either," he added. "Only what he told me when I hired him, which wasn't much. In general, I believe the teams are usually in charge of rescue missions, but as a sniper I'm sure Beau had targets that he had to eliminate before his mission was complete. I'm also certain his military career took its toll on Beau's life, and he's had to deal with his personal demons. Coping with being responsible for taking someone's life as an act of self-defense is one thing; doing it for no reason other than being ordered to is another. I know for a fact that most, if not all, Navy SEALs do not like talking about their experiences. I could see where he wouldn't want to necessarily broadcast the information to just anybody."

She pouted. "Yeah, well, I'll tell you like I told him earlier. I'm not just anybody."

Chuckling, he patted her shoulder. "I know, sweetheart. Guys generally don't like to be very open or exposed. Maybe he's just waiting until he knows you won't judge him too harshly for the skeletons in his closet. Maybe he's waiting to tell you when he knows you won't run away screaming."

"I would never do that." Caroline lowered her voice and clasped her hands together. "I just want to know him, not judge him. It's not my job to judge people. I gave April a chance or *three* before I finally decided I didn't like her, didn't I?" Eddie winced, and Caroline immediately regretted allowing those petty words to slip out. "I love Cade. Surely he knows I would never leave him because he was a sniper. A Navy SEAL. That's. . ." She searched for the right word. "Hot."

Her dad laughed aloud and kissed her forehead. "I think he will be very pleased with your reaction then, cher. I'm sure he has a good reason for not telling you the whole story yet. Don't be too hard on him. Just don't tell him I blew the whistle. I definitely don't want Beau as my enemy." He winked and straightened up. "I'm going to go back to the cafeteria to grab a cup of coffee and see if your mom is in there."

"Where did April go?"

"She said she was going to call some friends to help get her mind off of Remy."

Caroline smirked. "April has friends?"

He shook his head, but smiled. "Shocking, I know. Please call me if you hear anything. I gave them permission to give you updates on Remy."

Relief washed over her. "Okay, I will. Tell Mom I'm up here, okay?"

He nodded and walked to the elevators, not quite as morose as before.

Moments later, Kristy's voice carried down the hall. Caroline ran out to meet her and Runway.

"Oh, Caro," Kristy said, her arms extended toward her. "I'm so sorry about Remy. Thank God you are okay, and your dad and Cade." She looked around the room. "Where is he, anyway?"

"Thanks. He's out following a lead. I feel so responsible."

Caroline filled Kristy and Runway in on the events, including her confrontation with April.

"You don't think April is behind this?" Runway asked.

"No. If so, and she was, in fact, trying to take out my dad, she signed a prenup. She has nothing to gain from his death."

"Still, she *is* entitled to everything your father's company has earned since they got married. The prenup only covers what he had before they married," he argued.

Caroline hadn't considered that. April would probably get a massive amount of money if Eddie died. Caroline supposed April wasn't as much the obvious suspect as she initially assumed, but she couldn't be discounted, either. It did make perfect sense. If all of Eddie's dependents were dead, as his wife, she would inherit everything. That's why Caroline felt responsible. April only had Claire and Remy to deal with, then Caroline came into the picture as the oldest, biological daughter and seriously complicated things for April. Caroline noticed Runway's arm intimately draped around Kristy's waist.

Caroline raised her eyebrow. "So, how was *your* evening?"

Something big happened between them. That was evident in Kristy's blush. She shifted her weight, and looked at her feet while tucking her long, dark hair behind one ear. That never happened. Kristy never got embarrassed about these things. About anything. Caroline rarely had to ask because Kristy volunteered the information—in graphic detail. Something was very different about this time.

Kristy shrugged her shoulders and refused to make eye contact while Runway smiled at her, obviously intrigued by her embarrassment. "Not much. Just hanging out, that's all."

Caroline stared until Kristy finally made eye contact. Caroline wasn't sure what expression was on her own face, but she knew what she felt. Shock, awe, jealousy. Jealousy? Really? Was she jealous that her best friend had made love with this impossibly gorgeous man? He was beautiful, for sure, but Caroline didn't feel the same kind of warmth toward him as she did for Cade. Perhaps she wasn't jealous about the guy, but more the fact that Kristy had been intimate with Runway before Caroline had with Cade. When Kristy looked up, her eyes spoke before her mouth did. Kristy was in love, that much was painfully obvious.

"What? Why are you staring at me?" Kristy's annoyance emanated as she looked from Caroline, to the wall, and then the floor.

"Nothing. You wanna go grab a drink from the machine?"

"Sure." About to walk away with Caroline, clearly relieved to be changing the subject, Kristy almost escaped the jaws of humiliation, but Runway would not allow it. He seemed to enjoy her blushing and embarrassment as much as Cade enjoyed Caroline's. Runway snagged Kristy's hand and pulled her back to him, bouncing her up against his rock-solid chest. He whispered something in her ear, then longingly kissed her neck. She smacked his chest and pulled away from him, her face crimson.

"Uh-huh, how's it feel?" pointing at her cheeks. "Bet you won't make fun of me ever again for blushing like a little school girl." She elbowed her, and Kristy shoved back.

"So how was it? Good?"

Kristy shrugged. "We had a nice evening."

"Oh, whatever. I know you got some. Now spill it!"

Kristy smiled and nearly collapsed against the wall. "Oh, Caroline. You have *no* idea! I mean, I know you really *do* have no idea, but. . .oh wow. . .you *really* have no idea. He is. . . I'm just. . . He's completely amazing. In every way, shape, and form. He's just. . . Wow."

Caroline was truly shocked Kristy had given it up to a guy the first night she met him. But considering the guy in reference, who could blame her. "Man, I've never heard you at such a loss for words. He was that good, huh?"

Kristy grasped Caroline's shoulders and peered intently into her eyes to drive her point home. "Caroline, listen to me carefully. If Cade is *anywhere* near as good in bed as his best friend, you *have* to marry him. Now. You must. By far the most incredible experience of my life. I've never felt this way about anyone before. I mean, I've thought I was in love before, but I've never felt *this* way about anyone." She flailed her arms through the air. "If this is what it feels like to be in love, then I was pitifully mistaken." Resting her hands on her hips, she turned to Caroline. "I think I've seriously fallen for this man. Head over heels, hook-line-and-sinker, however you wish to phrase it. I'm in love."

"Wow! That's, that's. . .crazy. I mean, don't get me wrong, I'm happy for you, but are you sure? You just met him. Tonight."

"I can't explain it. I just know it's like nothing I've ever felt before. I know you have this affliction about timing, so call it what you will. Lust, love, whatever, I can't imagine not having Matt in my life from now on. The chemistry is there. Just like with you and Cade."

Caroline really was excited for Kristy. She deserved happiness. "That's great, Kris." She cleared her throat. "So, it's funny you mentioned me needing to marry Cade, like. . .now."

Kristy's dreamy expression instantly transformed to serious.

"Because I almost did something crazy tonight."

"Almost?"

"I might have mentioned that I was ready to have sex with him." Kristy gasped.

"Girl, you'd better get on the pill or something," she warned. "Even if you don't have sex with him, it can't hurt to start it now."

Caroline agreed and nervously shook out her hands as she paced. "I also may or may not have mentioned marriage—to him."

"What, did you ask him to marry you?" Kristy laughed, but when Caroline's sheepish grin was her answer, Kristy's jaw dropped. "You proposed to him?"

"Not technically, but kind of. More of an implication, really. I don't know what got into me. After seeing Remy on that stretcher, and briefly thinking it was Cade, I realized that I can't and don't *want* to live without him. I'm in love with him, and I can't see any reason for putting it off any longer, but then I almost ruined everything."

"Why? What did you do?"

Caroline dreaded telling her this part as she cringed. "I overthought things." Kristy groaned. "I know, I know. I was thinking and realized I don't know any more about him than I did a year ago. . .except that he was a Navy SEAL. I kind of flipped and chewed him out about how he keeps his past from me."

"Wow, a Navy SEAL? I can see that."

Caroline shrugged. "It all makes sense now." She sarcastically added, "Now that I know."

"I guess that means Runway was a SEAL, too." Kristy shivered with a smile. "That explains the scars. So what did Cade say? And don't avoid the question," she warned.

Caroline was intrigued. She wondered if Runway had the same type of scar Cade has on his chest. "What scars?"

"Uh-uh. Answer the question, girlfriend."

"He, um, he didn't really respond to the marriage part except to say he hadn't asked me yet." Caroline browsed the drink selection in the vending machine. "He told me he was taking it slow with me because he wanted to make sure I was completely over my last engagement before he got too serious. He wanted to give me time to heal or whatever. So, technically I didn't ask him. Instead, I went off on him. I felt really bad, but in my rant I did mention that I was ready to marry him."

"I know that boy didn't say he wouldn't marry you. Did he? I'll beat him if he did." Her voice softened as Caroline put money into the machine. "As much effort as I put into helping him stop you from marrying—" Kristy's voice abruptly cut off. Caroline let out an exaggerated sigh but didn't look up from the machine.

"Okay, Harry Potter, I know he's not your favorite person, but he's not Voldemort, so you can say his name." Caroline slammed the button and bent down to gather her drinks. "I swear, you and Cade both, it's like Taboo to say Trevor's name. You don't hav—"

When she looked up, Kristy was staring past her toward the information desk. Caroline followed her line of sight. Her jaw dropped, and her knees weakened. A pair of familiar, ocean blue eyes were acutely locked onto hers. She stumbled back in disbelief and slumped into a chair as her heart plummeted into her stomach.

FOURTEEN

Cade hung up the phone, disgusted with himself for not trusting Caroline's intuition last year when she suspected April. If he'd been monitoring her all this time, he could have possibly prevented this shooting tonight. He'd never have pinned April for being clever. He thought she was ditzy. . .dumb. Cade scoffed. Yeah, dumb like a fox.

Last summer, her issues centered around jealousy for the most part. Caroline showed up and took Eddie's attention from April. At least that's how it seemed. All part of her master plan, no doubt. Cade cursed, wishing he could remember everything from last summer. His focus was solely on Caroline and her safety from that dickhead, Trevor.

He remembered the incident from earlier this evening. Were the kill orders she was barking over the phone supposed to happen tonight? By the hands of someone he trusted? He'd fully intended to investigate first thing in the morning, but he never expected her to take immediate action.

Cade hastily rolled his window down for some air. He still couldn't believe he hadn't seen this coming. He should've known. He'd been too busy watching out for Kenneth Callahan, Trevor, and Ivan Baranovski, that he never imagined the prime suspect would be living in the very house he protected.

Cade shook his head again and pounded the steering wheel. April. Was she responsible for the shooting tonight? Or was she a decoy to cover a more obvious, more dangerous predator like Callahan? Either way, Cade had no doubt April was dirty. Or Ana Morales. Which name was real? Was April Jones Fontenot her real name, and she used Ana Morales as an alias, or was it the other way around? Where did she come from? How did she learn her way around weapons, and what were her connections to have the grounds to threaten someone the way she did?

And more importantly, what the hell was she doing with all the jars of blood, mutilated snakes and chicken feathers? Looked an awful lot like a damned voodoo ritual. Could that be what she was up to? Did Eddie know about her demented hobby? Cade rubbed his hands down his face to his chin. If it was voodoo, then they were in for a hell of a lot more trouble than just her sharp tongue and dangerous connections.

The question that nagged Cade most was who April was talking to before she shoved the barrel of that 9mm in his face? Someone he knew? Someone close to him preparing to betray him? Someone Eddie trusted?

Cade took a hopeful breath as he rested his faith in his private investigator, Tony. In the short amount of time Cade had to stop Caroline from marrying Trevor, the abusive bastard, Tony had found the game-changing information on Kenneth Callahan and his corrupted family's history. It wasn't over yet. Trevor and his vindictive father were still out there.

As Cade entered the hospital, headed to the waiting room where he'd left Caroline, he ran into Eddie, who was on his way to the cafeteria. Eddie asked him to take a walk so they could talk about April. Cade reassured him he was on it, but it didn't seem to do much good. The fatigue wore on Eddie at this late hour. His purple-ringed eyes were distant and sagged with a well of emotion. The lack of sleep didn't bother Cade, but it was punishing to Eddie.

"Mr. Fontenot, what can you tell me about April's past? Do you know much about her family or any reason why she would need an alias?"

Eddie shook his head. "I don't understand the alias. When I met her she was a beautiful young woman who seemed open and caring. She supposedly grew up in New Orleans. I think her mother was Hispanic, but she died when April was thirteen. April doesn't like to talk about it."

"If her mother died when she was that young, who took care of April? Who raised her?"

Eddie shrugged. "I guess her grandmother. We would drive to New Orleans often to visit, but I only met her once or twice." Eddie shrugged. "April's grandmother didn't care much for me, and I didn't care about impressing anyone who had decided upon her dislike before ever knowing me, so I usually found a reason to leave and come back to get April when she was ready. I don't know many details about her family. Now April goes by herself because I have too much going on here with work to take off every other weekend. Why? What are you thinking, Beau?"

"I'm not sure yet, sir. I'm not going to think anything until my buddy gets back to me with the information I need. Knowing her mother and probably her grandmother are Hispanic will help him with his research, so I'll let him know. It makes sense now that April referred to herself as Ana Morales. Did she ever mention her father? Is he still alive?"

Eddie sat still for a moment, thinking. Cade wondered if he'd heard him until Eddie finally spoke. "You know, I don't believe she's ever said anything about her dad. He wasn't able to come to our wedding, but then we just went to the courthouse with a couple of witnesses." He stood to go refill his coffee, but paused with a sheepish grin. "I mean, it was my third marriage, after all. I wasn't hell-bent on a formal ceremony, and she didn't care. She was just in a hurry to get married."

Cade spun the top from his water bottle, staring blankly in thought. He didn't look up when Eddie returned to the table. "We need to figure out who fired the bullet into your home."

Eddie nodded and shook a sugar packet. "I noticed the forensic teams gathering evidence around the property this morning. I sure hope they were able to find some traces of evidence that can lead them to this dirt bag, whoever he is." He stirred slowly.

Eddie took a sip of the scalding coffee, wincing as he added, "I know whoever it was couldn't possibly have been aiming for Remy. Of course, there is Callahan to consider. He's been fairly quiet for the last few months, so I suppose this could be his first move. Not likely, though. It's not really his style."

Eddie set his cup on the table and leaned back in his chair as he checked his watch and crossed his arms. "Surely he's a little more discreet than that. Firing into a party lacks the class that I would expect from someone of Callahan's stature. He's not a complete fool." Eddie shook his head. "No, Callahan is clever, and whoever had hired this hit man, or worse, fired the weapon himself, was not very smart, nor was he very skilled." Eddie paused, so Cade glanced up from the table. "I'm sure you will agree, rarely does a trained sniper miss his target."

Cade nodded. Missing was not impossible, but it was extremely rare for a skilled sniper. "Callahan had the resources to hire a professional last year."

Eddie grasped his coffee and started to raise it to his mouth. "This was an amateur job."

"Has April ever been interested in voodoo?"

Eddie thoughtfully puckered his lips. "No, not that I know of."

Deciding to breach that subject later, Cade frowned. "Why was she in a hurry to marry you?"

"Hey," Eddie huffed. "Back in the day, I was quite a catch." He took another sip of his coffee, and it burned the roof of his mouth. He jerked it away from his mouth, sloshing some of the scalding liquid on his hand. A string of colorful curse words slipped out.

"From where I'm standing, you still are." Emily approached their table, smiling over a box of assorted donuts.

132

Cade's stomach growled at the delicious, sugary smell.

She smiled big now. Cade understood how Caroline could be so irresistible. Her mother was a very beautiful woman. A youthfulness glowing beneath her gentle crow's feet and laugh lines.

Gazing at Emily caused a stirring inside Cade. He was determined now more than ever to be with Caroline and watch those same gentle lines adorn her beautiful face, and to hold her hand through whatever difficulties or blessings that may cross their paths—together.

"Hello, Emily," Eddie said. "My apologies for my language. I burned my mouth."

"You never did let it cool before you took that first sip," she teased. "I would have thought you'd learned by now." She playfully winked again.

Eddie glanced at Cade, and a wide smile spread across Cade's face. Eddie's sheepish grin was quickly squashed with a *shut up or I'll hurt you* expression.

"Hi, Mrs. Fontenot. Those donuts look almost as good as you do. How are you feeling?"

She smirked at Cade, appreciating the flattery, but was privy to his kissing-up. "Apart from a constant, dull headache, I'm doing well, Cade. Thank you. How are you? Shaken up, I'm sure?"

He shrugged. "Nah, I was especially glad Caroline was upstairs when everything happened. What'd the doctor say about your head?"

She puffed out a short breath. Clearly not thrilled about Caroline insisting she get checked out. "The doctor gave me all the necessary tests for a head trauma, and so far has no reasoning for my crazy visions."

After helping her into her chair, Eddie sat next to her at the round table. "No concussion or anything?"

Shaking her head she sighed. "Nothing. I'm just a freak of nature, I suppose. He said the can incident from this morning could have brought them on, but as far as damage goes, I'm clear." She chuckled. "It's a shame I couldn't have gotten something more fun, like mind reading or telekinesis. No, not me. I get the weird psychotic visions of people I care about being harmed."

Eddie grinned. "If you could read minds, I'd be in big trouble."

"Oh, please. You're easy to read anyway. I don't need the ability to read minds to know what you're thinking."

Offended, or embarrassed, Eddie playfully argued. "I'm not *that* easy to read. If so, things would be a lot different for me right now. Trust me."

Cade pretended to be oblivious to the lingering look between the former couple as Eddie changed the subject.

"I'm glad April's behavior hasn't caused you to rush back to Arkansas just yet. I tore into her after her nasty comments to you."

In true Emily fashion, she waved her arms to brush it off as she smiled at Cade. "Oh, it's no big deal. I've seen her kind plenty." She paused as she eyeballed Eddie. "What I don't understand is how or why you put up with it? What's she got on you?"

Eddie's eyebrows hitched up. "What's she got on me? Nothing. She's got absolutely nothing on me except a marriage license."

"Ahh, no prenup? I'm surprised, Edward. You even had me sign one. Well, at least your *parents* had me sign one, anyway."

Eddie laughed and shook his head. "You haven't changed. Of *course* I had her sign a prenup. That's why she's so bitter. Anyway, it's one thing for her to take her anger out on me, but she had no right to direct it toward you, Caroline, or anyone else." He swirled his coffee stirrer around in the cup attempting to speed the cooling process. "Besides, she hasn't always been like this. Only in the last year or two. I don't really know what happened, but one day she became very distant and short-tempered. Then I noticed her snapping at nearly everything I said to her. She's been a decent mother to Claire and Remy, but as a wife. . ." He flushed. "Well, the honeymoon phase is long gone. We'll leave it at that."

Emily covered his hand with hers. "Honey, it's obvious that she's unhappy with you for some reason, but burying your head in the sand

and pretending the problem doesn't exist, or will just go away in time, isn't going to solve anything."

He nodded.

"You need to sit her down and talk to her. Communication was never your strong suit. You and Caroline are very alike in that aspect. Confrontations have never been pleasant for either of you, specifically ones involving a romantic relationship."

Emily nudged Cade without looking at him. Caroline must've told her mother about their argument earlier. Great.

Tears welled in her eyes and she forcibly swallowed, blinking them back down. "If it hadn't been for you two, she would have married Trevor, and who knows what kind of trouble she'd be in now?" Emily squeezed Eddie's hand to get his attention. "Or what kind of trouble *you'd* be in. By now, you'd probably be in the Fontenot family vault if those nuptials had taken place."

Her steady eyes stayed focused on his. "I, for one, am thankful nothing happened to you. I finally see now that these last twenty-something years of brooding over how you left were simply wasted emotions and way off-base. You are an incredible man, Eddie Fontenot. I'm proud to see how responsible and committed you've become. April doesn't realize the man she has, or she surely wouldn't be treating you this way."

Cade wasn't sure he was still visible. Maybe he should leave. But he'd just gotten another donut and it might be rude to walk out in the middle of their conversation. And, frankly, he was afraid to distract either of them, and be responsible for ruining the moment.

Surprised, Eddie let out a gush of air. "Wow, Em. I had no idea you felt that way. I was under the impression you hated me. I was sure any ground I had recovered with you was lost today after April opened her fat mouth."

Emily scoffed. "I don't believe there is anything on that woman's body that could be classified as fat. Have you considered the possibility that the reason she's so grumpy and bitter all the time is because she's hungry? Have you tried feeding her a cheeseburger or taking her out for a nice five-course dinner?"

"That's funny. Caroline said the same thing. Almost verbatim. April is naturally thin, but she's always obsessing over her figure. She works out in her private room upstairs all the time. I don't even try to understand the female mind anymore." Eddie shrugged. "I'll be honest, I was really nervous about making that twelve hour drive to Chicago with you for the wedding. When Beau told me I was picking you up in Arkansas to drive you, I had no idea how you would feel about seeing me again after all these years. After the way I treated you and Caroline. I didn't know whether to expect you to ignore me or beat me unmercifully the entire way. I deserved the beating, but I'm glad you didn't. If I remember correctly, you pack quite a punch."

Cade snorted grabbing their attention. "So does your daughter." He gingerly rubbed his wounded left shoulder.

Emily ignored him and turned her focus back to Eddie. "I beg your pardon? When did I *ever* punch you?"

"Oh, you most definitely *did* punch me. When I first told you I was leaving. Remember? You thought I had cheated on you, which I didn't by the way, but you refused to believe me. When I tried to explain, you stood there silently, balled up your fist, and your right hook did the talking for you." He laughed, but she blushed and avoided eye contact.

"I don't remember that."

"Boy, I do," he winked. "Guess that's what I get for messing with a country girl."

The natural smile that graced her features emitted an inner beauty Cade had only witnessed from one other woman, and he ached to hold Caroline in his arms at that moment.

"You'd better believe it. You're lucky I'm a smooth talkin' woman. My daddy wanted to come down here and skin you alive."

Nodding in agreement, Eddie said, "Yes, lucky is right. I have been scared of only a few people in my lifetime. And your father was one of them. I've never seen anyone handle a Buck knife quite like he did."

Emily's eyes hazed with fresh tears. "Yes, he was very special. He could do it all. Fishing, hunting, you name it. If it could walk, fly or swim, he could catch it." She dabbed her eyes with a napkin.

"He could cook it, too. I think that's the only reason he let you marry me, because I liked his cooking. He thought some backwoods, coonass Cajun boy from Louisiana could never live up to his standards, but I did."

She slowly nodded and whispered to her hands in her lap. "Yes, you did."

Cade used the awkward silence as his opportunity to leave. He stood and started gathering his things, "Well, I guess I—"

"And then I blew it." Eddie interrupted, his attention fixed on Emily. "He must have been so disappointed in me. I never got to apologize for hurting his baby girl. I'll bet he hated me. When did he pass away?"

Cade halted and took a step back. This time he really did wonder if they could see him. They were oblivious of his presence. He walked away to throw out his trash, but he could still hear them. He stepped around the corner, out of sight, but still within range to hear and pretended to play a game on his phone. Cade hated snooping, but Caroline never talked about her grandparents, and he wanted to hear the story. He wanted to know everything about her, and a little insight about her family couldn't hurt.

"When Caroline was in junior high. It was a sudden heart attack." She sighed. "He didn't hate you as a person, Eddie. He hated you for divorcing me for no reason. As you know, he was a God-fearing man and read the Bible every day. In his eyes it would've been better if you had cheated on me. My parents both liked you until you left the way you did." Her voice was thick with emotion as she cleared her throat. "I miss them both every day."

"I'm confused. Is that the reason you never remarried? Because our divorce wasn't scriptural?"

Cade was curious too as he waited for Emily's answer. Caroline had mentioned that her mother never remarrying was a long story, but never clarified.

"Mostly."

Eddie's baffled voice raised, "Didn't you ever date? Surely, as beautiful as you are, you had men lined up to ask you out?"

"No, not really. I worked too much to have time for dating. My mother watched Caroline during the day, and in the evenings I was too tired to go out. Besides, I never met anyone that struck my fancy. That's the main reason my dad was so disappointed in you—because he felt that you ruined my romantic future. He didn't hate you. But I did."

Cade's stomach dropped. Lord knew how Eddie's must've felt. He couldn't imagine what it would do to him if those words ever slipped past Caroline's lips. It would be his undoing.

"I hated you for making me love you so much. I was crushed that you simply didn't want me. It wasn't another woman who lured you away, it was something about me that couldn't keep you. I hated you for capturing my heart, then crushing it."

Cade heard her sniffles and imagined the waterfall of pent-up tears flowing down Emily's cheeks. He vowed never to cause Caroline to cry that way.

"That's why I'm glad Caroline came down here last summer. If she hadn't, I never would have seen you again, and I never would have known it wasn't hate I held in my heart for you all these years."

Eddie's voice was soft, sincere. "Em, you don't have to—"

"No, don't. I need to say this."

"Alright."

"If I hadn't come down here. . ." She obviously struggled to speak without crying. "I never would've known that what I thought was hate, was really. . ." She paused, and Cade heard ice clink in her glass. She must have taken a drink. "Unfinished business."

Confused, Cade hadn't expected that answer at all. He imagined this point of this conversation traveling down a much different path. Apparently, so had Eddie.

"I don't understand. What kind of unfinished business?"

Emily's chair scraped against the floor as she stood. "The kind that we can discuss in private at a less traumatic time."

Cade's phone vibrated in his hand. A text message to call Tony. Cade briskly rubbed his face to clear his mind. Cade walked briskly out to his truck so no one could overhear his conversation.

"Hey man, it's Beau."

"Hey pod-nah. Where y'at?"

"I'm at the hospital waiting to hear about Caroline's brother. So what did you find?"

"Well, I traced back all the Morales families I could find here in the New Orleans area for the last fifty years. I came across several that I don't think are related. Just wasn't feelin' it, you know? So, as I was skimming the list, this one name kept jumping out at me. I did further research, and I'm still waiting for a couple of my contacts to get back to me, but I'm eighty-five percent sure I found the grandmother of Ana Morales."

"Awesome. Did you find anything about when or why she created an alias?"

"Yeah, that's the good part. If this particular name is the gold nugget I think it is, she's in with some dirty birds, bro. Big time, big name gangsters in the city. I'm talkin' the big boss man."

A chill shot up Cade's spine. "No way, dude. Big boss man? Like, how big?"

"Does the name Angelo Marcellino ring any bells?"

"The head of the Louisiana Mafia?"

"That's right, bro. If this is her, then she's hooked up. Definitely not to be taken lightly." I'll overnight you the information as soon as I get it all packaged up and pretty for you."

"Okay, thanks, Tony. I appreciate it. I owe you, man. Big time."

Tony's thunderous laugh blasted from the phone. "You know I'll collect sometime, pad-nah. I'll be callin' come gator season. Don't you worry."

Cade closed his eyes, pinching the bridge of his nose, and tried to put more of the pieces together. Gangsters. Angelo Marcellino. No wonder she needed an alias. She couldn't risk anything getting linked back to organized crime or they'd certainly kill her. Especially Marcellino. That explained how April could produce such heavy threats. It might also explain her access and familiarity with a weapon. This was not good. Not good at all.

He locked his truck and walked back into the hospital to the now packed waiting room where he had left Caroline. No one he recognized was in there, so he headed for the cafeteria. This new information put quite a spin on things. His mind raced.

How the hell did April get involved with the Mafia? Not just the Mafia, but with the Don himself. If Tony was right, things would only get worse. There was no doubt in his mind April and Kenneth Callahan were working together, and she'd helped him acquire the hit man last year. It made perfect sense, and the dots were slowly connecting. Cade just didn't understand why April would work with a pompous ass like Callahan. He would never trust a woman to do a man's job, so why would he work with April? The reasons why didn't matter at this point. Cade needed to find some proof before more people got hurt.

Deep in thought, Cade walked right past the elevators. He turned to head back down the hall when he heard a familiar female voice. He quietly slipped into an alcove and ducked behind a potted plant. He could barely make out April's phone conversation as she spoke in a hushed voice. He wanted to confront her, to let her know he was on to her, but he couldn't afford to do that until he found out who was betraying him. . .and why.

"You will do what I tell you to, or your family will be the one who suffers. Is that really what you want? Your poor, pregnant little white-trash girlfriend all alone with no money and no one to help her? You already agreed to this, and I don't think you want to try to back out on our deal. I'll have to unleash my not-so-pretty little friends on you. *Comprendé?*"

Her ominous laugh bounced off the walls in the quiet hallway. "Don't worry about her. I'll handle whatever she has to dish out. She doesn't know who she's dealing with. Just do your job." She huffed and stormed down the hall toward Cade. He held his breath and ducked deeper into the shadows of the plant. April was after the Fontenot family. He could feel it in his bones.

Yeah, now was not the time to confront her, but soon. He would find out her plans, what she was capable of, and who she was blackmailing. But until he had those answers, they were all in danger.

FIFTEEN

"Trevor? What are you doing here?" It was as if her mind summoned his presence. His name still fresh on her tongue. Once upon a time she would have launched herself over the chairs and into his arms to hug him tightly, and breathe in his woodsy smell. But his timing was horrible. She was, however, seriously confused by her happiness to see him.

Judging by her tone, Kristy was much less thrilled about his appearance. "Yes, *that* would be the question of the day. What, exactly, is Trevor doing here?"

Kristy stabbed Trevor with a cold stare. Surprisingly, this annoyed Caroline.

"Kristy, chill out. I'm sure he has a very good reason for being here. Don't you, Trev?" Caroline sounded like her mother.

Trevor cleared his throat, stopped glaring at Kristy, and glanced back to her, his eyes much softer and welcoming. "Caroline, I came to see if you were okay. I heard about the shooting, and I wanted to check on you."

That did it. All of her emotions rushed to the surface and she began crying as he gathered her into his arms. She didn't know what came over her, but the comfort of his embrace felt natural. Almost like nothing had ever happened and they picked up right where they left off before she ever came to Louisiana.

Kristy's voice, the voice of reason, burst through her moment of hysteria.

"Really, Caroline? I mean, *really*? Have you lost your mind? Trevor, get your hands off of her."

"Hells bells, Kristy, she's crying. I'm just comforting her. Mind your own damn business."

"Caroline is none of *your* business anymore, so back off." Kristy switched her piercing glare to Caroline, "C, what the hell is wrong with you?"

Caroline turned to look at her with a blank, innocent expression as she grabbed a tissue to blow her nose. "What?"

Kristy tugged on Caroline's arm to pull her from Trevor's embrace. "Don't you find it just a tiny bit suspicious that Trevor is here? After all this time? On the very night that someone tried to kill your brother? Or your dad? Or Cade?" Kristy's emphasis on Cade's name did not go unnoticed.

Caroline hadn't made that connection. Trevor was a jealous, hot-tempered, nymphomaniac, but not a killer. Right? But now that she thought about it, was it just coincidence?

"Have you forgotten about your oh-so-happy almost-nuptials when dear, sweet Trevor here *hit* you and spoke to you in front of everyone like you were trash?"

Trevor was glaring at Kristy again. "Don't you have somewhere else you need to be? Perhaps there's someone else to annoy?"

Her eyes narrowed. "If you think for one minute that I'm going to leave Caroline alone with you, then you aren't as smart as you'd like everyone to think. I want to know the *real* reason you're here, because, frankly, your timing is just too ironic to be coincidence. How did you hear about the shooting, anyway?"

"I had nothing to do with any of this."

"Prove it. Give us a rock solid alibi, Callahan, because at this moment you are *numero uno* on the suspect list."

"Since when have you had an interest in law enforcement, Kristy? Did the police department need newly designed uniforms?" Trevor straightened and crossed his arms as he confidently raised his chin. "I have a solid alibi, thank you very much. Not that I have to explain anything to *you*."

"Stop it! Both of you. Just stop it." Caroline looked at Kristy. "Lay off, okay. Give him a chance to explain before you start persecuting him."

Caroline turned back to Trevor, and her heart thudded in her chest. His sad, disheartened eyes pleaded to her. He still had feelings for her, and she wasn't sure how to feel about that. "Kristy's right. Your timing sucks. Tell me why you're here. How did you hear about the shooting, and why did you feel you needed to check on me?"

He warily glanced at Kristy before speaking. "I called my dad's office, and his secretary told me he was going to be out for a few days. When I asked her where he was and for how many days he'd be out, she told me he had instructed her not to give me any details. I had a sickening hunch where he might be headed, and I needed to come see for myself that you were okay. When I got to the plantation, I spoke with your friend, Delia, and she told me someone had been shot." His eyes scanned and appraised her body. "And here I stand." Trevor drank her in and whispered, "You look beautiful, C." He freed a loose strand of hair that was stuck to her lips, and wistfully admired her. "Even more incredible than I remembered." The same tone he used to seduce her with to get his way. Caroline held back a shiver.

She suddenly felt self-conscious. It was no wonder, she was freezing in this hospital, and her skimpy cocktail dress left too much exposed skin. She rubbed her arms to try to hide the goose bumps and shelter her braless chest. One good thing, when Trevor used to look at her that way, she felt anything but cold. Caroline nervously folded her arms across her chest in a pathetic attempt to cover herself.

Trevor removed his sport coat and draped it around her shoulders. She didn't want to accept it, but his smell brought back memories of their happy times.

Trevor was perfection in his lilac colored button-up dress shirt with the first two buttons undone, and his perfectly pressed charcoal slacks. His black hair tousled just enough to give an edge to his polished look, and his blue eyes contrasted with his black lashes and eyebrows. He stared at her with eyes ablaze, a slight tilt to his lips. He'd caught her checking him out much too long.

What was she thinking? Ten minutes ago she'd been ready to run away and marry Cade, and now she gawked at Trevor. She needed psychological help. This was ridiculous. While still physically attracted to Trevor, at least the desire to be with him was totally absent. Trevor was bad. Bad, bad, bad! He was abusive, but only when he lost his hair-trigger temper, and he was a control freak. But again, murderer wasn't on his list of attributes.

"I was coming to check on you lovely ladies to see if you got lo—" Runway stopped in his tracks and sized up Trevor who stood protectively next to Caroline. Territorial, even. Runway had never met or even seen Trevor, but he obviously knew enough to figure out who he'd come across.

Caroline quickly slipped Trevor's jacket off and handed it back to him.

"Thanks, Trev. I'm warm now."

Caroline looked at Kristy, who wore a self-righteous smirk on her face. She loved this uncomfortable, confrontational situation. Caroline, however, was not cut out for this kind of stress. She already had way too much on her plate. Runway settled next to Kristy and casually slid his arm around her waist.

"Trevor, I assume? What brings you down here to the swamplands?" Runway's voice was surprisingly friendly. Trevor's was, well, not so much.

"I don't believe we've met. I'm assuming you're a friend of the gardener?"

Runway didn't flinch at the slight.

"Nice," Trevor snipped. "I came to check on Caroline. To make sure she's okay after all the festivities tonight."

Runway's eyebrows raised. "Festivities?" He tipped his chin up. "Interesting word choice. Is that what you call it when an innocent teenager gets shot in the chest and now fights for his life? I could think of a few different words to describe it, but you Yanks are strange, anyway."

Shock registered across Trevor's face. "Wait. What? Your little brother is the one who was shot?"

Runway answered before she could, and it was rapidly getting on her nerves. "Yes, in fact it was. Also interesting that you knew it was her brother when all I said was that it was a teenager. Tell me, Mr. Callahan, was your mission accomplished, or did your sniper hit the wrong target? Beau told me you were low, but," Runway scanned Trevor's rigid frame and tilted his head thoughtfully, "I don't take you for the kind to kill innocent children."

Caroline should have stopped Runway, but she wanted to know Trevor's answer. Trevor looked at her without saying anything.

"Tell him, Trev." Her voice came out as a child-like squeak.

Trevor's hurt, shocked expression hardened when he looked at Runway. "I don't know what you think you know about me, but I had absolutely nothing to do with any of this. I honestly came to check on Caroline. That's all."

Runway grinned crookedly, and she would swear his eyes twinkled. "Ahh, no need for that. Caroline is in good hands. We've got her covered." Major implications were thick in his tone and he winked at Trevor.

Caroline groaned. She knew what that would do to Trevor. Beads of sweat popped up on his forehead and his Adam's apple bobbed. Runway definitely had Trevor's number, and Trevor now struggled desperately to rein in his temper.

"Easy, Trevor. Don't read too much into that statement," Caroline warned. "He's just trying to get to you. He only means that I've been thoroughly protected."

"I know what he meant, Caroline." Trevor's glare seared into her. "*Should* I read into it? Has something happened in the nine months we've been apart? Anything you'd like to tell me?"

Caroline's temper surged. She acknowledged the old Trevor resurfacing. "Nothing that's any of your business."

"So, Mr. Callahan, I'm sure Beau will be interested to know how long you'll be staying?"

He drew in a deep breath and looked at Caroline as he spoke. "Yes, because *Beau* is certainly the one person down here who I would like to please."

The suffocating tension in the room made it difficult to breathe. When no one said anything, he continued, more upbeat, yet still dripping with sarcasm.

"Oh, I don't know, I had some vacation time saved up that I had planned to use for my honeymoon last year."

Her gaze hit the floor, a sickening twinge of guilt sliced through her.

"Where *is* my gardener friend, anyway?" He dramatically looked around like Cade might be hiding around the corner. Trevor's voice softened, and he turned his attention back to her.

"Seriously, Caroline, I thought I could stick around for a few weeks. Feel the place out. It's kind of growing on me." Trevor gently lifted her chin with one finger and gave his perfect crooked smile. The one he always used when he wanted to get his way. Like the weakling she was, her defenses melted. "What do you think, Caro? Think you can show me around some while I'm here?"

She stared at him, not sure exactly what to say. Her head and her heart were at war.

This time Runway didn't answer for her. She looked to him for answers, but his face remained stoic. Kristy, on the other hand, vehemently shook her head before shooting daggers at Trevor with her dark, fierce eyes. This was all on Caroline, now. What the heck was she supposed to say? Why couldn't she think clearly?

"Um, I thought you hated it down here, Trev. Why would you want me to show you around? I've not been here that long, there's still plenty that I don't know about the area."

"It's okay with me if it's okay with you. Maybe we can explore together? I've never been to New Orleans. You could take me up to the city and show me around."

Words evaded her. The right ones, anyway.

"Or. . .we can just start with what you *do* know. It seems that I may inherit some property down here, so it would probably be wise if I knew a little about the area."

His dad, Kenneth, had bought all the land surrounding the Fontenot plantation with hopes of inheriting her dad's property, as well as Eddie's multi-generational business, through her marriage to Trevor. Only in the event of her dad's death, of course.

Rachel's message earlier in the evening flashed through her mind, and her senses instantly went on alert. The hair on the back of her neck prickled, and she felt an invisible force physically push her away from Trevor's hypnotic charm.

"Where *is* your dad, Trevor? You said he was out of town for a few days. So is he here? Is that why you're here to *check* on me?"

Trevor switched to reassurance mode. "Caroline, I swear, I have no idea where he is. I only assumed he had come down here. Since he didn't want me knowing his whereabouts, I immediately thought of you, and I had to know that you were safe. That's all. I had no idea about a shooting. I'm really very sorry about Rory."

"Remy."

"What?"

"His name is Remy. Not Rory."

"Right. Sorry. It's been a while since I've heard anything about him."

"You know, Kristy's right, Trev. It is really suspicious that you are down here at the exact time an attempt was made on a member of my family. And you show up only hours after the shooting. If you're truly not involved, then you are definitely in the wrong place at the wrong time. My dad's gonna flip out when he hears that you're down here."

Runway stepped up to Trevor, face to face. "Mr. Callahan, I think it might be best if you head back up to Chicago. But before you go, I have a few questions I'd like to ask you."

"I have nothing to say to you. I don't even know who you are."

"Of course. You can call me Matt, and I would like to speak to you in private."

Trevor's jaw clenched. He looked at Caroline, and she shook her head, warning him not to say or do something rash.

Runway saw her shake her head and smiled. "Aww, I'm not gonna hurt him, Caroline," he said, his eyes latched onto Trevor. "I just want to ask him a few questions regarding his whereabouts this evening around ten-thirty. I might get one of Beau's buddies from the station to jot down a few notes as an official statement. I promise, I'll play nice." The corner of his mouth raised when he looked at her this time, and he winked. "I'll only rattle his cage a little."

Trevor eyed Runway, no doubt taking in his muscular physique. Sizing him up to gauge his chances in a fight. Considering Cade smashed him up pretty good last year, Caroline didn't imagine Trevor stood much of a chance this time either. "Who the hell *are* you?"

"I'm a friend of Beau's. My name is Matt DeLuka."

Trevor looked him up and down. "Hmm. I didn't take the gardener for a switch hitter." He delivered the provocation with barbed precision. "No wonder Caroline was so happy to see me."

Runway smiled, but it didn't reach his eyes. "No need for jealousy, Mr. Callahan. Caroline knows she is free to choose anyone she wants. Beau doesn't force his girl to do anything she doesn't want to do."

Trevor shrugged his shoulders, but the tension was written on his face. She was sure Trevor fumed over Cade filling in his buddy, a stranger, with all the uncomfortable details, ruining Trevor's stellar reputation and making him out to be the bad guy.

"Caroline, I'm staying at a hotel in town. You know my number. Please call me sometime tonight or tomorrow to let me know how your brother is doing."

She nodded.

Trevor leaned in to give her a kiss. He cut his eyes over to Runway just before he reached her. That familiar crooked smile stretched across his face. She closed her eyes and prayed for strength. She knew she should stop him, and a part of her wanted one last kiss, but she turned her cheek at the last minute to prevent him from connecting with her lips.

Trevor lingered on her cheek and smoothed her face with his hand before he turned on his heel and walked out without looking back.

Caroline didn't move until he was out of sight, then she slowly looked at Runway.

Runway wore an unreadable expression. Caroline couldn't take the unbearable silence.

"Say something. Please."

"Hungry?" Runway asked.

Caroline let out a frustrated huff. "Am I hungry? That's all you have to say?"

"Yep. That's it. For now. I'm starved. Let's eat something, then go check on Remy. You should probably call your dad."

Caroline closed her eyes briefly, then looked to her best friend for support. Kristy simmered at Caroline with an incredulous scowl.

"What? Why are you glaring at me? I didn't do anything."

"Exactly. Don't play stupid, Caroline. You let him *kiss* you. What in blazing hell has gotten in to you? You should've clocked him."

"Kristy, come on. You know I can't do that. He was being nice. To me, at least."

She stared at Caroline before perceptively rolling her eyes. Was she that transparent? Or was it Kristy's incredible intuition.

"Yeah, I think Runway's right. Let's get something to eat. We can talk about this later when you haven't checked out of reality."

Caroline wasn't hungry. Her appetite left the room when she saw the handsome face from her past. Defeated, she followed Kristy and Runway to the cafeteria, but her mind was a labyrinth of confusion and she felt like she could puke up the toes right off her feet. She needed a good dose of Cade. Wherever he was.

In the cafeteria, Eddie, Cade, and Emily sat at a table, drinking coffee. Annoyance surged through Caroline upon seeing Cade. Why hadn't he let her know he was back? Where had he gone, anyway? However, she was relieved it had been Runway who saw her with Trevor rather than Cade.

Her dad looked at her expectantly, and Caroline shook her head to let him know she hadn't heard anything about Remy. She assumed, since he'd asked her, he hadn't heard anything either.

Her mom stood and opened her arms for a hug. Cade stood when Emily did, and Caroline tried, unsuccessfully, not to glower at him over her mom's shoulder. His brow crinkled, likely perplexed as she left him pledging her love and now frowning at him. This mixture of emotions tormented her beyond reason.

Runway's interrogation of Trevor perturbed her. Her irritation with Cade for not coming to her first when he got back to the hospital unnerved her. Add that to the confusion upon seeing Trevor, and she was a mess. Her hormones must be severely unbalanced this week. There was no longer be anything between her and Trevor. It was as simple as that. She was in love with Cade. So why was she so moody?

Maybe Cade was right. Perhaps she wasn't completely over her guilt for the way she left Trevor standing at the altar. That minuscule observation frustrated her plenty all on its own. She wanted to be done with him. She wanted to completely give herself over to Cade and live happily ever after. But after the rush of emotion, wondering earlier how Trevor was doing, and the attack butterflies when she saw him, and smelled him. . .

One thing was certain. She didn't need to be around either of them right now until she had a chance to objectively work this out in her mind. Only, she was afraid to leave Cade alone with Runway for fear of what Runway would tell him about Trevor. She needed to get her heart and her head on the same page. The crazy, irrational thoughts that repeatedly popped in her mind couldn't have been her own. Something weird was going on in her head. She had no doubts of her feelings for Cade. For some crazy, unexplainable reason she felt the need to protect Trevor.

But why?

SIXTEEN

Stupid gardener and his ridiculous hold on Caroline. What does she see in him anyway? He is no more attractive than I am. And his boyfriend's a prick.

Trevor opened the door to his tiny hotel room, and he was immediately blasted with the smell of stale cigarettes and moldy carpet.

Nice. What could he really expect in a town this size? They certainly didn't have five-star hotels down here in the swamps.

He bolted the door, tossed the keys to his rental car on the desk, and unbuttoned his shirt as he snatched the remote from the dresser. Trevor flipped through the minimal channels on the ancient tube television to see if he could find any news about what happened earlier. He glanced at his watch. It was late and he'd already missed all the news reports.

He settled for a rerun of *Friends* and plopped down on the squeaky mattress. Watching the sitcom didn't help his emotional well-being, considering he spent many nights watching this show with Caroline. Nights when they could've been making love like most normal couples.

He turned off the television, threw the remote across the room, and opted for a hot shower to release the tension in his shoulders from this crackpot day. But Trevor couldn't turn off the scattered thoughts shooting through his brain like static-filled comments from a CB radio.

Who shot Caroline's little brother? Were they really aiming for a teenager? Surely not. But who? The gardener? If so, the slip shot missed, damn it. That would've been a nice bit of luck for Trevor, but he doubted anyone wanted the gardener dead. He seemed to be the golden boy in this pothole of a town. Eddie Fontenot? Trevor figured plenty of people wanted Eddie dead, his dad included. But how would Trevor's dad benefit now that he and Caroline weren't married? Trevor had no access to her inheritance.

She looked great. Seeing her wearing the skintight dress reminded him how incredibly hot she was. It took everything he had not to jump her bones when he spotted her. As it was, he'd had to adjust himself behind the shelter of the welcome station desk. If Kristy hadn't been there, Trevor might have scooped Caroline into his arms to kiss a not-so-subtle reminder of how much she once loved him.

They were so close to finally being together forever, and Trevor blew it with his stupid temper. Why couldn't he control his anger around her? He'd never gone off on anyone like that before. Only with Caroline. She always knew exactly which buttons to push to set him off.

Caroline had been elated to see him. He remembered vividly the way she used to touch him, look at him, and kiss him with those pouty lips of hers. He knew she'd felt the same thing he had with that simple little peck. Trevor sighed and aggressively shook his head, flinging water against the shower curtain.

He had to stop, he was getting all worked up in the damned shower, and the last thing he wanted to do was handle business himself—again. This abstinence crap was for the birds. His frustration level was at its peak having not gotten any in the last three years. Granted, Caroline occupied two and-a-half of that. But she'd always gotten him good and ready, then left him hanging—literally. She was worth the wait, only Trevor didn't get her in the end. That piss-poor Cajun did.

Trevor had been out of the game for too long after Caroline dumped him at the altar, and his player skills were stumped. Trevor couldn't focus on being with anyone else because he couldn't get *her* out of his mind. He was getting old. He never used to think about anything during sex but the pleasure and satisfaction, but now he was like a damned woman, thinking everything through before he ever got naked. He went on a few dates, but he couldn't stop finding things about the women that annoyed him. He couldn't stop comparing them to Caroline.

Frustrated, he slammed the faucet down harder than necessary and stood drip-drying for several minutes. As he yanked back the shower curtain and stepped out to dry off, he heard something in his room. Voices. Trevor stormed out of the bathroom. The room was empty. But the television was on. Strange. He knew he had turned it off before he got in the shower because he had thrown the remote.

Another noise diverted his attention to the sink. Somehow, and for the life of him he could not figure it out, the faucet was turned on, a steady flow of water trickling down the drain.

Trevor shivered, noticing for the first time, the frigid temperature of this hotel room. It didn't help he was buck-naked, dripping wet in the middle of the room. He ripped the towel from the bar, wrapped it around his waist, and glanced back to the door to see if someone could have come in. The bolt was still securely locked.

With only the muted sounds of the television proving he wasn't in *The Twilight Zone*, he turned the old-fashioned air conditioning unit off and stared blankly at the trickling faucet. *This is ridiculous.*

He stomped over to the sink and firmly turned it off, making sure there wasn't so much as a drip coming from it. His senses heightened now, he was aware of every creak, pop, and groan of the old building. He stood in silence watching the faucet to see if it would come back on. Nothing happened.

He crept into the middle of the room to wait for any other unusual clues or oddities. An idiot, that's what he was, tiptoeing around like someone would hear him. He shrugged it off and dug through his bag for clothes.

The water came on again, full stream, gushing like Niagra Falls. This time it was the bathtub faucet. Chills crawled up his spine, and he was officially freaked out. *What the hell is going on here?*

He inspected the tub for faulty plumbing or fishing line attached to the faucet. Nothing. Trevor couldn't believe it. But it had happened. Something, or some*one,* had turned the faucet on again while he stood only six feet away from it. *Impossible.* Just as he reached to turn the shower faucet off, the water stopped. Trevor froze, his hand stretched in midair.

Feeling exposed wearing only a towel, he hastily dressed and stalked over to the door. He was certain someone was messing with him. *Probably that stupid redneck and his boyfriend.* Trevor turned off the television on his way to the door, and then tugged on the knob to test the stability of the locks. It didn't budge. One good thing about these old buildings, they were built to last.

Trevor sat silently in a corner chair with his back to the wall. He could see everything in the room without having to move his head. Something weird was going on. Someone trying to play him. Scare him. He wasn't falling for it. No way would he let that bastard get the best of him. Trevor would beat the gardener at his own game and show him just who he was messing with.

For twenty minutes, Trevor hardly moved. Nothing unusual happened. Nothing until something or someone thumped the windowpane. He threw the curtains aside and the water faucet in the sink started running again.

"What the—who's doing this? Who is here?" When no one answered, he walked back to the sink to turn it off again. "Answer me you coward!" As he passed the bathroom, he caught his reflection in the mirror. His face was pale. Maybe the old saying was true. He looked like he'd just seen a ghost. Though really creeped out, he still wasn't buying it.

"Ghost my ass. Whatever. It's just faulty plumbing and large bugs hitting the window. This is ridiculous." Trevor decided to get out of his spooky, dysfunctional room to get a much needed drink. He opened the door and remembered he'd thrown his key on the desk. He held the door open with his foot as he stretch to the desk to reach them. The door ripped past his foot and slammed closed.

Trevor tugged on the door handle, but it didn't budge. He yanked again with no luck. Frustrated, and creeped out, he told himself there was a logical explanation. He locked, then unlocked the bolt and forcefully jerked on the door, but it was no use. It wasn't opening. Panic officially set it. He picked up the phone to call the front desk, pausing when the door clicked and slowly opened with an ominous creak.

Trevor bolted out of the room and didn't look back. The only place he could think of to get a drink was the restaurant where Caroline had taken him the last time he was here—the place with the delicious gumbo. Hoping it was still open, Trevor drove to the restaurant ready for a nice, stiff drink to help him swallow what happened tonight. Yes, something strong was definitely in order.

Caroline had grown antsy sitting in the hospital. She decided to seek out Claire, to see how she was doing. They had a sudden emergency in their family, after all, and should lean on each other for support. Plus Caroline needed to rebuild the strong relationship she and Claire had together last summer. Talking was a good start.

Caroline should have told Cade where she was going. She'd promised to be good and not do anything irrational, but he would never have let her go by herself, and she needed to be alone when she spoke to Claire. He'll flip when he finds out she left, but hopefully he'll understand and not be angry. She didn't plan to be too long, anyway.

Caroline pulled up to the quaint, manicured drive of the two story house. She said a little prayer before she got out of the car. Before she had a chance to knock on the door, it opened and her little sister stepped out.

Claire scowled, her body language was not the least bit welcoming.

"What do you want?"

"Hi." Caroline self-consciously ran her fingers through her tousled hair when Claire didn't respond. "I came to tell you about Remy. He's in critical condition and I think you should come back to the hospital with me. Dad would appreciate it, I'm sure."

Claire rolled her eyes. "I don't give a damn what he would appreciate. Besides, I already know about Remy so you can rush back to the hospital and pretend to care about anyone but yourself."

"Can I come in so we can talk? I don't particularly want to be out in the open considering what happened tonight."

Claire shrugged, "I have nothing to say, and I'm not going anywhere with you, so you're welcome to leave right now if you're scared."

"And you're not?" Caroline asked, flabbergasted. "Claire, someone just shot our brother. Either one of us could be next."

"Then go away and leave me alone!"

Caroline pressed her eyes closed and took a calming breath. "Look, I don't understand what I've done. Why are you so upset with me?"

She scoffed. "Like you don't know."

"I really don't. I swear. What is so obvious that I'm not getting?"

"Oh, please. I thought you were smarter than that."

"Apparently not."

"Ever since your wedding didn't work out and you moved back here, my dad's been catering to your every need. I might as well not even exist."

"Oh, Claire. That's not true, and you know it. He loves you more than life itself."

"No, he loves *you* more than life itself. He loves *me* when people are around to notice. When he can be praised for being the doting father. You were the one he lost and finally found. His prodigal son. . .well, daughter. At first I didn't see it, but my eyes were opened and I see now I was a poor substitute that was just filling in until you came back." She mumbled, "Stupid me for falling for his little charade."

Tears sneaked into Caroline's eyes, the traitors, threatening to spill over and reveal her pain. "I don't get it. We had such a strong connection last summer. What happened to that? You came to me for advice. I thought we had a great relationship? I had Cade set you up with Josh. The man you want to marry, for Pete's sake."

Claire's eyes widened. "How the hell did you know about that? I haven't told anyone but my dad." Her eyes squinted, suspecting betrayal. "Did he tell you? Did he come to you blasting my business that is clearly none of *your* business?"

Caroline shook her head trying to recover from her slip of the tongue. "No, Claire, he didn't. I can just tell. I was preparing to get married not too long ago, remember? I can tell by the way you two look at each other. It's all over your faces. It doesn't take a fortune teller to see what the next step will be."

Claire stepped back to digest the explanation and shrugged. "Well, Dad's not happy about it, so I wouldn't be surprised if he talked bad about me behind my back. Anyway, it doesn't matter. Once I turn eighteen I don't need his permission anymore, and nobody can stop me."

"It's not my place to say anything about that. . .unless you want to talk to me about it." Claire smirked, making it clear she'd do no such thing. Caroline sighed. "What can I do to make you like me again? I miss you. I miss talking to you and spending girl time with you. I miss having a little sister to hang out with."

"Ha! You weren't too interested in hanging out with me when you got back from Chicago. You were all stuck up Beau's butt. . .not that I blame you. His cousin is even more amazing than he is."

Clair's immaturity was astounding. "Is that what this is about? Are you jealous that I didn't spend more time with you last fall? You were in school, your Senior year. You spent most of your time with Lindsey, anyway." Caroline dropped her shoulders. It was no use trying to defend herself, but she had to try. "Why didn't you say something when I first moved back? You knew I was in school in New Orleans this past semester, so surely you understand why I couldn't hang out then?"

Claire stared at her bare feet and shrugged. "I just wanted a little more of your time and attention, that's all. After the whole wedding mishap, I was so happy you were coming back here." The brief moment of sincerity and sweetness was quickly replaced with anger and malice. "Anyway, the truth surfaced and it was clear where *I* ranked in your life."

Claire had been around April for the majority of her life. The poor girl sounded just like her. Grasping for straws, Caroline went with sheer sincerity and spoke from her heart.

"Listen, Claire. I'm sorry if I hurt you. I'm sorry if I made you feel less important to me than anyone else in my life. I know this sounds like a stupid excuse, but please understand, I had big, life-changing things happen to me in a very short period of time. This move was a huge adjustment for me. Blood or not, I don't care, you're my sister, and I love you. I want you to know that I'm here for you no matter what. No matter how angry you are with me right now, I still want you to know—I *need* you to know—that I will always be here for you when you need me. Do you understand that?" Claire's eyebrows briefly peaked in the center, and she looked like she could cry as she bit her lip to resist, but that brief glimpse of authenticity was quickly replaced with an apathetic mask.

"Our brother is in the hospital fighting for his life. I came to check on you. To see if you are okay."

Claire slowly nodded.

"Do you want to talk about what happened?"

Claire shook her head. Considering she wasn't screaming for Caroline to go to hell, she jumped at the opportunity to keep her responding. "So, how's Josh?"

"He's fine."

Caroline managed a smile, though unsatisfied with her progress. "Well, I'm thankful for that. Cade, his friend, Matt, and Dad are going to find out who the shooter was, and when they do, he will be lucky if he's able to walk after they're through with him."

"What makes you so sure it's a man?"

Caroline shrugged. "I don't know. A hunch."

With a strange expression and a distant tone, Claire mumbled. "Don't get too confident. You never know who your enemies are these days. I don't trust anyone." She walked back inside, locked the door behind her, and left Caroline wondering what just happened.

In her car, Caroline ran the conversation back through her head as she drove toward the hospital. Claire's last comment about the shooter possibly being a woman unnerved her. Sure, Claire didn't come right out and say it, but the implication was there. Did Claire have any idea who was behind this, or was she just speculating like the rest of them?

Caroline's head hurt, and she was exhausted, but she wasn't ready to go to bed yet. It was late, and she couldn't ignore the twisting growl in her stomach any longer. She pulled into the parking lot at Dupree's already tasting the gumbo she was about to order. She'd finally learned the name of the restaurant after her fifteenth time eating there, and now she dreamed about it.

She parked in the crowded lot, and, as she approached the entrance, mouth watering in anticipation, an uneasy feeling settled over her. She chalked it up to her stressful day and went in anyway.

She propped on the nearest bar stool and grabbed a trifold menu before she looked at her surroundings. On her right, sitting pensively at the bar, leg shaking like a nervous chihuahua, was Trevor. Only two stools separated them, but he hadn't noticed her yet. She thought about darting out before he saw her. She should have. But instead, she studied him from the corner of her eye through the curtain of hair that she'd pulled from its ponytail and draped over her shoulder.

He wore jeans and a plain white T-shirt, and, except for the fact he was drinking a dirty martini with extra olives rather than just a beer, he could have fit right in with the locals.

She frowned. He usually never drank the hard stuff unless he was extremely upset. And she couldn't be sure, but his shirt looked to be on backwards. Why was he so disheveled? What had happened to him?

Against her better judgment, she scooted closer and got his attention. "Hey."

Moments passed before he moved, but when Trevor finally realized she was sitting next to him, he flinched, nearly knocking over his drink. "Holy hell, Caroline. You scared the. . ." He sighed and rubbed his face as he reached for his glass.

"Sorry."

His haggard, sagging face revealed he'd already had a few too many martinis.

"Yeah, sure."

"You okay?"

"Peachy." He answered before taking a large drink of his martini.

She couldn't help but notice his distraction. His outward appearance concluded his shirt was indeed backwards and his damp hair wasn't combed. He wasn't wearing a belt, either, which was very uncharacteristic of Trevor. Caroline smiled. He was a beautiful mess.

Trevor took another sip of his drink and spoke without looking at her. "So what brings *you* out so late?" Her gaze followed his to the mirror behind the bar. She blushed when she realized he had been watching her checking him out.

She rested her elbows on the bar, leaning her forehead into her hands in a pathetic attempt to hide her face. "I just talked to my sister. She's upset with me."

"Why?"

Caroline made eye contact and briefly lost herself in his crystal baby blues. Thousands of thoughts zipped through her crowded mind. Though she had no desire to be with him anymore, she still found him incredibly handsome. "Tell me, Trevor, why are you *really* here?"

He turned back to his drink and gulped the last of it as the bartender set another one in its place. "Cutting to the chase, huh, C?"

She glared at the bartender, the same girl who had served her and Cade the day Caroline discovered he was "Beau, the sexy gardener." The girl flashed a devilish grin as she held up the generous tip Trevor had left her and winked. Caroline rolled her eyes. Trevor obviously did not need another drink.

She brushed his hair from his forehead. He closed his eyes and leaned his face into her palm and she momentarily forgot the question. Her subconscious kicked her in the gut. Refocusing, she whispered, "I'm sorry."

His eyes flicked open, and he stared at her with an unreadable expression. She assumed he was trying to register what she'd just said because of the fog of his intoxication. He slowly sucked in a breath like he was about to speak, but then turned back to the bar and gulped his refreshed drink. The tender moment was over.

"I'm serious, Trev. Why are you here? Don't lie to me."

He turned to her with amusement in his bleary, glassy eyes. "Caroline, what happened to us? Everything was so perfect." He waved his hands wildly before gesturing between the two of them, "We were happy and in love for two years. Like an ignorant fool, I sent you down here. . ." He swirled his stick of olives in his drink, "And I watched you slowly slip away."

"Trev, that's not what happened, and you know it."

"Seriously, though. What did happen? I mean, we never had so much as a disagreement before you came down here."

"No, Trevor, we had plenty of disagreements, but they all happened *after* we got engaged. The entire two years before that were a show. We never had an argument because one of us, me, was afraid to be ourselves around the other. It wasn't an open, honest relationship. After we got engaged, the truth started rearing its ugly head. I'm really sorry for the way we ended. Just be glad it happened before we got married and not after."

"What makes you so sure things would have been that bad?"

"Because you were only interested in me for the sex. A conquest. It was painfully obvious, I just didn't see it."

Trevor studied his drink, pondering as he stroked his fingers along the thin stem of his martini glass. "Ahh. The sex." He sucked on an olive before pulling it from the stick and chewing it. He swallowed and took another sip. "Yes, sex with you would've been incredible. Mind-blowing, even." Trevor's forehead crunched into a frown. Clearly offended and hurt by that statement. He finished off the last of the cloudy vodka, shoved his glass forward, and waved for another. "But that is not the only thing I was interested in, Caroline." He faced her. "I was faithful to you. I'd cheated on other girlfriends before, but never you. You were different. I *wanted* to be faithful. I was completely devoted to you and in love with much more than just your body."

He stared deeply into her eyes. "Although, I imagined plenty of times what it would be like to kiss every inch of you. *All* the time. But. . .you always managed to stop me cold in my tracks." The bartender delicately placed a fresh drink in front of him. He smiled reminiscently, "You're such a good girl." He returned to his original fixed posture at the bar and took a sip. "Well, at least you *were*. There's no telling what that stupid Cajun's gotten you to do with him since you've been down here."

Anger pulsed through her, but she reminded herself it was the alcohol talking. "Don't forget the times you struck or manhandled me. Cade has never laid a finger on me in anger." Trevor flinched and took another swig. "I want to know the true reason you came down here. And don't give me that crap about you wanted to check on me. I'm not buyin' it."

Amused, he smirked as he stirred the olives around in the murky liquid. His third drink just since she sat down. "I think deep down I knew you wouldn't."

"Trevor. The reason?"

He sighed and took another big drink of his fresh martini. Just as she was about to lose her patience, he turned fully to face her. With his teeth, he pulled the blue cheese stuffed olive from the stirrer. His gaze latched back onto her. Chewing, he appeared to be mulling over what he wanted to say. She waited patiently as he swallowed the olive and took another drink to wash it down. "You're right, Caroline. I'm not here just to *check* on you."

SEVENTEEN

The hollow feeling in her gut was hard to ignore, especially since she hadn't eaten anything yet. Caroline managed to regain her composure enough to speak. "Trev, you're not the. . ." She exhaled and took a deep cleansing breath into her compacting lungs. "Please tell me you didn't shoot my brother."

"Of *course* I didn't shoot your brother, Caroline," he snapped. His dark brows pulled together. "How could you even suggest something that ludicrous?" Clearly appalled by her accusation, Trevor shook his head in disgust. Scowling, he shifted uncomfortably and stood to take his car keys from his pocket, smacking them onto the bar with a huff.

She had offended him, but overwhelming relief washed over her. "I didn't think so. I'm sorry, I didn't mean to insult you. I know you could never kill someone."

He chuckled. "It's okay. Honestly, I'm flattered."

"Flattered? Really? Care to explain that one?"

He ate the other olive from his stirrer and spoke with his mouth full, also very uncharacteristic of Trevor. "Do you know how many times I've actually fired a gun?"

She shook her head.

"Twice."

Caroline couldn't stop her smile. She never imagined Trevor being handy with any kind of weapon.

"The only reason I shot those two times was because I was dating a chick who was a cop, and I was trying to score."

Trevor slowly licked his lips, not realizing how provocative it was. She had to look away. Fond memories invaded her good senses. What the hell was her problem? Caroline cursed at herself for being stupid and straightened up. She scooped a handful of peanuts to munch on and turned back to Trevor. She was starving, but desperately wanted to hear the rest of this story.

"She enjoyed going to the firing range with all of her guy cop friends, and she wanted me to come. I went only so I wouldn't feel emasculated having a girlfriend who could handle a gun better than I could, but it was a disaster from the very beginning."

Someone two chairs down scraped his chair across the wooden floor causing Trevor to practically jump off his stool. Weird.

"Why are you so skittish?"

He mumbled something Caroline didn't catch as he brought his glass up to his mouth again. She'd seen enough. She carefully reached up, took his glass from his hands and placed it back behind her on the bar. When she had his undivided attention, she asked him to continue his story. Obviously the ever-smooth Trevor Callahan was flustered about something, and she figured keeping him talking was better than letting him get any more wasted.

"Well, this chick—we'll call her Heather—was not my girlfriend, but I was three dates in so I was still trying to make an impression."

She nodded as she remembered the impressions he'd made on her. Trevor was very suave when he successfully impressed her, but Caroline was no cop. She was a naive, small-town country girl who was blinded by his flashy ways in the big city. Caroline was quite certain this policewoman hadn't been impressed with his usual tricks.

"Well, when she told me she was going to the range with five of her fellow officers, one of which was her partner, and she wanted me to meet them, how could I refuse without looking like a jerk? So, I went." He snorted. His eyelids were heavy, and he was drawing out his words. "I should have stayed home. I ended up embarrassing myself and failed to make the good impression I was shooting for. No pun intended." He winked and reached around her for his glass again.

Curious now, she let him have it. She would have to drive him back to his hotel anyway. That wasn't something she looked forward to doing. She urged him to continue. "What happened? Did you shoot her partner or something?"

He shook his head, smiling. "No, not exactly. Now, see, that might have been better than what really happened. At least then it might have seemed like an accident or something. No, I simply managed to make myself look like a putz." His full lips puckered with the last word and he hiccuped.

This was potentially a very entertaining story.

"Her male friends were all ribbing me a little before we got to our station. Giving me a hard time about being born with a silver spoon in my mouth, never having to worry about money and such. Typical stuff, you know?"

She didn't, but she simply nodded so he would carry on.

"I started with a standard rifle. You know, one of those that have the big scope on the top. I guess it was some sort of hunting rifle or something. Anyway, it was the first time I'd ever held a gun in my hands, much less fired one." He was using his hands to show how he did it, and Caroline had to bite her cheek to keep from laughing aloud. He looked so goofy.

"I looked through the scope, I aimed the crosshairs so that they were on the bull's-eye, and I fired." He shrugged. "Sounds logical, right? Nobody told me to brace the butt of the gun against my shoulder before pulling the trigger. S'posed to absorb the recoil or some shit." He sat quietly, rolling the stem of his glass between his fingers and hiccuped again. He looked up with heavy eyes. "Anyway, when I pulled the trigger, that gun kicked back, and I thought I was blind. I literally saw stars. The scope launched back and practically impaled my eye socket." He subconsciously rubbed the place where the scope must've hit him. "It wasn't bleeding, but I had a quarter-sized blood-red whelp just above my eyebrow." He brought his glass to his lips. "Hurt like hell."

"So what did you do? Did they have to take you to the hospital?"

"No, not that time."

"Uh-oh."

He chuckled and took another drink. "Yeah. It gets better. After everyone stopped laughing at my expense, the owner of the firing range gave me an ice-pack. I sat back nursing my wound while my lady showed me up amidst her law enforcement peers." He ran his hands through his still-damp hair then brought them down to rub his face. "After I swallowed my pride and decided to try again, I chose a hand gun this time. I couldn't tell you what type or caliber it was. I don't have a clue, but it was one of those that has the sliding top part that you pull back to cock. It looked more my speed, and I was going to try to reinstate my manhood by proving that I could use it just as well as any of them."

"Let me guess. You completely missed the target?"

"Don't know. I never saw where the bullet went because when I pulled the trigger the sliding piece on top sliced through my flesh like a hot knife through butter. Apart from the excruciating pain I felt in my hand, there was blood everywhere. They wrapped it in a dirty towel and took me to the ER. I ended up with eight stitches in my hand. Guess I showed them, didn't I?"

She felt bad for him and put her hand on his to comfort him. "I can't believe you never told me this before."

Even though he was drunk, his blue eyes still mesmerized her. "Not something I usually brag about. Definitely wasn't my finest moment. Anyway, after that I chose never to touch a gun again."

The door to the restaurant jerked open, jingling the bells hanging from the top, and Trevor flinched again.

"Why are you so jumpy? You're acting very strange."

His head rocked back in amusement, and he muttered, "Strange. Ha."

"Yes, strange. Your shirt is backwards, and you're not wearing a belt. And your boots are untied. You never drink vodka martinis unless you are completely stressed out, and you've had more tonight than you've had since I met you."

"For your information, I had more than this after you left me at the altar."

She sat up straight and pulled her hand back at the low blow. Honestly, she worried that he was consuming liquid courage to do whatever it was he really came here to do. Perhaps his reasons for coming all the way down here involved something he really didn't want to do. . .like hurting her. She shook off that thought and reminded herself he was drunk.

"Oh, hell, Caroline. I'm sorry. I didn't mean for that to come out the way it sounded. I was in a bad place after you left, and I drowned my sorrows for a few months. I'm better now."

Caroline glanced at his glass and snagged his keys. She tugged on his arm as she said, "Yeah, I can see that. Come on, I'm taking you back to your hotel now."

"No!" He jerked his arm away. "No. I can't go back there. I won't."

She narrowed her eyes. "Okay, fine. Answer my question, Trevor. Why are you really here?"

He brushed the hair from her eyes, resting his hand on her cheek. He stared at her face for what seemed like forever, and his eyes settled on her mouth. "I came here to warn you. . ." He took a deep breath and involuntarily puffed out a silent belch that reeked of Vodka, but she was too stunned by his comment to be grossed out. "And to tell you I'm still in love with you, and I want you back."

Cade glanced at his watch and did the math in his head. He hadn't seen Caroline in way too long, and she was nowhere to be found in the hospital. Glad she wore the watch he gave her, he could find her if he needed to. She'd kill him if she knew the watch was a GPS tracking device, allowing him to know her location. She was much too curious to be alone in the swamps with no one looking out for her. The device was linked to an app on his phone and showed she was at Dupree's. She was probably just fine, but he wanted to go anyway. It was after midnight, and he knew she hadn't eaten anything. Still, he had a familiar uneasy feeling in his gut that he'd learned to trust.

By the time he pulled into the parking lot, his stomach churned near to hurling. When he was overseas, he had always gotten this same feeling before something bad happened. That fact alone made him restless. He stepped up the pace through the parking lot and as he approached the door, what he saw made his heart flop and his temper flare.

That bastard Yankee had his hand on Caroline's face, and he was staring at her like he was about to kiss her. Caroline just stood there with a blank look. It was an expression he had seen several times himself last year. A string of profanities that would make his momma smack the back of his head came streaming from his mouth. When did this trouble-making prick get in town?

Caroline had assured Cade she wasn't angry with him, so why was she here having drinks with her ex? Without telling him? What the hell was Trevor doing here, anyway?

Cade studied them. Trevor was drinking, but Caroline didn't have anything. Cade took a deep breath to calm himself before he approached them.

"Everything okay?" They hadn't even seen him walk up. Trevor flinched at the sound of his voice. Cade glared at him for a few long seconds before softening his gaze on Caroline. She had Trevor's keys in her hand and an apologetic look in her eyes. Callahan was clearly incapable of driving, and Caroline obviously felt obligated in some way to babysit his drunken ass. At least that explained her blank expression. She must have been trying to decide what to do.

Cade fought the urge to mark up his pretty-boy face again like he had last summer. That was too much fun, but Caroline wouldn't like it. She didn't like it then because Trevor was her fiancé, but now that she was Cade's girl, if that dickhead so much as gives her a dirty look, Cade would take him down.

Trevor had gotten physical with Caroline last year, and it had taken everything Cade had not to snap the son-of-a-bitch's neck right then and there. A part of Cade wished Trevor would raise his hand to her so he could demolish him. But, for now he would be the understanding, supportive boyfriend to Caroline and help her with this pest.

"Hello, Trevor. Enjoying the spirits of the bayou, I see. Need a lift?"

Trevor eyeballed him before finally rolling his eyes. Obviously annoyed with Cade's perfectly-timed interruption, he rocked his inebriated head back to look down his nose at him. "Why are you being nice to me, flower boy?" he slurred.

"Beau. Call me Beau or I might be persuaded not to be so nice."

He held his hands up to mock Cade's hostility. "Whoa, easy, Boy Scout. Jus' asking. No need to get your panties in a wad."

"Of course not, but when you're looking like you're about to kiss my woman, I tend to get a little protective."

Caroline pulled on his arm. "Cade, don't."

"No, it's okay," Trevor said. "He's right to be jealous. I should know." He narrowed his eyes, "Not a good feeling, is it, gardener?" Trevor reached for her left hand and pulled it to his lips. "But. . .from my angle, you're not married yet."

Cade's jaw muscles twitched. Those were the exact words he had said to Caroline many times last summer, specifically the night he asked her to kiss him for the first time. He wondered if she told Trevor about that or if it was a coincidence. Either way, Cade couldn't get mad. He'd done the same thing to Trevor, so he deserved a few jabs. He trusted Caroline. He watched Trevor as he finished off his last sip and followed it with an obnoxious belch. He was blitzed. Dude could start a bonfire with his alcohol-saturated piss, alone. "Come on, Callahan. I'll take you back to your hotel."

172

Trevor tensed and held his hand up. "Nope. Not necessary. I can make it just fine, thank you. I won't be going back there tonight anyway. Maybe I'll find a nice bench outside and crash."

Cade looked at Caroline for answers, but she shrugged. She didn't understand this joker anymore than he did. Cade grinned. "Don't be ridiculous. The mosquitoes would feast on your pickled blood, and you wouldn't make it through the night."

When that didn't get a rise from him, Cade tried something bigger. "Not to mention the bobcats and rattlesnakes out here." That worked.

"Bobcats? Really? I knew about the snakes, but you guys have bobcats here, too?"

The fear in the Yankee's eyes made Cade chuckle.

"Yeah, and those aren't as bad as the gators that sneak up to this restaurant looking for rotten meat that Tommy throws out for them from time to time." He pointed behind the restaurant. "There's a swamp about two hundred yards that way, and they come up here all the time." Cade shook his head. "No, you don't wanna sleep outside around here. You may wake up missin' a few body parts."

Trevor's bleary eyes bulged a little, and he pursed his lips as he digested this information for a few minutes. He stood, stumbling and shoving the bar stool back a few feet before loudly declaring, "Bullshit."

Cade shrugged. "Take your chances if you want, but you won't catch me sleeping outside in the bayou." Caroline peered up at him through her lashes, biting her lip to keep from laughing. He winked.

Trevor waved his hand, brushing aside the notion, and unsteadily dragged his stool back to its position to sit again. "You're screwing with me."

"Suit yourself. Don't say I didn't warn you."

Cade liked drunk Trevor. He was fun to mess with. But Cade got the feeling he wasn't the first one to mess with Callahan tonight.

173

"Well, thanks for the warning, but I'm not going anywhere near my hotel room right now. It's too. . .well, I just can't. Maybe I'll sleep in one of the hospital waiting rooms."

"I've got a buddy down at the police station that would be happy to lend you a cell to sleep in if you're interested." Cade winked at him. That brought back the old Trevor he remembered.

"No, thank you. Maybe you could go sleep with your pretty little boyfriend and let me borrow your cozy cabin for the night. How 'bout that, gardener?"

Was he talking about Runway? Had they met? Why hadn't Runway told him? A heads up that Callahan was down here would've been nice. "Aww, you sound jealous. What's wrong, Callahan? Daddy can't find you a suitable companion in Chicago?"

"I had one, but some coonass from Louisiana stole her from me."

"Guys, please. Now is not the time nor the place. We're all tired. Trevor, you're drunk. I really think it would be best if you go back to your hotel room and sleep it off. We can all talk in a *civilized* manner tomorrow after we've had some rest."

Trevor shook his head. "No. I'm not going back to that room. I'd rather brave the beasts than sleep in a haunted hotel."

Caroline's jaw dropped, and she and Cade looked at each other. She playfully jabbed, but Cade fished for more. He tried a little provocation. "Haunted? You believing ghost stories now, Callahan?"

Trevor shivered. This guy was seriously spooked. Trevor spoke slowly and more clearly now. "Yeah, laugh it up. Maybe I do believe the crazy ghost fodder you guys swear upon down here, who knows? Not me." He earnestly looked at Caroline. "You tried to tell me last year, and I laughed it off. I told you it was your overactive imagination, but I saw. . ." He pushed his unfinished martini toward the bartender and rubbed his hand down his face. "I experienced some unexplainable things today." He made a face and shook his head. "Never mind. Forget it. I'll take you up on that offer for the jail cell. I'm not going back to that room to sleep." He stood, pulled out his wallet and dropped a hundred dollar bill on the bar.

Trevor Callahan was one of the most spoiled-rotten, rich boys Cade had ever known. So if he was offering to sleep on a thin lumpy mattress in a concrete jail cell something was definitely wrong.

EIGHTEEN

A jail cell wasn't the worst option in this case, but Trevor could see this dude locking him up nice and tight just to be cute. If it got him away from the poltergeist, then he was down with that. Trevor had never believed in ghosts, and had ridiculed Caroline unmercifully last year for believing this crap, but he couldn't think of any other reason for the crazy things that happened. It didn't make any sense. Maybe he was hallucinating, or losing his mind, but right now, a cold, moldy mattress in a damp cell sounded better than going back to find out.

"Look, Callahan. I was kidding about the jail. You can come stay at my place if you don't want to go back to your hotel. I have a comfortable couch, and I'll probably be at the hospital most of the night anyway."

Nevertheless, Trevor considered it for a minute. "What about your boyfriend? Will he be there?"

"Probably. Runway and Kristy will both probably be there."

Trevor shook his head. "I'll pass. I think I'd rather sleep in jail than stay enclosed with those two, thank you very much."

"Seriously? You'd rather sleep locked up in a jail cell than crash on my couch near Kristy and Runway? Dude, you've got issues."

He had no idea. "Yes, I have issues. I'll be just fine. Really."

"He can stay at my place."

The invitation was offered by a pretty brunette with mocha brown eyes. She was not the least bit cautious about inviting a strange man, a strange *drunk* man, into her home in the middle of the night. Not the brightest light in the harbor.

"You don't even know me. A little dangerous, isn't it?" He looked her up and down before raising a curious eyebrow and mentally giving himself a high-five for his good fortune.

She smiled and placed her hand on his shoulder, causing his heart to melt the tiniest bit. "You're right, I don't know you, but I don't think you're dangerous. I overheard your conversation about guns." Her mouth curved up in an adorable crooked smirk. "I'm not worried." She held her hand out for him to shake. "Jessica Robicheaux. Pleasure to meet you."

Trevor was speechless, but, thankfully, Beau was not.

"Are you sure, Jessica? He's right, you don't know him. Do you think it's wise to invite him into your home?"

She shrugged. "Well, from what I understand, Caroline knows him pretty well, and she doesn't seem scared. I don't think he'll hurt me. Honestly, if he even makes it back to my place without falling asleep, I think once his head hits the pillow he'll be passed out for a very long time. Besides, I share an apartment with my brother, and he's a State Trooper. I'm pretty sure I'll be safe."

Great. Another cop. At least *she's* not the cop this time. "Thank you Miss—what's your last name again?"

"Robicheaux." She smiled and her eyes dragged from his face to his toes and back. "Just call me Jessica."

Even drunk, that small gesture sparked a little life into his libido. He cleared his throat and attempted to speak—and think—clearly. "Right. Thank you, Jessica, for saving me from the *beasts of the bayou,*" he mocked.

Caroline and Jessica laughed aloud, but the gardener only allowed himself a smirk. Oh well, he'd take what he could get in this state of mind.

"It must have been difficult for you to offer your couch to me, Beau. Thank you for that. I'm pleasantly surprised. Perhaps I was wrong about you."

He shrugged. "Perhaps. Welcome to the South, Mr. Callahan. We have manners down here."

Cade helped him to Jessica's car as he offered to drive Trevor's car back to the hotel for him. Trevor considered his options and asked the gardener to bring it to Jessica's place. That way Trevor would have wheels in the morning. Caroline followed him to the girl's apartment, and Beau helped him up the stairs as Jessica prepared the couch for him. He felt his stomach rolling, and knew things were about to get ugly.

"Um, bathroom. Now."

They scattered like ants to get him to the bathroom and he puked up the contents of his stomach in its entirety. After finishing the last few painful dry-heaves, which produced nothing but sore ribs, he rinsed his mouth and splashed the clean, cool water on his face. He stared at the pale green face in the mirror and cursed whatever it was in his room that got him spooked enough that he turned to martinis.

The drinks didn't even serve their purpose now because he was sick instead of relaxed and carefree. What had he been thinking, drinking so much? Especially since he had no intention of going back to that stupid hotel room. He had been so freaked out he didn't care. He would've slept on the grimy floor of the bar if they'd have let him. All he could think about was lying down and letting the room spin until he passed out. She was right, it only took a minute once his head hit that pillow.

The morning sun peeked through the sheer curtains in the kitchen and blinded Trevor. The rays had somehow managed to find the perfect hole in the blinds that shone directly on his face. It was God's way of punishing him for drinking too much.

He rolled over and tried to ignore the pounding in his head. Parched, his tongue was stuck to the roof of his mouth. But just the thought of drinking anything had him queasy.

He tried to lift his arm up to check his watch, but his muscles weren't working. His arm merely twitched and refused to cooperate. A hoarse groan surprised him until he realized it was his own voice. What was wrong with him? He hadn't been this hung over since his Sophomore year in college.

Ticking came from somewhere in the room and he peeled his eyelids apart to look for a clock. Moving only his eyes, he scanned the walls and it dawned on him that he had no idea where he was. He rolled over onto his back and nearly jumped out of his skin. An adorably sexy woman sat on a coffee table about two feet away.

"Good morning. How are you feeling?" She whispered these words, for which he was thankful. In her hands were two aspirin and a muddy-looking drink. "I mixed up my own special hangover cure for you. It's potent, but if you drink it quickly it'll make you feel better within the hour."

Trevor tried to speak, but his thick tongue refused to work. The hangover cure could be swamp water, but he'd drink anything to get rid of the jack hammering in his head. He slowly sat up, took the items from her, and chugged.

Trevor coughed, his mouth was on fire and his sinuses burned. "What the hell is in that stuff?"

She took the glass and smiled. "Just a few secret ingredients my dad taught me. I tweaked it a little."

"I can feel it burning all the way down to my gut."

She winked. "That's the Tabasco. Trust me, it works. I've used it many times. If for some reason this doesn't do the trick, I'll go get you some Yakamein. It's an old New Orleans hangover soup that works every time. It's hard to find these days, but Dupree's still serves it upon request."

179

For the first time, he really looked her over. She reminded him a lot of Caroline. Not so much by looks, but by personality. She was spunky and confident, but sweet and nurturing.

"May I ask you how old you are, Miss. . .?"

"Robicheaux. Jessica Robicheaux." She crossed her long slender legs, accentuating the tone and definition, and chewed her bottom lip suppressing a smile. He appreciated the tiny shorts she wore, but more so her amusement that he couldn't remember her name. This intrigued him. Most chicks would've been pissed.

"Right, Miss Robicheaux. You don't seem old enough to have been hung over all that often."

She took his glass to the kitchen and rinsed it out before she answered. "Call me Jessica, and I'm twenty-seven. Thanks for the compliment, though."

She looked like a Jessica. Flirty and feisty all in one tight little package. She wore a thin baby blue T-shirt to accompany those tiny cotton shorts and it was obvious she wasn't wearing a bra. A long-lost tightening clenched in his groin. He found her very attractive, and, though his mind was slow and hung over, his body reacted just fine. It was nice to finally have a distraction to take his mind off of Caroline.

"Really? You don't look a day over twenty-three."

She sat in front of him again and ran her fingers through his hair, smoothing the tangles that poked out in all directions. It felt great. Even though his body hurt all over, he managed a grin. "Thank you."

"You're welcome. You were looking like a peacock."

He chuckled. "No, I meant thank you for letting me stay here. I apologize for being such a drunkard last night and for puking in your bathroom. I'm not usually like this. It's embarrassing."

She held his gaze as if mesmerized by something. He could only imagine how awful he looked. . .and smelled. He was sure she was noticing what a mess he was. "You're welcome. I couldn't imagine you sleeping outside anywhere, much less down here. You're from Chicago, right?"

Choosing to ignore her city boy jab, he tried to recall if he'd mentioned it last night. "Yes, I am. How did you know that?"

"After I eavesdropped on your conversation with Caroline last night, I called my brother to do a little checking up on you before I invited you to sleep here. He's a State Trooper, remember?"

Ahh, yes. He vaguely remembered that little detail. A background check? Maybe she wasn't so naïve. "Anyway, I hope you don't mind. He didn't find anything but an impeccable record, so you're welcome to stay as long as you'd like."

Trevor wasn't certain, but that seemed like a loaded invitation. Her deep, probing eyes sparkled and penetrated the core of his libido, awakening the sleeping giant, sending signals he hadn't seen from anyone in a very long time. Amazing how one look communicated her unspoken desires.

They chatted about his embarrassing inebriation, what brought him down South—he edited that story—growing up in New York and Chicago, and how she'd always wanted to live in a big city. Much like Caroline had been before meeting the Cajun Casanova, Jessica was eager to learn about him and, surprisingly, very touch-oriented when she spoke to him. She was always touching his arm, or his knee, and, like Caroline, she didn't even realize she did it. He liked that. He missed that subtle physical contact. It must be a Southern thing.

Jessica was born in New Orleans, but her parents moved to Golden Meadow when she was four-years-old, and she'd lived here ever since. She worked part-time as a paralegal's assistant and part-time at the courthouse downtown. She had one "very protective" older brother, Brody, and her parents owned and operated a charter fishing company in Grand Isle, Louisiana.

Jessica and Caroline shared many similarities, but Trevor had a feeling Jessica was bolder and a teensy bit more in touch with her inner-vixen. He was suddenly very eager to find out.

"So, why is a beautiful young woman like you not married yet? I can't imagine why you are still on the market."

She pretended to be embarrassed while tucking her long, silky strands behind her ear, but she wasn't the least bit shy. "Well, I was engaged once, but that didn't work out."

"Why not? That is, if you don't mind telling me." He held his hands up. "I'm sorry, how incredibly rude of me. You don't have to tell me if you don't want to."

"No, it's okay. I don't mind. I found out a week before our wedding that the bastard was banging my maid of honor. So much for honor, or lack of it. Needless to say she was not only demoted from her position but from my entire life as well."

"Oh, that's low. I think your story trumps mine."

Her brow furrowed, and he could tell he'd opened the door for questions about a topic he wasn't interested in discussing. His issues.

"So, what happened between you and Caroline? Weren't you two gonna get married?"

He took a deep breath as he thought about the best way to explain it without making himself look like the jerk of the century. "Well, I didn't treat Caroline as well as I should have. I've learned my lesson."

"Did she cheat on you with Beau?"

Trevor rubbed the back of his neck in a poor attempt to hide his tension regarding this sore subject. Jessica was bold, he had to give her that. "Not exactly. At least, I don't think she did. Caroline is very. . . How can I say this respectfully? She's made a pact between herself and God to wait until marriage to be with a man. So as much as I would love to blame him for seducing her and stealing her away from me, I really don't think anything big happened between them. I thought it had, and I said some horrible things to her, but honestly I think they—she was innocent. I have no doubt he would've jumped her bones if she'd let him."

"So you guys never. . .?"

He shook his head and smirked at her apparent shock.

"The whole time?"

He shook his head again.

"How long were you two together?"

"Two and-a-half years. Not because I didn't try. She was always very consistent about stopping things before they got too out of hand."

"She's stupid."

Pleasantly surprised, but shocked, he chuckled. "Why do you say that?"

"Someone as gorgeous, successful, and sexy as you? And she let you slip away." She moaned. "I'd have licked you like a lollipop." She wet her lips and buried her fingers in his hair, squeezing. "Setting limits on someone as scrumptious as you, well that's just plain stupid." She sighed, "Oh well. You hungry?"

He was literally speechless. Had he not been hung over and had his wits about him, Trevor would have reciprocated her aggressive and bold flirting. For now, he'd play dumb until he got a better hold on her personality. "Um, I'm not sure if I can eat. Although, that drink you gave me is working. I'm feeling somewhat human again. What's in that stuff?"

She grinned. "Secret recipe. If I told you, I'd have to kill you."

He was liking Miss Robicheaux more and more. "Well, whatever is in it, you should patent it and sell it. You'd be a millionaire."

"I'll keep that in mind. Right now, we need to get you cleaned up. How 'bout a shower?"

The very thought of going back to that haunted hotel room made him nauseous. "No, I can't go back to my room just yet."

"That's fine, you can shower here. I'll get some of my brother's clothes for you. I also have a brand new toothbrush I've not opened that you can have if you'd like."

This woman fascinated him. "May I ask you another question, Miss Robicheaux?" She nodded. "I get that your brother is a cop, and you saw my record so you know I'm not a psychopath, but don't you think it was a little foolish, and dangerous, to invite a complete stranger into your home? Especially since your brother isn't even here?"

She pursed her lips, and he couldn't tell if she was offended or trying to bite back a grin.

He tried to recover. "Don't get me wrong, I'm grateful for your hospitality and for your taking care of me, but if you were my little sister or girlfriend I'd have half a mind to bend you over my knee."

Jessica raised her eyebrows, and her dark brown eyes sparkled with amusement. His insides tightened. She stood without removing her eyes from his and slowly walked over directly in front of him. Though propped up on the arm of the couch, still somewhat lying down, this woman was obviously not intimidated by him. She leaned down to be eye-to-eye with him. He was acutely aware of his morning hangover breath.

"Mr. Callahan, I am a first-degree black belt. You're gorgeous, chiseled, and obviously fit. I can see that you work out, but, no offense, I could take you. I'm not worried." She smiled and flicked the tip of his nose as she walked away leaving him with his mouth gaping open.

Damn! That was the hottest thing he'd ever heard. Her voice came booming down the hall as she headed for the kitchen. "Now, call me Jess or I'll put *you* over *my* knee, ya heard me? Get your lazy butt up to shower so we can eat and get to know each other better."

Eager to learn more, he decided to comply with her wishes. Besides, brushing his teeth sounded very refreshing.

"Yes, ma'am. Um, thank you."

This was a new one for him. He wasn't used to domineering women in his life. Could be interesting, and he was up for the challenge. Speaking of challenges, he still had to get up. He slowly graduated to a seated position, his head throbbing so badly he wanted to die. Once the room stopped spinning and he was sure his eyeballs weren't going to explode, he scooted forward to the edge of the cushion. His next step was to actually stand up, a feat he was unsure he could pull off.

Jessica returned and helped him up. He stood, wobbly, and looked down at her. She was a little taller than Caroline, definitely stronger.

They stared into each other's eyes. She really was beautiful. He felt something brewing between them, but before he could do anything about it he desperately needed to brush his teeth and shower. His eyes shifted to her mouth and back to her beautiful chocolate eyes. They were the deepest brown eyes he'd ever seen, full of compassion and desire. He leaned in and kissed the center of her forehead. He felt an urgency that no doubt seeped into his tone when he spoke. It had been so long since he felt this way, but he just met this girl, and he didn't want to blow it.

"Shower. Let me shower."

She nodded.

"And then. . ."

"Shower first," she interrupted. "And then we'll eat lunch. You need to regain your strength." She winked.

"Strength. Food. Food promotes strength. Yes, that would be good." She giggled as he stumbled into the bathroom to prepare himself for whatever adventure she had planned for the day.

Things were looking up for him down in the bayou. Now, if he could just figure out what the hell was in his room last night, maybe he could enjoy himself a little more.

NINETEEN

Driving back to his cabin as the sun was barely peeking above the horizon, Cade thought about Callahan and wondered about his true intentions. Caroline didn't say much about their conversation before he arrived. They discussed the ghost and Jessica's bold but foolish move to put him up for the night, but nothing more.

Cade chuckled. Callahan was hammered. Much better than his normal asshole self. He had followed Caroline back to the hospital, but after they parked, she climbed into his truck and fell asleep exactly where he wanted her to be for the rest of his life. . .in his arms.

He needed to find a way to keep her safe. But how? Too much uncertainty had Cade on edge. As long as Caroline was in town, she wasn't safe. He couldn't focus on the game when so much was at stake. Getting her to leave would be tricky with her entire family in danger, but he had an idea. He just needed to work out some details first.

Cade was expecting the package from Tony today containing the dirt about April. He itched with anticipation to find out what Tony had discovered. If April was linked somehow to the head of the Louisiana Mafia, he needed to know how, exactly, and tread very carefully. The last thing Cade wanted to do was piss off the Mob. It seemed he already had a target on his back, but obviously it wasn't their doing, or he'd be in the morgue.

Cade would have bet against her last year. But after learning more about April, he didn't think she'd be quite so careless. The jury was still out on her. Unfortunately, Eddie knew as much about April as everyone else did. Squat. She's bad, no doubt about it. Cade just wasn't convinced she should be the focused criminal in this case. At least he didn't think she was alone. Something was rotten, and he really needed to get to the bottom of it before anything else happened.

As he walked through the door of his cabin, his mouth watered at the savory smell of bacon.

"Smells good! Who's cookin'?"

Runway peeked around the corner. "Like you had to ask? The princess is still snoozing. How's Remy?"

"He made it through the surgery and is still in recovery. Doc says he thinks the lung will hold up and he'll be fine. The paralysis is still an issue, but both Dr. Johnston and Dr. Bailey think he'll be back on his feet before too long."

"Good. Kid's too young. He's just getting started with his life."

Cade grabbed a bottle of orange juice and plopped down on the couch. "Yeah, he's got a lot of livin' to do. So how was your evening with Her Majesty?"

"Fine. How is Caroline?"

Cade chuckled. Evasion was never Runway's style. He usually bragged at least a little after his female conquests. He must really have a thing for her. Couldn't blame him, she was beautiful, but she was a pistol. "Caroline's fine. So when's the wedding?"

Silence. Cade chuckled again as he chugged his orange juice. He almost spewed his mouthful of juice all over the room when Kristy's voice blasted from his bedroom.

"Mind your own business, Swamp Thing!"

"My bad. Thought you were sleeping," he hollered.

She walked in from Cade's room wrapped in only the sheet. He averted his eyes and heard the smile in her tone. "That's what you get for thinking."

"Geez, Kristy. Put some clothes on. You're making me blush," Cade said.

"I know. It's kind of fun. What, you don't like the view?"

He continued staring out the window. "Not when I'm in love with your best friend and you're in love with mine." Now she was the one blushing.

"Who said I was in love?"

He turned to her, focusing only on her face. "No one had to say it. It's obvious." He motioned to the sheet.

More embarrassed, she squeezed the sheet tighter around her body and slinked past him to pull her clothes from behind the couch cushion. "Speaking of that, where is Caroline now that her *ex-fiancé* is back in town?"

She was trying to get a rise out of Cade, but it didn't work. He knew Callahan had enough distractions on his plate keep him away from Caroline. Hopefully, Miss Robicheaux was the answer to his worries about Trevor.

"She's back at the house resting with her parents. Don't worry about Callahan, he's being cared for. Something spooked him in his hotel, and he got loaded at Dupree's last night. It was quite entertaining."

Kristy muttered something under her breath and went back to the room, but Runway wanted to know more. "What happened?"

"Dude, why didn't you give me a heads-up he was here? He knew about you and it caught me off guard."

"What'd he say?"

"He called you my pretty little boyfriend. Did you talk to him?"

Runway's lips twitched in agitation. "Yeah, we met." He set the plates of food down and they ate while he explained the introduction. Cade's head spun with the familiar sensation of controlled fury as he clenched his jaw. He wished he'd been the one to confront that little prick after personally removing his hands—and his lips—from Caroline.

Cade dismissed the Callahan issue at the sound of a knock at the door. Besides, he had much to learn about a different, more elusive, and possibly more dangerous enemy.

Cade opened the door to a smiling Delia who handed him a large envelope. "Hey, this came for you this morning. I was on my way to the grocery so I thought I'd bring it by."

Cade thanked her, closed the door, and tore into it, eagerly consuming the information.

"Incredible," he whispered.

Runway looked over his shoulder. "What is it?"

"Apparently, Ms. Morales has been keeping some pretty nasty skeletons in her closet. Wow. Just. . .wow."

"Who's Ms. Morales?" Kristy looked at them expectantly as she sauntered in fully-dressed and poured her coffee.

Not quite ready to let her in on this particular investigation, he tucked the papers back into the cardboard envelope and shrugged it off. "No one. It's not a big deal."

Much too quickly, she caught on to his vibe. "You listen to me, Beau. Caroline is my best friend, and I love her dearly." She stalked over and got in his face. "If you know something that involves her or her newfound family, you'd better tell me right now or I'll call her and get her over here to question you herself. Spill it, swamp rat!"

He watched keenly as Runway admired her. "You sure you're ready to deal with that? I told you she was a handful."

Without removing his gaze from her, he smiled, "Positive. I've never been more ready."

She sheepishly grinned at him before turning her focus back to Cade. "Tell me what's in the envelope, or I'll show you what a handful I can be."

He sighed. It wouldn't be such a bad thing to have Kristy in on it now that he had some hard evidence of April's past. He told her everything they knew about April up until now, then he thumped the package and told them both the staggering secret within.

The decision about what should be done was mutual. They had to get Caroline out of town until they could contain the fire from the explosion that was about to take place in Golden Meadow.

Kristy landed on a great idea. She would take Caroline and Emily to California with her when she flew back home in just over a week. That would give him a little more time to get to the bottom of this mystery.

"It's settled then. I will suggest it to Caroline, and you persuade her to go, Kristy. I have a good feeling about it."

Cade tucked the envelope under his arm, snagged the last piece of bacon and headed to his truck. Among other things, it was time to bring Eddie up to speed about April, who she really was, and what she was capable of doing.

"Beau." Eddie motioned for Cade to enter his office. "You look like you have something you'd like to talk about." He nodded toward the large envelope in Cade's hand.

"Yes, sir." Cade closed and locked the door. "First, may I ask if you know where April is?"

Eddie exhaled as he realized what news Cade brought. "She said she'd be running errands today. I honestly have no idea where, though."

"So, she's not here right now?"

"No. What's up, Beau?" Eddie's clipped response indicated that Cade needed to get to the point.

He approached Eddie's desk and placed the papers in front of him. Eddie put his glasses on and carefully read the information Cade knew would change Eddie's life. He quietly allowed Eddie to absorb the disturbing news. When he finished reading, Eddie tossed his glasses onto the desk and pinched the bridge of his nose, mumbling a string of curse words under his breath.

"Angelo Marcellino? Are you absolutely certain about this, Beau?"

Cade nodded. Tony was the best in his field. He'd had Cade's back plenty of times. "Yes, sir. I trust my source." He continued his unwavering stare. "With my life," he added.

Holding his gaze for only a few seconds longer, Eddie nodded. "Okay. What do you suggest our first move should be?"

"I have a friend who is an FBI Agent. I could have her check the system for anything we could use against April regarding her connections with Marcellino. Maybe he's got some unsecured skeletons in his closet as well. If we can make April believe we have something concrete that will blacklist her from her resources, perhaps she'll come clean and stop whatever it is she's trying to accomplish."

"Marcellino's been the notorious head of the Louisiana Mafia for as long as I can remember. If there was something to be found on him, someone in the FBI would have found it by now. Don't you think?"

"I certainly hope not."

"Alright. Find what you can, and keep me posted. I won't say anything to April until you tell me to." He leaned back in his chair and put his hands behind his head. "I'd be lying if I said I'm not worried what you're gonna find." He nodded to the papers. "I'd have never suspected any of this."

"She had us all fooled, sir. Caroline suspected her before I ever did." He stood by awkwardly.

Eddie smiled. "Is there more?"

He shifted his weight. "Yes, sir. There is something else. Something I wanted to ask you, but I'm debating on just doing it later. Now might not be the appropriate time."

"Since when have you ever been afraid to approach me with anything? Just ask me, Beau. I promise I won't bite." He winked as if he already knew what Cade was going to say.

He took a deep breath. "Mr. Fontenot, it's no secret I'm in love with Caroline. I have been since the first week I met her." Eddie nodded. "My sisters are all in town, and I'm taking her to my parents' house today to have lunch with everyone." For reasons he couldn't explain, Cade was extremely nervous. "I wanted. . . Well, I was hoping for your permission to ask Caroline to marry me. Today."

Eddie stood and walked around his desk to be face-to-face with him. His smile disappeared, and this serious look was one Cade had never seen before. This could be bad.

"Marriage? This soon? Caroline's been through an awful lot this past year. She had a nasty experience only nine months ago, then this whole thing with Remy. Do you really think she's ready to get married?"

Although he questioned him, Eddie wasn't doubting Cade's integrity. He was simply being protective of his daughter. Cade respected that.

"Yes, sir. I think she will agree to marry me."

"You think? You're not sure?"

Cade smirked. Eddie enjoyed this. "I know she will, sir. I'm ready to spend the rest of my life with Caroline, and I honestly believe she's ready to spend hers with me. I promise to take good care of her, Mr. Fontenot. May I have your blessing?"

His smile slowly stretched across his face, reaching his eyes. "Of course, Beau. You have my permission, and my blessing, to marry my daughter. When are you planning to do this?"

"I'm going to ask her tonight."

"No, I mean, when do you think you'll get married?"

Cade smiled. "I think I'll leave that decision entirely up to Caroline. She was pushed around so much with her last engagement, I think I'll let her make all the decisions for this one."

Eddie nodded. "Very wise choice." They shook hands, but Eddie didn't release when Cade did. He held tightly and gripped Cade's shoulder with his other hand. "Listen to me carefully. If you ever do wrong by her. . ."

Cade nodded. "Yes, sir. I promise to love, honor, and cherish her. Forever. You have my word."

Eddie hugged him. "That's all I need, then. Congratulations, son. Don't forget to ask her mother."

"Yes, sir. My next stop."

"Well, I saw her heading into the kitchen to have coffee with Delia and Delphine about a half-hour ago. She may still be down there."

"Thanks, Mr. Fontenot. I appreciate it."

Cade jubilantly breezed down the stairs on a cloud. He wanted to marry Caroline, but actually having her father's blessing made it real. Feeling prepared for anything, he entered the double doors to the kitchen and froze mid-step. There, sitting at the table laughing and drinking coffee, was the love of his life, smiling like an angel. So alluring, and best of all, happy to see him, as was her mother. He would have to wait to ask her mom for permission, but if the warm reception he received from Emily when he entered was any indication, Cade didn't believe that would be a problem.

"Good morning, ladies. How is everyone on this beautiful day?"

Emily smiled as Caroline answered. "Better now that you're here. What's got you in such a great mood?"

"You. Of course. Do you have anything planned for today?"

"I was planning to visit Rachel's grave again, before I go see Remy at the hospital." A breathtaking smile brightened Caroline's face. "His nurse called this morning, and he's able to stand and shuffle his feet with help. I want to be there for him. Other than that, I've got nothing. Why?"

"Good, because I'm taking you to have lunch with my family."

Her eyes grew big.

"My sisters are all in town, and they'll be there. You met Catherine and Cameron at the crawfish boil last summer, but you haven't gotten to meet Carly and Caitlyn yet." He smiled as he peeled a banana. "My mom's cooking crawfish bisque, and Catherine is bringing brownies."

"What are you supposed to bring?"

"You." With a larger-than-life smile, he winked, kissed her cheek, and took a bite of his banana. She was speechless. Feeling accomplished, he changed the subject. "So how have you been feeling, Ms. Emily?"

"I'm doing just fine, Cade. Thank you for asking."

"Have you had any more visions lately?" She shook her head. "Well, when you're not busy, I'd like to discuss the one you had of me earlier. I'm curious to hear the details of that one."

"Me, too," Caroline said. "Good luck with that. She's sealed up tighter than Fort Knox." Caroline made a face and mocked her mother. "It's nothing, really. I'm fine. It was no big deal, really." Caroline straightened up and brought her coffee mug to her lips. "Yeah, whatever."

Emily sternly replied with a less-than-thrilled expression, "Say what you'd like, but it really was nothing to worry about." She turned and smiled. "Cade, I would be happy to share the details of the ridiculous vision sometime when grumpy-butt isn't around to tease me about it." Caroline's jaw dropped.

"That's great. Are you busy now? We could go for a walk."

Caroline groused, "Oh, please. A walk in this humidity? She wouldn't last ten minutes. Don't bother. Y'all can stay in here. I'm going up to my room to get ready." She stood to walk away, but he caught her hand and pulled her close.

She looked up with pouty lips, so he gave them a small kiss to reassure her he wasn't blowing her off. "Don't take too long. I want a little alone time with you before I have to share you with my family."

This satisfied her and she hurried out the door to get ready. He took the seat next to Emily, and she knowingly looked at him.

"Mr. Beauregard, I am not a fool. I know you're not interested in discussing my vision from earlier. What is it you'd *really* like to discuss?"

"What makes you think that?"

"I was young and in love once, too. Your whole family will be at lunch today. I see the signs, so why don't you just ask me what you need to ask so you can go take care of my daughter?"

Cade could see how Caroline has stayed such a good girl this long. Her mother knew anything she was about to do before she could do it, so Caroline didn't stand a chance at getting into any trouble. "Yes, ma'am. I do want to know about your vision, but for now, you're right, I have something else in mind." He cleared his throat and wiped his sweaty palms on his shorts. "I realize you weren't here during the summer last year, so you didn't see how quickly and easily Caroline and I hit it off, but I am desperately in love with her." She nodded reassuringly. "I knew she was engaged to Trevor, and I'm not proud of the fact that I made a move causing her to doubt her feelings for him, but I'm not sorry I did. She's like no other woman I've ever known."

"I may not have been here last year, but that doesn't mean I'm clueless about the way you two feel for each other. She's told me about you from the first week y'all met. I could see something blooming, but I liked Trevor before I learned of all the bad things about him—which none of us would have known had it not been for you. Caroline acts differently around you than she did with Trevor. She's more relaxed and much more herself. I think you're good for each other, so my answer is yes."

Cade hid his surprise. "But I haven't asked you anything."

She smiled and placed her hand over his. "No you haven't, but, like I said, I'm not a fool. My instincts rarely fail me. I would love for you to marry my daughter."

A bit flustered, very unlike him, Cade sat quietly, not knowing what to say next.

"If it will make you feel better to ask, go ahead. Ask me."

He cleared his throat. "Are you sure those visions are a fluke?"

"You're stalling."

"Yes, ma'am. I am in love with Caroline, and I would love, well, I'm grateful for your blessing to propose to her."

She nodded. "Thank you, Cade."

Confused, he responded. "For what? I should be thanking you."

"Thank you for saving my daughter from making a huge mistake with Trevor, for helping her with Rachel, and for making her the happiest I've ever seen her. She truly does love you, and I am confident you are the best thing that's ever happened to her. So, thank you."

His excitement had him wondering if he could force himself to wait until the evening to propose.

He and Emily stood, hugged, and as he kissed her cheek, she whispered in his ear. "Know this, hot stuff. You hurt my daughter, and there will be hell to pay." She kissed his cheek and patted his back. "Now, go sweep her off her feet."

After changing clothes four different times, Caroline finally decided on a cheerful, yellow sundress that allowed her pasty white skin to have a little color. Blending in with his attractive family would be a challenge if she didn't look equally radiant. They were friendly, she didn't need to be nervous, but she still wanted to look her best. She squirted perfume into the air and walked through it.

Oh well, no use worrying about things that were out of her control. Cade loved her, so she was sure his sisters would, too. Hopefully. Caroline took one last look in the mirror when she spotted something move behind her. She whirled around and experienced a temporary bout of tunnel vision. She stumbled to the bed until the flashing subsided, and her heart slowed. The image of a set of piercing blue eyes flitted through her mind. She was pulled from this episode when footsteps hurried past her door.

Caroline poked her head out into the hallway just as a streak of blonde hair darted into one of the spare bedrooms. Instantly suspicious, she followed. She assumed she'd find April snooping around, but it wasn't April she stumbled upon. Frantically searching for something, with obvious difficulty, was the last person she expected.

196

"Need help finding something?"

Claire jumped like a skittish cat. Caroline had caught her in the middle of something. Her guilty expression was proof of that.

Caroline's heart broke. "Please don't push me away. I can help you if you'll let me."

"I don't *need* you," she snarled.

For the first time since she had moved back, Caroline saw the difference. Claire's normally shiny hair was dull and lackluster, dark circles underlined eyes that once sparkled, and she had lost weight. Caroline initially thought she had caught Claire simply trying to avoid a confrontation, but now she suspected there was more to it.

Caroline narrowed her eyes. "Claire, are you doing drugs?"

Claire stopped digging. "That's none of your business." She continued rummaging through the furniture. "Like you give a crap anyway" she grumbled.

"Of course I care. So which is it, Claire? Cocaine?" She squared her shoulders and crossed her arms. "Something less conspicuous maybe? Weed? Crystal Meth?"

Claire's head snapped up. "Those are mighty big words for a small town girl,' she hissed." You almost sound like you know what you're talking about."

"Oh, like you? You're almost eighteen so you think you're street-smart? You're forgetting I lived in Chicago. Golden Meadow isn't exactly a big city. I may be naïve and inexperienced in some things, but I'm not clueless."

Claire paused her scavenging, a creepy smirk crawled up one corner of her mouth.

Caroline stood her ground.

"Don't tell me, Miss Perfect dared to experiment with an illegal substance? I don't believe it." She stood face to face with Caroline, challenging her.

"No. I never did drugs, but I had some really good friends who did, and I watched them ruin their lives." Caroline waited a moment, studying Claire's listless eyes. She tried to infuse tenderness into her

197

voice. "People who are altered by drugs and addiction are impossible to reason with and incapable of making smart choices. You're better than this."

Claire rolled her eyes and walked back to the drawers. "Whatever. I'm not a drug addict, and I don't expect a self-righteous goodie-two-shoes like you to have any idea what you're talking about. I'm sure you've never taken anything stronger than aspirin. Besides, drugs are the least of my problems right now." She found what she was looking for and stuffed it into her bag.

Caroline blocked the doorway as Claire tried to leave.

"Get out of my way." When Caroline didn't move, Claire drew in a dramatic breath, exhaling loudly. "*Please.*"

Caroline motioned to her hand. "What's in the bag, Claire?"

"Outta my way!"

"The bag, Claire."

"I told you, none of your business."

"You're my sister, so it *is* my business."

"No, it's not. Move, Caroline, before I get angry."

"I can't let you ruin your life." Caroline reached for the bag, but Claire jerked her hand away.

"It's not your problem. Go back to your botanical beefcake and fertilize something."

Claire shoved her way past Caroline and scurried down the stairs.

Caroline's heart shattered. How did this happen? Claire wasn't even close to being this messed up last year. Was Caroline's coming back and taking Eddie's attention the spark of Claire's downfall? She's at a very impressionable stage in her life. Caroline was sure her life-altering presence and the danger she'd brought upon her family had been a huge strain on Claire.

Caroline needed to do something, but what? Ratting Claire out to Eddie would do nothing but push her further away. She would have to talk to Cade about this later. For now, Caroline did her best to push this emotional disaster out of her mind and prepare for an important lunch with the family she was dying to learn more about.

To gain more pieces to her puzzle. Clues to the mystery that was Cade Beauregard.

TWENTY

Cade pulled into his parents' driveway, and words escaped Caroline.. The beauty and grace of the antebellum home was unmatched. Simply gorgeous. This scaled-down house hadn't been a plantation, at least Caroline didn't think so, but it was definitely an historic structure. The two front winding staircases with black wrought iron spindles flanked two sets of regal white columns that extended to the roof of the second floor balcony. The wrap-around porch was an intricate design also fashioned from wrought iron that had been freshly painted a glossy black to perfectly contrast with the stark white exterior. Of course, the landscaping was exquisite. Much like when she saw Eddie's home for the first time, Caroline was overcome with emotion.

Cade was a descendant of General Beauregard from the Civil War, but she'd had no idea if his descendants would still inhabit his property. The general lived in New Orleans, or so she read. But if this was in fact one of the general's homes, she'd love to prowl around the building and dig for historical artifacts.

"What an incredible house. Why do you choose to live in that tiny cabin when you could've stayed here?"

Cade raised an eyebrow. "What would you think of a twenty-eight-year-old guy who still lived at home with his parents?"

"Hey, if *this* was home, I wouldn't judge you," she scoffed, playfully. "Look at me. You don't see me complaining about my address."

He shrugged and helped her from the truck. "That's different. I had been on my own for so long, I just couldn't bring myself to move back in to a place with rules."

Caroline nodded. That was an understandable reason. "Do your sisters still live here?"

"Well, Carly lives here when she's not at school. Caitlyn stays here when she's on leave, but she's stationed on a ship. Of course, Cameron lives here during the summer since she's in college now, too. . ." He shook his head in disbelief. "Which is impossible for me to accept. I can't believe my baby sister just finished her freshman year of college."

"I've met Catherine and Cameron, so it's Carly and Caitlyn I have to impress." She really talked more to herself, but it amused him. He put his arm around her neck, pulling her close to kiss her temple.

"Don't worry. They'll love you." Cade released his headlock and laced his fingers through hers. "Catherine's thirtieth birthday was last week, so we're kind of celebrating that today. I'm sure my mom will have a magnificent array of desserts. After all, thirty is a big one for women, right?"

"That's what they say. I'll let you know in about six years."

Catherine's voice chimed through the open door. "That's right, I forgot, you're just a baby. You don't know what it's like for us old gals."

An involuntary smile stretched across Caroline's face as she walked in to find Catherine perched at the bench in front of a gorgeous, antique upright piano in the living room. "I see no *old gals* in here. All I see is a vibrant, beautiful young woman."

Catherine smirked. "Good save, missy."

Cade's sister gracefully flitted across the room to give Caroline a hug and kiss on the cheek, the standard greeting down here, and

Caroline admired her natural beauty. Catherine's bright, welcoming smile offered comfort in what could possibly be awkward for an introvert like Caroline.

"Where's mom?" Cade asked.

"She's putting the finishing touches on the cake." Catherine quickly added, "*My* cake, garbage gut. I get the first piece, so don't even think about it."

Cade waggled his finger in protest. "I thought you were making brownies?"

Catherine pretended to be offended as she pressed her palm into her chest and dramatically gasped. "You expected me to bake for my own birthday party?"

Cade shook his head and led Caroline into the house. He spoke over his shoulder to Catherine. "Of course not, what was I thinking? Carly and Cait here yet?"

Catherine mumbled, "Yes, they're here. You might want to brace yourself."

Cade stopped in his tracks as they entered the living room. Mr. Beauregard stood quietly in the corner by the fireplace holding a drink while two girls sat on the sofa, one of whom held hands with a man who looked to be in his late forties. Caroline wasn't sure which sister it was, but Cade didn't look too happy. She stood with the man in tow behind her as Cade glanced to his dad. Mr. Beauregard's less-than-thrilled expression matched Cade's, but he remained silent as he winked and nodded a greeting to Caroline and took a sip from his highball glass. Cade's grip on Caroline's hand tightened.

The girl wrapped her arms around her brother in a tight embrace, and he released Caroline's hand to reciprocate. His sister stepped back smiling and looked at Caroline. She had a short blonde pixie cut, bright blue eyes, and stood shorter than her sisters. But she shared Catherine's welcoming smile and curvy figure. She offered her hand. "You must be Caroline. My brother's told me all about you. I'm Caitlyn Masters."

Caroline shook her hand, and looked at Cade for an explanation. She wasn't aware he'd told his sisters much about her. His expression surprised her though, and she watched Cade transform into the overprotective big brother, shocked and seething.

Caroline's heart raced and the back of her throat tightened. She hadn't seen him this angry since his brawl with Trevor. Rather than speaking, he simply observed Caitlyn with narrowed eyes, missing nothing. His gaze flipped to the man behind Caitlyn, who in Caroline's mind should have been trembling, but instead stood strong and proud.

Cade spoke to his sister again. "I'm sorry, I must have misheard you. You wanna run that by me again?"

Caitlyn was the sister stationed on an aircraft carrier in the Navy. Apparently she had gotten married, and this was obviously the first Cade had heard of it. Caught off-guard and noticeably unhappy with the sudden news, this didn't fare well for baby sister or her husband.

"Cade, don't overreact. This is my husband, Ryan Masters. We got married three months ago."

Cade's expression remained unreadable as he shook the hand stretched out for his, but he didn't release it after the initial shake. "Ryan Masters," Cade repeated, perceptively. "Guess congratulations are in order."

The show this guy put on fizzled a little as he released a small but noticeable exhale. "Thank you, Cade. I've heard a lot about you." Cade's demeanor suddenly shifted and his eyes turned hard. He'd recognized something about this guy.

"Beau. *You* can call me Beau."

Uh-oh. This couldn't be good. Cade said the same thing to Trevor at the bar, and he couldn't stand Trevor. Apparently the handshake was for his sister's benefit.

"Stop it," Caitlyn warned. "Please. This is my business, not yours. I'm happy. You should be happy for me."

Ryan looked confused. "Did I miss something?"

Caroline placed her hand on Cade's shoulder to calm him. On the outside he looked perfectly normal, but she could tell he was screaming on the inside.

"I'd like a word with you and your new husband," Cade said, never removing his eyes from his sister.

Mr. Beauregard stepped forward and spoke sternly, his voice commanding obedience. "Cat, why don't you and your sister show Caroline to the kitchen to see if your mom needs any help while your brother and Caitlyn *calmly* settle things in here?"

"Hey, Caroline, how are you, love?" Cade's mom hugged and kissed Caroline's cheek as she led her into the immaculate stone-walled kitchen. Her tall, slender frame flitted gracefully around the room in the turquoise maxi dress that flowed freely with her movements. Her golden hair was twisted up and secured with a clip showing off her toned shoulders. She didn't look much older than her daughters.

"Hi, Mrs. Beauregard. I'm great, thank you. I love your beautiful home."

"Please, call me Angie. Would you care for a glass of iced tea?"

"Yes, ma'am. Thank you."

She handed Catherine a tray with two glasses and a small plate of crackers and cheese. "Here, baby, y'all take this outside. You can show Caroline the back yard while Carly and I finish up in here." She leaned close and whispered, "She's learning how to make Maw-Maw's crab bisque recipe and she's a little nervous with an audience." Angie winked. "I'll call you back in when we're ready to eat."

Catherine led Caroline to the back patio where they could breathe. Caroline was grateful. The family tension made her nervous.

As they entered the backyard paradise, Caroline took in the full beauty of the skilled landscaping. She knew exactly who was responsible for this heavenly oasis. Cade's touch was everywhere in the flowering artwork. To her left, an archway lead to a secluded garden with a stone pathway slithering through the palms, azaleas, and fragrant citrus trees. In the middle of the remote area stood a huge oak tree that looked to be two-hundred-years old with its wide limbs crawling across the sky. Spanish moss dripped solemnly from the branches and a weathered, wooden swing hung low.

To her right, lay a large swimming pool complete with waterfalls, inviting Caroline to jump in and cool off. One end of the pool beneath a faux cliff was a swim-up bar area. It was unbelievable. Catherine led her to the center of the backyard near a huge three-tiered fountain with a large *fleur de lis* embellishing the top. The water feature was flanked by two stone benches that looked as old as the oak tree. Water cascaded down the layers of the fountain providing a pleasant, loud trickling sound that helped filter their voices as Catherine filled her in on the family drama.

"Caitlyn and Ryan got married three months ago because she became pregnant. She's about five months along now. Not that you can tell, she's not showing yet. I made her take a test in front of me before I believed her." Catherine giggled. She manicured a potted plant, breaking off the dead leaves. "Anyway, Ryan's a great guy, he's just a little old for her."

"How old is he?"

"Forty-six."

"She's twenty-four, right?"

"Twenty-five next month. My dad's pretty upset about it, and I'm sure our overprotective brother is even more so."

"How do you feel about Ryan?"

Catherine shrugged. "He's nice. He seems thrilled about the baby."

Caroline believed her, but she wasn't being completely honest. "Is he just as thrilled about Caitlyn?"

Smiling, Catherine shrugged her shoulders. "I don't know. He seems to be, I guess. He'd better be or Cade will rip his heart out." They shared a laugh and Catherine added, "The bad thing about this whole situation is that their relationship is fraternization. He's an officer in the Navy, and she's enlisted. That's the part my sister is most worried about because Cade's going to flip when he learns that."

"Why? Officers can't date enlisted? How come?"

"It's against Navy policy. Conflict of interest, if you will." Catherine hesitated and then looked at Caroline from the corner of her eye. "That's not all."

Confused, Caroline was certain whatever came next was the reason for the tension within the family. "There's more?"

"Yeah. Four months ago Ryan was married." Caroline gasped. "To the commanding officer of Caitlyn's ship." Caroline clenched her teeth so her jaw wouldn't hang open. "Who was also the aunt of Cade's late girlfriend, Jenny," Catherine added. "That's why he reacted the way he did when he learned Ryan's name."

As Caroline contemplated the uncomfortable situation Cade walked into, her stomach churned. The news of his little sister getting pregnant and married without his knowledge would knock him off his feet, but to find out she stole her husband from Cade's first love's aunt in an adulterous affair—that would tear him apart, not to mention the whole Navy fraternization issue.

"Caroline, I really like you, but I have to ask you a very important, very serious question."

Caroline agreed, suddenly wary of what she would ask.

"Are you in love with my brother?"

"Yes. I am."

"Completely?"

"What do you mean?" Catherine doubted her sincerity.

"I think you know what I mean. Is there any room left in your heart for someone else?"

Caroline's stomach fell and her throat muscles constricted. Was she that transparent? Surely Catherine was guessing and had no inclination about her irrational reaction to Trevor. "No. I love your brother. Completely."

"Are you *in* love with him? There's a difference, you know."

"Yes. Absolutely." She answered too quickly and Catherine studied her with a stone-cold stare. Caroline twisted her fingers into knots and released a frustrated breath. "I am madly in love with your brother, I just wish I knew more about him. He's so evasive about his past. Anytime I bring it up, he changes the subject. I don't want to push or be nosy, but he knows everything about me, yet I don't know much about him. It's exasperating."

Catherine pursed her lips. "Knowing everything doesn't necessarily mean you know anything."

Baffled by that cryptic statement, Caroline's brow furrowed.

"I mean, you know enough about him to realize he's one of the good guys, right?"

Caroline indicated she did, but avoided eye contact as she picked her cuticles.

"Cade and I are only a year apart, fourteen months to be exact. We are very close. I know him better than anyone else with a couple of exceptions. Trust me when I tell you he's a great guy and you have nothing to worry about. You don't have to know everything about his past to know he's perfect for you."

Caroline agreed, but still wished she could know what had happened that he was so reluctant to discuss with her.

Catherine's entire demeanor changed and her voice softened to a near whisper. "Did Cade ever tell you what happened to me?"

Oh, so this is the sister who was raped. Caroline remembered hearing about it last summer and it explained Cade's hatred for Trevor when he got physical with her, as well as his extreme over-protectiveness of women. Caroline shook her head.

"Bruce," she scoffed. "I thought I knew everything there was to know about him. After four years you'd think I would. He was the love of my life, my ex-fiancé, the man I wanted to have babies with. . . I thought I knew everything about him." When she didn't continue, Caroline looked up to see if she was okay. Cade's older sister glared, fire emanating from her tear-filled blue eyes. "I was wrong."

Her hands trembled as she shredded a leaf. "He was an ATF agent. Incredible, successful, gorgeous, and built like a tank." Wistfully, Catherine spoke to the trees. "He seemed perfect to me." She quickly recovered, "Oh, but he was a gambler." Catherine squeezed her eyes closed and shook her head, clearly remembering, and not so fondly. "I thought I was grown and ignored my momma's protests as I moved in with him. We lived together for nearly three years before I learned what kind of monster he *really* was." Emotion bubbled to the surface and Catherine stifled her reaction, swallowing hard to compose herself.

"Two weeks. . .two weeks before our wedding, he came home from the horse races drunk and angry 'cause he'd lost a lot of money. *Our* money. He started trying to take my clothes off, but I refused to have sex with him while he was drunk. He didn't like that."

Caroline's heart ached thinking about what this poor woman must have gone through. It was obvious she'd told this story before, it sounded rehearsed. She'd probably practiced it in therapy so much it was memorized verbatim.

"He raped me." She whispered through tears now, lips quivering and body trembling. "I pushed him away, begging him to stop, but he was so strong. So strong."

Caroline's eyes filled with sympathetic tears. No wonder Cade flipped when she'd mentioned Trevor forcing himself on her.

"The pain was so intense, I begged. I pleaded until he finally hit me and knocked me out cold. When I came to shortly after, I realized he had used his handcuffs to bind me to the bed."

Caroline was fully invested in this story. There was no going back, and she felt like a fool for doubting Cade. For complaining to his sister who was now spilling her worst nightmare to prove a point.

"He raped me over and over, hitting me, biting me, scratching me, pulling my hair. . ." Catherine drew in a sharp breath. "After a while my body went numb, but one of our neighbors must have heard me. The police showed up after he had taken everything he could from me but my life." She scoffed. "He almost got that, too."

Catherine wiped her fingers beneath her eyes, careful not to smudge her make-up any worse. "My body healed, but my heart. . .well, now that's a different story. I'm not sure I'll ever be able to trust another man again."

"Catherine, I'm so sorry."

Catherine smiled, but a warning flashed behind her glistening eyes. "Don't be. I didn't tell you my story for pity. I want you to understand that knowing someone's past or not knowing it doesn't make a difference. It doesn't change who they are inside." Catherine had fully recovered and spoke passionately, commanding Caroline's full attention.

"My ex didn't rape me because he was drunk and angry, he raped me because he was evil inside and I believed the man he allowed me to see. The act." Catherine smiled, but it didn't reach her eyes. "Don't be sorry. Just be sure you don't hurt my brother, or I will make sure you know what sorry feels like."

Caroline became very aware of her sweaty skin. She shoved back her nerves, refusing to show just how Catherine's warning affected her. "I won't. I promise. What did Cade do when he found out?"

"Yeah, he paid a visit to my fiancé when he got back in the states. Let's just say I wish I'd physically been able to do to Bruce what my brother did. Bruce had been checked into the ER with six broken ribs, a broken nose, two broken legs, and genital mutilation." Catherine grinned smugly, "He won't be raping any more women."

"Wow."

"Yeah. It's not wise to mess with a Navy SEAL, or anyone he loves. You're in good hands, Caroline. Just handle him with care. He's tough on the outside, but he's been hurt before, and I saw what it did to him. I don't ever want to see him go through that darkness again."

Caroline admired how honest and genuine Catherine was, but she desperately wanted to know what happened to Cade. She wanted to ask, but didn't want to push her luck.

"You're good for him. I see it in the way he looks at you. In how happy he is when he's with you," Catherine said. "He's. . ." she pondered, "lighter."

Caroline wished Cade could be as open with her as his sister. Then she wouldn't have anything to worry about because she'd already know everything about him. Catherine stared at her strangely for several long moments, and Caroline fidgeted uncomfortably wondering how long she'd been lost in her daydream.

"What's wrong?" Caroline asked.

"You know what? Come on," Catherine said. She grabbed Caroline's hand like a teacher with a toddler, and quickly pulled her across the yard to one of the stone garden benches beside the fountain. Catherine pushed her down on the bench, told her to stay, and scurried around their perimeter peeking through tree branches and around bushes. Caroline's back was to the house and she was confused by Catherine's suddenly erratic behavior, but didn't move. She glanced around to see why Catherine was acting so strange.

On their left, leading into the side of the fragrant garden with the winding stone pathway was a jasmine covered wooden trellis. Caroline closed her eyes and took a deep breath. So much had happened in the past hour and she needed to clear her mind so she could focus. The heavenly smell from the climbing blooms provided a moment of tranquility, allowing Caroline to briefly escape and imagine another time and place. A peaceful, relaxing one.

Catherine startled her back to reality by bracing both hands on Caroline's shoulders. She nervously looked behind Caroline into the kitchen before she spoke again, very quietly and focused on Caroline's eyes.

"Caroline, I need to tell you about Jenny."

TWENTY-ONE

"Has Cade ever mentioned anything about Jenny to you?"

"No, I told you he's never talked about anyone from his past. The first time I met him he told me he dated her for six years and that she died in a car accident, but he never said her name. Then he told me he really didn't want to talk about it. I Googled it, but wasn't sure if I'd found the right obituary until he slipped and said her name."

Catherine nodded and looked around again. "He'll lose it if he knows I'm telling you anything about her." She paused in thought, "But I think it might help seal any doubts you may have if you know at least the bones of what happened."

"Why won't he just talk to me about it? Why is he so secretive about her?"

"It's painful for him to talk about because she was his first love, his first *everything* really; kiss, girlfriend, lover. Cade was planning to marry her before she had the accident. It's painful for him because he blames himself—and the Navy—for her death."

"The Navy? Why? What happened?"

"That's a big reason why he won't talk much about his experience in the military. Bet you haven't heard too many stories about that time of his life, have you?"

"I haven't heard too many stories about *any* time in Cade's life. What I do know I had to drag out of him, or his friends told me when he wasn't around."

Catherine glanced over Caroline's shoulder again to make sure nobody was coming outside and began pacing. "Well, Jenny was one of my best friends in high school. I introduced them, and once they started dating they were inseparable. Cade joined the Navy right out of high school so he could have a steady job. Then, for some insane reason, he decided to try for the SEALs." Catherine mumbled, "I can't understand his logic behind that if he wanted to have a family. I mean, most Navy SEALs graduate from training fully expecting to return home in a flag-draped pine box."

Catherine exhaled and nervously checked the back door again before quietly continuing. Caroline stifled a laugh at the obvious body language Catherine used. Her brother may have been Special Forces, but Catherine would never make it in espionage.

"Jenny waited for him. She wrote him letters nearly every day. He came home for leave one Christmas, and they spent every day of the two weeks together. He went back to Afghanistan for some stupid top secret mission, so he wasn't able to contact us for months, but Cade had told me before he left that he was going to propose to Jenny once he got back." Catherine paused abruptly to look around and focused on the garden past the trellis, squinting her eyes to see better. After a minute, she continued in a whisper. "Anyway, he had this special thing all planned out for how he would surprise her, only she had an even bigger surprise for him. A month after my brother left, Jenny—"

"That's *enough!*" Cade stood beneath the trellis, framed by the white Jasmine, panting and radiating with anger and betrayal beneath the cascading pinkish-white flowers. A drastic contrast in beauty. Pleasant, pure and soft, versus hostile, dark and hard. Caroline had never seen this look. Ever. Even during the fight with Trevor.

Tears of rage welled in his eyes and he trembled as he glared at Catherine. "How—" Cade huffed, exasperated and fuming as the muscles in his jaw jumped with each clench. The anger was there, sure, but the apparent disappointment in his sister seeping through his wounded expression was heartbreaking, and Caroline wished she could disappear. Cade's chin quivered slightly while he tried to hold it together. "Why?" he whispered.

In her place, Caroline thought she would have been cowering like a frightened animal, but Catherine seemed to straighten her posture even further as she held her chin high. "I thought she needed to know about you and Jenny, and since you obviously weren't going to tell her, I—"

Caroline had never heard him raise his voice.

With fists and teeth clenched, his chest heaved with every hostile breath. "It's my story, and I'll tell it whenever I am damn good and ready." His face distorted and he turned his back as he rubbed his neck with one hand. He spun back around, "How could you?"

Catherine was persistent, but gentle. "She needs to know. You love her, and she loves you. It's a part of who you are."

He took a deep breath, and his glare softened, but not enough for Caroline not to find him intimidating. "Cat, I love you, and you're my closest sister, but you shouldn't have—" He tangled his fingers in his hair, threatening to pull out every strand in frustration. "Just. . .not tonight." His shoulders sagged. "Please excuse us. I need to talk to Caroline."

Catherine walked over to him and gave him a hug. "I love you, too." She whispered into his ear. He was briefly taken aback and held her gaze before he nodded as she walked inside. Caroline sat frozen, apprehensive of what he would do now. Cade slowly approached her, his expression still stressed, his jaw still clenched. But his eyes with a sadness that touched the depths of her heart.

"Hi."

"Hey, you."

He offered his hand to help her up and she gingerly accepted it, fearful he was angry with her, too. A crooked grin relaxed the hardened lines. "Welcome to my own personal soap opera. See, your family isn't the only one with drama."

"Cade, I'm sorry. I didn't press her for information. She asked me if I knew about Jenny after she had told me about what happened

213

with Bruce. I swear, I wasn't snooping around or fishing for information."

He held her face between his palms and smiled. "It's okay, sweet girl. I'm not mad at you. I wish my sister had given me a hint that she planned to dredge up painful memories today. I could have better prepared myself for what I walked into."

"Please don't be upset with her. She didn't plan it, it just kind of came up in the conversation. Besides, she didn't get far before you walked up. Why were you so angry?"

"It's not a time of my life that I want to remember. In fact, I've tried very hard to forget it." He blew out a steadying breath and held Caroline's hands. "I know Catherine was only trying to help."

"She really was." Caroline beamed. "I adore her." There was a pause, and though she wanted to know what happened with Jenny, now was not the time. Not after everything he'd just learned about his younger sister. "So how bad was the news from Caitlyn?"

He shook his head. "She got lucky. Ryan's ex-wife is Jenny's aunt, and, even though she hates my sister, she didn't want to embarrass me or my family, so she's willing to let it go. However, Jenny's aunt is requesting to be transferred to another ship. I can completely understand that. I'm assuming my sister told you the rest of Caitlyn's story? The baby?"

Caroline nodded, but couldn't get past what Catherine had almost told her about Jenny. She wished Catherine had been able to at least finish her sentence. "What did Catherine whisper to you before she left just now?"

He stared at Caroline impassively for a moment, contemplating whether or not to tell her. Weary lines crinkled his brow. "I have learned to trust Catherine's instincts about things, especially regarding women." He inhaled through his nostrils and briefly closed his eyes as he released the slow breath. When he looked at her, his eyes matched the concern in his tone. "She's afraid you will leave me if you never learn about what happened."

Caroline's heart sank. Was Catherine right? Was she so frustrated with his elusiveness that she'd consider leaving him if he didn't tell her? Cade must have read her mind.

"Was she right?"

A voice screamed in her head. *No. Absolutely not, Cade. I love you more than anything. I want to be with you forever.* But the truth squashed the words. Her reaction, or lack of one, hurt him. She could tell.

"Please tell me she's wasn't right. Surely you wouldn't run because of something from my past? It's over, done with, and gone. I'm over it. That's why they call it the past."

"If you can't talk about it, clearly you're not over it." She wanted him to hold her, but when she stepped forward fully expecting him to whisk her up into his arms, he didn't move. He was unsure. He doubted her love for him. After all they had discussed in the past twenty-four hours, he doubted her. She couldn't blame him. And she stood there like an idiot. *Say something.*

She reached for his hand. This time, he let her hold it. "It's not gone, Cade. It's you. I wish you'd tell me, but I don't want to force you." She hugged him, and he slowly, cautiously placed his arms around her, squeezing ever-so-gently. Her cheek pressed against his chest and she whispered. "I wouldn't leave you."

His grip tightened and he let out a whimper. His walls weakened.

"I love you, Cade. I want to know everything about you. If you were truly over it, you'd be able to talk about it easier. Especially with me." She rubbed her hands along his back, a back that had carried the weight of grief for far too long. "Talk to me, please. I'm a good listener. I can help you move on."

He kissed the crook of her neck and whispered, "You already have. I'm sorry I've not been more open about things with you. It's taken me years to get to this point, and I know I'm not completely healed." Cade led her to the bench and they both sat, facing each other. "I won't go into the details, but Catherine's right, you deserve to know what happened, at the very least." He brusquely rubbed his face and breathed deeply.

"Jenny was my everything. I'd planned to propose the night I got back in town, but I got held up in a meeting at the Pentagon briefing the brass about our last mission. I didn't make it to the restaurant in time." Cade cleared his throat.

Uncomfortable with dredging up heartbreaking memories, he ran his hands along his thighs. "She left the restaurant before I could get there, and I couldn't call because I'd been in a meeting, then rushed to get into the air." He licked his lips and blinked back aggressive tears pushing their way to the surface.

Already on the verge of losing it herself, Caroline hoped he wouldn't cry. Seeing him cry would push her over the edge.

"I should've called. I didn't have a cell phone at the time, but I could've borrowed one, or used a pay phone. I was just in such a hurry to get here, I didn't. . . I didn't take the time. . ."

Caroline threaded her fingers through his, wishing she could ease his pain somehow. This brought him back in the moment. "So, Jenny left, clearly upset with me, and she had a car accident on the way home. She drowned in a canal."

To anyone else it would look like he was observing the weeds popping up through the cracks between the bricks in the ornate foundation surrounding the fountain, but Caroline knew from the emptiness in his gaze that he was a million miles away. The memories of Jenny tortured him, and here she was pushing him to confront them.

Dredging this up was clearly excruciating for him, and she'd heard enough to know he wasn't purposely hiding anything from her, so she let him off the hook. "You don't have to continue. I get it. I love you." She kissed his hand. "And I promise to be more open-minded from now on. I'm sorry for pushing you to reveal a painful part of your life before you were ready. It was very selfish of me."

"Not selfish. Understandable. I'm sorry I've kept it from you for this long." He kissed the center of her forehead and pulled her close in a tight embrace.

"For so long I haven't allowed anyone to get close enough to rescue me from the darkness." The rumble of his deep voice vibrated through to her core. "I've just recently seen a ray of light at the end of that black tunnel." He pulled back, gently he ran his fingers through her hair and down the length of her jaw. "You, Caroline." His eyes sparkled. "You are the brightness that has given me hope and the zest for life to save me from myself. For that, I am forever grateful. I told you, you're my lifeline. I didn't know it was possible for me to love someone as much as I loved Jenny. More, even. I will always be indebted to you."

Her cheeks burned. She turned her mouth into the palm of his hand and kissed it before looking back into his golden eyes. "I'm crazy in love with you. I'll be honest, after hearing your story, I want you more now than I ever have."

He smiled and stood, pulling her up with him. "Baby, you have no idea how badly I *want* you to want me. I wasn't planning for all of the speed bumps tonight. It's put a kink in my chain, so to speak."

"What?"

He kissed her. A deep, hungry, passionate kiss that stole a part of her soul. The ground beneath her crumbled as she floated into his embrace. The magnetic force holding her to him was more powerful than anything she'd ever experienced. She truly wanted to be one with this man. Cade Beauregard was her other half. Of that she was certain. All doubts she had before regarding Trevor or marriage in general dissolved as she stood wrapped in his sheltering, passionate embrace. He smiled when she struggled to catch her breath after their mind blowing kiss.

So this was love. Lightheaded and warm, she couldn't keep her hands off of him.

He chuckled, "I will never again wait for that perfect opportunity. I'll make my own. I'm seizing the moment," he winked. Cade flashed his dazzling smile and knelt down on one knee holding her hands in his and causing her heart to leap into her throat. For the first time in her life, she wasn't frightened by this sight.

His gleaming, boyish smile eased her fears, and she almost couldn't wait for the words to pass his lips. "Rachel Caroline Fontenot, it would be my honor, and my extreme pleasure, if you would agree to be my wife and live the rest of your life by my side." He flashed that crooked smile again. "I want to grow old and wrinkly with you."

"Yes! Absolutely!" she squealed. But then she paused. "On one condition."

His brow furrowed, and he stood. "Sure, what is it?"

She smiled. "Can we make lots of babies first? You know, before the whole old and wrinkly part?"

He hugged her tightly, spinning her around in a circle. "You got it, babe. We can practice, and practice, and practice as much as you want to. I will happily and eagerly fulfill that condition."

"Great! Let's start this weekend!"

"What? This weekend? Don't you want to get married first?"

"Yes! Let's get married this weekend! I don't want to wait any longer. I want to be with you and start our lives together."

"Okay, slow down. I don't want to rush you into a wedding. You've been through that already, and I won't put you through it again."

"You're not rushing me. I'm rushing you. I am in love with you, and I believe I have been since the first week I met you. It's just taken me forever to realize it. Like you said before, chemistry is chemistry, and we are great together. The only reason I hesitated before was because I didn't understand why you were so secretive about your past. I just didn't know. Now, thanks to your sister, I know you have nothing to hide but painful memories. You're perfect."

He shook his head. "I'm not perfect, Caroline."

Caroline hugged him tighter. "You're perfect for me," she whispered. "That's close enough."

"Now *that* I'll agree with." He kissed her again, taking her breath away. "How about this. . .you and your mom go to California with Kristy and spend a week or two while I get some things taken care of here?"

Caroline frowned. "Two weeks?"

He chuckled. "It's not that long, and I'll be able to sleep at night knowing you're not in danger. Someone is after your family and if you're not here, they can't hurt you." He pulled her close. "I'll ask Runway to accompany y'all, which I'm sure won't be difficult with Kristy there," he mumbled.

"I can call in a few of my other SEAL team buddies to help, and, with the local police, we'll get this nipped in the bud before you get back." He beamed.

Caroline favorably considered his suggestion. "That's a good idea. Kristy's been bugging me to come out to Cali with her, anyway. And I'd love to get in some beach time."

Cade agreed. "Besides, I'm sure Kristy wants to make your dress. That will give her time, and allow me a chance to get the marriage license, find a nice place—wait, where do you want to get married? Do you want me to check with the church?"

"No, let's get married in New Orleans. We could do it at that historic hotel we stayed in last summer when you took me on the most romantic date of my life. Maybe this time I'll actually get to follow through with my seduction."

"Honey, you won't find any objections from me. I've been waiting for a replay of that moment for a year."

"I would love a small intimate ceremony with just our close family and friends. We could ask the preacher, Mr. Stevens, to perform the ceremony in the hotel rather than the church so we could just go straight upstairs and focus on the honeymoon."

He frowned playfully. "Why, Miss Fontenot, are you using me for my body?"

She wrapped her arms around his neck. "Maybe. Will that be a problem, Mr. Beauregard?"

"No, ma'am."

"Good, you'd better eat your Wheaties and start training for this marathon, Sailor. I've got a thirst that needs some serious quenching."

"I'm in my prime," he grinned wickedly. "Bring it on."

She kissed him again, as if her life depended on it as they walked hand-in-hand to announce the glorious news to his family. Her new family.

After the congratulations and hugs from his family, and the surprising and amazingly sweet toast from his reticent father, she and Cade went for a long walk on his family's property and talked. He shared about his childhood, what it was like growing up in the bayou with four sisters, and joining the Navy. She asked him about his sports, his hobbies, and his band. He asked her about her childhood, where she grew up in Arkansas and went to school, what sports she played, if any, and the boys she dated. She shared the story of her first kiss and asked about his.

"There is no kiss in my life, first or not, that could ever compare to the way I feel when your lips touch mine," he said. If his words hadn't left her breathless enough, his lips did when he pulled her into his sheltering arms and kissed away every care or worry she ever had. "I may as well have never had a kiss from anyone else but you because yours is all that matters." Cade hugged her tightly and whispered, "I promise to kiss you every day for the rest of your life."

TWENTY-TWO

"This place is incredible. Paradise on Earth." Emily closed her eyes and breathed in the salty Pacific air welcoming them to the Santa Monica Pier.

The trendy L.A. eatery located by the pier offered popular dance music and signature drinks. Runway ordered them fried calamari with a refreshing cocktail sauce.

Their outside table allowed the crashing waves to add a pleasant ambience. Caroline relished the soft breeze that smelled of the briny ocean as it kissed her skin, and in that peaceful moment, she lost herself in the low-lying sun's reflection on the water.

She imagined walking barefoot along the beach holding Cade's hand, kissing him as the setting sun cast a golden-orange glow, spreading warmth throughout her body. The shrill tone of her cell phone disrupted her fantasy, causing her to flinch, spilling a full glass of water.

"Oh, man! Grab your phones. I'm sorry."

Kristy laughed, "That's it, you're cut off. That water is clearly too strong for you." She unwrapped her silverware and tossed her cloth napkin on the liquid. "Or maybe you're just not used to the weight from that new rock on your finger," she teased.

Embarrassment burned Caroline's face and neck. "Yeah, just call me Grace."

Runway eyed Caroline carefully as she snatched up her phone and wiped the screen on her shirt before frantically spreading cloth napkins over the mess. She hadn't heard from Cade or her father since she arrived and her imagination ran wild. She was a nervous wreck.

"Calm down. It's just a little water. We're fine." Runway winked, "Only sugar melts."

"Oh, well I should move then," Emily quipped as water dribbled onto her leg.

Caroline grinned and anxiously answered her phone while they shared a laugh.

Her dad was just checking on them, more so Emily than anyone. As Caroline wondered about their story, she realized she longed for her parents to get back together. That would probably be possible if April wasn't in the picture.

The meal was delicious, but Kristy was eager to take everyone on a tour of her favorite city. Runway generously paid for the meal, and they all walked toward the beach.

Kristy looped her arm through Caroline's and sighed contentedly as they strolled along the bike trail near the pier. The waves serenely whooshed onto the beach. "Isn't the West coast just amazing?"

"Gorgeous."

"Clear, fresh air, the tranquil ocean, toes in the sand. Much better for the soul than blazing heat and soupy humidity. Don't you want to move out here so we can hang out every day again?"

Caroline snorted. "I wish, but my Cajun fiancé would disagree. There aren't many alligators or crawfish boils out here." She stopped to lean against a railing on the pier and looked out over the water. Runway had told them Navy SEALs had salt water in their veins. The ocean was a mandatory staple in their lives. Runway chose the Pacific; Cade, the Gulf of Mexico. She was glad, though. Otherwise, she never would have met him. Her mother tapped Caroline's shoulder and pointed to the horizon where two dolphins arced and played in the water.

"Mom, how did you and dad meet?"

"What?" Caroline's question had caught her mom off guard.

"Well, you're from Arkansas, and Dad's lived in Golden Meadow his whole life. I just realized I never knew how your paths crossed."

She smiled. "I was nineteen. I had gone to New Orleans with my church youth group for mission work in the lower ninth ward. We ate lunch in the French Quarter." She slowly rubbed her arms, her eyes distant with the memory, "It was freezing in the restaurant. I'd gotten up to go to the restroom, not paying close attention, and didn't realize I'd walked into the men's room. He was drying his hands and looked up, shocked, then amused." She hugged herself and smiled wistfully. "He was so handsome, and my heart raced from his appraising look."

"I thought he was in the ladies room, so I stared at him expectantly, waiting for him to realize and bolt out. Only he stared back, smiling curiously." She thoughtfully puckered her lips. "That crooked grin, reddish-brown hair, and those intelligent green eyes that sparkled with amusement. . ." She fooled with her necklace and smiled. "I was smitten. Then I saw the urinals," she chortled.

"My face turned five different shades of red, and tears sprang to my eyes. I'd never even kissed a boy, and there I stood, humiliated." Emily shook her head and dabbed at her eyes. "Oh," she breathed, "if I'd been thirty-seconds earlier. . ."

Caroline laughed. She'd done better than that. At least when her mother trespassed, she hadn't run face-first into his wet, just-showered, exposed manhood.

"He handled it well. Asked me to calm down before we walked out so people wouldn't call the cops on him," Emily laughed. "Then he asked for my name and if he could take me out to dinner." She stared out at the ocean, her eyes glistening with the reflection of that sweet moment.

"Similar to mine and Cade's first meeting."

Kristy and Runway laughed, but Emily raised an eyebrow. "Yes, I heard about that. Something about a shower?"

Not realizing she didn't know the whole story, Caroline sobered up quickly and gave her the edited version. "Apparently, I made an impression on him," Caroline stated proudly.

"Mmm-hmm, or vice versa," her mom said.

They approached Runways' car and Caroline interrupted his laughter, "Runway, have you heard from Cade today?"

"No, I haven't. Have you?"

Caroline shook her head, worry crushing her. She'd called him a couple of times that afternoon, but he didn't answer. Unwelcome goosebumps cloaked her skin. A sinking feeling twisted her stomach.

""He's okay, Caroline."

Caroline searched Runway's eyes for reassurance. "But he usually calls. . ."

"He will. He's probably busy following a trail. Beau can take care of himself. He's more worried about you right now than you are about him. Trust me."

"But. . .I'm with you," she stated matter-of-factly.

He flashed his megawatt smile and opened the door to his luxury, ruby-red Aston Martin convertible. "Yes, bella, you are. And Beau would have my head if I let anything happen to you. Please get in and buckle up." Caroline rolled her eyes and squeezed into the tiny back seat. She felt safe with him, but niggling anxiety lurked in the back of her mind.

Kristy insisted Runway drive them to Beverly Hills to show off where she worked. They strolled along the Hollywood Walk of Fame pointing out the stars of their favorite celebrities. Kristy and Emily dashed into a trendy department store, but Caroline opted to wait outside with Runway. She wasn't in much of a shopping mood.

Cade's face flickered through Caroline's mind and she experienced the same tunnel vision with flashes as before. A surge of fear plunged into her throat, and she stumbled, but Runway quickly steadied her. She tried to play it off by checking her phone again. It was eleven o'clock in Louisiana. She hoped Cade was sleeping soundly in his bed. When she looked up, Runway's watchful gaze revealed he'd observed everything, catching more than just her fall. His penetrating green eyes bored through her, but he didn't push her for information.

"You okay?" She nodded. His stare lingered, but he only clenched his jaw. "What would you like to do tomorrow?"

"I think I'd like to just hang out on the beach. Relax and bury my toes in the sand."

Runway agreed and smiled. but it didn't reach his eyes. "I think that would be a great idea. The ocean is very tranquil and calming. I know a great Tavern on Hermosa beach where we can have lunch. Also, there's a long pier where you can walk to the end and feel like you're standing in the middle of the ocean. It's a lovely place to free your mind. I went there a lot after I got out of the military."

Either Runway was surprisingly intuitive or she was painfully obvious. She avoided eye contact, afraid he would see everything that was in her thoughts.

"I know we've only known each other briefly, Caroline, but I am here for you if you ever need to talk. I can read people pretty well, and I can tell you have a lot on your mind.

"Thanks. Just worried about my family," she mumbled.

Caroline wiggled her toes, grinding tiny pebbles of sand between them, and buried them deeper into the cool earth. She loved the beach and everything about it. The smell, the water, the waves, even the sand that unwelcomely sneaked its way into all the little cracks and crevices of anything that touched it.

The shrieking seagulls scavenged for their dinner along the beach full of snacking sunbathers as pelicans surfed the breeze before swooping into the ocean for theirs. A soft breeze swept over Caroline's body chilling her bikini-clad skin. A drastic change from the Louisiana summer, but not cold. The goose bumps confused her and she brushed off the uneasy shiver. Runway's words echoed in her head. *"It's a great place to free your mind."* That's exactly what she needed.

"How about a rum runner for old time's sake?" Kristy asked.

"Sounds great."

"I'll get them. You ladies stay put," Runway said.

Caroline put her cover-up on and gathered her things. "I'm going out to the end of the pier." She smiled at him, "I want to see what you were talking about."

"Why don't you both go and I'll bring your drinks out to you." He kissed Kristy and sprinted off to the Tavern as Kristy and Caroline walked toward the pier. It stretched far out into the ocean for probably a hundred yards. When they got to the end, Caroline did as he'd suggested and blocked out the rest of the world with her hands like race horse blinders. He was right. A sense of tranquility washed over Caroline.

"Kris, you've got to try this," she murmured. "It's awesome."

The orange and turquoise sunset was now a muted gold as the apricot sphere on the horizon sank into the depths of the sea. Simply breathtaking. Behind them, however, were menacing gray thunder clouds rolling in to ruin their lovely evening. The waves were already rebelling with their choppy clapping sounds as they slapped the thick posts supporting the pier.

"Did I ever tell you why Trevor had come in town?" Caroline asked.

"No. Why?"

Caroline shrugged and turned around to sit on the railing at the edge of the pier. "He told me he was still in love with me and wanted me back."

"Figures," Kristy scoffed. "Bastard."

"Cade showed up and saved the day. Trevor ended up going home with Jessica Robicheaux. I think they've been seeing each other." Caroline turned, feet still on the bottom rail of the pier, and stretched her arms out. Water as far as she could see.

Kristy rolled her eyes. "Still the same old Trevor."

"Not my problem. Not anymore." Caroline tilted her head back and closed her eyes to let the ocean breeze soothe her worried soul.

"He's a Callahan. That whole jacked-up lineage has issues with you." Kristy retorted.

At the mention of that name, someone jerked Caroline's left shoulder, pulling her down and spinning her around in one motion. She gasped, almost falling before she could steady herself and grasp the railing. Her heart lurched into her throat, stealing her voice. She clawed at the constraint around her neck. At the entrance of the pier, in the split second before she realized who had assaulted her, she saw Runway's alarmed expression as he dropped their drinks and sprinted toward her. Through the cloudy mist of the apparition, she made out the disturbingly familiar, piercing blue eyes.

TWENTY-THREE

"You!" she managed to choke out just before she catapulted backwards over the railing into the rough, icy water of the Pacific Ocean. The angry waves tossed her body about until she slammed into the large pilings like a rag doll. Her head ached, but she fought to remain conscious. Kristy's scream resonated as Caroline struggled for composure to stay afloat, but the cloudy face with the menacing eyes glared murderously as he pushed her straight down into the water. The unusual force thrusting her to the bottom of the ocean was too powerful to fight, and the increasing pressure crushed her chest, causing a painful pop in her ears. Caroline yelped, sucking in a mouthful of salt water.

Runway's hand appeared in the shadowy water before his face did, and Caroline frantically reached for him. The fear in his eyes didn't help, but a brief moment of relief filled her when he grasped her wrist. The invisible force tugged against him, squeezing her throat tighter, pulling her deeper into the inky darkness. She fought against this evil, but all the oxygen was expelled from her burning lungs and she was losing consciousness. She gave one final burst of kicks to assist Runway's rescue, but her efforts were wasted against the relentless force claiming her body.

The frigid Pacific water pierced her skin like a thousand tiny needles, numbing her from the inside out. She no longer felt pain. She watched him smile malevolently as the merciless sea finally relinquished its punishing hold on her, and she succumbed to the darkness.

"Runway, how's it going?"

"Beau, something's happened," he said, tensely.

"What?" Beau's blood ran cold, weakening his knees.

"Before you flip out, Caroline is fine. She's in the ER getting some tests run, but she is okay."

"The ER? What the. . . Runway. Come on, man. What the hell happened?"

"We were on the beach, and she and Kristy walked out on the pier while I ran to get drinks. When I got close to the base of the pier Caroline was standing on the bottom rung of the rail with her arms spread looking out over the ocean. She and Kristy were fine. In a matter of seconds, Caroline twisted around, and reached up with both hands to grab her throat like someone was choking her. I dropped the drinks and ran as fast as I could."

Cade spit out every curse word he could think of and dragged his hand down his face.

"I ran with everything I had, but she launched over the railing. Kristy reached for her, but wasn't fast enough."

Cade shouted and slammed his fist on his steering wheel.

"I started running before she fell, so I made it there in twenty seconds or less, and immediately dove in after her." Runway sighed, his voice lowering. "Beau, she was terrified, but no one was touching her when she flipped over the rail."

"Who the hell was trying to choke her? What do you mean no one was touching her? Were there other people on the pier?"

"No, it was just her and Kristy, and they were standing about three feet apart. Caroline was up on the rail, Beau."

"So you jumped in, then what happened?"

"I swam down to reach her, and you know we've gone really deep before. She was way too deep to have just fallen in seconds before I got to her, and she was fighting to swim," Runway added. "She was

229

at least twenty feet down, Beau. Her body should have floated before she reached that depth. The water was choppy from a storm rolling in."

"Dammit," Cade shouted.

"The paramedics said she suffered a mild case of hypothermia, and had a large bump on her head where she must have hit the pilings. But that's not the part I'm most worried about."

Cade's temper surged. "Then why don't you tell me what *is* the part you're worried about, Runway? Come on, man! I'm aging by the second."

"When I got to her and started swimming back up, there was resistance. Like she was stuck on something. I checked and her foot wasn't hung on anything, but she started sinking downward again. I swear something was pulling her from my grasp. Like someone had her by the ankles pulling against my efforts to save her."

Cade released a slow hissing breath as he pictured an unseen force trying to steal Caroline away from him. There had to be another explanation. "Was it the current in the water? You said it was choppy. Maybe she got caught—"

"It wasn't the current." He let out a reluctant sigh. "Listen, I know you don't want to hear this, but I think it was George. Kristy said when Caroline whipped around she whispered, 'You' like she recognized someone. Then Caroline clawed her throat, as if trying to pull someone's hand away or loosen his fingers. I think he choked her before shoving her into the water. Then he followed her, pushing deeper and deeper. When I saved her, I think he was holding on to her feet to keep me from bringing her back up."

Cade trusted Runway, but an invisible enemy was difficult to swallow. Caroline was clumsy, after all, maybe she fell. And it probably took Runway a little longer to get to her than he'd like to admit. Cade gripped his phone, the flimsy plastic groaning from the pressure. There had to be a logical explanation. He'd always believed that ghosts couldn't touch people. Haunt, yes. Hurt, no.

"So why did he stop? If he was pulling against you, how were you able to save her? If it was George, he doesn't need to breathe. He could have just kept her down there until both of you drowned."

Runway paused. "I don't know." His clipped tone lowered, pleading with Cade to believe him. "I swam with every ounce of strength I had, refusing to let her go, so maybe he ran out of energy." Runway cleared his throat. "She's been acting strange since we got here. She's worried about you. I think there's something going on, but she's not talking to me about it."

Cade rubbed his forehead in frustration, finishing with his fingers in his hair. He released the breath he'd been holding. "I'm sorry, man. I don't blame you. You did great. She's alive, and for that, I'll owe you forever. Thank you."

"So what now?" Runway asked.

"Come home." Cade wouldn't sleep until Caroline was in his arms again.

Caroline relished the feel of Cade's strong arms around her again as he hugged her tightly. She hadn't made it completely off the escalator before he crashed in to her, sweeping her off her feet. He held her so tight she thought she might break. But she didn't dare stop him.

"I'm so glad you're okay," he breathed. "I'm never letting you go again."

Caroline pulled back to look at him. His haggard appearance spoke volumes. The circles beneath his red-rimmed eyes, two-day stubble, and his constant forehead crease confirmed his worry. "Cade, I'm okay. Runway took care of me like you asked him to. Let's go home."

The drive from New Orleans was quiet. Too quiet. Cade hadn't asked her anything about what happened. She wondered if he believed what Runway told him. It didn't matter if he believed her. She knew what she saw, and it was no hallucination. She didn't feel like talking about it, and Cade was exhausted, so she squashed bringing up that topic.

"So were you able to find anything more on the shooter?" Caroline asked. She hoped her disastrous trip wasn't in vain.

Cade's silence lasted longer than it should have, and Caroline wondered if he heard her. She opened her mouth to repeat the question when his quiet voice halted her mid-breath. "Yes."

He brushed his hand through his unruly hair and huffed. "And no."

She frowned. "What does that mean?"

"We found a piece of jewelry near a tree on the side of the house where the shot was fired. A bracelet. Claire said it looked like one of April's."

She knew it! But there was no possible way April could've been the shooter. Caroline saw her beforehand, all dressed up in a red formal gown, and immediately after the shooting. Not a hair was out of place. Confusion set in, and Cade didn't seem eager to share any more details.

"And?" Caroline pressed.

"My buddy on the local police force did some checking in to April's record." Cade gave a sideways glance and focused back on the road. "April's gone."

Caroline's jaw dropped. "What? What do you mean *gone*? Like, dead? Or missing?"

"Missing." Cade's grip on the steering wheel tightened.

"Eddie doesn't know where she is?"

Cade shook his head, jaw tight, and eyes glued to the road. "April has an alias. Her other name is Ana Morales. Neither name has any record of life. No credit cards, no birth certificates, no social security cards. . . *Nothing*."

He uneasily looked at her and pursed his lips. "It's like she never existed."

TWENTY-FOUR

The next week crawled by as Caroline anxiously awaited the happiest day of her life. The day after Cade proposed, she'd woken up and admired her new engagement ring. To avoid misplacing it, or having a ghost steal it like what happened with her last engagement ring, she refused to take this one off her finger. Thank goodness she hadn't lost it in the ocean when whichever deceased Callahan tried to kill her. She pushed the cold blue eyes from her mind and studied her ring. It was perfect. Cade knew exactly what kind of ring she would love. A single round diamond with a halo of emerald stones set in 18K gold.

Eddie gave Caroline Rachel's gorgeous ring to wear as her *Something Old*. In pristine condition, it hadn't belonged to its owner long enough to look worn. The dainty round diamond was flanked by small, round emeralds. Cade later told her the ring was why he chose to have emeralds in the halo of her setting. He said it was simply too ironic that she and Rachel shared the same birthday, name, birthstone, and physical features. He wanted to continue the similarities.

Her *Something Borrowed* was her mother's locket. Caroline's grandmother had given it to Emily when she was a little girl. It had Emily's parents' wedding portrait in it, and Caroline had never gone a day of her life when she didn't see her mother wearing this locket. It was a very special piece of jewelry her mother cherished, therefore

233

Caroline would cherish it as well. Her *Something New* was a pair of Kristy's favorite designer shoes to wear with her gown. Kristy knew Caroline hated high-heels, so she chose an exquisite pair of low-heeled D'orsay wedding slippers in silver glitter fabric. Perfect for Caroline and surprisingly comfortable.

Kristy had worked diligently to tweak the beautiful gown she'd handmade for Caroline's wedding last summer. Caroline didn't know how Kristy managed it, but it looked like a completely different dress. Once strapless, now with lace cap sleeves that came to a V-shape in the back. Kristy adjusted and customized the gown to fit Caroline's relationship with Cade so no thoughts or memories of Trevor would barge in during her special occasion. Just above the hem of the dress were clear and pearl beads hand sewn in an intricate design resembling anchors with wings—in honor of Cade's time in the Navy.

Her wedding day had finally come. Caroline smoothed the snowy white fabric on the hanger and adjusted her bodice in the mirror. She had been thrilled to see Remy at the rehearsal dinner last night. He defied the odds and walked in with a smile, using the designer cane she'd bought for him in California. Caroline was glad Remy would be here for her special day. She didn't expect to see April after what Cade had told her, but she did wonder if Claire would make an appearance. Kristy slipped the wedding gown over Caroline's silky undergarments and fluffed the billowing skirt around Caroline ankles.

"Wow, Kris. You really are amazing. This is incredible. Cade is going to love it."

Kristy smirked at Caroline's reflection as she smoothed the bodice of her own royal blue gown. "I know. The adjustments I made to this gown make you look as modest and innocent as you really are. They accentuate your purity and wholesomeness while also boosting your assets." Kristy winked.

Emily walked in wearing a huge smile. "As if she needed any of that. Cade would love her if she had buck teeth and ten kids already."

"Gee, thanks. You're right, though. I'm a lucky girl."

Kristy aggressively cinched the corset-style lacing at Caroline's waist, catching her attention in the mirror. "No crazy thoughts about Trevor today, right?"

"Of course not. If there were I wouldn't be getting married."

"Good. I'd really hate to have to kick your butt and risk ruining my masterpiece. Does he know you're getting hitched today?"

Caroline shrugged. "Don't know. Probably not. I didn't tell too many people. I wanted it to be a small, intimate ceremony with no interruptions or possibilities of anything going wrong."

"Things like attempted murder and such?"

"Yeah, among other things," Caroline mumbled.

Kristy lowered her voice, "Has Cade said anything about what happened in Cali?"

"No. I haven't brought it up." Caroline caught Kristy's attention in the mirror. "I don't think he believes me. I think he thinks I just tripped."

Kristy rolled her eyes. "Oh, that's crap. I was there and there was no tripping to it. You flew over the railing of the pier."

"I know." Caroline brushed her fingers across her neck. "But I don't know how to make him believe it. He wasn't there." She shivered. "I just hope nothing like that ever happens again. I may not be so lucky next time."

Kristy hugged her. "You're going to be fine. We'll get to the bottom of this. For now you concentrate on your special day." Kristy winked, "And your special night."

Emily adjusted a lock of Caroline's hair. "I'm glad you are doing this, sweetie. I truly believe you and Cade are meant for each other. He will make you very happy."

Kristy placed the delicate, three-quarter-length veil on Caroline's head and smoothed it around her shoulders, down to her behind. "There. Perfection."

"Oh, my goodness, Kristy. You're so talented. This gown is incredible."

"You make my job easy. You look gorgeous, C. More beautiful than I've ever seen you before." Kristy's eyes misted, surprising Caroline. She'd rarely seen Kristy cry.

Kristy hugged her, handed her the *Something Blue*—a fragrant bouquet of royal blue delphinium and powder blue hyacinth—and helped her to the door where Eddie waited anxiously. He was dashing in his tux and shook his head in wonderment. "Hello, sweetheart. You are a beautiful bride. Cade is a lucky man."

"Thanks, Dad. Did Claire come?"

His gaze dropped. "No, cher. She said to give you her love."

Sure she did. She gave her best smile. "Okay, we'd better get moving so Cade doesn't think I changed my mind."

"Yes, ma'am. We certainly don't want that to happen."

Eddie looped his arm through hers and led her through the doors of the same historic hotel on Poydras Street she and Cade had stayed in last summer.

They had been lucky enough to catch a last minute cancellation. The elite wedding and reception package included a honeymoon suite "fit for royalty," complete with matching his and hers bathrobes, champagne and hors d'oeuvres in their room, breakfast for two, and a keepsake holiday ornament. Everything had fallen into place, as if the stars had aligned just for them.

Cade stood beneath an arch covered with white roses strategically placed in front of marble columns. His golden-brown hair, trimmed, and face smoothly shaven, he flashed a blinding smile that stole the breath from her already heaving lungs. Caroline's heart raced upon seeing his handsome face, and she struggled not to speed walk the rest of the way. Instead, she concentrated on not snagging her heel on the hem of her dress or the crimson rug lining the aisle.

Cade's relaxed stance and clasped hands would have fooled her if it weren't for him rapidly tapping his thumbs together. She grinned as he nervously shifted his weight, drinking her in with each step she took. His matching blue carnation boutonniere accented his designer black tux and crisp white, silk handkerchief. She was sure Runway, who stood by his side, had something to do with Cade's attire. The afternoon sun cast its muted beams through the frosted glass in the high Palladian windows creating a romantic glow throughout the room. The end of each row was dressed with royal blue and white satin ribbons intricately wrapped around small bouquets of white roses. The rows of white fabric chairs were filled with the smiling faces of those closest to the Beauregard and Fontenot families. With the surrounding perfection, and her alluring fiancé eager to spend eternity with her, Caroline questioned reality.

"Dad, am I dreaming?" she whispered.

"No, sweetheart. This is completely real."

"He looks incredible."

"Yes, but nowhere near as much as you do."

They approached the altar where Mr. Stevens, the preacher from the church she and Cade had been attending, asked, "Who gives this woman to be married to this man?"

Her dad's chest expanded as he drew in a deep breath, smiled, and patted her hand that was wrapped around his arm, made everything about this moment worth coming down here to meet him last year. He answered with a resounding, "Her mother and I proudly give her to this fine young man." He kissed her cheek, and placed her hand in Cade's.

The ceremony was everything she could have imagined. She once thought she wanted the big fairytale wedding, but that's not what she wanted at all. The small, intimate ceremony blew away any fairytale she'd ever heard, and the groom was even better. She glided through the motions, performing as if she knew exactly what to do, but all she could think about was that she could now spend every moment of every day with the man standing before her. Who would have ever thought that the voice she heard below her window that morning last summer would now be vowing to love, honor, and cherish her until the day she died?

"Caroline, for years I've avoided facing the demons in my past. I chose to exist in a sea of depression and darkness. I was afraid to let anyone in. To expose the shredded nerve in what was left of my heart. And then I met you."

The corner of his mouth tilted and his eyes sparkled. "Your vibrant personality, enchanting smile, adorable innocence, and fiery spirit lit up my world. You showed me how to have fun again, how to care for someone besides myself, and why I want to wake up every morning. I'm forever grateful your crazy curiosity led you to me that hot day last summer. You captured my heart by simply being yourself, and you made me the luckiest man in the world when you chose me." Cade kissed her naked ring finger. "Thank you for finding me. For accepting me. For loving me." His voice cracked and Caroline nearly came undone. "I will love you until I take my last breath. For eternity. In this life and the next."

How could Caroline follow that? She could hardly talk, much less think of something equally as amazing. She swiped her tears.

"I love you so much." Caroline brushed her fingertips across his smooth jaw. "More than our bodies collided that day. Our souls joined and we were meant to be together. I was naïve. . . and maybe a little too stubborn," Kristy quietly laughed and coughed, causing Cade and Runway to chuckle. Caroline playfully rolled her eyes before gazing deeply into Cade's. "I wanted you then, but didn't know it. I'm so happy you persisted and showed me the light. I'm yours forever, Caden Luke. For eternity."

They exchanged rings and Cade paused to look at her.

"I've been waiting a long time to do this." He lifted her veil, dipped her back, arching her over his knee and whispered, "*Mi aime Jou.*" And then he kissed her into oblivion.

Friends and family gathered around, clapping, whooping and hollering, especially Cade's alligator hunting buddies.

"I love you, too," Caroline said, after she caught her breath. She fanned her burning face, certain she was blushing.

Cade smirked and kissed her nose. "Yep. I've still got it."

They dined on fine gourmet Southern fare and danced on the designated black and white marble floor until it was time to cut the cake.

Cade was very careful as he delicately placed a small bite of strawberry-filled cake into her mouth. But she wasn't so kind. She graciously stuffed his mouth while smearing icing across his cheek. He didn't mind, but then he kissed her immediately afterward and rubbed the icing back onto her face, much to the thrill of the guests.

As the celebration wound down, Caroline's nerves frazzled. This was it—the beginning of her honeymoon. Everything she held dear, her heart and body to be given to Cade.

They hugged their parents goodbye and headed to the elevators. Cade eased her anxiety with a passionate kiss while they rode the car up to the honeymoon suite. She was barely aware that the doors opened as he scooped her into his arms and carried her across the threshold of their suite.

He set her down and turned on soft music. She ogled the foyer to their elegant suite. To her left stood an antique grandfather clock facing a red fabric-covered bench on her right, and straight ahead was a majestic fireplace flanked by two wall sconces that resembled torches. Between two aged emerald green divans, a round wooden coffee table held a tray of luscious fresh fruit and chocolate with two crystal flute glasses and a bottle of expensive champagne.

Caroline wandered into the bedroom while Cade carried the tray into the kitchen. She turned her phone off and dropped it in her purse before checking her reflection in the mirror. Could be the lighting, but Caroline noticed a change in her appearance. Happiness shone through the stress from the past few weeks and she inhaled. Tonight she would finally get what she'd dreamed of for so long. To experience the unmitigated pleasure of making love to the man of her dreams. Her soul mate. She eyed the bed in the reflection behind her. She ran her hand along the carved wood of the headboard.

The polished mahogany four-poster bed framed a luxurious golden silk damask bedspread that she sank into when she sat. Candles radiantly flickered in brass wall sconces, the flames licking at the walls, casting shadows that danced to the rhythm of the music. The soft glow emitted an enchanting mood of passion and sensuality. Caroline's body zinged with heated anticipation. Cade popped open the bottle of champagne and filled the glasses. His eyes blazed with flaming desire. A slow burn descended, warming her insides down to her loins.

Her face flooded scarlet, and she fidgeted with her arms, not quite sure what she should do with them.

Cade placed the glasses on the counter beside her, and gently held her hands. "Baby, look at me."

She forced herself to focus on nothing but his golden eyes.

"Breathe. Everything is okay. Are you nervous?"

She nodded.

"Don't be. I promise tonight will be the best night of your entire life. You just have to trust me."

"I trust you," she whispered.

"We'll take it slow. You can set the pace. No pressure. But first, let's dance."

"Dance? You want to dance?"

"Yes, ma'am, I do." He held out his hand "May I?"

"Of course." She kicked off the shoes cramping her tired feet.

He took her hand and spun her around as he looked her up and down.

"Have I told you how incredibly beautiful you are?"

"Once or twice." He pulled her close and they swayed to the music.

"Don't tell my wife, she may get jealous."

"Hmm, I was under the impression that you weren't into jealous girls. Perhaps you should've shopped around a bit more."

"Not an option. She stole my heart the first time I met her," he looked deeply into her eyes, "and I never got it back."

Caroline swallowed and licked her lips. "That's unfortunate, Mr. Beauregard."

He pressed his warm, smooth cheek to hers, whispering in her ear. "Not really. I don't want it back. It's yours to keep."

"I shall take great care of it then," she breathlessly replied.

He kissed her neck, just below her jaw, and his kisses trailed down her neck, gently brushing her collar bone. His hands roamed her body, igniting her arousal. Her heart fluttered and she thought she might spontaneously combust.

She suddenly wasn't nervous anymore. She was quite ready for this milestone in her life. Adrenaline pumped through her blood and combined with her nerves, her body quivered with fervor. She felt gloriously sexy and bold—liberating.

"Cade?"

"Hmm?" He muttered between kisses.

"Make love to me."

He pulled his head back and smiled. "Yes, ma'am."

He led her to the bed scattered with fragrant pink and red rose petals. He pulled her into his arms and they slow-danced as he sang along to a love song softly in her ear. She closed her eyes and allowed herself to get lost in the moment. She could listen to his smooth voice forever. After his serenade, Cade moved behind her and slowly unlaced the back of her dress. He ran his hand across her bare shoulders as his lips trailed behind it, kissing that particular spot between her shoulder blades, causing shivers to rock her body. This triggered something within him. He groaned and gently pushed her dress the rest of the way down.

She closed her eyes and leaned her head back. He took the opportunity to kiss her throat. He walked around in front of her.

Instantly self-conscious, her cheeks burned. "This is the lingerie Kristy gave me."

His eyes blazed with passion and a smile slowly crept across his face. "She has great taste. I'll be sure to send her a thank-you card." He smirked and cleared his throat.

She wasn't positive, but he seemed nervous, too.

His fingers followed his eyes as he caressed his way down across her stomach to her garter belt.

"Your skin is so soft." His eyes sharpened, his tone authoritative. "Please tell me if I do anything that you don't like or if I hurt you in any way. I'm serious."

She nodded, trying hard not to explode from desire.

He slid his fingers along the smooth part of her exposed thigh above her thigh-high stockings, releasing the straps holding them up. "You're so sexy. Just beautiful." His whispers were raspy. "And you're finally mine."

Cade rolled the stockings down each of her legs. She took a deep breath. Her heightened senses were overwhelming. He was literally driving her wild. Caroline pressed her hands upon his chest and forced him back against the edge of the bed, and removed his bow tie. She kissed his mouth, biting his lower lip, while her hands carefully worked on the intricate buttons of his designer shirt. He helped her as he unbuttoned his shirt and removed it along with his undershirt. Soon, they were both breathing heavily, in their underwear standing next to the luxurious bed of roses.

His voice was husky and thick with arousal. "I need you, baby." He nipped at her earlobe and whispered, "Are you ready for me?"

"More than I've ever been ready for anything in my life."

He scooped her up and set her down in the middle of the bed, bracing himself above her. Kissing her neck, Cade worked his way down to her toes. He paid attention to every freckle, scar, and attribute, showing proper attention to the sensitive places of her body until she writhed beneath him. She explored every inch of his chiseled body, pleasuring him while reveling in his responses to her touch. And then he helped her reach a height of ecstasy she never knew was possible. It truly was the greatest, most culminating, unsurpassed, incomparable and most memorable night of her life. The best part about it was that this was only the beginning.

242

Caroline woke in the arms of her husband, and it was as if she was looking through a new pair of eyes. The world was a different color. Everything was brighter and more vibrant. The air smelled sweeter, the sheets felt softer, and the man lying next to her was the most divine form of happiness she had ever had in her life. And he was hers.

She woke him with delicate kisses along the curves of his back, causing him to roll over with a million dollar smile on his face.

"Good morning, beautiful. How is my lovely bride this fine day?"

She exhaled, contented. "Fabulous. How is my charming husband?"

"I've never been better." He leaned in for a kiss.

She would have been overcome with the moment, only she had morning breath. "Wait, I need to brush my teeth."

"No, you don't."

"Yes, I do. I have morning breath."

"So do I, so that cancels it out, therefore neither one of us has morning breath."

Unable to control her giggles, she tackled him, causing the sheet to slide off the bed. She sat on top of him gazing at his defined chest muscles when her eyes rested on the unusual scar covering his heart. He noticed and took a deep breath.

"Go ahead and ask. I know it's killing you."

She smirked. "Is that a fact? And just why do you think that?"

"Because I know you and that unmerciful curiosity of yours."

"Okay, fine. What is that?"

"It's a scar from my Budweiser."

"Your what?"

"My Navy SEAL trident pin. It's what we get when we graduate SEAL training."

"They burn you with it?"

He smirked this time. "How did you know it was a burn?"

"I'm a nurse. I know my wounds and scars."

"No, the Navy didn't do it. A couple of other guys in my team and I branded ourselves with our tridents to serve as a reminder to always have each others' backs."

She silently stared, begging him with her eyes to continue. Kristy had mentioned that Runway had the same scar, but she couldn't imagine what could've been so terrible that these guys would willingly inflict this type of pain upon themselves.

His mouth twitched as he spoke just above a whisper. "I was a sniper." When she didn't react, he continued. "I've killed people, Caroline. Most were bad people. A huge threat to this world. But I still took human lives. Some were innocents." His soulful eyes stayed steady, but he couldn't hide the sadness. "Collateral damage."

She had a million questions, but the pain in his eyes had her choose her words carefully. "So what's the story behind the scar?"

Long moments of silence passed. She began to think he wouldn't answer her. "We lost a guy from our team, but his family lost a husband and father. He was my responsibility because I was the sniper, and I was supposed to cover him. I failed."

"Cade, I'm sure it wasn't your fault."

He shook his head. "No, it was my fault. I was supposed to take out the sniper from the tower in the village we were raiding. I shot and missed, alerting him to mine and Runway's positions, so we had to move quickly. While we were in transit to our new position, the sniper took out Morgan. It was my fault. He had twin sons, and his wife was pregnant with his daughter. He was only twenty-five years old."

"It wasn't your fault. It was just his time. When God is ready for us, it doesn't matter where we are, what we're doing, or who we're with. It's going to happen when He's ready." He pressed his eyes closed and pursed his lips, clearly disbelieving her last statement.

"It was my job to make sure it didn't happen that day." Cade ran his fingers through his hair before resting both hands behind his head. "Anyway, Runway, Ty, two other guys and myself decided we would die before letting another brother fall like that, so we burned this reminder into our chests over our hearts."

She cringed. "Didn't that hurt?"

"Like crazy."

"I can imagine. How did you heat it up to brand yourselves?"

"With a cigarette lighter and a pair of pliers. It must've worked because we all came back unharmed."

She kissed his scar and rested her cheek on top of it, secretly wishing she could heal all of his wounds—emotional and physical. She wanted to see what other scars he had and learn how he got them. She wanted to kiss every single one of them. She reveled in the glory that she had the rest of their lives together to find them. She would immensely enjoy searching his body for these little insights into his past.

"So you never told me what your nickname was."

Cade let out an exasperated breath. "Tell me why you want to know so badly."

"I'm just curious what all your buddies decided to call you. Obviously Runway didn't choose his own name and is somewhat embarrassed by it. But it's entirely fitting of him."

"Well, mine isn't the least bit fitting to me."

She stuck her bottom lip out in a pout. "Please?"

He shook his head. "Nuh-uh."

"Why not?"

"Because I don't like it. Besides, I'm afraid you'll use it when you're mad at me. No way."

Her jaw dropped. "I will not! Tell me. Was it really that bad?"

"It was bad for me. If you knew what it was then you would understand. I hated it, and, like I said before, the people who really knew me didn't call me that because they knew how I felt about it."

She laughed. There was only one thing she could think of that Cade hated so much and others respected enough not to mention it around him. "What was it, Voodoo or something?"

His face remained serious, and he said nothing, but the muscles in his jaw clenched.

"Oh my gosh. I'm right, aren't I? It was *Voodoo*?"

He nodded. "Yeah. It was. I got it because I was from New Orleans."

"I thought you were born and raised in Golden Meadow?"

"I was, but people who aren't from here just group all of southern Louisiana into New Orleans."

"Wow. I can see why you hate it now."

He smiled. "I told you. Now promise me you'll never call me that?"

"Technically, I guessed it." His eyes grew wide, and for a moment she thought he was angry with her. "I promise," she quickly added.

"Even when you're mad at me?"

"Even then. But I can't promise I won't call you other names when I'm angry." She snickered.

"Deal."

She traced her finger down to the V shape of his waistline and noticed another scar in the shape of a crescent on his lower left abdomen right next to his hip bone. "What's this one from?"

He sat there quietly as if he was debating whether or not he wanted to tell her. "It's from a piece of shrapnel that pierced through my body armor."

She didn't want to push too much, but she didn't understand what most of that meant. "Must have been some large shrapnel to have made it through armor?"

He nodded. "It was nothing compared to what was behind me."

She frowned, confused.

"I was running from enemy fire trying to get to what we called a safe zone, which was the point where, once I was past it, they could blow up whatever was behind me. I kept falling down as I was running to get there, and I couldn't understand why. Once I crossed the line and was behind cover, I noticed my pack had three bullets from an AK-47."

To think that Cade had been shot with something as powerful as an AK-47 was terrifying. If those bullets had been two feet higher they would have hit his neck and killed him. She masked her terror and calmly replied, "Well, it obviously wasn't your time, was it?"

He smiled, pleased with her reaction. "Guess not. Maybe God knew I would meet you someday."

"Yeah, He knew how badly I needed you in my life."

"You are the best thing that's ever happened to me. I'm honored and so damned happy to be your husband."

"So is that why you hate talking about your time in the military so much?"

He shrugged. "There are plenty of reasons for that, but yeah, that's one of them. To know how many times I faced death and escaped, but so many other guys weren't so lucky. It just doesn't seem fair, you know?"

She nodded. "Yeah, I guess." She smiled playfully. "Now you get to spend the rest of your life making babies with me."

Quicker than she understood how, he had her flipped over onto her back towering over her, pinning her to the bed. "Speaking of that, maybe we should practice again. . .for good measure."

"Practice makes perfect."

TWENTY-FIVE

Cade couldn't imagine his life getting any better as he lay next to his new wife, feeling completely satiated and overwhelmed with emotion. He'd married a complete package of goodness. Physically, she was flawless. Her petite body, curvy and plump in all the right places, firm and smooth with porcelain skin and as soft as the rose petals in which they had made love. Her hair thick and soft, emerald eyes bright and full of life, and those supple, kissable, pouty lips provided pleasure he had never experienced in all his life.

Yeah, her physical being was most enjoyable, but her spirit had him over the moon. She could transport him from sullen and moody to chipper and playful with a simple smile. Her purity, spirituality, curiosity, and tenacity was everything he knew he couldn't live without. After all this time, his wounded heart was complete. Caroline was his missing link, and whether it was coincidence that they met, or fate, he didn't care. He thanked the powers above for making it happen and vowed to keep her safe. He just hoped she would cooperate and let him protect her. Although, how the hell could he protect her from something he couldn't see? Cade rubbed his face, smoothing his fingers over his jaw. If there was a ghost trying to hurt her, there was nothing he could do about it. He wished he believed her. He wanted to. She hadn't mentioned it, though, and wasn't too affected by it. She was as spunky as ever.

Cade smiled. From the moment they entered the suite as husband and wife, they had made love more than they'd slept. After the last marathon romp, she'd drifted to sleep. He swallowed his rising chuckle so not to wake her. Caroline wasn't kidding when she told him she had a thirst that needed quenching. Like a caged bird flying for the first time ever, she was an endless fountain of energy. Cade was glad he'd kept himself in shape all these years, otherwise he might have disappointed her. He admired her as she slept and wondered how he had gotten so lucky.

Unfortunately, that thought brought him back to the dark reality that someone—with a heartbeat—was still out there trying to eliminate the entire Fontenot family. He silently slid from the bed and tiptoed across the room, cursing under his breath as his joints crackled and popped. All those years of abuse and his body was finally paying the toll.

Cade pulled his pants on and scrolled through his contacts on his cell phone until he found the name of his FBI contact. If anyone could help him find something on April or Marcellino, it was Tonya. Her dad had been a career FBI agent and was involved with bringing down some of the most notorious gangsters, with Marcellino being the only big fish that got away from him. Tonya was a former marine and was overseas when her father mysteriously disappeared. His body eventually turned up in the swamps, but it had been so badly mutilated and eaten by animals that he'd had to be identified by his dental records.

From that moment, Tonya vowed to find Marcellino and take him down. She could do it, too. Cade had seen plenty of men in combat, and Tonya made many of them look like pansies. Fast and able to handle any weapon within her reach, she was also beautiful. Tonya could stop men dead in their tracks as she gracefully entered a bar in her stilettos. Little did they know she could incapacitate them in a matter of seconds. The woman was positively lethal.

Cade stepped out of the room to avoid waking Caroline.

"Special Agent Floyd."

"Hey, Tonya. It's Beau."

"Well, hello, sexy. How's it going? Miss me?"

"It's great. Of course I miss you, but I'm actually on my honeymoon right now."

"Really? Congratulations, Beau. That's great. Damn. Why the hell are you calling me? You should be in the throes of passion right about now, shouldn't you?"

He shook his head, smiling. "Don't worry, there's been plenty of that. My new bride is effectively wearing me out."

"Ahh, just like a squid. Slacking on the PT." She clicked her tongue to scold him. "Need me to come down there and beat you back into shape?"

"No, thank you. I don't need some ex-jarhead ordering me around. There is absolutely nothing wrong with my physical endurance. I'm in excellent condition and handling things quite well, thank you."

"Hey, ain't no *ex* to it. Once a marine, always a marine. I can still outrun your lazy ass."

"Anytime you feel like racing, come on down to the swamps. I'll deflate that ego of yours put you back in your place."

"You got it, bud." She chuckled. "So, what's so important that it's pulled you out of bed with your woman?"

"I have some names for you if you have time. I think one of them will interest you a lot."

"Yeah? Who you got for me?"

"Will you have time to do this? I don't want to get you in trouble."

"You kiddin'? You're talkin' to Betty Bureau here. I live and breathe this stuff. You know I can't turn down a lead. Besides, not much action right now. I just closed a case, so I've got some free time."

"Alright. The first name I have for you is Ana Morales. A-n-a M-o-r-a-l-e-s. Tony did some digging for me last week and discovered her mother's and grandmother's names and that they were working for the next name I need you to dig up."

"Okay. Hit me." Cade could tell Tonya was writing as she spoke.

"Angelo Marcellino. No need to spell that one out, right?"

She was silent for a moment, and Cade checked his phone to make sure he hadn't lost the connection.

Her voice low, all traces of playfulness gone. "Marcellino? Really? Beau, you don't want to get involved with this guy. Trust me. I've seen firsthand what this monster is capable of. He's got more powerful people in his back pocket than the POTUS. Tell me you're not in any trouble with the mob?"

"No, it's not me. At least I don't think it is. Someone's been trying to hurt my wife's family, and her stepmother's name is an alias. Her real name is Ana Morales, but her legal married name is April Fontenot. My guy down here did a search for records and came up empty. It's like she never existed."

Cade paced the hall as he spoke. "Tony had gotten me some information before her records had been wiped clean, and her family members, at least her mom and grandma, have been involved with the Marcellino family for three generations. I need some dirt on Marcellino to find April and make her sweat a little. Make her think she's the reason we've got enough to put him away. She's smart, but careless. Just see what you can find for me, okay, cher?"

"Yeah. I'm on it. I'll meet up with you once I find something. I don't handle this kind of stuff by phone, especially if Marcellino's involved. Go relax and enjoy your honeymoon. Don't call me again, or I'll have to kick your ass on your wife's behalf."

"Yes, ma'am." He hung up, smiling, and smelled coffee.

Caroline stood sleepily in front of the coffee pot, stirring her cup slowly. She turned as he entered and her face lit up. If he never saw anything else as long as he lived, he would be just fine.

"Hello, lover." She smiled, and her cheeks flushed.

Carnal desire rushed through him. "Damn, I like the sound of that." He slinked his arm around her waist and pulled her close, bumping his nose to hers. "Hey, beautiful. How are you feeling this morning?"

She shrugged, but the reminiscent smile that spread across her delicate features suggested more. "I'm a little sore, but I kind of expected that. How about you?"

"Never better. So, are you glad you waited?"

She placed the coffee cup on the counter and hugged him, kissing him deeply, then she whispered, "Waiting for you was the best thing I've ever done in my entire life. I can't imagine sharing something like this with anyone else. You are a very good teacher, Mr. Beauregard."

He kissed her with an overflowing heart and vigor he almost didn't recognize. "You make me feel like a giddy, hormonal teenager all over again. Being with you is like my first time every time. I love you so much."

"I love you, too."

Cade pulled her into a tight hug and squeezed. "You are my heart, and I will die before I let anyone hurt you."

Caroline released a surprised huff. "Um, let's hope *that* never has to happen. I don't want to live without you. We still have to grow old and wrinkly together, remember?"

He smiled. "How could I forget?"

She released him and reached for her coffee, her eyes training on the spoon as she stirred. "So, did I snore last night?" She looked up and a flame danced in her emerald eyes stirring Cade's libido. "I was so exhausted after you rocked my world. . .*four* times." She winked.

Turned on, he couldn't resist the opening she left hanging. "No, you didn't snore, but you farted a couple of times."

Her jaw dropped, and, with a gasp, she smacked his shoulder. "I did not!" Her face turned an adorable fuchsia when she realized the possibility existed. "You're lying. I didn't fart in my sleep. . .did I?"

252

He chuckled. "No, you didn't. I'm only kidding, but seeing the mortification on your face has made my day."

She smacked him again. "You punk. I can't believe you did that to me. You're so mean."

He grabbed her by the waist as she tried to run. "Oh, baby, you know I love messing with you. You could stink up the whole room, and I wouldn't love you any less."

"I would be so humiliated if I ever farted in front of you."

He shrugged. "Nah. It's human nature. Everyone does it, and people who say they don't are liars. Just wait till I get to watch you have a baby. You won't be embarrassed by anything after that." He smiled again as her eyes grew big and her rosy cheeks glowed.

"Nuh-uh. No, way. You will be up by my head through the whole thing. No way will you watch that."

He raised an eyebrow while folding his arms across his chest, rising to the challenge. "You're kidding me, right? Let someone try and stop me. I wouldn't miss the opportunity to see my child enter the world and take its first breath. That'll be the third best day of my life."

"What was the first best day?"

"The day you stole my heart with your reaction when you realized it was my house you had snuck into and my naked body you'd slammed into. Adorable."

"Gee thanks," Caroline huffed. "Glad you enjoyed my humiliation. And the second?"

"Yesterday, of course. The day you became my wife. The day I made love to you. The day you had saved just for me."

She leaned up on her tiptoes and gave him a small, sweet kiss. "The best decision I ever made. You were totally worth the wait."

"As were you, sweet Caroline. You weren't my first, but you'll definitely be my last."

"So, speaking of babies. . ." Cade's eyebrows rose in surprise at her implication. "Wanna practice some more?"

"I thought you said you were sore? I was afraid I might have gotten a little carried away last night. Too rough." Cade's voice lowered and he felt his libido stir to life. "Seeing you naked does things to me."

Caroline's pupils dilated and a lovely shade of pink bloomed across her face and chest. "No, I kind of liked it when you got rough." She suggestively bit her lip.

Cade's knees weakened with his instant arousal. Her gaze hit the floor and she smiled while fidgeting with her hair. "I like seeing your reactions and how I affect you. . .the sounds you make. It turns me on. I'm a little sore, yes, but I can't think of a better way to work it out, can you?"

The invitation in her eyes was nearly his undoing as he listened to his insatiable wife tell him how much she enjoyed making love to him. Every man's dream, but his reality. Cade shook his head in wonderment. "You'll be the death of me, woman. But what a way to go."

She drug him into the room by the waistband of his pants and took advantage of him in every beautiful way possible, making him the luckiest, happiest man on the planet.

As they walked around the city, Caroline inhaled the warm breeze off the Mississippi River, appreciating the relief it provided from the heat as the gentle gust combed through her hair. She brushed away the sweat dripping down her temple as they carefully continued down the busy, sunken sidewalk. Fleur de lis-shaped sun catchers glinted in the windows of shops, and Caroline admired the weathered brick buildings with creeping vines climbing along the mortar and around the balconies. The open french doors offered muted jazz music that trickled from the live band performing inside. Caroline loved the beautiful, infectious sounds of New Orleans in the summertime, Cade pulled her over to a vendor's stand.

"You ever had a snoball?"

"Yeah, we used to get them at the state fair, only they were usually in a cone-shaped paper cup."

He shook his head and smiled. "No, cher. Not a sno*cone*, a New Orleans snoball. I promise it's like nothing you've ever tasted before. It's finely shaved ice, and the only place I've ever seen them like this is here. I'll show you."

He ordered a small piña colada snoball for her, and for himself, a large chocolate, stuffed with soft-serve vanilla ice cream, with condensed milk poured over the top. Cade smiled like a seven year old kid as he handed the man his money and accepted their treats.

"What? Why are you looking at me like that?"

She couldn't suppress her smile as she stretched up to kiss him. "You're cute, that's all."

"Here, taste this. You'll love it."

Caroline's taste buds exploded in happiness. "Yum, that's delicious, but it's so much sugar. Too sweet for me. I don't think I could eat a whole cup of it. I'd barely make a dent in it before I'd have to throw it away."

"No, you just put it in the freezer for later, that's all. I do it all the time."

They enjoyed their shaved ice snoballs as they walked through the French Market. The amount of people piled into the structure should've been claustrophobic, but strangely enough she wasn't bothered by it. They browsed the crafts and locally-made merchandise, and Caroline admired her new wedding ring beneath the bright jewelry lights as she scoured the sterling silver selection.

As they exited the pavilion headed back toward the French Quarter, the unforgiving summer sun beat down on the asphalt. The heat drifted from the asphalt and radiated the pungent odor of the mysterious fluids flowing along the street curb. Sweat trickled down her temple as Caroline covered her nose to mask the abhorrent odor. A huge contrast to the baked sugary dreaminess of the beignets only a short walk away.

Caroline enjoyed the intricate French architecture and the endless balconies filled with hanging ferns that framed the worn cobblestone streets. Saxophones and trumpets throughout the Quarter blended with the clopping of hooves from the nearby mule-drawn carriages. She imagined what those streets must have been like when they were newer, covered with horse drawn carriages, or perhaps filled with looting pirates and busty harlots. Or maybe later in history with jazz music filling the alleys crowded with dancing flappers and flashy new automobiles owned by wealthy stock brokers. Aristocrats and their mistresses partying on the balconies with drinks in hand, laughing and smoking cigars as they spoke of their riches before the crash in twenty-nine.

Caroline broke from her daydream upon spotting the voodoo shop she had wanted to enter the last time she and Cade wandered the French Quarter.

"Caroline, please." Cade shook his head. "Keep walking."

"I'm just looking."

She took a step, but a dark-skinned, small-framed woman with salt-and-pepper hair that was twisted into a tight bun caught her attention. The woman, with watchful, cautious eyes that sat too far apart on her small face stood stock-still in the middle of the crowded street before the voodoo shop. Her curious and determined focus was on Caroline.

"Cade, that woman is staring at me."

Cade morphed from protective to rigid in one fluid motion. He stepped between Caroline and the stranger.

As the petite old woman approached him, she spoke in French, or possibly Creole. But she wasn't talking to Cade. She mumbled to the air above Caroline's head.

Caroline's heart skipped a beat, her skin prickling with goose bumps. Cade spoke the same language to the woman and suddenly they were immersed in a heated foreign conversation. Caroline had no idea what they were saying to each other.

"Cade, what is she saying? What are *you* saying? Tell me what is going on."

They were talking so fast Caroline couldn't even keep up with which one was speaking. Cade stopped talking to the woman and turned to look at Caroline. His eyes darted all around her and then settled on her face.

Frustrated and completely freaked out, Caroline shouted. "Cade, you'd better tell me what is going on. Right now."

He huffed and stepped back as the woman approached Caroline. She slowly reached out and wrapped one tiny hand around Caroline's upper arm while the other arm swept the air around her as if feeling for something.

"She says you have a dark spirit looming over you. I told her not to come near you, but she's insistent that you let her cleanse you of this spirit. She said something about an aura."

The woman rolled her eyes and spoke in heavily accented English. "Not something about an aura, it's *everything* about an aura."

Caroline let out an exasperated breath. "You speak English? Why didn't you just speak it to begin with? Why did you have to freak me out like that? What do you see? What kind of dark spirit?" Caroline thought about what happened in California. That had definitely been an evil spirit.

The lady placed her waving hand on the side of Caroline's face while keeping the other securely locked around her bicep. "Young lady, do not be alarmed. I will not hurt you."

Cade muttered under his breath, clearly uncomfortable with the woman touching her. "Come on, Caroline. We're leaving. This woman is crazy."

The mysterious woman straightened and turned to him. "Crazy? I see you. I see what burdens you."

He scoffed. "Piss off." He stabbed the voodoo woman with a hard stare. "If you touch her again, I'll break your arm. Understand?"

They turned to walk away, his arm securely around Caroline's shoulders.

"Cade, wait. What about—"

"Those you've lost do not blame you for their passing."

Cade stopped mid-step and spun around, chest heaving with each breath.

The woman continued in her steady tone of voice. "You need to let it go before it eats you alive."

Caroline couldn't tell if he was shocked, angry, sad, or worried, but she felt a little sorry for the poor woman on the receiving end of his frightening glare.

They remained in an apparent standoff.

"I can help you let them go," the woman stated.

"You keep your black magic and go to hell."

He grabbed Caroline's hand and pulled her away. But the woman grasped his arm. As quick as Caroline blinked, Cade had ripped his arm from the woman's grasp, had her hands bound behind her back with one hand while her head was locked into the crook of his other arm.

"You must let me help her before the spirits get to her first." The woman's raspy voice did not betray her bravery. She spoke calmly and quietly, without a trace of fear.

Caroline's stomach dropped. "What? Did you say spirits? As in more than one? Who are they, can you tell? Is it Rachel? She was murdered, but I didn't think she would be considered a dark spirit. Why is it following me?"

"Caroline, don't. Just don't, okay?" Cade warned her. "For once I need you to resist your curiosity and just walk away." He released the woman and aggressively ran his fingers through his hair, his eyes pleading. His voice was a whisper now. "Please."

Ignoring Cade, the woman studied Caroline's face. "Come with me, child," she said. "I will show you."

Caroline wasn't threatened or scared. The woman was approachable, friendly, and her smile was warm and maternal. Not at all the way she had pictured a voodoo priestess.

Caroline looked at Cade, who vehemently shook his head. "Caroline, please. You know how I feel about this. Don't do this."

"I'm sorry, baby. I have to know." She apologetically pursed her lips and squeezed his hand before following the woman into her voodoo shop. Cade shoved both hands into his golden locks, let out an exasperated heaving breath, and grudgingly followed them, cursing with every step.

TWENTY-SIX

Cade stared at Caroline in silence, pacing as they waited for the woman to join them in the back room of the voodoo shop. He was upset with her, but, if she ever wanted to sleep peacefully again, she needed to know what the woman was talking about.

"Please don't be upset with me."

"You're making that kind of impossible for me right now," he snapped. "You *know* how I feel about voodoo, yet here we sit. You also knew there was no way I would let you come in here alone. I honestly can't believe you've put me in this situation. I swear if that woman touches you, I'll break her bones one at a time until there's nothing left but a deformed heap of flesh."

"Cade, that's a little harsh, don't you think? She's friendly. I don't feel threatened at all. Why are you so judgmental before you know anything about her?"

He spun around and faced her, rubbing at the back of his neck. He eyed her incredulously. "Why *aren't* you? I've lived here all my life, and nothing. . .*nothing* I've ever heard about this crap has ever been good. Sure, she seems friendly enough, but how do you know it's not a ploy to draw you in so she can use her black magic on you?"

"Really, Cade. You sound ridiculous."

"Do I?" He clenched his teeth and prowled furiously. "Dammit, Caroline." He slammed his hand against his chest. "*I'm* not the one being ridiculous. Can't you see that?" He dropped his arms and paced more. The cramped room seemed smaller the more he prowled around it. "I had a hell of a time convincing you that Rachel's ghost was real, and even after you finally started believing it you still refused to admit it. Now, this lady you've never met tells you something even crazier, and you're gung-ho about following along?" His nostrils flared as he sucked in a big frustrated breath, "It's just not right, Caroline."

She defiantly crossed her arms. "And you didn't believe me about the incident in California! So we're even," she fired. He clamped his mouth shut. "This woman sees something that may answer the questions I have about the evil that tried to drown me. I want to know what it is." Caroline reached for him, but he jerked away from her. "Let's just see what she has to say. I promise, the first sign of danger, we'll leave."

He shook out his hands by his side. "It's not safe in here. I can feel it in my gut."

Cade crossed his arms over his chest, and glared at the wall, shifting his weight. Brooding and angry, the muscles in his jaw flexed with each clench of his teeth.

Caroline hated that they were arguing on their honeymoon, but she needed to know what the woman saw.

The silence was broken when the woman entered and cleared off a chair in the back of her store. She asked Caroline to sit as she disappeared behind the beaded curtain.

Caroline sat apprehensively and took in her surroundings. It wasn't what she'd imagined except for the various styles of voodoo dolls hanging from a display. She expected those. The other things in there were typical earthy items for sale, such as incense, candles, and essential oils. A large cross was displayed in the corner along with paintings, wall hangings, dresses and other sundries for sale.

The woman came from the back room with an arm full of various items. "I am Lucinda. I am not a voodoo priestess as you are probably wondering, but my sister-in-law was. This was her store before she passed, leaving it to my husband." Lucinda noticed

Caroline's interest in the cross. "That's mine. My mother-in-law would roll in her grave if she knew I invaded her altar with it, but I care not. How are you feeling? Are you well?"

Caroline wasn't sure how to respond. "Uh, I'm fine. Thank you."

She smiled and looked at Cade then back to Caroline. "You two are just married, yes?"

Caroline nodded, surprised she knew that.

"Congratulations. Marriage is a beautiful thing. I was married to my Carlos for twenty-five years before the cancer took him. He died young with little suffering, but not before he taught me his ways."

"I'm sorry to hear that he passed."

She smiled. "You are a sweet girl. I can see why he is so protective of you." She turned to Cade. "You can stand down, soldier. I'm not going to hurt her. Quite the opposite, actually."

"I'm not a soldier." His voice was stone cold, but Caroline knew him well enough to know he was at least somewhat intrigued with how she knew so much about his very private nature.

Without looking at him she waved her hand in the air, continuing with the set up of things she'd brought out. "Soldier, sailor. Browns, blues. It's all the same difference to me."

His eyes narrowed as he tilted his head and continued nervously shifting his weight while repeatedly clearing his throat. Caroline wondered if the sandalwood incense was getting to him, too. Noticeably upset and cautious, he motioned to the items she brought in. "What's all this stuff?"

Lucinda answered while looking at Caroline as if to explain it to both of them. "You've heard of the sixth sense, yes?" Lucinda said. "Most holistic people believe that healthy humans project particles of energy suspended in an oval-shaped field around the body. An aura. It's the electromagnetic field that surrounds the body. This energy has color. We call the place in the center of our forehead the third eye chakra which allows us to see more of a person than just what's on the outside."

Caroline struggled to keep up with Lucinda's heavily accented English.

"Each person has different colors from the frequency and type of energy the body projects, which sometimes reflects the strongest personality traits."

Lucinda placed a bowl of candy, headphones, plastic cords with clips, and an oxygen mask on a table in front of Caroline and adjusted the strap on a pair of video gaming goggles.

"Sometimes, if a person is being haunted by a spirit, it is possible to see the aura of that particular spirit floating above the person, depending on how strong the spirit is, of course."

Cade shook his head and mumbled obscenities under his breath.

Lucinda ignored him and focused on Caroline. "You, dear, have three spirits fighting for your energy. If not expelled, those spirits will deplete your energy source, causing major health problems or possibly an accident that could be misinterpreted as clumsiness."

Caroline's blood iced over. She'd become quite clumsy since arriving in Louisiana.

"Most people generally have the spirit of a loved one who is watching over them. This spirit is sometimes credited as a guardian angel, so to speak, but those are on a completely different spiritual plane." Her face became serious. "You have three very powerful spirits connected to you, two of which want to cause you harm."

On top of her most recent *accident*, Caroline recalled her fall into the duck pond last summer when Cade swore that it had looked like someone threw her backwards into it. Could it have been these dark spirits the whole time?

"Who are they? Why are they so strong, and why are they stuck to me?"

"I do not know. I will help in any way I can, and we will find out."

"What's going to happen to me?"

"I see auras, cheri, I don't predict the future."

Caroline glanced up to Cade. He pointed his fierce, cold glare at the woman, as if he was mentally willing her to tell him more. He was curious now, but still beyond asking for help. Caroline wasn't above that. She wanted to know more and learn everything she could, especially since Lucinda seemed to be concerned for Caroline's safety.

"How did you learn about this?"

Lucinda busily connected something to Caroline's fingertips. "I told you. My Carlos taught me. He was a very unique, spiritually gifted man."

Cade spoke up. "Carlos? Hispanic? I thought you were French?"

She replied without looking at him as she connected plastic tubing to a large tank. "I am Creole. I married a man from Guatemala." She smiled at Caroline. "My Latin lover. Carlos came from a long line of spiritually talented people. His *granmè*, his grandmother, was Haitian. They moved to Guatemala when Carlos's *madré* was a young woman, so they adopted the Hispanic culture, but still acquired some of their Haitian heritage. Some of his family were good," she cut her eyes to Cade, "Like my Carlos and me." She went back to connecting the tubing. "Others in his family were bad."

"Bad?" Caroline frowned. She didn't like the sound of that. "Like spell-casting, hexing, witchcraft, scary voodoo, evil kind of bad?"

Lucinda nodded, and Caroline tried to ignore the hair rising on her arms and neck. She glanced at Cade whose brow was pinched deep in thought.

"What's that you're connecting to my fingers?"

"I will explain everything once we have it all set up." She picked up a tiny bottle of eye drops and stood. "Now, we need to put one drop of this in each of your eyes."

Cade abruptly stood up. "Like hell. Absolutely not. You're not putting anything in her eyes. We don't know you, we don't know what that is, what you're doing, or what will happen. You're not touching her. Do you understand?"

She sat down and leaned back in her chair, obviously amused. "I admire your security over your bride, but you need not be hostile with me. I told you; I mean her no harm. I will explain." She took a deep breath and used her hands as she described what she wanted to do. "Every healthy human body has five senses: sight, touch, taste, hearing, and smell. We depend on those five senses to provide daily functionality. If one of those senses fails, the others are usually heightened, right? My Carlos, who was a skilled ophthalmologist for years here in New Orleans, developed these eye drops as an experiment for the clairvoyant or spiritually gifted. He conducted this particular experiment on me, so I know personally that it is safe and harmless."

"If they're so harmless, put them in your own eyes right now," Cade challenged.

Moving slowly, she put a drop in each eye. Nothing happened. She didn't scream or act differently. Cade stood down. . .for now.

Caroline was intrigued. "How exactly does it work?"

"First, we must over-stimulate all of your senses. Once I put these special drops in your eyes that only minimally dilate your pupils, you will watch a video with bright colors and constant flashing picture changes thoroughly keeping your mind stimulated. I will place headphones playing classical music over your ears and a mask over your nose to stimulate your olfactory senses with the fragrant smell of peppermint to awaken your mind and heighten all of your other senses."

Cade snatched the mask from her grasp. "Needless to say, I don't trust you. I want to smell it before you put it anywhere near her nose."

She nodded. "Absolutely." Lucinda ignored him as he sniffed the mask and continued talking. "Next, we'll place a piece of sealed, store-bought, sour candy in your mouth to trigger gustation, the sense of taste. Finally, the fingertip pads vibrate, stimulating your sense of touch. With all five senses stimulated, it will open up your sixth sense, your third eye chakra, allowing you to see what I see."

"What exactly is it that you see?"

"Carlos always told me I am a natural sensitive. I can see auras. I used to need the eye drops and stimulation of my senses, but as I practiced and became more familiar with the sensation, I was able to train myself to see these things without help." She smiled. "The world is a very colorful place for me."

Caroline was astounded. "You can see our auras right now?"

She nodded, then turned to Cade. "The more positive the energy, the clearer the aura. Your aura is a bit cloudy, which means you have some negative energy."

"I am not negative about anything," he rebutted. "I just married the woman I love, and I'm on my honeymoon. I'm very happy."

Lucinda smiled and stepped closer. "Oh, young man, no need to lie to me. I know your secret."

TWENTY-SEVEN

Cade frowned, his eyes tightened in warning. "Tread carefully, madam."

"You are happy on the outside, yes, but on the inside you are in pain. You harbor much guilt. You feel responsible for the deaths of several people you loved." He closed his eyes and turned away from her. "The layer of color closest to your body is bright and clear, proving your happiness physically and spiritually, but as the colors spread farther, the layer farthest away representing your spiritual well-being is a murky green. You need to deal with your grief and let it go before it cripples you."

His cautionary voice was barely audible, but he may as well have had a megaphone. Caroline's heart shriveled from his pain, the intensity of his warning.

She shrugged, unfazed by his threatening tone. "I know enough to tell you it wasn't your fault. You have a bright white spirit attached to your soul, and she seems happy. Whatever happened to your loved ones. . .they don't blame you, so you shouldn't blame yourself."

Caroline changed the subject quickly before Cade lost it. "What about me?"

Lucinda smiled. "I see many things."

Caroline smiled in response. "Like what?"

"You are a sensitive, yourself."

She was confused. "What does that mean?"

"Your aura suggests that you are sensitive to spiritual gifts. I take it you haven't discovered your gift yet?"

"I don't have a gift. Trust me, I'm the most unobservant person on the planet."

"That's probably because you look past the obvious. Perhaps nothing has triggered your superconscious. Gifts such as these are usually inherited from a parent. Do either of your parents show any spiritual talents?"

Caroline looked at Cade who was distant and clearly still digesting what Lucinda had said about him, and shook her head. "I don't think so. Like what kinds of talents?"

"Have either of them ever been extremely intuitive, had premonitions, or visions of any kind?"

Her heart flopped. "My mom has always been intuitive, knowing what I was thinking before I did it. Not in a mind-reading kind of way, but more like knowing my next move before I made it. She just recently began having visions after getting a bump on her head." As Caroline pointed to her forehead to show her where, she realized the can of milk had hit her mom's third-eye chakra. "Is that what triggered it for her?"

Lucinda slowly nodded her head and gently touched Caroline's abdomen. "Your torso is bright pink with a clear red outer lining. That means you are in love, a new romance. You just got married, so that's accurate. The outer red lining signifies sexual and passionate energy. Considering you just celebrated your wedding night, I can see why."

Caroline's cheeks burned, but Cade's fleeting amusement skittered across his tense face.

Lucinda smiled and continued. "Your abdomen is orange which relates to your sensuality, physical pleasure, and adventurous nature. You are a very curious and energetic person, yes?"

Cade snorted, confirming her diagnosis. "The orange spreads down to your reproductive organs, and you have bright white flashes around your womb. This usually means it is fertile, signifying that you will be blessed with children in the not too distant future."

Caroline's gaze flashed to her new husband who wore a broad grin. He liked that bit of news. She was glad to see him lightening up a little. "You also have a blue-green aura color spreading throughout your body meaning you are very intuitive and caring and also indicating your sensitivity toward your sixth sense. You love to help others."

"Yes, but what about the dark spirits you saw?"

Lucinda's gaze saddened. "The spirits have black undertones and are fighting to subdue your energy. They were both jealous, hateful, vindictive people in life. The other bright colored spirit I see is protecting you from them. She is not as strong as they are, and they will eventually overpower her, but you are better connected with her. She inhabits a purple area of your aura which means she has connected to or come to you in your dreams. Is that correct?"

"Yes, exactly." Two of the spirits Lucinda referred to were surely Rachel and George, but who was the third one? The other dark spirit. "I get how you can see who's stronger or good and bad by their brightness, but how do you know if it's a male or female spirit?"

"Years of practice and the constant studying of people. Once I learned how to do this, I was obsessed. I became passionate about helping others, so I sat outside the shop and watched for people like you. I can tell much about people from their auras. Your husband, for example; he has many very strong colors. He knows who he is and is confident. He is a hard worker and has a love for the earth and nature. The blues scattered throughout his aura show his love of the water or sea. He has strong principles and well developed basic instincts. In his head is dark brown indicating common sense, however the muddy green around it shows his continuous guilt and blame. He is very hard on himself. His bright spirit friend, she likes to hang around this muddy section."

Lucinda turned to Cade. "She is the one you blame yourself for losing, yes?" He hesitated, then nodded once, choking back the emotion. Lucinda had gotten to Cade, no denying. There was no way anyone could have known these things about either one of them without some kind of supernatural powers. The woman was incredible.

"So what is all this stuff you have hooked up to me going to do?"

"Once your senses have been completely over stimulated you will see for yourself."

Caroline was nervous but eager. "Okay, let's give it a shot."

Cade pleaded with Caroline in a last ditch effort to change her mind. "Baby. . ."

"I need to do this for peace of mind," she pleaded with him to understand.

"What are you expecting to find? If she's right and there are three spirits attached to you, you already know who they are. Why do you want to subject yourself to this. . .witchcraft?"

"Three spirits. I don't know who the other dark spirit is." She hugged him, kissing his cheek. "Please, Cade."

"Fine," he huffed in defeat and wrapped his arms tightly around her.

He turned to Lucinda. "Consider this your final warning. If you hurt her in any way, now or later, I will hunt you down."

Lucinda nodded calmly, unbothered by his threat. "She is perfectly safe with me."

Once again, Caroline was amazed at his self-control. Cade was furious about this whole situation, but he wasn't taking his anger out on her the way Trevor would have.

Lucinda put the drops in Caroline's eyes and hooked her up. The music and video was indeed stimulating, and after about fifteen minutes her fingers went numb from the constant vibrations. The extremely tart candy caused her salivary glands to be in overdrive, but with the peppermint scent in her nose, her taste buds were confused. It was a very strange sensation. Once the thirty minutes were over, Lucinda removed everything and lifted Caroline from the chair, walking her over to a mirror. Caroline didn't know what to expect, but from what she could tell nothing was different.

"What's supposed to happen?"

"Concentrate on the third eye chakra in your forehead." Lucinda's voice, more soothing than before, might have been an indication of a change.

Caroline focused, and her eyes began to shift until she felt as if she was going cross-eyed. What she saw next was like nothing she'd ever experienced in her life.

Caroline gasped quickly following with a smile, amazed. "This is insane."

"What is it? What do you see?" Cade urged, worry thick in his voice.

She pulled her gaze from her own colorful reflection and focused on Cade. An earth-toned rainbow haloed him.

"Cade, you look beautiful."

He laughed.

"No, really."

She used her hands to trace the colorful lines around his head and shoulders. That's when she saw it. The bright spirit above his left shoulder next to his ear. "Cade," she whispered. "I see her."

"Who?"

"The bright spirit Lucinda was talking about. Jenny."

"Caroline, that's not funny," he warned.

"No, I'm serious. It's a really bright, white light ball next to your head. Right here." She placed her hand in the crook of his neck between his shoulder and ear.

"No, *I'm* serious. This isn't funny. If you're messing with me. . ."

She focused on his eyes. "Cade, I'm dead serious. Whatever those drops did, combined with the stimulation, it worked."

Tears welled up in his eyes as he turned away from her. He needn't have been embarrassed by his emotions. She wanted him to know that.

"It's amazing. Looking at her light, she really does cause me to feel warm and happy. She's still looking out for you."

With his back to her, he nodded.

Caroline turned back to the mirror to look at her own aura, and her eyes shifted again to adjust. The colors Lucinda described were bright near the purplish area by her head. Rachel's light wasn't as bright as Jenny's was for Cade. Perhaps it had to do with Rachel being dead longer and Caroline never knowing her personally. Her light seemed to grow bright then dim, then bright again.

"Why is her light pulsing like that?"

"Because she's struggling to protect you from *them*." Lucinda pointed to the shadowy areas by her shoulder.

A minuscule area, but very defined. Like oily stains on her shirt in the reflection. When she looked down at her clothes, they looked normal. She had to be looking in the mirror to see the colors of her own aura. The shadowy spots remained constant, not pulsating. Caroline had to do something quickly before George and his evil cohort, probably Peter Callahan based on her graduation day nightmare, overpowered Rachel. Her life may depend on it. She wondered what happened to the three generations between George and Kenneth Callahan and why they weren't haunting her, too. Two evil spirits was plenty.

"How can we get rid of them?"

"You have to find out the cause of their distress in the afterlife and figure out a way to set them at peace. There is a reason they are after your soul. You need to find a way to prevent them from getting it by helping to release their spirit."

Cade stepped up. "Wait a minute. How the hell can a spirit hurt a living being? I thought once you died you had no power in this world anymore? This is all just a little much for me to believe. I mean, I believe in ghosts and suspended spirits and all, but having one that can hurt a living soul? Really?"

"Well, he can't physically hurt her himself. But he can cause her to harm herself or cause another soul to bring harm upon her."

"You mean like possession?"

"Not the Hollywood depiction, but some other form of it, yes."

Caroline shuddered, remembering Trevor's fury toward her last summer when he thought she'd cheated on him with Cade. He'd gotten physical with her and later told her he didn't understand why. He'd said it was like someone else was controlling his arms. She also thought about Henry. How he had been a lifelong friend of Cade's who tried to force himself upon her. He'd acted out of character, with no reason to want to hurt Caroline. A sharp chill rocked her spine.

"Actually, they can."

"Oh?" Lucinda asked.

"I had one push me off a pier and try to drown me a couple of weeks ago."

Lucinda studied her. "Then there is no time to waste," she added quietly. "They are stronger together and powerful beyond my knowledge."

Caroline's sharp intake of breath stuck in her throat and she wanted to vomit.

Cade noticed and pursed his lips. "Right. What can I do?" He was determined now. There would be no stopping him.

"Find out everything you can on these dark spirits. I can see that you know who it might be?" They both nodded. "I can perform a ritual to release their hold on your spirit, but first you must do something for me. Find out how and when they died, if someone had a hand in their death, and any family members that are still living. There is a reason they are stuck here, and their dark, shadowy aura tells me it has something to do with their past life hurts or some sort of unresolved karma. Their surviving family may have clues that can help us set them at peace."

She and Cade stared into each other's eyes for several moments with unspoken dialogue. They both knew what kind of unresolved karma Peter and George Callahan were both dealing with—betrayal, jealousy, and hatred toward the Fontenot legacy. This meant talking to Trevor and, most likely, his dad, Kenneth Callahan. Not something Cade wanted her to do ever again.

As she stared at him and his colorful aura, Caroline could almost feel his heart breaking at this very thought of involving the Callahans again. She was on the verge of blowing off the whole thing and taking her chances, until something unusual happened. The spirit lingering by Cade grew extremely bright, causing her to squint her eyes. It was as if Jenny was trying to tell her something, maybe even screaming at her. Perhaps Jenny was reassuring her she would help them fight George Callahan's evil spirit. Caroline sure hoped that was the case, because she was going to need all the help she could get.

TWENTY-EIGHT

Caroline and Cade snuggled in silence on the chaise in the sitting room of their suite. The afternoon at the voodoo shop had been stressful. Cade had put up with her insanity and now the awkward task before them. But there was something else. Something that promised to be more difficult than anything she'd gone through before.

"Caroline, what's on your mind—besides the obvious."

She shrugged and stood up to pace. "Talk to me, sweet girl."

She stopped in front of him and squatted down to look into his worried golden eyes. "Cade, I-I'm sorry. . .for the whole voodoo shop thing. I know how you feel about it. I really appreciate your support. That means a lot to me."

He nodded, smiling. "I knew about your curiosity when I married you; I just wish that your stubbornness wouldn't override your good sense. It turned out okay. No harm done. Apology accepted." He rubbed his palms down his thighs. "I owe you an apology, too."

"For what?" She asked, perplexed.

"For not believing you about what happened in California. For not being there for you emotionally when you got back." He pulled her into his lap. "I'm so sorry, baby. I believe you now. Will you tell me what happened?"

She snuggled against his neck, enjoying his warmth and his clean scent, glad he finally accepted that she wasn't crazy. "It's okay. The important thing is that I'm here now. With you."

"Was it George?"

Since he wasn't going to let it go, Caroline put her difficult task on hold and revisited that frightful moment again. Maybe talking about it would help her make sense of what happened, too. "I don't know. I felt someone tug on my shoulder, but when I turned, no one was there. Then, I saw a flash of something. A cloudy face, and I recognized who I thought was George. . ." she stared at the wall, "but now I'm not sure. My throat ached, and I couldn't breathe. I clawed at it, but there was nothing to grab hold of. The next thing I knew I was flying over the railing and sinking like led. I hit my head, but whatever had me was pushing me deeper and deeper while squeezing my throat."

She frowned. "It was so cold. Then I saw Runway. I frantically reached for him and he grabbed me under my arms, but something fought him. Something, or some*one*, was pulling me down by my feet against his efforts. It was terrifying." Cade's watchful eyes hung on her every word. "After my nightmare, I'm wondering if it was Peter Callahan."

He pulled her closer and kissed her forehead. "How can I protect you from something I can't see? How can I keep you safe?"

She didn't know how to answer that. But at the moment she wasn't concerned with George and Peter Callahan. Something much more important centered her thoughts. She sat up and slipped off his lap to kneel in front of him. Caroline opened her mouth to speak, but she paused and snapped it closed.

He studied her face and frowned. "What's wrong?"

Chickening out, she shook her head and said, "No. Forget it. I changed my mind."

He leaned forward and held her hands. "No, don't do this. Don't shut me out. What is it? I can see that something else is really bothering you."

She sighed, closing her eyes tightly as she blurted it out. "Cade, I really need you to tell me about Jenny."

He flopped back on the sofa, mumbled something under his breath, and rubbed his face. "I thought my sister forced us to deal with that already?"

"Tell me about your relationship with her. I want to know more."

His brow furrowed, "Why do you want to talk about this now? On our honeymoon? This is supposed to be a happy, joyful time all about us. Why bring up a tragedy from so long ago?"

"Because you need closure, and I need you to have that closure. It will help you to talk about it."

"I *have* let her go." His tone was sharp around the edges. "Isn't it obvious? I'm married now. I've moved on." He turned his head away, glowering at the oil painting on the wall.

"Cade, look at me."

He drew in a deep breath and met her gaze.

"I know you love me. I know you've moved on with your life. But I'm still sharing you with another woman as long as you continue blaming yourself for Jenny's death. Lucinda was right. You've got to let that go and accept that it was an accident. It was out of your hands."

"Caroline, you don't understand. I was the reason she left the restaurant upset. It was my fault she ran off the road into the canal. It was me who couldn't save her. It was me who caused her death— and my baby."

She stood up abruptly and shouted. "No. You didn't. How can you even think that? You weren't driving the car, she was. It was an accident. It was just her time."

His jaw twitched, and he closed his eyes. "Caroline, please stop saying that."

She straddled his lap now to claim his undivided attention. She squeezed his shoulders a few times before running her hands up to place them on each side of his face, forcing him to look at her. "Please, baby. Humor me. Talk to me about her. It will help heal the wounds that were left so deeply in your heart." She traced his lips with her thumb, admiring their fullness. "You can't fully devote yourself to me if a part of you is still in that canal where she died."

He closed his eyes and rested his forehead on her chest. "Why?" he pleaded. "Why are you making me do this?"

"Because it's the right thing to do. Because you are a steel fortress of pent up emotion. Someday you're going to explode. I love you. If I can't help you move on, who can?" His eyes shifted with sadness. "You've taken such great care of me. Let me take care of you. All I'm asking is that you talk to me, please. I promise not to interrupt. I will just listen and let you get it out."

He kissed her with a vigor that could have been interpreted as aggression, but she knew better. It was just his very passionate way of conceding to her request. He leaned back against the sofa and ran his fingers through his golden curls.

"I don't even know where to begin."

She waited for him to look at her before she spoke.

"How about from the beginning? When did you first meet Jenny?"

"Oh, wow. That seems like a lifetime ago." He sighed again. "Catherine had her over one night in the summer, and she and I hit it off. We stayed awake until four in the morning just talking about everything. She loved sports, fishing, hiking, camping, and music. She was like one of the guys, only beautiful."

He gave her an apologetic look. "Do I really have to do this?" She nodded, smiling. He sighed and reluctantly continued. "We were just friends for a long time, but I realized I was wanting to spend more and more time with her. She was all I could think about from the time I woke up until the time I went to sleep. When I wasn't *with* her, I was doing something *for* her. She had a beautiful voice." His smile curved at the corner, "She's the one who encouraged me to play the guitar so she could sing with me while I played.

"We dated all through school, fantasizing about our future together, and after graduation, I joined the Navy. I wanted a steady income, benefits, and stability. I needed to learn a trade, something I could use when I got out." Cade shook his head as he rubbed his forehead. "I don't know what I was thinking when I decided to try for BUD/s training. Everyone told us, me and Runway, that it was nearly impossible for someone to have a family while being a SEAL. I knew my relationship with Jenny was strong, and I got cocky thinking that ours would be different. We would defy the odds." He looked at her and gave a sad, crooked grin. "We almost did, but I was a fool."

Caroline tenderly ran her fingers through his hair as he continued the story. He wrapped his arms tightly around her torso. "Jenny came to my SEAL graduation in Coronado, and it was one of my proudest moments. I went on my first assignment and thought I was hot stuff. I was excited about all the covert ops and top secret missions we were involved in, but that quickly got old. Jenny was a trooper. She wrote me constantly, and all the guys would heckle me whenever I'd get her letters. She'd spray her perfume on the paper so they always smelled like her." His eyes glazed over, lost in thought.

He smiled, "The only guy who didn't heckle me about her was Runway. He always supported my relationship with her. He was like the brother I never had. We were very close. We even joked about doing the whole blood brothers thing where you cut your hand and mesh your palms together to share blood. We decided against that, because in our line of work we didn't need any unnecessary wounds to deal with. We just agreed to always be there for each other. Through our entire tour, we were inseparable." Cade rested his head on the back of the sofa, his eyes trained on the ceiling.

"To make a long story short, I was home on leave for Christmas and spent every day of it with Jenny. Leaving her to go back to Afghanistan was the hardest thing I'd ever had to do. I didn't want to go, but I had no choice. It was my last mission. I had decided not to re-up, or reenlist, when my contract was up in six months. I'd planned to propose to Jenny. Like an idiot, I didn't tell her before I left. Pride, I guess. I wanted to have a ring when I popped the question." He slowly shook his head in disgust. "I guess I didn't want her to take it any harder than she'd have to if for some reason I didn't make it back home. I can't imagine the stress she must have gone through wondering each time I left if she would ever see me again."

He coughed, trying to disguise the emotion clogging his throat. Caroline kissed his forehead, distracting him into another passionate kiss, before she pulled away for him to continue.

He sighed, resigned. "I sent an email about two weeks before I was planning to come home, telling her to meet me at our restaurant at seven. I told her I had a surprise for her and not to be late. Only, I got stuck in a top secret briefing at the Pentagon." He shrugged, "Standard procedure. We always had one after a mission. However, the President was on his way to join this particular meeting. He took a long time to get there, and it prolonged my time in Washington. I was over four hours late." He closed his red-rimmed eyes and a rogue tear escaped.

"The restaurant owner expected me, but didn't want to say anything and ruin my surprise. He told me how upset she had been, how she'd rushed out of the restaurant before he could catch her to tell her what I had planned. Then. . ." Cade cleared his throat again and looked everywhere but at Caroline. "He handed me the gift bag she'd left behind on the table."

His tears fell freely down his cheeks. Caroline wasn't sure what to do, so she hugged him, crying along with him and continuing to gently run her fingers through his hair. He cleared his throat again and again, struggling to keep from losing it.

"It's okay, baby,' she whispered. "I love you, and I'm not going anywhere. Just get it all out."

He wept against her shoulder as she held him through it all. His arms were a vice grip around her waist as if she might slip away from him at any moment. When he could finally talk, he pulled a handkerchief from his pocket and wiped his face and nose.

"She had been planning to surprise me with the news that she was five months pregnant with my son."

Caroline swallowed her gasp to keep from reacting so he would continue.

"She had kept it a secret from almost everyone. She was afraid I would find out and she wanted to show me in person rather than tell me in an email. She knew how badly I wanted to have a family someday." Cade inhaled a shaky breath. "There was a handwritten note in the bag full of baby stuff. She wanted to name him Lucas. After me." He sobbed again, broken words through his panting. "I didn't know. I swear, I just—I didn't know."

Caroline's heart broke for him, and she wanted to give him permission to stop, but this was probably the first and only time he'd ever spoken about Jenny's death. Of his son's death.

"I drove like a bat out of hell to find her before she decided to leave me forever. I knew she was angry with me for not showing up, and she was probably worried I'd be upset with her for not telling me about the baby. My friend at the restaurant said she had left crying hysterically."

Cade shook his head, his watery eyes distant with the painful memory. "I drove so fast, I don't know how I managed to see her car. A flash of light from my headlights reflected off her side mirror, maybe."

Caroline thought of the bright white light she had seen today from Jenny's spirit. Had that been the light that grabbed his attention? Was Jenny already gone, and had somehow flagged him down?

"I saw the flash of light come from the murky water in the canal, and I knew. I felt it in my gut. I just knew it was her car. I pulled over and launched out of the car so fast I barely got it in park. I dove in and swam to the passenger side, and of course it was locked. I swam around the car to the other side. I would have normally jumped over the top, but I didn't want to push it any further into the water than I had to. When I got to the driver's side, it was also locked, but I could see her face through the top part of the window that wasn't under water yet. I screamed her name and pounded on the window with my bare fists, but the glass wouldn't break. I tried everything I could to bust the window out, but the pressure from the water made it impenetrable. I wasn't strong. . ."

His sobs deepened now as they wracked his body. "I wasn't strong enough. The airbag hadn't deployed, and she was strapped in with her hands resting on her belly, unconscious, beautiful. I pounded on the glass, yanking the door handle, and watched, screaming for help, as she drowned."

Caroline couldn't stop her own tears from flowing.

"That will haunt me for the rest of my life. I felt so helpless. There I was, this big, bad Navy SEAL, capable of killing someone with my bare hands. I could shoot the whiskers off of a squirrel from twenty-five hundred yards, but I couldn't bust out a damned car window. I wanted to die with her. I wasn't strong enough to save her and, obviously, not strong enough to lose her."

Caroline cradled his head, absorbing his tears and sobs as they cried together.

He straightened up and wiped his face again with his handkerchief. "I asked her parents not to mention the baby in the obituary. Her death was tragic enough, we wanted to be able to mourn them both without the whole town knowing our business." He nervously flipped the cloth over in his hands and his voice cracked. "Now you see why I don't like to talk about it?"

"Yes, I do, but if you don't allow yourself to grieve, you'll never be able to truly move on with your life. Jenny would want you to move on."

He clenched his jaw as he rested his head back on the sofa. His blank, rejected, disbelieving stare was proof he struggled to accept that.

"I saw her spirit, Cade. She was bright and warm. I think Lucinda was right; she doesn't blame you for her death, so you shouldn't blame yourself."

"I wish I could have seen her." He brushed a strand of hair from Caroline's face. "It must have been incredible to see what you saw."

She nodded. "Can I ask one more thing about your story?"

"I'm not sure what else I can tell you."

"What happened with Runway? What's his story? If you two were so close, why haven't I heard anything about him until now?"

He cringed. "That is a completely different story in which I also blame myself." He hesitated, knowing she wouldn't let up if he didn't tell her, so he gave in. "Runway knew about the baby." Caroline swallowed her gasp. "Catherine had sent him an email asking him to help make sure I made it home because Jenny was pregnant and they needed me. She also asked him not to tell me, which he never did." Cade shook his head.

"We were raiding a compound one time, and I stepped on an explosive. Before my foot came up to detonate it, Runway shoved, more like propelled, me out of the way taking the brunt of the explosion himself. Luckily it was a small explosive, perhaps a dud, and he only suffered the fringe of it rather than the full explosive capabilities, but it ruined his shoulder. He had to have multiple, painful reconstructive surgeries to repair what they could of it, but it basically ended his SEAL career. They offered him desk duty, but that's like clipping an eagle's wings. His entire career that he'd worked so hard to achieve was ruined because of me."

His voice cracked with emotion. "He said he did it because he didn't have anyone waiting for him at home like I did. Since I had my parents and sisters, Jenny, and the baby I knew nothing about, he'd saved my life for them. It was very honorable, but after Jenny died, I didn't appreciate him like I should have. I was angry that he hadn't told me he knew about the baby, as if I could have done anything about it. When you're sealed in a top secret briefing, there's no getting out. No calls, no memos, no contact with the outside until it's over. He turned down the offer of desk duty and got out the same time I did. He went back to California, and I came back to Louisiana. I never quit feeling guilty about blowing up his shoulder and ending his career. And though I knew I was wrong for being angry with him, I never apologized. At least not until you came back from Chicago and I knew someone was trying to hurt you. Then I called him for help. It was the first time I'd talked to him in years."

"I'm sure you would've done the same thing for him if he'd been about to step on a bomb. Blood or not. He was your family, too."

Cade leaned his head back and pressed the heels of his hands into his eye sockets. "Oh, you're killing me with this emotional stuff." He stood and lumbered to the kitchen to pour a glass of water.

"Yes, of course I would've done the same thing for him. Without the slightest hesitation. But I had never intended to make the SEALs a lifelong career. I always said if I made it through my last tour alive I was going to get out and have a big family with a dog and a swing set. Runway had always planned to die as a SEAL. After Jenny died, I wished it had been me that stepped on that explosive so I might have died honorably without having to endure the pain I was going through.

"For so long I've held a grudge against the Navy for keeping me from her and not allowing me to leave the briefing room to make a phone call. I've held a grudge against Runway for not telling me about the baby and for not letting me be the one to blow up. I've held a grudge against myself for not being able to save them when I was right there watching them die." He took a long drink, placing his glass heavily on the counter. "It should have been me that died. Not Jenny."

Caroline immediately shook her head and approached him. "No. Not you. God had other plans for you. He knew I would need you in my life. He wasn't punishing you, He was looking out for me. You are my guardian angel, Cade. Only, you're not a bright, white spirit I'm hanging on to. You're flesh and blood. A glorious heartbeat standing right in front of me, and we're going to make lots of babies, have a dog, and a swing set. We're going to watch our children playing in the backyard while we sip iced tea on the porch getting old and wrinkly together. That's how it's supposed to happen. You told me once that you believe everything happens for a reason. Remember? Jenny died so you would find me, save my family and me from the Callahan's, and get married so we can complete each other. You are my missing puzzle piece, and I am yours."

Cade jerked her up, pressing her against his body. "Yes you are."

TWENTY-NINE

Trevor stood in the shower letting the hot water beat down upon his tense shoulders. No one should be this stressed out on vacation. Maybe it was time to head back to Chicago. He wondered if Jessica would want to come with him. One thing was for sure, there would be no cold showers needed when she was around.

The last two weeks with Jessica had been amazing. Her State Trooper brother had been in Baton Rouge for training, so Trevor had jumped on the chance to be with her. He'd been staying with her since he'd been spooked at the hotel and they'd had sex nearly every day since. She was always in the mood. At times he wondered if she was more obsessed with sex than he, not that he was complaining. What man didn't dream of a horny beautiful woman? But sometimes he missed the instant blush that would flood Caroline's cheeks when he would kiss her in specific areas, and the flush of heat when he would run his lips across that tender place between her shoulder blades. He grinned at the memory. He thirsted for the embarrassed look she would get when he would talk about all the things he could teach her. He missed her. Period.

He wondered what Caroline and the gardener were doing right now. Well, maybe not. He had seen them together from a distance around town several times last week, but he hadn't seen them in the last couple of days. It was unlike her to slip away for that long without at least checking on him. Having had her attention since he'd been here was nice.

He enjoyed being on the other angle of the love triangle, watching Beau squirm as Caroline made a point to check on Trevor. He'd wanted to ask Beau how he liked wondering what the woman he loved was thinking while spending time alone with a man who was trying to steal her away. Trevor liked Jessica, but he would love nothing more than for Caroline to rush back into his arms as the home-wrecker stood behind her wondering what he did wrong.

Whatever Beau did, he swept her off her feet, right into his arms and, now, probably into his bed.

Trevor needed to talk to Caroline to get some closure. Either closure or to rekindle the love she once had for him. He knew she loved him at some point because she'd agreed to marry him. She'd spent more than two blissful years with him. He simply needed to remind her of the Trevor she once knew before the gardener butted in and sealed the deal. He hated to hurt Jessica, but Caroline was the main reason he'd come down here. His dad could've handled the ridiculous property assessments. That wasn't Trevor's job, anyway. He'd lost Caroline to this marshy wetland, it was time to win her back. Game on.

He mumbled to himself, "Look out, C. Here comes Trev."

He shut the water off and dripped in the tub for a few minutes as he cleared his sinuses with the steam from the scalding water. When he stepped out of the tub, his hot skin prickled and instantly chilled. On the mirror, written in the fog from the steam, was an unmistakable message.

Failure! Get Out!

Had Jessica written that? Surely not. Trevor wracked his brain. Had he accidentally called out Caroline's name during their quickie before his shower. He was sure he hadn't and Jessica wasn't the type to play games, leaving messages on mirrors. She was bold enough that she would just come in and tell him to get out if she wanted him to leave. Who the hell came in there without him hearing it?

Trevor wiped the mirror with his towel, clearing the evidence, and wrapped it around his waist as he stepped into the hall. His hair dripped water down his shoulders and back, but he didn't care. He needed to get to the bottom of this. If there was a ghost haunting him down here, he was about to kiss Louisiana and the entire southern part of the country goodbye, and get the hell back to Chicago where he belonged. At least there the ghosts seemed to like him enough to leave him alone.

"Jess?"

"Yeah?" He heard dishes clinking as she loaded the dishwasher.

"Did you come in while I was showering?"

"No, why? Did you need something?"

"No, just wondering. I thought I heard someone come in."

She peeked her head around the corner. "If I'd come in the bathroom while you were in the shower, I would have gotten in with you." She winked and went back to doing the dishes. He forced a smile, but the uneasy feeling in his stomach made him want to hurl.

"Your brother isn't home, is he?"

"Uh-uh. He's in Baton Rouge 'til next weekend. Why?"

"Just curious."

She walked up to him this time, concerned. "You okay? You're pale. You look like you just saw a ghost."

A hysterical laugh escaped his mouth. "I do? That's funny."

Her brow furrowed, and she looked at him cautiously. "Yeah. Hilarious." She held her stare for a few minutes as she studied him. "Listen, I don't do crazy, so if something's up you need to tell me."

"Nothing's up. Still high on endorphins, I guess."

She smiled and kissed him, tugging on his bottom lip with her teeth. "Yeah? There's more where that came from, baby." She ripped the towel from his hips and smacked his bare cheeks, squeezing them with her nails. Normally, he would have had an instant erection. Normally.

Could it be possible that the hotel wasn't haunted after all? That it was him who was haunted? He'd quickly dressed in a pair of boxer briefs, and while brushing his teeth in the bathroom, Trevor stared blankly at the spot in the mirror where the words had been written, trying to make sense of it.

Movement behind him caught his attention. The decorative hand towel hanging on the towel rack behind him slowly slid off of the bar, as if someone pulled on the bottom of it. The towel had been hanging on this rack untouched for the two weeks he'd been there. No way was it just slipping. He swung around. It wasn't moving but it had clearly been disturbed. He quickly rinsed his mouth and when he glanced up, the towel slipped over his head and wrapped tightly around his neck. He clawed at the fabric, finally ripping it from his neck and hurried into the bedroom to throw on some jeans.

He needed to talk to the one person he knew would listen to his crazy rant, and he hoped with every freaked-out bone in his body she was home.

He bolted for the front door. Jessica called for him, but he yelled over his shoulder that he'd be in touch before slamming the door. Muttering to himself in near hysterics, he revved the engine and laid rubber, squealing his way out of the driveway.

"Please be home, Caroline. Please be home. I need you."

The instant those last three words passed his lips, the gas pedal pressed down on its own. Trevor wasn't in control of the car anymore. Trying unsuccessfully not to panic, he gripped the steering wheel with as much strength as he could and stood on the brake. The car bucked and jolted, but didn't come to a stop. He pumped the brakes and pulled the emergency brake. When that didn't work, he yanked the keys from the ignition. Trevor sent up a hasty prayer just before the engine died. As the vehicle slowed, he put it in park, causing it to lurch forward, slamming his forehead into the steering wheel.

Breathing heavily through the fierce throbbing, Trevor launched himself from the car, keys still in hand, and gawked at the possessed vehicle. Beads of sweat dripped from his face with each jarring pump of his heart trying to escape from his chest. What the hell had just happened? Through the ringing in his ears and the pounding in his head, he heard his name clear as a bell. He instinctively looked up. Trevor's racing heart leapt into his throat, blocking his air supply. He bolted back in the car and fumbled to get the key back in the ignition after locking the doors. He turned the key and nothing happened. He pumped the gas, curse words flying as he looked back to the front of the car.

Floating in the beam of his headlights was a cloudy figure of a man with jet black hair parted down the middle, wearing old style dress, and a fierce expression on his face. A man who looked identical to Trevor. An evil chuckle resonated within the walls of Trevor's car as a sinister smile slowly spread across the doppelgänger's face and his crystal blue eyes glowed.

Before Trevor could rationalize his fear, the figure was sitting next to him in the passenger seat. Trevor's vision blurred, and the darkness pressed in.

THIRTY

Caroline walked hand-in-hand with Cade down St. Charles Avenue marveling at the large, beautiful homes that had survived the below-sea-level bowl of New Orleans for over a hundred years. Blossoming azaleas and gardenias colored the streets and Magnolia blooms welcomed bees and other insects to their sweet nectar. Majestic oaks lined the path with their crooked branches outstretched, touching like lovers holding hands and shading them from the midday sun. The familiar moss she'd grown to love hung solemnly above them waving gently in the slight breeze, reminding Caroline of the metallic icicles she used to hang on her mother's Christmas tree each year. A painting come to life just as the bayou had been the first time Caroline had explored it.

"What I wouldn't give to be able to go back in time and walk these colorful streets in the eighteenth century. Maybe the early nineteenth century. It must have been a sight to see." After her experience with Lucinda, Caroline was more in touch with her spiritual side than ever. She could almost feel the ghosts of the original French settlers brushing past her on the street. With every gust of wind or cold patch she walked through, she felt an energy she'd never experienced before. Was Lucinda right? Did she really have psychic abilities?

She stopped and observed graffiti written on the side of a bus stop. *Joie de vivre.* She attempted to say it aloud, and Cade laughed at her pathetic attempt at French. He corrected her and promised they would work on that.

"What does it mean?"

"It basically means an enjoyment of life, or an exultation of spirit. It's kind of the theme or spirit of New Orleans and the people from here." Cade grasped her hand and they continued walking. "The settlers who first came here over three hundred years ago were French, and the spirit of New Orleans is a sort of living legacy to those who founded and nurtured the city in its early years." He winked. "Partying is in our nature. It's who we are." Caroline loved his playfulness and how animated and excited he became as he gave her history lessons about the city he loved so much.

The extraordinary architecture brought Trevor to mind. He would love analyzing these old structures and how they've lasted all these years. Caroline scolded herself for allowing Trevor to invade her thoughts on her honeymoon.

She wrapped her arm snugly around Cade's tapered waist. "I love it here," she mused. "If I didn't love Golden Meadow so much, I swear I could move right into one of these mansions on St. Charles today."

"Is it the city, or the houses you love so much?"

"The houses. I would love to have a colonial or antebellum home. I think they're beautiful."

He kissed her forehead. "Maybe someday we can build our very own house like this to hand down to our kids."

She hugged his arm. "Oh, Cade, I would love that, but I'm sure it's really expensive to build a house this big and beautiful. We may end up living in your cabin for the first five years of our marriage. I guess I should get a job when we get back." She had very little enthusiasm regarding that subject. Caroline really didn't want to work as a nurse, but since that was what her degree was in, she needed to stick to it and do her part in their relationship.

"Don't you worry about money. My SEAL team leader during my first tour was a master at investments. He taught me some valuable lessons, so we're set. Besides, my family comes from money, and so does yours. I'm sure if they knew they could keep us close, it wouldn't be too difficult to get help building our dream home."

"What do you mean we're set? You have money? I didn't know that? How did I not know that?"

"I don't exactly flaunt the information. That's why I do odd jobs that I enjoy rather than some big time career that I hate. My income while in the military built up while I was overseas because I never needed to spend it on anything. So when I learned how to invest it, I pretty much quadrupled it. You don't have to work unless you just want to. I personally would love for you to be a stay-at-home mom so I could enjoy your company any time of the day." He turned her to face him and gently ran a finger down her cheek. "But only if that's what you want."

"It may be a while before I'm a mom. I recently started taking birth control after all the talk about sex," Caroline sheepishly grinned. "Kristy's suggestion," she shrugged. But I'm okay with being a stay-at-home wife. I could get used to enjoying your company on a daily basis, Mr. Beauregard." She reached down and patted his firm backside. Ever since she'd gotten a taste of what marriage had to offer, she increasingly understood how that was all Trevor could think about. Cade was scrumptious, and she could easily become a glutton off the fruits of his labor.

After lunch, Cade expanded upon what his friend Tony uncovered about April. Caroline still couldn't believe it. She knew April was a conniving bitch, but would never have guessed she had connections and especially an alias. Still no trace from April or her wherabouts. No one had heard from her. Not even Eddie.

When Cade wasn't teaching her about some little tidbit of New Orleans history, or divulging new information about April, Caroline noticed him quiet and lost in thought. She wanted to ask what was on his mind, but after he had opened up so much this week, she didn't want to press her luck.

Cade asked if she minded making a stop before they headed home. She nodded, eager to see what else he had in store for her. They entered an old cemetery, most famous in New Orleans for housing many local celebrities, dating back to pirates who sailed with the notorious Captain Jean Lafitte in the early 1800s. The aged, above-ground marble vaults shadowing the manicured lawn stood timeless, the cracks and fading inscriptions adding to the haunting feel of the legendary attraction. A shiver crept up her spine as her eyes fell upon a somber bouquet of dead flowers atop a small tomb belonging to a child. Caroline wondered how long it had been since anyone visited the poor baby.

It was eerily quiet in the busy cemetery as they moved gingerly along the concrete path, broken from the sinking, marshy soil. She was amazed by the close proximity of the trees between each vault and how the roots managed to not bust the concrete. The once-white structures, now grayish-black from the punishment of Mother Nature, were meticulously lined in rows, each one guarded by its own wrought iron fence. Caroline wondered from what, or *whom*, exactly, they needed protection.

Fascinated, her attention was quickly stolen by a small blue butterfly landing upon her shoulder. It was right next to her face, and she was like a child, so excited to be this close to it. Amazingly, the butterfly stayed on her shoulder for the full remainder of their visit, occasionally fluttering its wings.

Cade stopped in front of a specific vault and stared in silence. Caroline followed his mournful gaze. "Richardson" was emblazoned above the slots of tombs. He reached for Caroline's hand and placed his other hand on Jenny's tomb. Caroline's friendly butterfly flitted from her shoulder to rest on Cade's. He noticed the butterfly and his eyes met Caroline's for a moment of silent understanding. Not that she could've spoken if she'd wanted to because of the softball in her throat, but she remained steady as he clutched her for support, for the strength to get through this.

"Hey, Jenny. It's been a while since I came here. I'm sorry. It's just been so painful for so long, it was easier for me to be a coward and bury my feelings instead of face them." Tears welled in his eyes and he struggled to speak.

Caroline's tears dripped from her chin, but she didn't dare let go of Cade to wipe them.

"I need. . .I need to tell you how sorry I am."

His voice cracked and Caroline nearly lost it.

"I'm so sorry, Jenny. I'm sorry I couldn't save you, and I. . .I hope you can forgive me. I've finally found someone who managed to drag me from the hole I buried myself in after losing you, and it's. . ." He coughed and squeezed Caroline's hand. "It's taken me forever to accept this, but it's time for me to set you free now. You will always hold a special place in my heart. Forever." Cade squeezed his eyes closed and swiped beneath them, but it was no use, the teardrops flowed freely. "Goodbye, Jenny." He leaned forward with tear-streaked cheeks and kissed her tomb as he whispered, "Thank you."

He abruptly turned to Caroline, his face drawn and more serious than she'd ever seen him. She worried she'd pushed him too far and he was angry with her, but if he could only see himself the way she saw him in this moment, he would understand why she could never exist without him. His hazel eyes, windows to the depths of his soul, illuminated with sincerity causing the green swirls to be more pronounced with his emotion. He pressed her fingers to his lips, softly kissing each one while never removing his eyes from hers, and smiled. Her knees quivered, her heart pounded, and her breathing became labored from the intensity of his focus. He was beautiful. And free.

"Thank you, Caroline. For helping me reach this point—this point of healing. I'm positive I would never have breached this wall if it hadn't been for you. I know I'm repeating myself, but I will continue to tell you this as long as I live. Thank you for saving me. . .from myself. For towing me from the dark waters—for being my lifeline. I love you so much." He pulled her into a tight hug with one arm and kissed her hairline. "God knows I'm the luckiest man in the world to have you."

"I love you, too." Caroline looked up and cocked an eyebrow, "And just to set the record straight, you saved me first."

They kissed and the butterfly remained steadfast on Cade's shoulder. It stayed perched there all the way back to the car. Just as he started to scoop it up to place it on a tree branch, it flitted away into the dusk sky. Caroline wouldn't say it aloud, but both she and Cade knew the butterfly was Jenny's way of showing her approval with him letting her go.

They held hands in silence the rest of the way home, closer spiritually than they'd ever been before. She was more in love with him than should be possible. In her mind, their intertwined souls were one, their heartbeats keeping time together.

When the familiar crunch from the oyster shell driveway ceased, Caroline still couldn't pull her gaze from Cade to even look at the plantation house.

"This was the best, most amazing week I've ever had," he said. "I can't wait to spend the rest of my life with you, especially now that I have the green light to touch you wherever I want."

She smiled, amazed that she could still blush after the things they had done on their honeymoon.

His hands continued roaming as he leaned in to her neck. "Now that I can do this. . .and this. . ." he whispered. His hot kisses on her neck, and his fingers creeping up her thigh, had her ready right there in her dad's driveway.

Cade exercised his superhuman control, and pulled away, smoothing her hair.

She released a controlled breath. "Let's go say hello so we can continue this in the privacy of our cabin."

He grinned. "I love hearing you refer to it as ours. Everything I have is yours now. Everything." He gave her one last melting kiss before they got out. Her heart fluttered with anticipation of making love in his bed, *their* bed, for the first time ever.

A car she didn't recognize sat in the driveway. "Who do you suppose is here?" she asked.

Cade shrugged. "No clue."

Delia met them at the door, her bony arms stretched out and a million dollar smile on her face.

She spoke very low, just above a whisper. "Welcome home, Mr. and Mrs. Beauregard. We are so happy to see you."

Curious, as always, Caroline whispered back, "Thank you. Who's here, and why are we whispering?"

Delia closed the door behind them, her eyes wary. When her mouth opened it wasn't Delia's voice Caroline heard.

"Caroline. Thank goodness you're home. I'm so happy to see you. I need you—I mean, uh, I desperately need to talk to you."

Her heart leapt into her throat. "Trevor? What are *you* doing here?"

"I'll be in the kitchen if anyone needs me." Delia ducked her head and scurried from the room.

Trevor's smile fell, and he scowled as he gauged her reaction. "It's a pleasure to see you too, Trevor," he mocked. "What can I help you with since you're obviously desperate to have come to my father's house uninvited? Please, sit down, let's talk."

Cade stepped between her and Trevor. "That's enough, Callahan."

The last time Cade stepped between them, things got ugly fast.

"She may not have answered the way you'd hoped," Cade said, "but she did ask you a legitimate question."

"Still overly protective, I see." Trevor's gaze landed upon her with authentic speculation. "My, my, Caroline. Your face is flushed. I don't remember ever seeing you with a glow like that around me. I would almost guess. . ." His crystal eyes darted to her left hand, and bulged at the sight of her wedding rings.

Embarrassed, and for some crazy reason, a little ashamed for not telling him, she cringed in preparation for Trevor's outburst, but he surprised her.

He stepped back a couple of steps, stunned. "Wow. Seems I've missed out on a very special occasion in the Fontenot household. Expected, I guess." Trevor cleared his throat and licked his lips. "I suppose congratulations are in order."

His lingering stare gouged her guilty conscience. He was genuinely wounded by the unexpected news. She should've at least told him about the wedding, even if she didn't invite him.

Trevor held his hand out to Cade. "Congratulations, Beau. You've got yourself an amazing woman."

Cade apprehensively shook his hand and thanked him, his guard never dropping.

Trevor stepped around Cade and held his arms out to hug her, pausing beforehand to ask permission. "May I?"

"Um, sure." She opened her arms to hug him back, relieved to feel nothing at all in response to his touch or smell. "Thank you, Trevor."

He pulled back without releasing her. "You're welcome, C."

He pursed his lips in a smile, but sadness dulled his eyes. "I really am happy for you. I'll admit, I'm a little jealous, but I'm glad you finally got your happily ever after."

Things wouldn't exactly be happy until she found out who was trying to hurt her family.

She thanked him again and he released her, stepping back.

"Well, I've enjoyed about as much as I can of my time down here. I'm headed back to Chicago. It's time to get back to reality and sleep in my own bed."

Trevor shuddered. Something was up with him, but she didn't want to ask. She had more important, more pleasurable plans for her evening.

"Me too," she mumbled.

Cade glanced at her, smirking.

Trevor frowned. He was putting on a good show, but he was more than just 'a little jealous'.

Cade stuck his free hand out to shake Trevor's again. "Well, Callahan. It's been a pleasure. Much more so this time than last."

Trevor eyed him cautiously, but then genuinely smiled. "Agreed. Take care of her."

"Count on it." Cade answered confidently.

She remembered that she needed to talk to Trevor about his family, about George and Peter, and shed some light on why they wanted her soul. "Um, Trev. Before you go, I have a few questions I wanted to ask you."

"Sure." His brow furrowed. "What's up?"

"First, you seemed very eager to talk to me about something when we walked in. What was that about?"

He shrugged. "No big deal. I had to explain to your dad that I wasn't the one who shot Remy."

He was hiding something, but more importantly she had to get questions answered before he left. "Can you tell me what you know about your ancestors?" Rachel's journal mentioned that Peter had died of pneumonia. "Specifically, George Callahan, and how he died?"

The color in Trevor's face drained.

"Trevor? Are you okay?"

He nodded.

"You're lying," she accused. Trevor took a step back and looked away.

"Did something happen? What's wrong?"

"Yeah, Callahan. You look like you're gonna hurl. What's got you so spooked?"

Trevor nervously rubbed his face and chuckled. "Interesting choice of words you used there, Beau."

"You're spooked?" Caroline said. "Come on, let's go sit down and talk. I want to know what happened to you."

They sat in the formal living room where Trevor told them about the unusual things that had happened to him. He explained his erratic behavior the night she found him at the bar, what happened at Jessica's apartment, and then the apparition he witnessed the night before that could only have been the description of George Callahan.

Caroline explained everything she knew about George and Rachel's relationship. How he'd been jealous of Rachel and Jackson's marriage, and how he flipped when, after Peter's death, the partnership between the Callahan's and Fontenot's crumbled. That betrayal eventually lead to George's obsession, his thirst for revenge. The ultimate revenge being the rape and murder of Rachel, all in hopes to eventually acquire, by force if necessary, everything the Fontenot family had worked to build, and destroy it.

"Don't you see, Trev, ruining and ending the Fontenot legacy was George's driving force when he was alive. He pounded it in to his kids and grandkids, who then pounded it in to theirs. When you and I didn't. . . Well, when we didn't get married and you didn't inherit my family's fortune, George's plan dissolved."

"No. That's ridiculous. My father told me a different story. My love for you had nothing to do with a stupid vendetta. Your family has skewed the story somewhere down the line. That can't possibly be what happened. There has to be another explanation for all this."

Caroline pulled Rachel's journal from the bookcase to prove George's psychotic jealousy and rage caused him to murder Rachel. Trevor read each handwritten page until finally closing it and pinching the bridge of his nose.

"This is all very disappointing."

"Trevor, the dreams I had last year that I told you about—"

"The same ones I criticized you about? That I made fun of you for, blaming them on your overactive imagination? Yes, I remember them, and I'm so sorry for being such a prick."

"They were very detailed and graphic. Yes, George raped Rachel, impregnating her, but he didn't know about it. I think if he'd known she was pregnant, especially with his baby, he wouldn't have killed her. I know that doesn't make you feel any better about the current situation, but perhaps there was some good in him."

Trevor shook his head. "This journal said George was double-crossed. Is that correct?"

She shrugged and nodded. "In my first dream I heard George say something about it before he raped her, and in another one when she and Jackson were talking, but none of the dreams ever explained *how* he was double-crossed."

Trevor frowned pensively. "Last year my dad told me George was supposed to inherit half of your family's company, but when Jackson and Rachel had their baby, Jefferson Fontenot changed his mind and decided to keep it in the family."

Eddie's smooth voice rang through the room as he rounded the base of the stairs. "I don't know if that's truth or not, Trevor. Forgive me for eavesdropping, but I was always told that George couldn't stand seeing Rachel and Jackson together because he was in love with her. When he found out they were having a baby, he couldn't take it anymore and moved up north."

"Well, I guess we have two different sides of the story. Either way, George Callahan felt cheated, and apparently he can't even deal with it in death."

Eddie agreed.

Thinking back to what Lucinda told her to find out, Caroline broke the tension. "Trevor, do you know how George died? Or even how old he was when he died?"

He stared blankly at the table, his compelling eyes glassing over with the memory. "After you left last summer, when I fought with my father, we didn't talk for months. Finally, I went to visit him at his office one day, and I had apparently interrupted something intense. He was uptight and skittish, like a feral cat. He told me I should leave, but I didn't listen."

Trevor's head rocked back with amusement. "It's interesting now, thinking back, that he told me I *should* leave rather than just throwing me out. Normally I would have simply been escorted out. He was acting very weird. . .constantly checking his phone and looking at the door as if he was expecting someone. I demanded his attention and asked him to tell me why he'd hired a hit man and how the hell he'd become involved with the Mafia." Cade stiffened and squeezed Caroline's hand. She glanced at him, his eyes scanning the area undoubtedly looking for April, but Trevor didn't notice. "He looked directly at me and told me he was just keeping with tradition." Cade stood protectively near the foyer, still able to hear the story and keep watch.

"That triggered my curiosity, so I did some digging." Trevor looked at Caroline, his solemn eyes serious. "Every man in my family, including George, mysteriously disappeared, and each man's body was later found at some random dump site. George was supposedly found at a construction site, his body burned beyond recognition due to an alleged gas explosion."

Caroline gasped and stiffened, remembering when she smelled the smoke at the hospital. Was George hovering around her then, too?

Trevor's face crumpled in thought. "The funny thing is, for the stage of development at that particular site, the gas lines hadn't been connected yet. No one ever found the responsible party, but everyone suspected. They were all just too afraid to talk about it."

Trevor huffed and rested his elbows on his knees. "I'd always thought my grandfather died of a sudden heart attack, but my father spilled it that day. He said, and I quote, 'in case I never have the opportunity to tell you later in life.' He informed me that he tried to keep me out of the loop so I wouldn't be associated with the Mafia in any way, so if authorities questioned me I could plead not guilty. But when Beau, here, found my dad's dirty little secret, he let the cat out of the bag. My dad was furious with you all, which is why I came down here when I realized he had gone somewhere and instructed his secretary not to tell me when I asked. I just knew he had come to hurt you or your family."

He offered his hand to Eddie. "Mr. Fontenot," Trevor placed his palm over his heart and spoke earnestly, "I don't know who shot your son, but I honestly don't believe it was my dad or anyone he hired. If he'd hired someone to do it, your son would be dead."

Eddie nodded. "I've thought of that, too. Thanks, Trevor. I appreciate your honesty. I hope your dad hasn't gotten himself in too deep that he ends up dragging you down with him. Take care of yourself when you get back up there, and let us know if you ever need anything."

Trevor nodded. "Thank you."

"So, why do you think George is haunting you?" Caroline asked, refusing to let it go.

He shrugged. "I couldn't tell you. I thought it was the hotel that was haunted until something happened at Jessica's. Then, when I heard. . .George, if it really was him, say my name while floating in my headlights, I knew it was me, not the place. I am really hoping he's stuck down here in Louisiana so when I go back home to Chicago, I'll have a little peace. This shit's really creeping me out. Excuse my language." He stood, nervous and twitchy, and briskly walked to the front door. "I need to get back to Jessica's place and get my things. She probably thinks I've been eaten by a gator by now."

"Are you just going to leave her? You two have been inseparable for weeks, won't you miss her?"

Caroline had hoped Trevor and Jessica would get together. She really wanted Trevor to find happiness. Plus, it would ease Caroline's guilty conscience about the way she left him, ending up with Cade after all, and not telling Trevor about her wedding.

Trevor shrugged and smiled that crooked smile that she'd always loved. "Maybe I'll ask her to come with me. She said she's always wanted to live in a big city, so something tells me she won't have a problem with that idea."

He chuckled and gave Caroline one last hug, smoothing her hair from her face as he spoke. "Goodbye, Caroline. I really am happy for you." He whispered, "Don't forget me."

She nodded.

"Beau, Mr. Fontenot. So long. Please give my regards to Emily."

With that, Trevor turned and walked out of Caroline's life forever. Part of her was sad, the other relieved. Thanks to Trevor, she at least had a few more clues to add to the mystery of George Callahan. Mysteriously killed by the Mafia, definitely not a pleasant way to die, and no justice for his death. That explained why George was stuck in the afterlife as a dark spirit, and Peter was betrayed, causing hardships for his ancestors. But with Eddie still alive, why in the world were the ghosts only after her?

THIRTY-ONE

The internet was a wealth of information, and one can find most anything he needed online. But what Cade had just learned worried him. When Lucinda, the surprisingly helpful voodoo sorceress, mentioned her Guatemalan husband, Carlos, that day in her shop, Cade had wanted to keep her talking so she might reveal more information to help his research. While Caroline was hooked up to stimulation for half an hour, he interrogated Ms. Lucinda.

She was informative but very meticulous with how she answered, so not to reveal too much. Lucinda's husband had one younger sister and his mother had been a voodoo priestess in Guatemala. She wouldn't say too much about Carlos's sister except that her name was Maria and she died in her early forties, leaving behind a teenage daughter. Carlos and Maria's mother, Corina, raised her granddaughter here in New Orleans. Lucinda didn't have much to say about her in-laws, but from her facial expression, rigid posture, and timbre of her voice when she mentioned them, he could tell there was bad blood.

While Caroline slept, Cade researched male licensed ophthalmologists in New Orleans. He scrolled through pages of names and found one that made his skin crawl. He figured *something* was screwy with Lucinda's whole situation, but he never imagined it would be this. The name he found, that he was sure was her husband, was Carlos Morales. This information was congruent with the report

Tony had sent, but Cade wanted to double check the names to make sure it wasn't a coincidence. He immediately called his FBI friend,

Tonya to inform her of what he'd learned, and she filled him in on what she'd found thus far. It turned out his gut feeling was spot-on. Corina Morales, Lucinda's Guatemalan mother-in-law, had two children, Carlos and Maria. Carlos Morales was the brother of Maria Morales, the voodoo priestess and mother of Ana Morales, aka April Jones Fontenot.

Lucinda's words echoed in his mind. "I'm not a voodoo priestess, but my sister-in-law was." Even worse, "Carlos came from a long line of spiritually-talented people. Some were good, like my Carlos and me. Others in his family were bad." He assumed Maria was in the evil category of spiritually-talented people and frequently abused her power, which was why Lucinda wasn't fond of her. Cade's stomach churned.

April's grandmother and mother were both voodoo priestesses, and she was raised by both of them at different stages of her life. What exactly did they teach her? April didn't seem very spiritual, so maybe she chose not to dabble in the same practices as the women who raised her. One could only hope.

Tonya had also found April's connection with the Marcellino family. Corina, April's grandmother, met and worked with Marcellino when he briefly lived in Guatemala during the 1960s. She and her teenage daughter, Maria, came back to the states with him, and she lived in his house as his maid. Whether Corina was actually his maid or not, no one really knows. She could have been using her voodoo to help the Mafia take people out.

Researching crimes associated with the Marcellino family over the years, Cade noticed an abundance of fires and "accidental" explosions. He recalled the gas explosion in the kitchen last summer when Delphine suffered second degree burns, damaging a major part of the Fontenot kitchen. He and Caroline had thought it was the ghost, but Cade wondered now if April had been responsible.

He sighed in frustration as he massaged his temples. This was not good. So April, or Ana, was raised by Corina Morales, an evil voodoo priestess who worked personally with Angelo Marcellino. No wonder she knew how to handle a weapon. Was she trained by the crime family to handle explosives, too?

Cade worried about April's endless supply of dangerous people to 'do her bidding' as he had overheard her say on the phone. He asked Tonya if she knew who Ana Morales's father was. She said, "No, but I do know Ana was born during the short two years while the Marcellino family lived in New York." Considering New York had one of the largest populations in the country, April's father could be anybody. For now, Cade would keep researching why she was working with the Mafia and who she was after. The simple fact she was working with someone he most likely trusted didn't sit well with him either. He needed to find out who it was.

Caroline walked into the small kitchen wearing a thin, satin robe. Cade's body promptly responded knowing she had nothing on underneath it. He admired the contours of her delicate curves as she poured herself a cup of coffee.

"Good morning, beautiful. How'd you sleep?" She grunted. "That good, huh?"

"I slept okay, just not long enough." Her heavy lids framed her sultry gaze. "Someone kept kissing me in certain areas of my body last night making sleep a non-issue."

He continued working on his computer with a wicked grin. "Sounds to me like a wonderful problem to have."

She carefully pushed his computer aside as she placed her coffee cup on the table. Demanding his full attention, she straddled his lap and kissed him. "If it was a problem, I wouldn't be here right now." She smiled. "Good morning, lover."

His heart pounded, and the pheromones swirled through his body. "Damn, baby. You have no idea what that does to me."

She smiled wickedly and squirmed in his lap. "I have some idea."

Caroline ran both hands through his hair and kissed him as he cupped his hands around her hips, pulling her body even closer. He moved his lips to her ear and whispered, "Say it again."

She sucked in a deep breath, her voice raspy, "Lover." Grinding against him now, she tugged on his bottom lip with her teeth and tangled her fingers into his hair. His caveman gene was beating down the door to his self-control as it balanced on a thread. With her sitting on his lap, he was ready to take her on the kitchen table, but this game was fun. With her inexperience, he wanted to let her hold the reins and set the pace, all the while showing her how much fun things could be. Though, she'd apparently already mastered the game. He learned last week that she was bashful and modest in public, but behind closed doors the vixen came out to play.

When she released his lip he gently tugged her hair. Her chest heaved with each breath as he slowly kissed her exposed neck. "You naughty little minx," he murmured. "I should bend you over this table and show you my appreciation."

She seductively licked her lips. "What are you waiting for, Sailor?"

He untied her silky robe and slipped it off her shoulders, exposing her beautiful curves.

His phone rang. He let out a gush of air and rested his forehead on her breastbone. With the second ring, he shook his head. He continued, sliding his hands up her naked back that arched into him, and pulled her puckered rosebud into his mouth while his hand massaged her other breast. "Ignore it," he mumbled through suckles.

She giggled and stepped off of him. "It's okay. This ship's not going anywhere." She bent over directly in front of him to retrieve her silky garment and sashayed down the hall, calling over her shoulder. "Answer your phone, it might be important." Damn.

That woman could bring him from zero to eighty with just a look. He snatched up his phone, answering curtly.

"Yeah, Beau."

"Dude, I'm really sorry." Runway's words were urgent. "You know I wouldn't call if it wasn't important."

"Yeah, I know. What's up?"

"I have something you'll want to see. You're not going to like it."

"On my way."

Runway had moved to one of the extra rooms in the plantation house so Cade and Caroline could have the cabin to themselves. Cade felt bad about kicking him out, but he said he wanted to move so he could be closer to Eddie and Emily in case anything else happened. He also said after April's aborted mission to blow Cade's head off, he needed to watch her a little closer, too. After what Cade learned this morning, that was a wise move, only. . .April was off the grid at the moment.

Cade jogged the entire way to the house, and Runway was already waiting for him on the porch.

"What's up? Is everyone okay?"

Runway nodded, but the seriousness in his eyes made Cade's skin prickle. "Yes, everyone is okay. April is in New Orleans. Tony spotted her this morning. Apparently all her information for April Fontenot is back on record, but there's nothing for Ana Morales."

"Okay. Why is that urgent?"

"Come see for yourself."

Cade climbed the stairs two at a time and turned the corner into Eddie's office. Eddie absently stared at a duffle bag on his desk like he was waiting for a monster to pop out of it.

"Mr. Fontenot. Everything alright?"

He shook his head without removing his eyes from the bag. "No, Beau. Everything is not alright. Not at all."

Cade started to ask what was in the bag, but someone knocked. Eddie jumped like he'd been shot, while Runway pulled his weapon and stood behind the door.

"Geez, what has got you guys so spooked?" Cade stalked to the door, watching Runway in his peripheral vision to make sure he had back up.

"Hello, Mrs. Fontenot. How are you this morning?"

"Cade, you're my son-in-law now. Please, call me Emily, or Mom, but cut the formalities. Is Eddie in here?"

Cade glanced at him, and Eddie nodded. "Yes, ma'am. He's right here."

"Okay, good." She paused for a moment, torn about something. "I would like to speak with you, too. I'm sure you're busy, but if you could make time I would appreciate it. It's important."

Cade smiled. "Sure thing, Mrs. Fo—Ms. Emily."

Eddie walked up next to Cade, smiling at Emily like a man in love. Cade pretended not to notice and motioned for Runway to show him the bag in question. Eddie and Emily spoke softly, and Eddie's body language, leaning against the door frame with his hands in his pockets and his head tilted toward her, was like a teenage boy hanging out at his girlfriend's locker in high school. What would April think if she saw Eddie grinning at Emily like a fool. Probably wouldn't be pretty.

"Eddie couldn't find his razor this morning, so he dug through his closet for an unopened package of razors he's left in an old suitcase from his last trip. He picked this bag up to move it out of the way and noticed it wasn't empty. When he unzipped it, he discovered this," Runway whispered.

The duffle bag was full of personal items belonging to other people. He recognized Caroline's hair brush, a toothbrush, lip balm and a razor that must've belonged to Eddie. There was one more item inside that disturbed him a great deal. A pair of his own boxer briefs complete with military stenciled name. He cursed loud enough to catch Eddie and Emily's attention.

"Sorry for the language, but *damn*."

Emily pushed past Eddie into the room. "What is it? What's

310

wrong?" Eddie filled her in on how he'd found the bag. She looked confused. "Well, whose is it?"

Runway and Cade looked at each other. Cade had filled him in about the voodoo priestess, but he hadn't had the chance to tell him April's genealogy yet. Eddie's voice was solemn. "It's April's."

Emily gasped. "No. That little thief. Why did she steal our stuff?"

Eddie's face turned hard. "There's something of yours in this bag?"

She nodded and pointed to the lip balm. "Yes, that's mine. I've been looking for it for weeks now. I finally just bought a new one."

He grasped her shoulders and stared intently into her eyes. "You're sure that's yours?"

She picked it up to examine it. "Yes, it's my favorite brand, and see here where the label is peeled? I was frustrated that it wouldn't roll up anymore. Why? What is going on?"

Cade sorted through the items in the bag, pointing out to whom the things belonged. The toothbrush being the only mystery. He looked at Runway, and his best friend shook his head. The only ones with nothing in the bag were Runway, Claire, Remy, and Kristy. Cade couldn't imagine April wanting to hurt Remy or Claire, considering she'd practically raised them. She's cold, but he didn't think she was that heartless. Especially after her shocked reaction when Remy was shot. That left Runway and Kristy, and Runway said it wasn't his, so. . . "Kristy," Cade said.

Runway's head popped up in surprise to look at him, and his jaw clenched. He cursed softly. Now they each had a vested interest in bringing April down, but why was she doing this? What was she hoping to achieve? Emily's concern broke the silence.

"Edward Joseph Fontenot, you'd better tell me right now what the heck is going on."

"April has an alias. I didn't know it. Beau discovered this information and told me about it the day of the graduation party. Her real name is Ana Morales, and she's somehow connected with the Louisiana Mafia."

"Well, actually," Cade said, "there's more." Three sets of eyes bored into Cade. He took a deep breath and explained his and Caroline's unusual experience with Lucinda and what he learned from her, along with the information Tony sent him. Then he told them about contacting Tonya and what she'd found out about April's relatives.

"You see, April has lived with the Marcellino family since she was born. She's travelled with them, trained with them, and possibly learned the ways of her mother and grandmother."

Emily crossed her arms and raised an eyebrow. "Learned their ways? I suggest you elaborate on that before I unleash my crazy."

He sighed, not wanting to go too deeply into this and cause a panic. "Her mother and grandmother were both voodoo priestesses."

Emily's jaw dropped. "Voodoo priestesses?"

He nodded. "Yep. The hexing, spell-casting, curse-bestowing kind. Tonya believes they may have been working with the Mafia to help torture or take out those who betrayed them. This is all about to get really ugly."

Emily turned to Eddie and cupped his cheek. "Oh, no, Eddie. What have you gotten yourself into? What have you gotten us *all* into?"

He turned away from her with clenched teeth and slammed his fist into his desk. "Emily, I swear this woman will not touch you. Not you, or Caroline, or anyone in my family. So help me, I will stop this, even if it kills me."

Emily's nostrils flared. "And what good would that do anyone, Eddie? Huh? If you died, she's still going to come after the rest of us. Even if you take her out, her henchmen will follow through eliminating everyone who was involved. Voodoo *and* the Mafia? I can't imagine a much worse combination."

Cade remembered something Lucinda had said about Caroline's parents being spiritually sensitive. "Emily, these visions you've been having, did any of them have anything to do with April?"

She shook her head with a baffled expression. "I don't think so. I mean, they were all just ridiculous nightmares. None of them have actually happened. I saw you get shot, for heaven's sakes."

He shifted uncomfortably, flashing Runway a look, because they had lied to everyone about that.

"Wait, you think these visions are voodoo?"

Cade shook his head, but wanted to know more about what Emily saw. "Start from the beginning, and tell me what your very first vision entailed."

She sat down. "Well, the first vision happened in the backseat of the car after graduation as Caroline, Kristy and I drove down here. It was very disturbing, and I tried not to flip out for Caroline's sake. Someone's hands were wrapped around Caroline's throat trying to strangle her."

Cade's stomach dropped. It was the same nightmare Caroline had before her graduation. He'd teased her unmercifully about dreaming of dancing potheads. She'd said George or Peter, whichever it was grabbed her throat before he pushed her off the pier. "Caroline told me about a nightmare she had that was very similar," Cade said. "She said a man had his strong hands wrapped around her throat, and a crowd was cheering and stomping to drums. She also told me she smelled the scent of burning herbs. Do you think her dream and your vision were related somehow?"

Emily's brow furrowed. "Oh, Cade, I don't think so. Nothing I've envisioned has come true. The one I had of you didn't, thank goodness. I saw you and your hot little friend here walking through the woods, and April found you. She put a gun in your face and pulled the trigger. I saw you fall, yet here you stand."

He glanced at Runway, who nodded his head. "Well, Ms. Emily, your vision wasn't entirely untrue. It wasn't a wild hog we ran into in the woods." He glanced at Eddie whose brows were bunched in curiosity. "It was April. Her target practice in the woods caught our attention, so I snuck over to the building where she was while Runway stayed in the woods to cover me, and I overheard a phone call. She called someone I probably know from the reference she made to alligators being nothing compared to the monsters she would unleash on him. I desperately wanted to know who was betraying me."

He looked at Eddie and gave a single nod, "Betraying *us*. So I stayed to hear more. After I observed the odd, random items in the shack, and wondered what the hell kind of black magic she was involved in, I started to make my move and disappear into the trees when she popped her head and weapon-yielding hand through the broken window above me. She told me I'd heard too much and pointed the gun in my face.

"Runway shot at her, but he missed and hit the window above my head, causing the glass to fall and slice my shoulder open." Cade smirked at Runway and added, "Thank goodness he's a lousy shot and missed me. Either way, I'd dropped and covered my head, sure she had shot me. When I looked up only moments later, pinned by the glass pane that had impaled my shoulder, she was gone. Runway saw her vanish into the woods headed south of the plantation house."

"Why the hell didn't you tell me about this earlier, Beau? Didn't you think this was something I'd like to know?"

"Yes, sir, I realize that, and I apologize. I didn't want to ruin the party, and after Remy was shot, I wanted to talk to my FBI contact and get all my facts together before I told you. Just in case I was wrong about her. That's why I asked you if she'd ever mentioned anything about voodoo. I really am sorry."

Eddie mumbled a stream of curse words as he paced the room. Emily stayed frozen in her chair, clearly in shock. "That was my vision. Why didn't you tell me?"

"I didn't want to scare you any worse than you already were. Did you have any other visions or dreams?"

She nodded her head, fighting back the tears. "I had one indecipherable vision just after Remy was shot, but I couldn't understand it. It was cloudy with flashes of light if that makes any sense."

Lucinda and Caroline described what the spirits looked like to a spiritually sensitive person, which validated Emily's gift, so he did understand her vision. Cade wondered just how powerful her clairvoyance was, but didn't know how to answer the questions she would have.

"Was that the last vision you've had?"

The tears flowed freely as she pursed her lips together and shook her head. They gave her a minute, but Cade struggled to keep his control. Suddenly her fierce eyes beamed into his. "Cade, whatever you do, whatever it takes, do *not* get Caroline pregnant right now. Do you understand me?"

His confusion knit his brow. "You do realize we just returned from our honeymoon? Caroline told me she was on birth control. I mean, we both want kids and. . . Why? What did you see?"

She covered her face with both hands and wept. Eddie squatted in front of her. "Em, you need to tell him what you saw. He might be able to help and at least take measures to prevent whatever it is from happening." Eddie handed her his handkerchief to wipe her face, and she took a deep breath.

"I woke up in a fright last week to an eerily quiet room. After the dream I'd just had, I wanted to call Caroline and warn her, but I didn't know about what? And I didn't want to bother y'all on your honeymoon.

"At first I thought I was dreaming, it was much too quiet, but when I stood I was very dizzy. It was still dark out, so I looked at my watch and realized it was 3 a.m. Anyway, I noticed the full length mirror was pointing downward. I don't know why, but I straightened it."

Emily's chin quivered as the waterworks started again. "I saw. . .Caroline's reflection in the mirror, and she was very pregnant. She had on the wedding rings you gave her, and she looked incredibly happy. Glowing even. A warm sensation filled my body with the thought of being a grandma some day. Dreamy and euphoric. . . Until Caroline's face in the mirror distorted in excruciating pain."

Emily spoke between sobs. "I felt helpless. There was nothing I could do, I didn't know what caused the pain. Then she grasped her belly and suddenly she was ankle deep in blood. Then the blood was up to her hips. I gripped the mirror. Like that would do any good," Emily scoffed. "I yelled for help, not expecting anyone to hear, but my first thought was where all the blood was coming from? Was it a miscarriage? A normal human doesn't have that much blood in her body, so maybe the symbolism of the blood. Why was I dreaming about my pregnant daughter drowning in a pool of blood?" Emily's whisper may as well have been a shout. "I realize it was probably just a dream, but it was terrifying."

"Ms. Emily, I don't—"

"She can't get pregnant until all of this has been taken care of. Okay?"

Cade hesitated, not thrilled with this command, but he finally nodded.

"Cade, promise me."

"I'll start wearing protection, just to be extra careful."

This appeased her, and she relaxed.

Cade wasn't comfortable discussing his sex life with his in-laws, and the idea of anyone dictating when he started his family didn't sit well. But he understood. "For now, let's not tell Caroline about this. Don't lie to her; if she asks you, tell her, but just don't volunteer the information. She already blames herself for Remy being shot, even though he'll be fine. She thinks she's the reason everything bad is happening to her family. She doesn't need to know April is targeting everyone in the family. I don't think she'd be able to refrain from confronting April right now, and if she tips April off that we're on to her, that might ruin everything. We're lucky that right now April thinks we're clueless about her past." Cade grumbled, "Though she's obviously suspicious now if she's clearing her record."

"There's one more thing you should know. It may be irrelevant, but April was there," Emily said, hesitantly.

"What?" Eddie's posture became that of a fighting gamecock. Chest puffed out, head alert, shoulders squared and ready to attack.

"April's up to something, but I don't think she knows your bad dreams are actually pre-cognizant visions." Cade nodded to Eddie, "If we want to get to the bottom of this, discretion is key," Cade warned. "She's sneaky."

She waved her hand like it was no big deal. "I didn't read too much in to it. The woman's hated me since I stepped foot in Louisiana. She shook me, shouting, 'Stop. Turn the horn off before you wake the whole house.' I asked her what she was doing there, but her malicious grin should've tipped me off. She asked if I'd had a bad dream. I said yes and thanked her for her superficial concern. She replied, 'You're welcome, of course. Next time try to keep your screams muffled with your pillow or something.' Then, she left. But not before she whispered, 'Sweet dreams'."

"Wait a minute. This was last week?" Cade asked.

Emily nodded. "Yes, while you and Caroline were on your honeymoon." Emily looked at Eddie. "Why?"

"April's been gone for almost three weeks."

Emily frowned. "What the. . ." Her fingertips darted to her mouth and worry creased her soft features. "I didn't imagine it. She was there. Hateful as ever."

"Runway, I want you to come with me when I go confront the guys to find out who is working with April. I might need some backup."

Eddie stepped up. "What do you want me to do?"

"For starters, I would find April and confront her about her alias, without revealing everything you know about her. If Tony saw her in New Orleans, then that means she hasn't left the country. She may pop back in as if nothing ever happened. Then, if it were me, I would tell her I wanted a divorce."

317

Eddie nodded with a lingering look at Emily. "I couldn't agree more."

THIRTY-TWO

As they drove down to Grand Isle to meet up with Chris, Henry and Ty, Cade refreshed Runway's memory about April's phone conversation the day she'd nearly shot him. Runway knew Ty from their tour together overseas, but he'd never met the other two. Cade was certain Ty wasn't the one working with April. Ty would never betray him like that. They had the burn scar to prove it. Cade's first suspicion was Henry, after the way he had threatened Caroline last year, and Cade nearly shot Henry's balls off. But Cade wasn't assuming anything. Chris could be just as guilty as anyone, and their innocent, long-term friendship would be a great cover.

"Why are you so sure it's one of these two guys who is working with April? Aren't there other alligator hunters in this area?"

He nodded. "Yes, but these guys are the only ones who could get close enough to me and the Fontenot family to pull anything off. My gut's telling me it's one of them."

"Your gut has saved us on many occasions, so I'm with you one hundred percent."

"Thank you." It really did mean a lot to him to have Runway by his side again after Cade had been so hard on him before. It wasn't Runway's fault for not telling him about Jenny and the baby. He was just following orders from Cade's sister, trying to keep it a surprise for him. He'd been an ass to Runway, and needed to apologize, but didn't know where to start. Cade gripped the steering wheel and squeezed, twisting until the leather groaned in protest.

"Something on your mind?"

Runway knew Cade better than he knew himself. Cade shook his head and laughed. "If you keep ripping your fingers through your hair like that, you're gonna pull out those curls, Goldilocks," Runway teased.

Cade gave him a look, and Runway nudged his shoulder with his fist. "Talk to me, brother. I know something's bothering you. Is it Caroline?"

Cade shook his head. "No, she's fine. It's me." He sighed, "I owe you an apology, Matt. I treated you like crap for so long and you didn't deserve any of it. Yet, I call you out of the blue one day after not speaking to you for years, and you drop everything to help me on good faith alone."

"Beau, you don't owe me anything."

Cade huffed. "Except my life. Twice now."

"Twice?"

"Yeah. First the bomb, and then when April shoved that damned 9mm in my face."

Runway's head rocked back in recollection. "Ahh, yes. When I nearly shot your head off, myself."

They laughed together. "Seriously, dude. You're a great friend. The best. And I'm sorry I haven't pulled my weight. I'm really glad you're here."

He slapped his hand on Cade's shoulder and squeezed. "You're awesome, Beau. Don't beat yourself up. I'm glad you called me last year when you did. It gave me a reason to come see you and pick up where we left off. Plus, I met the woman of my dreams because of you. Trust me. We're even. I've got your back anytime, any day, and I know you've got mine. We're brothers, that's just what we do."

The thousand pound anvil of guilt lifted from his chest. Caroline was right about dealing with regrets and not burying them. It made a huge difference in how he saw things.

They pulled up to the daiquiri shop where Caroline had first met his friends. Chris, Ty, and Henry were all outside.

Henry took one last drag before standing and flicking his cigarette into the parking lot when he saw Runway and Cade.

"Hey, Beau. Been a long time. Still mad at me?" Henry asked.

Cade shook his head. "Keep your distance from my wife and we're good," he warned.

This was why part of him didn't suspect Henry. The obvious villain, Henry's honesty and straightforwardness debunked his involvement. Chris, on the other hand, was superficial. More talkative and outgoing, you always had to wonder about the validity of his stories. Sometimes Chris played up the truth to make himself look better. Henry told it like it was.

Henry smiled, his accent bleeding through, "You right, podna. I was worried you was gonna pass a slap at me."

Cade laughed and put him in a head lock. "Nah, we good, we *shive*. It's cool. You just need to get laid. Get your *poupoune* somewhere else from now on."

"Seriously, though," Henry continued. "I wasn't myself last year. Don't know what happened. Won't happen again."

Lucinda had mentioned the possibility of dark spirits taking control and causing harm.

Henry motioned to Runway. "So what's up?"

Cade introduced Runway to Chris and Henry, before Ty shook his hand with a sly grin.

"Lookin' smooth, Runway. I see the fashion industry still has you by the balls. Keeping it in business, huh, hot stuff?"

Runway took it in stride, responding coolly, "Still single, huh, Ty? Need some pointers?"

Ty fluffed his shirt. "Nah, ain't nothing wrong with my game. I just don't have time for a woman right now."

Runway raised an eyebrow. "Sure. No time. I believe you."

When the laughter settled, Cade looked at Chris, who was uncharacteristically quiet. When he caught his eye, Cade said, "Can I talk to you for a sec?"

He seemed nervous, which fueled Cade's suspicion. Chris nodded once and followed him to a tree on the other side of the parking lot.

"'Sup, Beau?"

Cade made it a point to keep eye contact. Any shift in Chris's eyes indicated he was lying. "Keeping busy. Got married last month."

"Congratulations, dude. That's awesome."

"Thanks. Does the name April Fontenot ring any bells with you?"

"That's Eddie Fontenot's wife, right?"

"Yep. Ever met her?"

Chris fidgeted and broke eye contact. He slowly shook his head. "Nah. Seen her, but never officially met her. Why?"

"Ever talked to her before?"

Splotchy hives popped up on Chris's neck. He was scared. Good.

Chris cleared his throat. "No, dude. I told you I've never met her. Why?"

Cade squinted. "You seem nervous, Chris. Why? Are you intimidated?"

Chris defensively moved away. "Hell, yes. You're interrogating me. Who wouldn't be intimidated?"

Cade smiled. "I just asked you a simple question. I'm not interrogating you." Cade hardened his tone and squared his shoulders as he stepped closer. "You want me to?"

Chris stepped back again and laughed nervously. "No, of course not. What's up, Beau?"

"Someone I trust has been working with April Fontenot in a ploy to hurt Caroline's family. It's someone I'm close to, who thinks he can deceive me, and apparently is supposed to take me out. I'm gonna ask you again. Have you ever talked to April Fontenot?"

His eyes snapped up to look at Cade. "No way, dude. I don't know anyone who could take you out."

"You didn't answer my question. Are you the traitor trying to hurt my wife's family?"

Chris avoided eye contact and pursed his lips.

"Why, dude? Just tell me why?"

Chris shook his head. "You don't understand."

"Try me."

"You know Lindsey Connor?"

"Yeah, she's Claire Fontenot's best friend. What about her?"

"I got her pregnant. She's only seventeen. I asked her to marry me, but her parents said hell no because I'm broke and have a very unstable, low paying job. They think I'm a loser."

"Are you insane? You're twenty-seven-years old! What the hell are you doing sleeping with a seventeen-year-old?"

"She don't look seventeen. She told me she was twenty-one."

"And you believed her just like that?"

"Come on, man. What was I supposed to do, card her? She came on to me, and I ain't had a girlfriend in four years. I sure as hell ain't turnin' away a beautiful girl who wants to play with my dick."

"Dude, you *are* a dick! This isn't a joke. You could be labeled a sex offender for the rest of your life. Are her parents pressing charges?"

"No, they said they wouldn't press charges if I agreed to stay away from her. They're making her have an abortion. An *abortion*, Beau. I'm Catholic, I don't believe in abortion. They're killing my baby." Chris ran his palm across his shaved head. "April heard about it from Claire and called me. She told me if I helped her she'd talk Lindsey's parents in to allowing her to have the baby and let me and Lindsey get married. She said she'd give me some money to help us get started with our lives."

Seething, Cade narrowed his eyes. "And if you chose *not* to help her?"

"She threatened to report me as a sex offender and ruin my chances of ever having a peaceful life or a family again."

Cade cursed.

"After I agreed, I thought about it and realized nothing was worth this kind of blackmail, so I told her I wanted out. She threatened to end me and my family if I didn't follow through with the plan."

"Damn it, Chris! What was the plan?"

He sighed. "She wanted me to kill Eddie Fontenot."

Cade spit and kicked dirt over it as he pursed his lips. He had suspected that.

"Then she wanted me to kill you."

Cade rocked back on his heels. He had figured that, too, but hearing the confirmation still shocked him.

"She said you were too nosy and caused her too much trouble. I told her to go to hell. She can do whatever she wants to me, Beau. I ain't helpin' her no more."

Cade gripped Chris's shoulders with both hands, forcing himself not to squeeze the little shit like a tick. "Did you shoot Remy?"

"Who? No! I didn't shoot anyone, Beau, I swear. She wanted me to shoot Eddie, but I couldn't do that. I may be a player, dude, but I ain't no killer. Who's Remy?"

If Chris hadn't been the one who shot Remy, then who was? Another mystery. Cade was back to square one. "Remy is Caroline's teenage brother." Cade stared intensely into his friend's muddy brown eyes, demanding his undivided attention. "Chris, do you swear that you didn't aim for Eddie and accidentally shoot Remy? Swear it?"

He returned Cade's glare without any sign of guilt, his voice pleading. "I swear, Beau. I didn't shoot nobody. I promise."

Cade released him forcefully, pushing him back and cursing a blue streak. This hole was getting deeper and deeper, and unfortunately, he'd fallen even farther behind with answers. Runway tipped his chin in question to which Cade shook his head. In usual Runway fashion, he broke the tension with a joke as he joined them.

"So, when did the party move over here? Who wants a drink?"

Chris jumped on that opportunity. "I do. I'll get 'em." He couldn't get away fast enough. Runway studied Cade's face without saying a word. He sensed the frustration, and Cade started to tell him what happened when his phone rang.

"Beau?"

Tonya's voice blasted from the ear piece of his Smartphone. "I don't care what the hell you're doing or who you're doing it with. Drop everything and start driving up to meet me. I'll head your way and we'll meet in the middle at that sandwich place just off the highway in Larose. This is too big to discuss on the phone."

She hung up, leaving him staring blankly at Runway, who must have heard her because he said, "Let's roll."

They waved to the others as they jumped in Cade's truck and headed north to the city without explaining their hasty retreat.

Cade called Ty while driving to meet Tonya. He wanted to make sure someone he trusted was watching over Caroline. He didn't think anything would happen, but at this point he'd rather be safe. Cade was worried about April and just how far she would go. The woman had connections.

He wished Tonya could have told him what this was regarding. It was sensitive information to need to meet in person, but it must have been time-sensitive as well. She'd never before told him to drop everything and start driving. His stomach ached. That was never a good sign.

"What kind of information do you think she's got?" Runway asked.

"I don't know, but whatever it is I have a really bad feeling. It must be big, because, you know Tonya, she doesn't overreact to very many things."

"Yeah, she's one of the most levelheaded chicks I've ever met."

They pulled into the parking lot about five minutes after she did. When Cade got out of the car, she marched over to him, hugged him quickly, and greeted Runway with an approving once-over.

"Here." She slapped a manila folder to Cade's chest and held it for a moment. "Brace yourself."

Cade cursed under his breath. The last time he'd heard those words, he found out his little sister was married and pregnant from an adulterous relationship and possibly facing a dishonorable discharge from the Navy. He took a deep breath and opened the folder. Not sure exactly what he was reading. "Looks like a birth certificate."

She rolled her eyes. "Men. You can't see past the surface." She turned it over and pointed to the bottom. "It's Ana Morales' birth certificate from the University Hospital of Brooklyn."

He was impressed. Tonya thought to start with Ana's birth. Cade would have gone directly to the time when she moved to Louisiana. He guessed that's why Tonya was the F.B.I. agent and he wasn't. He skimmed the birth statistics until his eyes rested upon the specifics. Five years before he was born, which coincides with April's approximate age. Born in Brooklyn, New York, birth name Ana Marie Morales. Her mother's name was Maria Sophia Morales. When Cade read her father's name, he thought he might puke. He'd been shocked plenty in his life, but this had his hackles up. Everything made sense now, and this one tiny little fact was all the motive April needed.

"You couldn't just tell me this over the phone?"

Her chin stubbornly jutted out. "Not when Marcellino is involved. I told you, I don't do business by phone." Tonya's Georgian accent seeped through with her frustration. "Because of her grandmother's loyalty, Marcellino also took care of Maria and Ana because *that* jackass refused to take responsibility." She pounded her finger on the name at the bottom of April's birth certificate. "He denied ever having anything to do with Maria Morales, even though she claimed he had an affair with her while he lived in New York. Angelo Marcellino may be Ana's surrogate father, but this dude's blood runs through her veins."

Cade studied the birth certificate, legitimately embossed with the seal of the New York State Department of Health, and still couldn't believe his eyes. The name listed as the biological father of Ana Morales was none other than Kenneth Callahan.

THIRTY-THREE

Caroline attempted to follow the ridiculous speed limit in Golden Meadow as she drove across town with a moronic grin on her face. Could the stupid light take any longer? There's no one else at this intersection. Her heart fluttered as she thought about Cade. After her behavior at the voodoo shop, she wasn't sure he was ready for this news. Lucinda had given her a few meditation exercises to help clear her mind and strengthen her spirit. She'd only done them a few times, but so far nothing special came from them. At least she hadn't had anymore freak accidents. Lucinda was adamant about her practicing the exercises daily, but Caroline wouldn't remember do do them until she was driving. Can't exactly meditate while driving.

She hoped Cade wouldn't be angry. They had only been married for a few weeks, and things had been absolutely magical. Especially the sex. He'd suddenly started wearing condoms, which she thought was strange, but it didn't make a difference in the pleasure for her. She was on the pill, but if he was that serious about not wanting a baby yet, why hadn't he used condoms from the beginning? It didn't matter. She was perfectly content just being with him in every way—or position—possible. A wicked smile stretched across her face as she replayed the different ways they'd made love.

Her nerves jumped like electricity pulsating through her body, and her foot grew heavy as she got closer to the cabin. She was anxious. When she pulled into the driveway, it seemed still in the cabin. Usually she could see the lights from the television or Cade walking around inside. But there was no movement. A moment of panic shot through her. Where could he be?

She went inside and put her things away, clutching the manila folder in her hand. Cade would be very interested in what was inside this little beauty; more information than he'd ever imagined.

She freshened up and headed out the door into the misty afternoon. As she approached, the mist gave way to sprinkles. She rounded the corner and heard voices on the porch. With their backs to her, Eddie and Emily stood just feet away. She should have made herself known, but the terse tone from her mother kept her rooted in place.

"Don't call me that," Emily snapped.

"Call you what?"

"*Love.*"

"Okay. I apologize, sweetheart."

"Don't call me that, either. You don't love me, and I'm not your sweetheart. April is." Emily stormed off the porch past Eddie and stopped just short of the woods.

"Emily, wait. Where are you going?"

"I don't know. Away from here." She ran from him, impressing Caroline with her agility and speed.

She'd made it into the camouflage of the trees before he finally caught up and stepped in front of her, breathing heavily. Caroline held her breath and edged closer, ducking behind a tree.

She huffed, resigned. "Go back to your wife, Eddie."

The sprinkling rain had fattened up and spattered on the leaves, but Caroline couldn't move. She tucked her folder into her rain jacket while her father stood oblivious to the steady drops drenching them and focused on Emily's tear-filled eyes. The firm set of his mouth deepened in frustration. He stared out into the woods and Caroline thought he might walk away. Instead, he abruptly pulled Emily into his arms and kissed her.

Caroline nearly cheered aloud. Emily would never admit her feelings for Eddie had rekindled. Caroline knew that much about her mother. But her actions spoke louder than her words. Emily broke away and cried into Eddie's chest, clutching his shirt as if hanging on for dear life.

"Why?" she screamed. "Why did you have to leave us? Why did you have to continue your life without me?" Emily pounded on his chest. "What was it about me you hated so much? Why did you have to be so wonderful when I came back here? Why do you have to be married?"

He stayed quiet and let her beat upon him until she finished screaming, resting her head on his heaving chest, crying.

The heavens had opened up and they all stood in a downpour, but Caroline didn't care. Caroline had wished for this moment her entire life, and now she had the good fortune to witness it. Emily pulled away and apologized continuously for taking her frustrations out on him.

"It's okay. I deserve it."

She shook her head. "No, you don't. I knew you were remarried when I came down here. I thought I would be strong enough to handle it. I was stupid. I should have stayed in Arkansas where I belong."

"You belong here with your family, Em."

"I have no family, Eddie. My family just got married. My parents are gone, I have no siblings, and my husband left me twenty-four years ago. I'm alone, and I'm just feeling sorry for myself. I apologize for dumping it all on you."

The rain slackened to a light drizzle, though they already looked like drowned rats. Well, at least Caroline did.

"Can I ask you something?" Eddie said. "I want an honest answer. How come you never remarried? And don't tell me you were too tired. Was it *really* because our divorce was unscriptural?" She dropped her eyes confirming his statement, and Eddie's face contorted, riddled with guilt. "I'm so sorry. I never imagined I would ruin your life by leaving you. I thought I was giving you a second chance to be with someone more ready to settle down, someone more responsible and stable." He hugged her again. "I never intended to force you to spend your whole life alone."

After a pause, Eddie grinned. "That kiss was pretty damn incredible."

Caroline grimaced. She wished she could leave now, but that was impossible without being detected. Watching them kiss was one thing, but if they started making out, Caroline would lose her mind.

Emily agreed, unable to hide her smile, and looked him in the eyes, her voice stern. "Yes, but it was wrong. You can't be kissing your ex-wife while your current one is probably on her way home. It's just. . .wrong."

He stared at her reminiscently for a moment. "I don't understand how something so wrong could feel so right."

His eyes dropped, and he reached for her hand, but she crossed her arms.

"I'm so sorry," he whispered.

She looked at him with indignation. Caroline knew that look well. "Would it have been so different before you ever met Caroline? Do you honestly think your feelings for me would be this way if Caroline had never knocked on your door?"

He said nothing.

"I thought so."

He shook his head. "Don't be like that. I never knew that you wouldn't remarry. I assumed you had men lined up to date you."

She snorted. "Right."

"Didn't you ever have a date?"

"I dated one guy about a year after you left. It didn't work out."

"What happened?"

She shrugged. "He wasn't my type."

"You have a type?"

"I guess."

"What was wrong with him?"

"Nothing." She waved him off, annoyed. "It just didn't work out."

"There had to be some reason you didn't like him other than he wasn't your type?"

"No."

"Tell me," he pressed, blocking her path as she tried to walk around him.

"He wasn't *you*, okay," she shouted. "You are the first and only person I've ever loved in this life, and you broke my heart. Now I'm down here again, in your world, and I've let myself fall for you all over again. It's my problem, not yours." She stalked past him toward the house, Eddie watched Emily walk back to the house, letting her get a nice lead, before he followed her in. His hurt squeezed Caroline's heart.

Soaking wet, confused by her mother's behavior, and still needing to find Cade, Caroline rushed back to the cabin to change into dry clothes and blow dry her hair before she drove back to the plantation house. No need to get caught in a rain storm again.

Caroline clomped up the steps, exhausted and drained from the heat and humidity amplified by the rain. "Hello?" she called as she entered the foyer.

Delia bustled through the heavy kitchen doors. "Ms. Caroline. Great to see you."

She smiled and hugged Delia before following her into the kitchen. Delia poured her a glass of sweet tea.

"So whatcha did today, boo?"

"I've had the most incredible day, you just wouldn't believe. It's been amazing."

Delia smiled, her eyes sparkling. "Tell me all about it. I need some good news."

Caroline looked around. "Where's Delphine?"

"Her sister's been very ill. She's in the hospital, and it ain't lookin' good. She's had ALS for a while, so Delphine is spending as much time as she can with her before she passes."

"Oh, how sad." Caroline's eyes swelled with tears. "That's terrible. She must be so upset."

Delia stared at her for a moment as if Caroline had lost her mind. "Don't cry, love. Her sister has been sick for a few years. Delphine's had time to prepare for this, and her sister is at peace with it." Delia studied Caroline for a moment when a knowing grin slowly graced her face. "It's sad, yes, and she's taking it pretty hard, but she'll be alright. You want some water or Sprite? Something decaffeinated?"

Confused, Caroline looked at her glass through blurry tears. "No, is something wrong with the tea? It tastes fine to me."

She raised an eyebrow. "Nothing wrong with the tea, cher. Just checkin' on you. How's your appetite? Hungry?"

Just the thought of eating right now made Caroline queasy. "Ugh, no, thank you. I couldn't possibly eat right now. I had fried catfish for lunch, and it's threatening to make a reappearance as we speak."

Delia smiled and took a sip of her tea. "Mmm-hmm."

Cade's voice filled the foyer. "Caroline? You in here?"

Her mom's voice was behind his. "I know I heard her come in. Maybe she's in the kitchen."

She rushed out to meet them, suddenly bubbling over with joy. "Hey, guys."

A huge smile swept over Cade's handsome features sending her heart aflutter. "Hey, beautiful. How was your afternoon? You went to your appointment?" She nodded, smiling. He looked her over. "What'd you have done? Nothing looks different."

"Huh?"

"You got your hair done, right?"

"No, silly."

"What kind of appointment?" her mom asked. Concern etched deep in her frown. "Where'd you go?"

"Easy, momma bear. I just had a well-woman check up, that's all. My appointment was actually a couple of weeks ago, but I rescheduled it so I could get married and. . .stuff."

Emily smiled in understanding, causing Caroline to blush. If her mother knew Caroline had witnessed the passion between her and Eddie earlier, she'd be the one blushing.

Cade enjoyed her comment way too much. He smiled as he wrapped his arms around her waist and pulled her close. "I missed you. You're my new addiction, and right now I'm suffering from a serious withdrawal." He kissed her, but with her mom watching, Caroline cut it short.

"You're new addiction? As opposed to your old one?"

He shrugged. "Nah, it's always been you, but now I get a much stronger dose." He waggled his eyebrows playfully.

Emily cleared her throat, ending their verbal foreplay. As Caroline hugged him, she peeked over Cade's shoulder to talk to her mom. "So, where's Dad? April's not back, is she?"

Her mom's smile fell. "What? What do you mean? I don't know what you're talking about. Why do you ask?"

Alarms went off in Caroline's head. Emily was scared. What had her so frightened and defensive? The tension blanketed the room. "Okay, am I missing something? You look guilty. Did you and dad hook up or something?" Caroline flashed a devilish smile. She couldn't help it. Since she'd had her first taste of sex, she was a fiend now. Caroline giggled, releasing Cade and walking over to face her mom. "Come on, Mom. Spill it. Did you and dad have an. . .*intimate* moment?"

She blushed. Emily Fontenot was blushing and nervously fidgeting with her hair. "Caroline, don't be ridiculous. Your father is married, he doesn't just go around being *intimate* with people." Caroline knew better. She held her disbelieving stare until Emily let out an exasperated sigh. "Fine. We kissed. That's all. And then I told him to go back to his wife."

"Y'all kissed? That's. . .awesome."

"Caroline, really. It's not awesome. It was just a kiss, a poor lapse in judgment." Emily studied the floor and mumbled, "It's not like we confessed our undying love for each other."

Caroline waited for her to look up. "You did, didn't you? You're in love with him again, and you told him."

"Maybe," she smiled.

Caroline hugged her mom tightly and whispered, "This is almost the best news I've heard all day."

"Almost?" Cade said.

She threaded her fingers through her hair and stared at her shoes. "Yeah, almost."

"What was better than that?" Emily insisted.

Smiling, Caroline looked up, giggly excitement thrumming in her chest. "Cade. Buckle your seatbelt. Ready or not, I'm pregnant!" She squealed in delight. "We're gonna be a family."

Cade stood in shock, and her mother's hands covered her gaping mouth. Both rendered speechless.

Caroline's goofy, expectant grin faded, waiting for one of them to say something. Her mom's tears streaming down her face weren't happy tears, and Cade's unreadable expression worried her.

"Did y'all hear me? I said I'm pregnant." They didn't move. "Well, don't everybody jump at once."

Cade hugged her, squeezing her so tightly she couldn't breathe. He pressed his cheek to hers. "I heard you, sweet girl," he whispered. He sucked in a deep breath. "I'm gonna be a daddy?"

Tears exploded from Caroline, and she burst into joyful sobs. "Yes. You're gonna be a daddy."

She pulled back to look at his face, expecting elation, but that's not what she saw. Worry creased his features. Emily bawled like Caroline had just announced her death sentence. Anger pulsed through her veins.

"Gee, Mom. I expected excitement, not. . .disappointment," Caroline retorted. Emily sobbed so hard she couldn't talk. She simply shook her head.

"Baby," Cade said. "I am sure your mom is excited for us. She's probably just worried about you. Pregnancy can be hard on a woman's body." He spoke sternly. "Right, Emily? You're just concerned for her health?"

She nodded and swiped her tears. "Of course. I'm your mother. It's my job to worry about you." She cradled Caroline's face in her hands, caressing her cheek. "You'll find out soon enough, I'm sure."

Caroline smiled. "Yes, I'm sure you're right. I just thought you would be more excited to find out you're going to have grandchildren to spoil."

Emily smiled, laughing. "Yes, I'm excited, but let's not get overzealous. Let's start with one and, in time, work our way up to more."

Caroline smiled and shook her head. "No can do. This is a two-for-one special." She turned to her confused husband. "We're having twins."

His face lit up, but his brow still furrowed. Caroline didn't realize it was possible to look excited and worried at the same time. "You're having twins?"

She handed him the manila envelope with the ultrasound pictures in it. "No, baby. *We're* having twins."

"Are you sure? You can't be that far along."

"I'm sure. Apparently I was ovulating on our honeymoon, and that was three weeks ago. When the urine test was positive, they did an ultrasound, and there were two heartbeats."

He studied the pictures, and his eyes welled up. Unable to hide his excitement any longer, he dropped the folder and spun Caroline around while kissing every exposed inch of her face.

Emily, however, was crying again. Still. Her sadness broke Caroline's heart. She couldn't understand why her mother wasn't elated.

"Mom, what is your problem?"

Cade interrupted by hugging her again, kissing the top of her head. "Wait, I thought you were on the pill? How is it that we're having twins?"

She shrugged. "Apparently it takes about a month for the pill to fully take effect and prevent pregnancy. I've never needed them before, and we got married kind of quickly, so I'd only been taking them for two weeks. I guess since I have a degree in nursing the doctor assumed I knew that. Oops." She smiled. "Ironically, I've been taking prenatal vitamins since last July to make my hair grow back faster after they shaved my head from my accident." Caroline caressed his face. "I'm not sorry. I can't wait to be a mother to your beautiful children."

Cade vigorously kissed her, weakening her knees. When she came up for air, her head spun, but thankfully he didn't let her go. She leaned her head back and watched the ceiling slow to a stop. While her neck was in that vulnerable position, Cade took full advantage and kissed every inch of it.

"Man, I moved out of your cabin so you guys could have some privacy, and now you're over here making out." Runway walked in the room, his grin lighting up the room. "Are you trying to make me jealous, dude?"

"Payback, man." For all those times I had to watch you and Kristy going at it at my place."

They shook hands. "Hey, bella."

She smiled. "Hey. Did Kristy make it back to California okay?"

Runway's beaming smile split his face. "She did. She called me this morning." He curiously looked Caroline over. "How was the honeymoon? You look ravishing as always. If I didn't know better, I'd say you're glowing."

She smirked. "Pregnancy tends to do that to a woman."

He was better at faking his happiness than her mom and Cade were upon first hearing the news. Caroline picked up that he wasn't as thrilled as he could've been.

"Wow, that's great! Congratulations, bella." He clapped Cade's shoulder. "Congrats, Pops. A baby. That's awesome, brother. I'm really happy for you."

Cade smiled, clearly enchanted by her surprising news, and held up two fingers without saying a word.

Runway's eyebrows popped up, and he switched his gaze back to Caroline. "Twins?" She nodded, excitedly. "Double trouble. Two little Beau's running around."

They all laughed, all except for Emily. She continued to cry, looking as if she'd just been told Caroline had less than nine months to live.

Runway noticed and intervened. "Ms. Emily, would you care to join me in the kitchen for some of those delectable fudge brownies I spotted earlier?" Without smiling or answering, Emily simply agreed and looped her arm in his, walking hunched over like an old woman carrying the burden of the world. What was her problem?

Cade pulled Caroline into his comforting embrace and smoothed her hair. "Let's go home and celebrate," he whispered. "It's not everyday a man's beautiful wife breaks the news that they are having twins. I don't think it's hit me yet, but when it does I'll be the happiest man on the planet."

Maybe it was the hormones or her mother's disappointment, but Caroline needed reassurance. And Cade's words were music to her ears. "Thank you. I needed to hear that. I just don't know what's gotten into her. I'm beyond happy, and I love you so much. I can't wait to have your babies." He dropped to his knees and pulled her hips to his face as he kissed her flat belly. Caroline's throat constricted and she lost it. Her heart swelled with pride. "You'll be a wonderful father. I just know it." Tears streamed down her face.

Standing quickly, he ran his fingers through her hair at her temples and pressed his lips to her forehead. Slowly, he worked his way down, capturing each tear with feather-light kisses until his lips covered her mouth. His passion removed all doubts she had of his eagerness to become a father again. He wasn't angry, he was enlivened. Ecstatic. She wanted to have his babies right then to see the joy on his face as he held them in his arms for the first time. Eight more months would last an eternity. His fervor and excitement melted her bones, and she succumbed to his warmth, letting him sweep her into his arms.

"I love them already," he whispered with a smile as he carried her all the way home.

The End

ABOUT THE AUTHOR

The Bigger Picture Photography
Location Credit to House Plantation in Hockley, TX.

Judy McDonough is a southern author of the Paranormal Romance series titled The Bayou Secrets Saga. A U.S. Navy veteran, the Arkansas native was stationed in New Orleans during her enlistment where she met her husband. In twelve years, they've lived in Louisiana, Tennessee, and now reside in Texas with their three young boys, two dogs, three kittens, and a bearded dragon.

Fascinated with the supernatural and haunting elements of the South, her writing style will always include some facet of the extraordinary whether through her characters, their settings, or the situations in which they find themselves. Judy's always had a passion for creative writing, so she finally made the time to bring her dreams to reality when she wrote, Deadline-Book 1 in The Bayou Secrets Saga (available now). Lifeline is the second novel in The Bayou Secrets Saga, and Flatline (Book 3) will be released in 2015. Judy has several other projects in her cue, and she's just getting warmed up.

Join her mailing list to keep up with the latest updates and new releases. She will only send out a newsletter quarterly, so no worries about your email getting cluttered. Here is the link to sign up for the mailing list: **http://eepurl.com/yuIVX**

Visit her website for more information and juicy deleted scenes. **www.Judy-McDonough.com**

Follow Judy through her social media sites to stay in the loop! As always, please be so kind to leave a review to let others know how you liked LIFELINE.